Highway 23

Highway 23

The Unrepentant

A Novel

Patrick Carlin

iUniverse, Inc.
New York Lincoln Shanghai

Highway 23
The Unrepentant

iUniverse books may be ordered through booksellers or by contacting:

iUniverse
2021 Pine Lake Road, Suite 100
Lincoln, NE 68512
www.iuniverse.com
1-800-Authors (1-800-288-4677)

This is a work of fiction. All of the characters, names, incidents, places, organizations, and dialogue in this novel are either the products of the author's imagination or are used fictitiously.

ISBN: 978-0-595-42639-3 (pbk)
ISBN: 978-0-595-86966-4 (ebk)

Printed in the United States of America

This book is dedicated with love to my best friend, my brother George. Who was born hip to the jive. Without his help and encouragement over the years this would ~~been have~~ never have been written. Thanks, George.

CHAPTER 1

▼

It's springtime in Oscoda, Michigan. Songbirds are singing, beavers are busy and fawns are on the scene. The Au Sable River at full flow, working its way toward Lake Huron, is sending no fisherman home with an empty creel.

Springtime, in Oscoda, wild flowers bloom along the trails and in the inviting clearings in the woods where young couples with a blanket can spend an hour or two getting in touch with Mother Nature and each other.

Springtime, and the Commanding Officer of the 646th Aircraft Control & Warning Squadron is not happy.

Captain Richard Becker, a content air reservist, felt great reluctance when called to active duty. Sitting at his desk, brittle and military, he sags within. Flipping through a folder labeled BASE ROSTER, scanning its pages, he takes a deep drag of the tail end of his cigarette before grinding it out in his "Souvenir of Washington D.C." ashtray.

He stares at the picture of the Washington Monument, half hidden under a scattering of butts. "Those were the days," he exclaims. He slams the folder shut. Leaning on the arms of his chair, he pushes himself erect and walks to the window.

Gazing out the window, he mutters, "Goddamn Korean War." Across the squadron's main street, the mess hall with its manicured lawn and its path lined with stones painted white kindles memories. Memories of a different war, his war. He recalls World War II.

World War II was good to Becker. As an aide to General Barney "Balls" Cooperton, he had only two duties; providing the general with an endless supply of bottles of Scotch, and keeping the general's steno pool stocked with willing, busty, young typists. Becker spent the entire war in D.C. lining up pussy and scoring booze, pussy he never got a chance to sample and booze that his stomach refused to tolerate.

Glancing at his battered, old, maple desk, and surveying the well-scrubbed, yet heavily-worn wooden floor of his office, he has visions of his old office, with its huge, polished mahogany desk. And that carpet, he reflects, almost feeling the plush, deep purple, wall-to-wall carpeting, I didn't need cushion insoles, like now. He sighs.

Those were the good old days. That was a good war. Yes. World War II had been good to young Lieutenant Becker.

The potential typist seated across the desk from Becker inhaled. The thread strength of the prospect's blouse was being tested, wonderfully, to its limits. The young woman's hair, platinum—almost standard issue in 1944—glittered. Her lips and fingernails, an enticing, bloody carmine, beckoned. He wanted that woman. Picturing her, Becker still feels desire. He recalls her expensive aroma. Must be French perfume, he had thought at the time.

Becker frowns in both the present and the past. Busty's reply to his dinner invitation whirls through his brain. Her breezy, dismissive words, "Give me a call when you make general, Lieutenant," rankle yet, in spite of the years.

That night Becker got too close to combat for comfort. Slouched on a stool at the bar of the Officer's Club in Georgetown, attempting to drown Busty's brush-off with Scotch and milk, Becker watched trouble brew. Outdoors, a ripe, full moon on the rise, shined on the city. Indoors, the club jammed with soldiers, sailors and marines, two-thirds of them wearing campaign ribbons, cooked. Men outnumbered women eight to one. The jukebox blared and the packed dance floor bounced to the beat. Unruly energy, soaked in a sea of smoke, alcohol and testosterone, simmered.

Seven marine flyers overcame the jukebox in their area and gave a semi-drunk, raucous rendition of "The Marine's Hymn". The main singer stood on the booth's table, directing the others.

At a nearby table ten rowdy, young, ensigns, fresh out of school and feeling fit were celebrating a birthday. They gave the marines a Bronx Cheer, hooted at them and sang "Anchors Aweigh". As the notes were fading and the candles were about to be lit, war erupted between the U.S. Navy and the U.S. Marines.

The main singer, a just-drunk-enough marine lieutenant, poured himself a shot of vodka and lurched and staggered his way to the navy's table, never spilling a drop. "That's enough of that anchor-clanking bullshit," he bellowed. "Here's a toast for you swab jockeys. 'A thousand gobs laid down their swabs to whup six sick marines. A thousand more stood by and swore, 'twas the bloodiest battle they'd ever seen.'" He threw down his shot and started to walk away, when the ensign nearest to him stood up and shouted in his face, "Fuck you, Jarhead!"

Grabbing the ensign's head, the marine buried it in the cake. Another ensign hit the marine in the side of the head with a full bottle of beer. The booth full of marines exploded. All three bartenders vaulted the bar to break up the fight. They were too late. In the area of the ensigns' table, ass was being kicked, bottles were being broken and used, and guys were getting cut. Screaming women scrambled for the doors. Other fights broke out and more fighters were jumping into the main battle. Somebody struggled their way to the pay phone and called the cops. The cops notified the Military Police.

A squad of eight MP's headed by a 250-pound, bulldog-faced, warrant officer packing a 30-inch, custom-made, ash baton stormed into the brawl. "You don't get to bust up Brassheads often, guys," Bulldog gleefully shouted to his men. "Let's get to it." Hearing that message, Becker headed for cover.

He hunkered down, out of sight at the far end of the bar … the unattended bar. While the MP's were busy, merrily and vigorously dispensing instant night-stick justice, (one of them cold-cocked a major and another opened up the scalp of a lieutenant commander), Becker seized the moment. Sweating like a pig on a broiling Iowa afternoon, and so afraid of being seen or caught that he nearly shit, he grabbed two bottles of Scotch and scurried out a side exit. He was proud of himself for almost a month.

The following morning he left one bottle on the general's desk. One bottle or two, he told himself. What the general didn't know wouldn't hurt Lieutenant Becker.

General Cooperton thanked him and assured him that he'd soon be making captain. He took the general at his word, bought captain's bars and shined them. He pinned them on exactly two years after the surrender of Japan, while in the air reserve.

Becker had joined the reserve at war's end, anticipating an easy government pension. Desk warrior on weekends and solid businessman on weekdays: a good plan. It was simple, but simple was good enough for him. Then Korea acted up. He wasn't sure what happened. He knew Korea was about Communists, but resented the United States' involvement. *North or South, they look the same to me. Ought to let 'em kill each other. Too goddamn many of 'em anyway,* he'd often think. The Korean War had burst Beckers' bubble.

"Goddamn Koreans," he shouts. His heartburn begins to kick in with a churning in his gut. The burning acid is on the rise. Turning abruptly from the window, he crosses over to his desk and quickly pours a glass of water. As an afterthought, he dials the brass desk calendar to June 7, 1952. "Saturday. Hope it's a slow day."

Standing in front of his desk, he opens the bottom, right hand drawer and retrieves his Alka-Seltzer. Shaking out the last two tablets, he drops them into the water. He makes a mental note to have his adjutant get more. Sucking in his stomach, he pulls his shoulders back and calculates. Only fifteen pounds over-weight. Not bad for a thirty-six-year-old. He raises the glass to his ear. He enjoys listening to the fizz. It soothes him. Gulping the comfort of the bubbling drink, he drops into his chair.

Wheeling backwards, he puts his feet up on the desk and stares at the photos hanging on the far wall. None are level. Nestled among the P-38's, P-40's, B-17's and other World War II aircraft photographs is a black and white of a drab, gray, concrete block building. "Grand Opening, 1946" is written in the lower left corner. Even from his desk, he can read the sign on top of the commercial structure. The sign dwarfs the building. It reads, BECKER'S.

When activated, Becker was forced to sell his dream and forget his future. Worse yet, he had to sell at a loss. Memories tug. He loses himself in the photo, recalling Memorial Day sales with red, white and blue bunting throughout the store, Washington's Birthday, with him dressed as President Washington, and Midnight Harvest Moon sales with pumpkins and corn stalks all over the place. He sees the merchandise filling the sales floor, the stained pine bedroom sets, the Formica and chrome kitchen tables and chairs, the sectional couches with match-ing chairs and love seats. Time blurs images, working its own magic.

Becker has forgotten what a giant pain in the ass the store had been and how much ulcer-inducing aggravation it had produced; money-grubbing suppliers demanding cash on delivery; employees with a litany of excuses for time away from the job and lists of complaints, gripes and grievances when they were at work; big department stores trying to squash him, with one of them under-cut-ting his prices every time he advertised a sale, and worst of all for him, the cus-tomers.

Becker thought of his customers as thieving bastards and he despised their nit-picky antics, citing tiny imperfections in items as reasons for discounts. He kept a large stock of cheap lamps, mirrors and rugs *and* a sales manager with a sharp pencil to thwart these chiselers. No, it wasn't much of an operation, but stomach-churning and all, it had been his.

The only thing that took some of the sting out of his call to duty was that as the C.O. of a radar squadron he could hope to make major in a year.

"Major Becker," he speaks the words reverently, relishing their sound as the syllables of his elusive dream trail off his tongue. His stomach rumbles. He gets to his feet, planning to look the picture over more closely. "But I'm here damn near two years with no sign of promotion. How did things go so sour?"

"Here's the reason," he growls, snatching the BASE ROSTER folder from his desk. "Malcontents! Misfits!" Becker slaps the folder back onto his desk with a resounding whack! A knock on the door halts him in mid-rant. Getting control of himself, he opens the door for his adjutant, Second Lieutenant Harry Sumner. Sumner, one year out of the ROTC program at Ohio State, is a born ass kisser with a deep, almost holy respect for rules and regulations.

Sumner is one of those unfortunates who looks bad in anything he wears, especially his uniform. His khaki trousers show too much sock. His shirt, where it's tucked in, blouses back out and his belt line is so high you'd think his voice would squeak. He wears no glasses, but squints and blinks his eyes frequently, as if light is his mortal enemy. Sumner is almost a caricature. Half the guys on the base can do acceptable imitations of him. Even Becker enjoys observing Sumner's many idiosyncrasies. But Sumner excels at following orders and he can be counted upon never to come up with an original thought, qualities that Becker expects from his subordinates. Since taking over the 646th Becker has watched his large expectations dwindle to small hopes.

Thank God for a kindred spirit, Becker reflects. He observes Sumner placing the steaming mug of coffee on his desk, and thinks, Just like a waiter at a fine hotel. Amused by his waiter thought, he almost smiles. He sits down, gets comfortable behind his desk and sips his coffee. "Sit down, Harry."

Sumner immediately pulls a chair close to Becker's desk and sits. "Captain?"

"You know how many men we have in this squadron?"

Sumner squints, blinks twice and searches his brain for the data. He hesitates, looks blank for a long moment, then recovers. "Er, umm, two hundred and five enlisted men, sir. And then there are ten officers and um fourteen noncoms." He does some slow addition and finishes, "That's two hundred and twenty-nine, total, Captain. Uh, according to yesterday's morning report, sir."

Becker nods, grunts his displeasure and slowly continues. "I've been sitting here wondering how two hundred men can generate so much grief?"

"Yes, Captain."

"It's only June and I've already busted as many fuckups as I did during all of last year."

"Last year we weren't at full strength, sir. We only had a hundred airmen, Captain."

Becker's frown returns, tripping Sumner's the-captain-is-upset alarm. Bells ring, red lights flash and sirens wail. Sumner quickly tries to cover his ass. "That could account for part of it, sir, couldn't it?"

Becker's frown deepens. A scowl is on the approach. He wants no rationalizations for the increase in infractions. "We still get more than our share of fuckups." His tone marches in step with his irritation. He continues, "We've got twenty airmen basics on a base that calls for no troops under the rank of airman third class."

"We're picking up eight new radar operators this morning, Captain. Fresh out of radar school, all airmen third class."

"I already know that." Becker belches. "God, I was waiting for that one." He pounds his sternum. "Who's driving the bus?"

"McKinny, Captain."

"Another goddamn eight ball. What about Weller?"

"Still on emergency furlough and Jordan's absent without leave. Again."

Becker lets out a long, slow breath. His stomach acid sloshes around, stirred by this latest vexation. "What time do we pick up the new troops?"

Sumner checks his watch. "They'll be at the bus depot in Bay City at oh-nine-thirty, sir."

Becker wonders how quickly the new troops will sink to the level of his current crop of misfits. Jabbing at the roster folder with his index finger, he asks, "You got any ideas on how to deal with these malcontents?"

"I don't know, sir. Umm, maybe we could just ship out some of the worst ones? Flynn, McKinny, Jordan, Dennis?"

Becker's scowl arrives. "All I'm getting are orders for Japan and Europe. Think I'm going to reward a dirty son of a bitch like Flynn with good duty like that? I wish to God, I could have shipped him to Greenland last year with that crazy medic friend of his."

"What about the stockade, sir?" Sumner hopes he's hit a winner. Watching Becker redden, he feels that the stockade may not have been a satisfactory suggestion.

"Miller and Dennis are down at Selfridge right now. The Inspector General was on the horn yesterday, asking me what the hell was going on up here, as it is. No, we don't need the stockade. What we need are requests to ship troops to Alaska, Greenland or Timbuktu, for that matter." Becker shakes his head, trying unsuccessfully to will away his acid woes. He looks at the old Seth Thomas above his door. "You might as well saddle up," he orders, adding, "and bring me back two bottles of Alka-Seltzer … and don't let McKinny kill the new men on the way back."

"Yes, sir. Alka-Seltzer and make McKinny drive safely." Sumner jumps up and salutes, happy to be off the slide on Becker's microscope.

Becker returns Sumner's inept salute, watches his attempt to leave the office in a snappy manner and shakes his head. He may not look sharp in his uniform, he gives a sloppy salute … he's a brown-noser and he's not very bright … might even think we've got a radar site in Timbuktu … but goddammit, he knows how to follow orders. I wish I had two hundred like him in this outfit. The door closes behind the lieutenant and Becker pulls a sheet of paper entitled SHIT LIST from the top left hand drawer of his desk.

Heading up Becker's SHIT LIST is Airman Basic Edward P. Flynn, his prime nemesis. Flynn is sampling the accommodations at the Saginaw County Jail, the result of a fistfight with a deputy sheriff.

Becker muses, Wasn't too long ago a thing like that would have put a man on a chain-gang. Nowadays, all the bleeding hearts don't have the stomach for real discipline and real punishment. He pictures Flynn doing a lively dance at the end of a rope and manages a small smile. At the very least, they ought to keep him thirty days.

Next on the list is A/B George Dennis. He's halfway through a sixty-day stay in the stockade, down at Selfridge for altering ID cards and making phony Class A passes. God only knows how many of my minor airmen are running around drinking, thanks to this clever, little asshole. Becker starts to get red, slams his fist down on the desk and hits his wrist on the edge. He pulls it back and rubs it, still bitching; the little bastard did it right under my nose. Got those blank passes right out of my orderly room. Once again he thinks about the Inspector General's call and the pseudo-sympathy permeating the I.G.'s voice. I look like a goddamn clown. No wonder I haven't made major.

He continues down his list. "Jordan, AWOL again," he laments to no one. Tossing his shit list back into the drawer, he slams it in disgust. "Right under my goddamn nose." He feels pressure pushing in on all sides of him, smothering him. It's the same feeling of being suffocated that he experienced back in Buffalo, running the store.

A small amount of honest introspection might have revealed that whether he was flying his desk, weekends in the reserve, running his furniture store or commanding the 646th, he enjoyed bossing people around, but lacked the qualities of a real leader, intangible qualities that troops or employees sense. "This guy understands," they tell each other of real leaders. "He's one of us."

Real leaders make those serving with them feel that everything is going to be all right because the leader says so and knows what he's doing. Real leaders instill confidence. It's a knack; a knack for getting the most and the best out of those under your command, whether in the military or the corporate environment. Some come by the knack naturally, almost seem to be born with it, while others develop the knack. Still others know of the knack but can't quite master it. And a dismal few don't even recognize the knack when they see it in action.

Becker is a member of the dismal few. This, coupled with his lack of empathy, hooked to a zero reading on the common sense meter, make leadership a tough chore. Jesus! Whatever made me think that running an outfit would be easy?

Jumping up out of his chair, he heads for the door. "I need some air," he exclaims. He tears the door open and slams it behind him, rattling the walls and shaking his photos to further unevenness.

Rushing out onto the orderly room porch, he stands there in the sunshine. A loud rumble rambles around his stomach as he takes in the mess hall. He gives himself a memo, Get the medic to requisition six bottles of Alka-Seltzer, Monday morning.

Might as well try some breakfast. He heads for the mess hall.

CHAPTER 2

▼

The daredevil behind the wheel of the small, blue Air Force bus barreling north on Highway 23 is the fourth name on Becker's shit list, A/B Thomas McKinny, formerly A2/c Thomas McKinny, Intercept Control Tech, Charlie crew.

McKinny, twenty-two when the war started, grabbed his chance to get away from farm life in Nebraska, where he'd worked like a grown man since he was old enough to reach the pedals on the family tractor. He enlisted in the Air Force. The recruiting sergeant promised McKinny that after four years as a radar operator, he'd be a cinch to get a job as an air traffic controller in civilian life. As the youngest of three sons, never able to wedge a few words into a family discussion, McKinny grew up taciturn. "Okay, Sarge," he declared and signed up. Girls are charmed by McKinny's quiet, "aw, shucks" Gary Cooper manner. He is unaware of this.

Only one thing lubricates McKinny's vocal cords—alcohol. Unfortunately, as loquaciousness enters the front door of his brain, good judgment zooms out the window and off into the wild, blue yonder.

McKinny recalls the night that cost him two stripes, took him out of Radar Operations and dropped him into the motor pool.

It was March. He'd been drinking since late afternoon, into the night with two of his crewmates at Sally Benton's house in Oscoda. Four of Sally's girlfriends were there. While slow-dancing with Sally in the living room by the light of the moon, McKinny waved a silent goodbye to his friends as they left with two of the girls. The two remaining girls sat on the couch drinking their beers.

Sally whispered in his ear, "Tommy, I wish you could get a couple of the boys at the base to date Jenny and Alma."

"Well, they're not really great looking, Sal. Not like you."

Sally kissed his cheek. "You're sweet."

"You know, now that I think of it ... I know two guys from radar school on Baker crew. They ain't seen a girl for almost three weeks."

As McKinny's tongue kicked into high gear, the last wisp of his usual good judgment evaporated into the cosmos.

"They're on thirty-day restriction," he continued. "Think the girls would sneak on the base to see these guys?"

"Sounds exciting. I'll bet they would. Let's clean up around here. It's after midnight. My folks are due home soon."

McKinny downshifts, powers through a curve and returns to his reminiscence.

He's helping the girls through a hole in the fence, everyone stumbling and laughing. They weave their way to Baker crew's barracks, Jenny and Alma carrying a case of beer between them, he and Sally passing a half-gallon bottle of wine back and forth.

They enter the barracks and march down the aisle dividing the two rows of cots, singing, "Rose, Rose, I love you with an aching heart." Jenny and Alma, their church keys flying, are opening long-necked bottles of beer, giving them to each airman they awaken.

In his reverie, McKinny hears himself shouting, "Where's Pip? Where's Jonesy? I brought 'em a couple of hot-to-trot, young heifers."

Suddenly, flashlights, two air policemen and the Officer of the Day burst into the scene. The barracks goes bright and he and the girls are taken away.

At the end of his recollection of the disastrous night, he's standing at attention in front of Captain Becker being told that not only was he being demoted to airman basic but he was also being transferred to the motor pool. He was no longer an intercept control tech; he was now a truck driver.

Eddie was right, McKinny thinks. I do get to fuck off a whole lot more in the motor pool than up at Radar Ops. He hits a straight stretch of road and jams his foot down on the accelerator. He remembers Eddie's advice.

It was the day after his squadron punishment and although he had sustained a two-stripe bust and had been transferred, McKinny had not been restricted to the base, so he did the natural thing. He took his troubles to the Huron Hotel's bar, where he spent the afternoon mulling over his new circumstances, watching his life spiral to nowhere and trying to drink his problems into submission. He didn't succeed. He returned to the base talkative and downcast. On the way to his barracks, he met Eddie and surprised him by answering Eddie's greeting of,

"Hi, Tommy," with a dreary, "I feel lower than snakeshit at the bottom of a gully."

McKinny knew that Eddie and everyone else on the base had heard all about his adventure, demotion and transfer to the motor pool. He also knew through squadron gossip that Eddie thought of him as a right guy, who always had his shit in order and his logs up to date at shift change. Being on different shifts, he didn't see that much of Eddie off-duty.

Just a little bit drunk and a lot upset, Tommy had allowed Eddie to steer him to the PX, where the two of them sat at a table, drinking coffee, smoking and talking for two hours.

Telling a rambling tale of all he could remember of what was being called "the females on the base incident", Tommy then went into all the things that were bringing him down. Noticing Eddie's surprise at the depth of his despair, Tommy realized, even with the alcohol drifting through his brain, that Eddie, just like the folks back home in Nebraska, had mistaken Tommy's usual non-talkative manner for rigid self-control. I'm not a stoic, he thought, and Paw was wrong to call me that. I've got feelings and I feel shitty.

Tommy continued to sing the blues, mentioning everything from his unhappiness at having to go back to the farm with his air traffic controller dream down the toilet, to his fear that Sally's beauty contest entry form would get rejected if the news got out.

Tommy dominated the first hour and a half of the conversation with Eddie nodding his head from time to time, offering encouraging words like, "I can understand that," and "Sure, I'd feel the same fuckin' way."

Toward the last half hour of their discussion, as some of the effects of the alcohol began to diminish, Tommy started to drift into his natural quiet mode and Eddie sprang into action.

"So you lost a couple of stripes. Stripes ain't shit ... unless you're buckin' for general. You don't feel any dumber, do you? And shit, Tommy, come on. You had to expect somethin'. Jesus Christ, man! You had pussy in the barracks. You coulda started a fuckin' riot." Eddie laughs at the thought and Tommy makes an effort.

"And as far as Sally's concerned," Eddie continues, "you said the girls were picked up by their parents here on the base. That means the provost marshal is treating it as a 'base incident.' There'll be nothin' in the local papers. It's like a fight in the dayroom; nobody's business but ours. Besides, most of the shit we worry about never happens. And that's no bull-shit. I read that somewhere. Some famous guy said that.

Eddie then went on to extol the merits of the motor pool. "One of the guys on my crew knows Sergeant Kazmarkian, says he's a good guy, not chickenshit. If I was in your shoes, especially with what you said about drivin' tractors and farm shit, I'd have as much fun as I could workin' in the motor pool and I'd never let Becker see me without a big smile on my face. And who knows, things change, you could wind up back in Radar Ops. You still got two years on your enlistment. So cheer up, Tommy. Assholes like Becker are everywhere. You can't avoid 'em. You just gotta outwit 'em. And that's so fuckin' easy, it's fun. And you know what? I'll bet you get to fuck off a whole lot more in the motor pool than up at Radar Ops."

McKinny knows every turn and twist of Highway 23 and he defies centrifugal force on most of them. The eight new radar operators watch the bean fields and jack pines whiz by with wide eyes, trying to listen to Sumner. McKinny is making mental comments, using the bus to emphasize them as Sumner drones on about the rules and regulations of the 646th.

Standing near the front door, hanging onto a pole, he's trying to look impressive. He is deep into his usual spiel. "And remember this, men. We're in a bind …"

You're always in a bind. Watch this, McKinny thinks as he hits the brakes hard, downshifts into a tight turn and accelerates suddenly coming out of it.

"Bingo!" Sumner loses his garrison cap. It rolls along the floor toward the back of the bus. One of the new men scoops it up and hands it back.

Sumner puts his hat back on, glares at McKinny and continues, "As I was saying, we're in a bind for good radar operators here at the Six-Four-Six and promotions come quickly for those who know how to follow orders."

They come even faster for brown-nosers like you, flashes through McKinny's mind. He gooses the bus. Sumner sways.

"*De*-motions also occur and some radar operators find them-selves in the mess hall or the motor pool. Isn't that right, McKinny?"

McKinny jumps on the brakes, and lays a hard left off the highway onto the gravel road that leads to the base's main gate. Sumner is pitched into the door.

McKinny looks over at him, grinning at the lieutenant's struggle to stay erect. "Yes sir, that sure is right." He floorboards the bus and the din from the spewing gravel reminds McKinny of the old joke, "What's the noisiest thing in the world? Two skeletons fucking on a tin roof, during a hail storm." Doing his best to sound like two skeletons fucking, he roars up to the main gate.

At the guard shack, under the sign that reads, 646th AIRCRAFT CONTROL AND WARNING SQUADRON, McKinny locks the brakes. The bus screeches to a halt. Sumner tumbles up into the wind-shield. McKinny pops open the door and shouts past Sumner, to the air policeman on duty, "Hey, Smitty. Eight new scopedopes on board."

"You're late, Tommy. Becker called twice."

Fuck Becker, McKinny's mind shouts. He slips the shift lever into first, slides his foot off the clutch, and digs out in a cloud of dust and another barrage of gravel. He's in front of the orderly room before he can get into third gear. The new men disembark. One of them, a joker, gets down and kisses the ground. Sumner pulls himself together and calls the men to attention.

Captain Becker struts out of the orderly room, strikes a Patton-like pose, surveys the new men and barks, "I'll keep this simple. We go by the book here at the Six-Four-Six because the book works. Follow orders, don't break rules, respect regulations and you'll make rank. Fuck up and it's your ass. Two of you will be assigned to each radar crew. A memo on the squadron bulletin board explains your duty hours. Basically, it's nine days on and three days ..." Becker stops speaking. Down the street, near the motor pool, a sheriff's car is parking behind the base bus.

"Sumner! Take over here," Becker shouts, heading for the black, gold and white Hudson.

The Captain has a good idea who the passenger might be. The deputy and A/ B Edward Flynn are standing beside the car when Becker storms up. Flynn, his hands cuffed behind him, is wearing wrinkled khakis. His tapered shirt is torn. His non-pleated oversees cap, spread wide, rests on the bridge of his nose. His dark green aviator shades only partially hide a black eye. He's smiling and his greasy ducktail haircut is shaggy.

"Hiya, Captain." Eddie smiles bigger. "Sorry I can't salute."

Becker ignores him and glowers at the deputy. "Three days was all you could keep him? I told the sheriff to rip the sheet on this guy."

The deputy unlocks Eddie's cuffs, watching for him to rub his wrists. Eddie doesn't. "Dirty little bastard," the deputy mutters. "Sorry, Captain," he grunts, "he's all yours."

"Thanks for the lift," Eddie shouts after the departing deputy. Turning toward Becker, Eddie goes into his military act. He snaps to rigid attention, salutes and almost shouts, "Airman Basic Edward Flynn reporting for duty, sir!"

Boiling, Becker grudgingly returns Eddie's salute. "Dismissed," he orders. "Now get your ass over to my office and put yourself at attention in front of my desk. Pronto!"

Eddie strolls into the orderly room, says, "Hi," to the morning report clerk and stands at attention three feet away from Becker's desk. He knows this drill. He's looking at the pictures of the old fighter planes on the wall when Becker blows into the room, looking apoplectic. Slamming the door behind him, he starts pacing up and down in the space between Eddie and the desk, breathing deep, quick gulps of air.

Eddie watches with concealed glee. This is gonna be a good one, he decides. Maybe a classic.

Captain Becker turns abruptly and gets right up into Eddie's face. Eddie goes into his straight ahead, I don't see nothin' zombie stare, repeating his mantra, There you stand, you silly son of a bitch, chewin' my ass, and you with less brains in your head than me.

Becker starts railing. "Flynn, there are so many things about you that I hate that I don't know where to begin. But I think the thing that I hate the most about you is your I-don't-give-a-shit attitude."

"Whatever the captain says, sir."

"Don't give me that happy horseshit. You're going to stand at attention in my office until a shit detail comes up. And if a shit detail doesn't come up, I'm going to make one." Getting redder, Becker shouts, "You got that?!"

"Yes sir," Eddie shouts. "I'm gonna stand at attention until a shit …"

"That's enough," Becker interjects. "As soon as I dismiss you, you get into your fatigues, get your ass over to the mess hall and tell Sergeant Arbo that I want you to clean out the grease pits. Dismissed. And get a haircut."

Eddie continues to stand at attention. "Which should I do first, sir?"

"What the hell are you talking about?"

"Your orders, Captain. Should I clean up the grease pits first or get a haircut? I'll have to go to town for a haircut."

The big vein in Becker's forehead starts wriggling. "Forget about town for thirty days. I'm putting you on restriction. Now get the hell out of here! I'm calling Arbo in five minutes and you'd better be in that mess hall. And I'm putting you on permanent KP. Forget about Radar Ops."

"Yes, sir." Eddie salutes and holds it. Becker looks at him and thinks, I've got to get rid of this misfit. He's killing me. He returns Eddie's salute.

Eddie leaves Becker's office, closing the door quietly. He grins and heads for the barracks.

CHAPTER 3

▼

Staff Sergeant Rocco Arbo runs a first-rate, immaculate mess hall, but you'd never know it to look at him. He has enough mustard, ketchup and assorted food stains on his fatigues to be mistaken for a huge burger with the works.

During World War II, stationed in England with the Eighth Air Force, Arbo did his cooking for a bomber squadron. Many faces disappeared from his chow line before their tours were up. Arbo remembers most of them. To him, they'll always be young kids.

At war's end, he joined the reserve, went to culinary school for two years on the G.I. bill and landed a job as a chef in a high-line restaurant in Miami Beach. He doesn't mind being back on active duty because it keeps his ex-wife out of his hair.

On his walk from the barracks to the mess hall, Eddie lights a cigarette and allows his mind to travel back to February 1951, when he pulled his first KP in the 646th.

As the last of the four KP's to show up for duty, Eddie was assigned to pots and pans. The first guy in always signed up for outside man, a cushy job, hosing the empty garbage cans, setting up the loaded "food only" cans for the pig farmer to pick up, helping unload any deliveries, sweeping and mopping the loading dock and working the serving line during meals.

The next two guys in signed up for dishes, washing and spraying the trays and sending racks of them, along with cups and utensils through the dishwashing machine. They also work the serving line, along with the two cooks on duty and the outside man, so their work piles up during meals, but nothing like pots and pans.

Pots and pans was the toughest. Every ladle, strainer, mixing spoon, whisk, milk pitcher, pot, pan, flat tray and deep dish flat tray with every baked-on, caked-on, greasy, burnt, sticky piece of crud on it wound up with the pot-and-pan man.

The menu gods did not smile on Eddie that day. Morning chow had been French toast and bacon, which equaled many flat trays either full of burned-in bacon grease or caked, burnt French toast batter, along with the usual onslaught of milk and orange juice pitchers. Arbo's cooks used utensils like Kleenex, so every meal brought a rain of scoops, spoons and mixing paddles.

Noon chow had been baked beans, franks and coleslaw, along with brownies for dessert. That meal resulted in deep dish trays with residues of molasses and brown sugar fused to the sides of them, and flat trays with rows of hard-baked gunk on them from where the hot dogs had roasted. The brownies brought on flat trays with burned spots of brownie dough welded to them.

For evening chow, Arbo's favorite, he went with lasagna, garlic toast, baked eggplant, salad and deep-dish apple pie. This meal gave the flat trays an encore. Arbo's cooks had painted the slices of bread with copious amounts of melted garlic butter, resulting in a plethora of remnants on the trays. All the apple pie tins were Crisco-greasy and the deep-dish trays were full of baked-on lasagna leavings and crusted eggplant debris.

Throughout the day, Arbo had observed Eddie plowing through the mound of pots and pans relentlessly. He watched as Eddie filled the wash-and-rinse sinks with near-scalding water, taking note of Eddie's use of the scraper and the Brillo pad. He saw how Eddie changed the water when necessary and noticed how he left the worst of the trays for last at each meal.

After evening chow, when Arbo had asked Eddie to hang around a few minutes, Eddie immediately became suspicious. "Wonder what's up," he thought. As he watched the mess sergeant duck into the walk-in refrigerator, his thoughts became defensive and combative. "I put in a good day's work," he was grousing to himself, when Arbo popped out of the refrigerator with a quart bottle of Miller High Life in each hand.

Listening to the sergeant shout, "When there's work to be done, we do that. And when there's fucking off to be done, we do that too!" Eddie's attitude changed. Arbo then handed one of the bottles to Eddie.

Eddie laughed, and after taking a drink said, "Thanks, Sarge."

"Just call me Arbo."

"Arbo it is. I'm Eddie Flynn." Eddie and Arbo shook hands.

"I know. Becker said keep an eye on you. Said you're a fuckup." Arbo smiled. "I could use four fuckups like you every day." Arbo sipped his beer.

"Thanks for the compliment." Eddie offered Arbo his pack of cigarettes. Arbo took one. They both lit up and Arbo sat down in his swivel chair, vaulting his feet up onto his desk in the same motion. Eddie made a seat out of a stack of three cases of canned peaches.

"You know, Eddie, you deprived me of the pleasure of using some of my best lines today."

"How's that?" Eddie took another swallow of beer.

"I'm expecting a fuckup, so I'm all set with shit to say like, 'Jesus Christ, kid, you've got to change that fucking wash water. That sink's got more shit floating in it than the swimming pool at an officers' club.'" Arbo took another sip of beer.

Eddie laughed. Arbo nodded. "Most of the guys like that one. Another one I use is, 'Get some hot water in that sink. If that water gets any colder, penguins'll start hanging around in here. I don't want no one dying of the drizzling shits after eating in *my* mess hall.'"

"I like the 'drizzlin' shits.' It's a nice touch."

Arbo grinned a big, self-satisfied grin, leaned back in his chair and blew a cloud of smoke at the ceiling.

You could even say you saw Willie the Penguin on the loadin' dock, smokin' a Kool, lacin' up his ice skates.

Arbo let his chair snap upright. "You'll probably hear me use that." From there, Arbo went on to comment on Eddie's use of hot water, Brillo pads and his general experience at the sinks, ending with, "You even found time for smoking breaks. How'd you get so good with the pots and pans? Sent away? Reform school?" Arbo laughed at his own question and Eddie took a long drink.

"Drink up," Arbo had said. "There's plenty more where these came from. And where these came from is the officers' mess slush fund."

"So you wanna know how I got to be a pot-and-pan champ?" Eddie took a drag of his cigarette. "It was June. School was out. My mother says, "Listen, mister, you're not going to spend any more summers running the streets of New York."

"Running the streets of New York," the phrase that Mrs. Flynn used was as active and lively as it sounded. Eddie's mother used it without an inkling of its full scope. Running the streets, for a kid like Eddie, offered far more activities than any summer camp. A partial list would include playing stickball, playing blackjack on McCarthy's stoop, hanging out and bullshitting in the ice cream parlor, swimming in the river, grabbing fruit off produce stands (one store, the

Pick and Pay Market was renamed the Pick and Run by Eddie and his pals,) swiping coins from newspaper stands, sneaking on the 125th Street ferry to New Jersey, climbing the pipeline up the palisades and slipping into the amusement park, jumping the turnstiles and riding the subway all over town, sneaking into downtown movie houses, shoplifting at department stores, hanging on the corner smoking, spitting and cursing, and after sundown, girls could be taken up to Riverside Park or the guys could play cards on the corner, underneath the lamppost. No two days of summer were ever the same for Eddie and his bunch, no one was overweight and they never complained about being bored.

At the extreme tip of the top of this incomplete list of enjoyable things to do, hitching ruled as the uncontested favorite. Eddie and his friends could stick, like dogshit on a sneaker, to the back of anything that rolled, from a trolley to a taxi and they could jump onto slow-moving trucks, taking them on the run.

Along with hitching went hitting the milk truck. Hitting the milk truck involved stealing cases of chocolate milk from Sheffield Farms milk trucks, easy prey as they snailed their way up the long hill on Broadway from 125th Street to 118th.

Kids hitting the milk truck found a sturdy, full-length step bumper to stand on and an array of handholds. Taking advantage of the large hinges, bulky levers and door handles on the back of the truck, two agile climbers would be atop the truck in an instant. "It's like a jungle gym on wheels," Eddie once remarked.

On the milk truck's roof were four open hatches overflowing with shaved ice, used to keep the cases of milk, cream, half and half, cottage cheese and the prize, chocolate milk, cool. Scraping away the ice and rummaging in the hatches, the roof guys would pull out a case of chocolate milk (sometimes quart bottles, sometimes half-pint cardboard containers), and pass it down to two kids standing on the bumper.

The bumper-riders would each keep their inside hand free to grab the case and hold it until another kid could dart out from the line of cars and trucks parked by the curb, take the handoff of the case and melt back among the parked vehicles. A well-oiled team could nail three or four cases before the hill died at 118th. Sometimes, "Civic Sams," as Eddie called them, would blow their horns and point to alert the truck drivers. They were usually too late with their warnings.

The milk trucks were hit so often that the company sometimes had a second man ride shotgun, watching for trouble. This made hitting the milk truck a bit more difficult but much more fun.

Many a stickball game would be interrupted when a kid would shout, "Hey, it's two o'clock. Let's go hit the milk truck."

A typical day in the life of Eddie the street-runner would be like this sunny day in June, 1943. With his father dead and planted for over a year and his mother working downtown from nine to five, Eddie has had time to polish his skills at unsupervised fun. He's in good form.

He's sitting in the bushes, in the traffic divider on Broadway, between 120th Street and 121st with two of his classmates, Big John Malloy and Jerry Casey. They'll be 8th graders in September.

Eddie has just stolen a pack of Luckies from a nearby candy store and the three of them are practicing inhaling and blowing smoke out of their noses. Jerry whips out a Buck Rogers comic book that he slipped into his shirt and the boys start talking about the future.

"I'll be sixty-nine in two thousand," Jerry states.

"Nobody gets that old," Eddie adds and they laugh.

A southbound trolley is approaching the stop at 120th. It's a Tenth Avenue trolley, an easier hitch than a Broadway, a newer model with fewer places for hands to grip and a bumper that folds under if a kid stands on it. Although they were more challenging, Bees were still hitched with impunity by the kids, but Tenners were more fun.

"Hey, here comes a Tenner," Jerry shouts. "Wanna go hitchin'?"

"Fuckin'-A," Eddie answers, flicking his cigarette butt out into the street, like the guys in the movies.

The Tenner leaves the trolley stop with the three boys hanging on the back of it, kicking at each other, laughing and goofing.

With no potential passengers waiting at the 116th Street trolley stop, the Tenner goes zipping past a crowd of Columbia students coming out of the subway kiosk. Big John shouts, "Fuck Columbia!" Jerry spits a juicy loogie in their direction and Eddie shouts, "Fuck the world!"

Later that afternoon, Eddie takes a large chocolate cake out of the front window of a bakery on 83rd Street and goes running up Broadway balancing it on one hand, like one of those competitors in a waiters' race. Big John and Jerry keep pace with him. The baker and his teenage assistant drop out at 85th Street.

At 86th Eddie and the guys cut west and don't stop until they hit Riverside Drive. They sit in the grass in Riverside Park and eat the cake with their hands, sharing with the pigeons and squirrels. They wash their hands in a fountain, wipe them dry on their dungarees and walk up to Broadway to head home.

Hitching back uptown, they catch a pickle truck with a canvas back. They climb inside and break open a barrel of dills. Passing 110th Street, they throw pickles at the people sitting on the traffic divider's benches. Jerry knocks an old guy's hat off.

After supper Eddie plays blackjack with the guys down on the corner of 122nd and Amsterdam. He quits at ten o'clock, eighty cents ahead. "How come you're quittin' winners," one of the guys whines.

"Because I gotta get up and serve the seven o'clock Mass tomorrow, asshole," he answers. "See you guys tomorrow."

"Looks like a pretty good summer comin' up." He heads up Amsterdam, jingling the coins in his pocket.

"Then she starts in about how my friends are all pieces of shit. You know, like that."

"You bet I know," Arbo agreed. "My mother used to think any girl I dated was a whore. A couple of times she was right."

Eddie laughed, took another drink and continued. "Anyway, long story short, my mother made a deal with a guy who runs Catholic summer camps. I'm gonna spend the summer at a lake in New Hampshire, not as a camper, but as a worker. And I'm gonna be a waiter, not a pot-and-pan man, not at the kids' camp, but next door at a lodge where priests from the city come up to vacation, play tennis, shoot golf. The place had its own nine hole golf course … and a softball diamond."

"Sounds better than summer in the city." Arbo sipped his beer and took a drag of his cigarette.

"It coulda been okay. I get seventy bucks at the end of the season and the waiters and the kitchen crew divvies up the summer's tips from the priests. About two hundred bucks apiece, my mom tells me. I figure, what the fuck and say I'll go along with it."

"How'd you fuck it up?"

"I was doin' good for two weeks. Waitin' tables was easy duty. I'm carryin' one plate with two more up my arm, shit like that. I ain't even breakin' a sweat. Then the kitchen manager's buddy shows up. The kid worked for him before. These guys are like Batman and Robin. Next thing I know I'm in the kitchen and this kid's waitin' on the priests. I know I'm gettin' fucked but I say, 'To hell with it.' I'm still in for the tips, my mom made a deal, and the lake beats swimmin' in the Hudson."

"Hello, pots and pans." Arbo finished the rest of his beer.

"Not yet," Eddie had said, taking a drag from his cigarette and chasing it by killing the remainder of his beer. He ripped out a loud, smoky belch.

"Sounds like it's time for another," Arbo said. He went back into the walk-in and came back with two more quarts. Eddie took a bottle and continued with his story. "The kitchen wasn't that bad. There were five of us, so you only got pots and pans once every five days. We only had sixty priests at a time stayin' there. It was okay for a couple of weeks."

"Well then, how'd you fuck it up?"

Arbo took a drink of beer and Eddie continued, "We had an old cook, nice old guy, retired navy, always drunk, but a good cook. Cooked potatoes every night, Lyonnaise potatoes, mashed potatoes, potatoes au gratin, diced potatoes, scalloped potatoes … and on Sunday, potato salad. Every dinner took two milk cans full of peeled potatoes, the big milk cans. With five kitchen workers and five waiters taking their turns, you came up for potatoes once every ten days." Eddie stopped and took a long drink.

"Once every ten days ain't too bad."

"No it ain't. But two days in a row finished it for me. The kitchen manager wanted to take his pratboy to town with him to pick up supplies so I get stuck with peelin' potatoes in his place, right after doin' my own day. I go to this jerk and I bitch about it and he tells me, 'Tough shit. Like it or lump it.' I decided to lump it. I put the tops on the milk cans like they're full. I put the sack of potatoes away, except for one big potato. I carved eyes and a mouth in it and put it on top of one of the milk cans. Then I stabbed the potato peeler into it.

I spend the afternoon swimmin'. I forgot all about it 'til the kitchen manager comes back and I hear him screamin' and goin' apeshit. They served the priests rice that night. Hope they all got constipated."

Eddie dropped his cigarette in the butt can. Arbo took a swallow of his beer. "What about the pots and pans?"

"Next mornin' I'm in the main office gettin' my walkin' papers, ready to be shipped back to the city, when the phone rings. It's Mister Dalton, the owner. He needs a pot-and-pan man at his girls' camp in Vermont. I talk to him on the phone and agree to the switch. It's a guaranteed hundred and fifty bucks at season's end and I'm off to the Pine Lake Camp for Ladies."

"How old were you?"

"Fourteen, and I didn't get no nookie. The guy who ran the joint and his wife were on me and this other kid like flies on shit. We couldn't go nowhere alone. If I woke up at night to take a piss, the guy would pop up in the latrine. Jack was sixteen. He was sent up from another camp as a dishwasher. One of the senior girl counselors liked him, but I'm sure he never got a chance to bang her."

"And you never got nothin'?"

"Oh, I got some nice feels from some of the girls when they'd work meals as servers but that was it. I got my hundred and a half so the summer wasn't a total loss."

Arbo and Eddie drank three quarts of beer each that night, with Arbo telling Eddie not to ever marry a stripper, how full of shit commissioned officers were and his plans for opening a pizza joint after the war.

They locked up the mess hall, laughing and singing. "Ta rah, rah boom tee-a, did you get yours today? I got mine yesterday, that's why I walk this way."

Eddie's almost to the mess hall. He quits daydreaming and flicks his cigarette butt toward the open #10 can nailed to the wall near the entrance. It hits the can and rims it but doesn't go in. Eddie picks up the butt, drops it in the butt can and enters the mess hall.

Fifteen minutes later, Eddie's sitting at a table with Arbo. Eddie's eating bacon and eggs. They're both drinking coffee laced with vanilla extract. A large bottle of vanilla extract is on the table. Arbo is laughing. Eddie is in mid-story, "I never knew the asshole was a deputy until we were already dukin' it out."

Arbo breaks up. "Becker must've went apeshit when the sheriff delivered your ass."

"Better'n ever. Reddest I ever seen him. His big forehead vein was jumpin'."

The wall phone rings. Leaning back in his chair, Arbo grabs it without looking. He puts on his best military voice. "Mess Sergeant Arbo here."

He takes a big drink from his vanilla extract bottle and swallows loudly. "Yes, sir, Captain, he sure is here. I'm getting him ready for the grease pits right now." Hanging up the phone he turns to Eddie. "You know, Eddie, officers are just like seagulls."

"How's that, Arbo?"

"They're both fulla shit and government protected."

The two of them laugh. Eddie wipes up the remains of his eggs with a scrap of toast and stuffs it into his mouth. "I guess I better get my ass in gear."

"Yeah. Becker's coming by in an hour and he says if you ain't in the pits, it'll be *my* ass." Arbo jumps up squawking loudly, high-stepping toward the kitchen, his head dipping back and forth, with his hands on his hips, flailing his elbows like wings. The two KP's wiping down the serving line laugh heartily.

Fuckin' Arbo, Eddie thinks, grinning.

Eddie takes his tray, cup and utensils over to the sink, rinses them and puts them on the counter next to the dishwasher. He goes to the utility room and picks up two buckets and a scraper with a flexible, six-inch-wide blade. Spotting a small trowel, he takes it along. Might as well do a decent job, he figures and heads for the back door.

Out behind the mess hall, Eddie opens the manhole that leads down into the grease pits. The stink that greets him is almost visible. He lights a cigarette. By the time he's finished bringing his gear down to the pits, he's acclimated to the odor.

He's down in the pit almost two hours with no sign of Becker, when a shadow passes the manhole. "The asshole's come to gloat," Eddie concludes and he starts to sing, "Come and Tie My Pecker to a Tree".

On his walk from the orderly room, Becker relished the thought of looking down into the grease pit at an unhappy, sweating, pissing and moaning Flynn. His thought of punishment, being so much more rewarding when viewed, was interrupted with Eddie's singing. He wasn't singing when I first got here. That little bastard knows I'm up here. How?

"First time I met her, she was talkin' to her mother,
Crabs on her belly was a fuckin' one another,
Come and tie my pecker to a tree, to a tree,
Come and tie my pecker to a tree."

Eddie sings it, just as he learned it at radar school down in Biloxi.

Becker steps farther from the manhole and lights a cigarette. I'll just wait him out.

"Last time I seen her and I haven't seen her since,
She was jackin' off her daddy through a barbed-wire fence,
Come and tie my pecker to a tree, to a tree,
Come and tie my pecker to a tree."

The grease pit is an echo chamber. Eddie enjoys the way he sounds and gets into it.

"Went to the cat house and they tried to hide her,
And I seen two bedbugs jackin' off a spider,
Come and tie my pecker to a tree, to a tree,
Come and tie my pecker to a tree."

Captain Becker stands next to the mess hall, smoking, fuming, looking at the sky, trying not to hear the singing, trying to relax.

Louder than before, the voice from the manhole booms:

"Floatin' down the river on a shithouse door,
Me and your momma and another old whore,
Come and tie my pecker to a tree, to a tree,
Come and tie my pecker to a tree."

Becker can stand no more. He surrenders. Ignoring the nearby butt can, he stamps out his cigarette on Arbo's pristine lawn and stomps over to the manhole. Peering into it, he yells, "How do you like it down there, Flynn?"

"Beats the shit outta Radar Ops, Captain," Eddie shouts back.

Becker's face vanishes. Eddie goes on with his job. He feels good about his retort, just as he felt good not rubbing his wrists when uncuffed, knowing that the shit-eating deputy was waiting for him to do exactly that.

The mindless task of scraping grease and putting it into a bucket allows Eddie's brain to ramble through the past, through the battlegrounds in his war with authority.

He was not yet four when he decided, almost intuitively, to never give authoritarian assholes the satisfaction of seeing that whatever punishment he was absorbing was causing him even mild discomfort.

He flashes back to Lucy's birthday party in first grade as an example of a brush with an authoritarian asshole. I think I'll call Authoritarian Assholes, A As, he thinks. No, I'll call them Double A's. He drifts back to that day.

Lucy's mother comes in with the cake, "Happy Birthday" is sung, six candles are blown out. It's time to cut the cake.

The boys, there are only three of them, are farthest away from the cake. They start to jostle their way through the cluster of twelve girls surrounding the table. Eddie and the other two boys are shouting, "Me first! Me first!"

Lucy's mother, a no-nonsense kind of woman with her hair pulled back into a tight bun, takes charge. "You three," she commands, "you just stand there until the ladies are served. Ruffians!"

She takes her time with each girl, cutting large pieces from the cake and taking a large piece for herself. With only three skinny-ass pieces on the platter, she offers it to the boys. The first two boys take their cake and say, "Thank you." Eddie looks at the last piece of cake on the plate, smiles his best "Fuck you" smile and declares, "No thanks, not hungry." His defiance undiluted with even a speck of hurt.

Eddie laughs out loud, thinking of the stricken, frozen look on Lucy's mother's face.

Lucy's mother calls Eddie's mother. Eddie's mother has to pick him up early from the party. Eddie's father comes home three-quarters blasted, gets the report from Eddie's mother concerning the party, and Eddie gets a beating. He refuses to cry.

Down in the grease pit, Eddie feels energized. "When I get punished, I usually got it comin'. So what the fuck ..."

He puts in a good day's work, skips evening chow and heads for the barracks.

CHAPTER 4

▼

The barracks are almost deserted. Dog crew, finishing a three-day break, is not due back on duty until 0800 Sunday. Its members are scattered from Oscoda to Detroit in search of fun. The only two guys in the barracks are Eddie's buddy, A/3c Bob Porter and A/2c Norm Stanton.

During tourist season, Bob is Eddie's partner on what Eddie calls "Beach Patrol." They've had some memorable three-day breaks with girls like the "Benzedrine Nurses from Flint" and "Cadillac Baby."

Like Eddie, Bob wears Levis and Pendleton shirts off base and like Eddie, he hears the words, "Get a haircut, airman!" whenever he crosses Captain Becker's path. Unlike Eddie, he's not apt to tell you to go fuck yourself, or punch you in the mouth if you piss him off. An unbiased observer would tell Bob that Eddie is bad company. He and Eddie are both twenty and equipped with altered ID cards and Class A passes thanks to the skills of their friend and former crew member, A/B George Dennis.

Last three-day break, when Bob and Eddie went to Detroit, they stopped by Selfridge Field, where Eddie smuggled a pint of Seagrams past the stockade guards. George was surprised and grateful.

Bob's from San Jose. He's one of only eight enlisted men in the 646th who has a car on base. It's a '49 Ford coupe, deep maroon, de-chromed and lowered in front. With its V-8 engine and stick shift, Bob goes through tires like Captain Becker goes through Alka-Seltzers. The car is almost paid for and Bob once told Eddie, "If my car was a girl I'd marry it."

Bob's in the latrine combing his hair, talking to Norm. Norm is wearing his khakis. He's buffing up his shoes. Norm is conscientious, has a regulation haircut and always wears his uniform off base. He's twenty-one and has legitimate ID. He's from Los Angeles, did well in high school, had a year of college at UCLA and is taking a correspondence course in Ancient History. Norm's only been in the 646th for four months. Although he's twenty-one and Eddie's twenty, Eddie thinks of him as, "A nice kid, kind of square but okay." Eddie once told Bob, "You guys may both be from California, but any similarity ends there."

"I didn't see a perch anywhere this afternoon," Norm remarks.

"And you're not going to see any tonight either." Bob laughs. "The Tawas Perch Festival isn't about perch. I wouldn't know a perch if I saw one. It's about girls coming up here from all over the area …"

Eddie slams the barracks door and yells, "Where the fuck is everybody?!?!"

Bob spots Eddie in the mirror. Norm sees him an instant later. "Eddie," they shout, almost in unison. They leave the latrine and greet Eddie midway down the barracks.

Norm grabs Eddie's hand and shakes it. "Boy am I glad to see you. I wasn't looking forward to starting day shifts tomorrow without you."

Bob is pounding Eddie on the back, shaking Eddie's other hand. "Welcome back, Eddie. Phew! You smell rank!"

"Great pals. One guy's glad I'm back because he don't want to work too hard and the other guy says I stink." They all laugh.

Bob notices Eddie's black eye. "Nice shiner."

"Three days old and healin' already. I like the little patches of yellow around the purple edge. Kinda colorful." He walks a few steps down the bay to his bunk. He opens his foot-locker, gets out his toilet articles, fresh boxers, socks and a T-shirt and throws the stuff on his cot.

Norm and Bob continue talking. "Captain Ross told me you might get thirty days." Norm looks worried.

"Norm was shitting green. Afraid he'd have to work intercept control tech," Bob reports, adding, "How *did* you get out so fast?"

Eddie sits on the side of his bed and starts taking off his shoes. "Sheriff's daughter due home from Michigan State on Monday. Sheriff's house is attached to the jail. Goodbye, Eddie." He grins. "At least, that's my theory. Where are you guys headed?"

"The dance at Tawas," Bob answers. "It's the last night of the Perch Festival."

"Holy shit!" Eddie pitches his brogans under his bunk. "I forgot all about that." He rips off his socks and grabs all the things off his bed. "Lemme hit the showers." He sprints for the latrine.

Eddie takes a steamy, fifteen-minute shower, working every speck of rancid grease off his skin and out of his pores. He brushes his teeth, takes a shave and while clipping and cleaning his fingernails, he recalls his 8th grade sex education talk with his mother. He's standing in the bathroom, looking in the medicine chest mirror, combing his hair, almost ready to go out for the evening; his mother standing by the bathroom door addressing him. "You know, Eddie, now that you're out of grammar school, you'll be dating," she starts.

I've been dating, he wisecracks to himself, picturing Rhonda and Babs, two girls from 120th Street who let himself and his buddies get away with a few things at the movies or the park. He doesn't want to be having this talk and interrupts, "Mom, I go to parties with girls, and movies. I know how to be polite around girls."

"Well, there are also men out there, who …"

"Come on, Mom. I know about queers."

"That's not a nice term."

"Call 'em fruits, then. Who cares about them? You got anything else to tell me? The guys are waitin'."

"Well, there are also scarlet women."

"Mom, in a few months I'll be thirteen. You wanna teach me somethin' about the birds and the bees, tell me somethin' I don't already know." Eddie slips his comb into his pocket and smiles at the mirror.

Mrs. Flynn relaxes. She's far more at ease discussing social graces with her son, rather than sex. "All right. I see you smiling in that mirror. I'll teach you something practical. Don't think looks are going to get you anywhere. You'll pass in a crowd, but you're nothing special in the looks department. If you want to get along with the ladies, do three things: learn to dance; develop a gift of gab; and always keep your fingernails clipped and clean."

"Okay, Mom. Clean fingernails, develop a gift of gab and dance lessons."

"You do that and you'll have just as many dates as the pretty boys. Most women aren't that interested in a man's looks. Good-looking men are usually vain. Anyway, remember what I'm saying. I really do love you, Eddie. I only want what's best for you. Sometimes I worry so."

"You got nothin' to worry about, Mom. I'm cool. I'll be okay." He goes to her and kisses her cheek. "I love you too. Now get outta here and let me clean my fingernails. Some of the girls'll be at the movies tonight."

Closing the door behind his mother, he starts cleaning his nails, figuring, the fingernail part is easy and the guys all say I'm a bullshit artist. That takes care of

Mom's gift of gab suggestion. All I gotta do now is learn to dance. If Rhonda lets me cop a feel tonight, I'll ask her if she wants to teach me how to dance.

While he's dressing, he tells the guys his story, including a verbatim imitation of Becker's tirade. Toward the end of his tale, Norm's face takes on a cloudy look.

"If Captain Becker put you on thirty days restriction to the base, why are you getting ready to go to town?"

"Because I'm a shithouse lawyer." Eddie digs into his jar of Dixie Peach Hair Pomade and slathers it through his hair. "I know more about the Uniform Code of Military Justice than Becker does. When he put me on permanent KP, he automatically cancelled my thirty-day restriction." He smiles at himself in the mirror, then turns to Norm. "Why is that, Norm?"

"I don't know." Norm shrugs.

"Because either one of those punishments has to come my way as an Article Fifteen or Squadron Punishment. It used to be the old One-Oh-Four. According to the code, you can only serve one punishment at a time. Becker fucked himself with his own book."

Smiling triumphantly, Eddie puts the finishing touches on his ducktail. "So what do you think of that?"

Bob is in awe. "Man, that's great, Eddie."

Norm is not as impressed. "I think you're crazy. It's futile to think you can win against the Air Force. You remind me of Sisyphus."

Bob shakes his head. "Sisyphus? Is this another one of your ancient history lessons?"

"It's Greek mythology." Norm changes into Professor Stanton. "The gods punished Sisyphus by having him push a huge boulder up to the top of a mountain, only to watch it roll back down. He had to repeat this process over and over through all of eternity."

"Like washing your car and having it rain every time you wash it," Bob remarks. "That's punishment."

"I read about Sisyphus. He was okay in my book," Eddie states. "Pushin' that fuckin' rock up the mountain over and over, watchin' it roll back down. He had persistence. Sisyphus was a cool guy." Eddie turns his gaze directly on Norm and continues, "Anyway, Norm, if I was old Sis, I'd fuck the gods on my off-duty time. If it took me a century to push that big turd up the hill, I'd take five centuries on my way back down. I'd be one slow-movin' motherfucker, lookin' at the scenery, smellin' all of the flowers." Eddie starts bobbing his head, front to back and side to side, enjoying himself.

Bob begins laughing, fueling Eddie. Eddie runs on and continues the head moves, "Checkin' out all of the nubile maidens, Mister slooow-motion …"

Norm interrupts, "But in the end, Sisyphus loses. He must continue to push the rock. Sisyphus loses to the gods." Norm is smiling like a guy in a toothpaste ad, proud as a brand-new parent.

"Wrong, Norm," Eddie counters. "Sisyphus wins in the end. Myths are called myths because they're bullshit. If they were real they'd be called facts. So gettin' away from the bullshit part of the story, let's get logical and talk about friction. I had to study that shit in high school, in physics. Each time that big son of a bitch rolls down the hill, parts of its mass will be lost, due to hard knocks and friction. Some of the parts'll be tiny, others will be large hunks, but eventually, after enough trips that big motherfucker'll be worn down to a pebble that old Sis can pick up and throw over the goddamn mountain. And that, Norm, is fuckin' physics."

Norm looks like a two-week-old party balloon.

Trying to cheer him up, Eddie sticks his comb back into his pocket and in a cowboy movie voice announces, "Now let's hit the trail. There's pussy out yonder and I aim to get me some."

"I still think you're crazy," Norm persists.

"I'd be a lot crazier to miss this dance. Last year there were chickies up here all the way from Detroit."

Norm frowns. "Your name will still be on the "Restricted To Base" list at the main gate."

"Correct, Norm." Eddie checks himself out in the mirror. "That's why I'll be in the trunk when you and Bob drive through."

"You mean when you and Bob drive through." Norm looks at his watch. "The base bus leaves at eight-fifteen. I'll meet you guys at the dance."

"Come on, Norm," Bob coaxes, "nothing's going to happen."

"No thanks. I'm trying to make airman first, not airman basic." Norm turns and starts to walk toward the barracks' front door.

Eddie shouts, "See you at the dance, Norm." He and Bob go out the back door to the enlisted men's parking area.

Bob rolls through the main gate with no strain. Two miles south of the base, he pulls onto the shoulder of Highway 23, parks and opens the trunk. Eddie climbs out displaying two bottles of beer. "Well, would you look what I found wedged under your spare?" Eddie opens them with his keychain church key.

Bob takes a bottle. They clink their bottles together, "Hot beer's better than no beer," Bob toasts. Eddie shakes a couple of cigarettes out of his pack and they light up.

Eddie stretches. "Lemme straighten up." He drags on his cigarette. "You know, back there in the trunk I was thinkin'. It's lucky for me you guys were runnin' late. I was gonna shower and hit the sack. I'd've missed the dance."

"We weren't running late. We were in Tawas all afternoon. You're just lucky Norm ate a lot of junk and then went on the Loop the Loop." Bob starts to laugh a little.

"He puked?"

"I hate to laugh but he looked so funny. He got off the ride and first he smiled, then he frowned like he does." Bob starts laughing more. "Pink cotton candy, a Dairy Queen, two hot dogs with relish and a couple of beers. I had to laugh, man, all over his shoes and pants, a mess. Then he got pissed off 'cause I was laughing. Anyway, it's all okay now."

"So if Norm didn't ride the Loop the Loop, I miss the dance. Here's to the Loop the Loop." Eddie chugs his beer and throws the empty across the highway. The bottle arcs high over the road then descends a hundred feet into the jack pines. They hear the sound of breaking glass. "Musta hit a rock." Eddie grins, "That's a good sign. Let's go give Tawas a break."

Bob kills his beer and tosses his bottle in the direction of Eddie's throw. The guys get back into the car and drive the remaining fifteen miles to Tawas, listening to a rhythm & blues station from Detroit. They hit Tawas at ten after eight.

CHAPTER 5

▼

At ten after eight, sixty miles south of Tawas, a better than good-looking seventeen-year-old with shoulder-length, jet-black hair, brushes her bangs away from her eyebrows. Joan Whitman's dark brown eyes, focused on Highway 23 are glistening. Her mouth is a firm, straight line and she's frowning. She's doing a solid seventy in her black 1950 Chevy coupe. The car's a stick shift with zebra skin seat covers and a hot engine.

Joan, called "Icegirl" in her yearbook by the boys in her graduation class, allows no latitude on dates or at dances, no cheap feels or furtive rubs. The boys consider her aloof; an unfair label. The problem Joan has with the neighborhood boys is not a mystery. Charlie Chan doesn't have to be called in. The solution is simple. She finds them dull, predictable and spoiled by their indulgent parents. For Joan, they have no spark.

She enjoys dances. As a rule, she attends with her close girlfriends and leaves with them. She dates infrequently, sometimes with a boy that her father suggests. And as an only child, she hears a lot of suggestions.

She once complained to her mother about a boy her father had thrust upon her, a boy from what he called "the proper social strata."

Her mother had commiserated, "I'll admit, you're fishing in shallow waters around here, honey, but this is nothing but a dance-date. If the boy's a pain, just give him a hearty handshake when you say good night." After sharing a laugh, her mother had continued, "But you are right about these dates that your dad comes up with. I can control him. I'll keep him on a tighter leash in the future."

Joan had thanked her and her mother added, "Seriously, dear, you must hold out for someone who makes your heart jump, someone who excites you, someone who is vibrant, someone who makes you giddy. Don't settle for less than love, Joanie."

Despite her good looks, Joan is popular with the other girls in the neighborhood and at school because she is not competing with them for dates or for a spot on the cheerleading squad.

Sandy Johnson and Laura Winslow are sitting in the front seat with her, singing along with the radio. Sandy, a natural honey blonde, is sitting in the middle. Sandy sometimes dreams of being a race car driver. Having to take Home Economics instead of Auto Shop, an exclusively male course, angered her. Sandy would rather tinker with an engine than help some boy unzip his fly.

Sandy's brother used to let her help him work on his car without treating her like a little, kid sister. She cried most of the night when he left for Hawaii to take a dream job, working for a millionaire, speedboat-racing enthusiast. He left Sandy his best socket wrench set, a set he knew she was fond of. They write letters on Christmas and on birthdays. In high school some of the boys resented her because not only could she out-drive them, she could out-wrench them.

Although feminine, she's not frilly. There's enough of a strong, almost jockish manner about her to intimidate most boys. She skipped the Junior Hop to go to a short-track auto race in Akron with her father. Joan wanted to skip the hop and go with them, but her father prevailed over her mother, a rare event. Her mother had explained, "It really is too late to back out now, dear. It wouldn't be fair to the boy."

Sandy dates as often as Joan. Though she's only eighteen, she feels older and beyond the boys at the local ice cream parlor. To Sandy, it's more trouble than it's worth, fending off attacking hands at a drive-in movie. She'd rather be at the movie with Joan and Laura, making smart remarks, giggling and eating unbuttered popcorn. She's been Joan's Blood sister since they cut their thumbs and pressed them together in fifth grade. In sixth grade, Sandy quit the Girl Scouts when Joan got bounced for not ratting out a girl who had eaten a box of cookies. Sandy and Joan have *no* secrets from each other.

The third girl, Laura, a bottle blonde who doesn't care who knows it, is a year older than the others. Considered wild by some, she's a Tri-Delt sorority girl at Michigan. She lost her claim to a spotless reputation when she was a junior, dating the second-string quarterback. She let him get across the goal line. He had loose lips and the nickname "Hot Pants" circulated among the snotty girls at school. Then, guys who'd been tagged out between first and second base by Laura began saying they'd hit a homer. She was at a low ebb. Joan and Sandy felt that Laura was being treated unfairly and went out of their way to include her in their activities—ice skating, bowling, and movies. They were rewarded with a good friend.

In subconscious, or perhaps conscious, retaliation against braggart boys bullshitting about the success of their dates with her, Laura became a first-rate cockteaser. She delighted in taking a boy half the way there and then sending him home with an acute case of aching lover's nuts without even the courtesy of a mercy hand job.

Laura refuses to go steady, preferring two or three quality dates with a boy while he's trying to make a good impression, to getting bogged down as somebody's steady, always sitting in a parked car evading amateur, invasive gropes. She kisses on the first date and if she's in a good mood, she'll let a guy grab a handful of tit.

She's had marriage on her mind since she was a bridesmaid at her sister's wedding two Junes ago, but she claims that she's not desperate. Laura taught Joan and Sandy how to smoke. She wears an uplift bra, fire engine red lipstick and never gets asked for ID.

The three of them are wearing pleated skirts, sweaters, loafers and bobby socks. Laura's skirt is just a bit shorter than Joan's or Sandy's. They're from St. Clair Shores, down near Detroit.

Sandy, Laura and The Four Aces finish singing "Tell Me Why" and the disc jockey goes into his pimple cream pitch. Sandy turns down the radio. "For a girl who's going to be eighteen in two weeks, you don't look very happy."

"I'm not, San." Joan's frown deepens.

"Don't frown like that. You'll get wrinkles," Sandy warns.

Laura tries for a laugh. "Eighteen's not bad. It's not like you're looking at thirty or thirty-five."

"I know, Laura." Joan tries to smile. "I don't mind the age. It's Roddy."

"Roddy?" Laura looks puzzled. "You dated Roddy?"

"Just twice, a dance at the club and a movie, last time he was home from Yale. I only did it because my dad begged me to give him a chance."

"So now your dad wants you to invite Roddy to your party?" Sandy checks the radio. The DJ is off the pimple cream and into a Coca-Cola commercial.

"Worse than that, Sandy. My dad says Roddy wants to give me his frat pin at my party. It's crazy. I didn't even invite him. I don't like him. He's a drip."

"Two dates and you're getting pinned? Those must have been some dates." Laura grins mischievously. "You give Roddy any pie?"

"Pie?!" Joan laughs. He tried getting fresh, in his car after the movie, and I slapped him a good one. I should have punched the creep."

"Lots of girls in our sorority would love getting pinned by a Yalie," Laura states and thinks, I'd like to land a guy with a solid future.

"Well I'm not one of them." Joan's jaw tightens. "I'm tired of my father trying to run my life."

Sandy looks wistful. "Getting pinned is like getting engaged."

"Don't remind me. I'm too young to quit living."

"Oh listen." Sandy turns up the radio. "They're playing 'Wheel Of Fortune'."

She and Laura begin to sing along with Kay Starr. This time Joan joins in.

"Will the arrow point my way? Will this be my day?" they sing. Joan punches the Chevy up to seventy-five.

CHAPTER 6

▼

In Tawas, Main Street is blocked off. Money-raising booths sponsored by civic groups and clubs line both sides of the street. Bob drives half a mile south of town, turns onto an abandoned logging trail and carefully makes his way to a clearing, where he parks. Walking back to the highway, he and Eddie break off a few small twigs that had come too close to the Ford's paint job.

A photo of the town would make the cover of any wholesome magazine. It's late twilight, not a cloud in the sky and just enough breeze to flutter the plastic white, blue and red pennants strung among the strings of colored light bulbs. A long red and white TAWAS PERCH FESTIVAL 1952 banner stretches from the second floor of the Huron Hotel across the street to the top of the Tawas Theater's marquee.

Along Main, the guys kid around with some of the girls running the booths. Eddie wins two packs of cigarettes at the Rotary Club Ski-Ball game. At the Elks Club booth, Sally Benton's sponsor in the beauty contest, Bob pays a buck and gets his picture taken with his arm around Sally. She's wearing a silver evening gown, and her 1952 PERCH FESTIVAL QUEEN sash is easily read.

"You can show that to potential girlfriends," Eddie jokes. "Show 'em what high standards you got in chicks."

The Iosco County Kiwanis decorated the VFW hall, hoping to capture an underwater feel. Off to a head start with the already pale green walls, they pasted up much larger than life-size, papier-mâché perch and tacked blue and green streamers to the walls, letting them hang down vertically, like seaweed. A few well-placed green lights helped achieve the desired effect.

On stage, several large nets filled with blue and green balloons surround the band's area. A backdrop of a tropical underwater scene completes the stage decoration. With the house lights dim, only the band area brightly lit and an eerie green glow from the walls, the hall does resemble a surrealistic grotto.

"Nice and dim," Eddie notes. "If a guy had enough beer in him, he could think he's underwater."

The jukebox is playing at a moderate volume. Les Paul and Mary Ford are finishing "The World Is Waiting For The Sunrise". Eddie selects a table near the stage, off to the left, next to the jukebox. Bob takes a seat and looks around the hall. Eddie goes to the juke and punches up two tunes. He returns, tosses the two packs of cigarettes on the table and adjusts his chair. The hall is only half full but the beer counter across the dance floor is busy. Nat Cole starts a tune and six couples head for the dance floor to take advantage of Eddie's first selection. Eddie readjusts his chair. "There," he declares, "now I got a perfect bead on the front door."

"Looks good," Bob agrees. "I'll get a pitcher ... and check things out."

"Okay. And Bob? Let's wait a while before we make a move on any of the local honeys. They're around all the time."

"All right with me. I'm in no hurry."

Eddie checks the band. They're ready to blow, just waiting for "Mona Lisa" to run its course before they cut the juke and greet the folks.

Billed as The Tunetimers, the band works Saginaw, Bay City and the Thumb area, doing weddings, parties, dances and some club dates. They're known as a fun band, six middle-aged guys in matching red blazers, all good musicians, along with Ilsa, the singing accordionist. Ilsa's a slightly chubby, bubbly thirty-year-old with blonde braids who looks like she just stepped off the wrapper of an imported chocolate bar. The band can do ninety percent polkas or five percent, depending on the crowd. They do all the current tunes and the old stuff as well. When the trumpet player puts down his horn, he can sing. A duet by him and Ilsa will not offend any listener's ears.

The Tunetimers open their first set with "Slow Poke". Eddie lights up and turns his attention to the front door, unconsciously tapping his foot to the beat.

Bob gets back to the table with the pitcher of beer ten minutes later and twenty minutes after that Norm shows up. Bob rags Norm about taking the bus and Eddie comments, "It's a good thing Norm took the bus. He's just in time to buy a pitcher of beer." No dollar bill will ever break a speed record jumping out of Norm's pocket, so Eddie and Bob delight in making him spend a buck whenever they can. Eddie once commented, "If you were livin' back in the old West,

Norm, and you were as slow drawin' your gun as you are with your wallet, you'd be a Swiss cheese-lookin' motherfucker." All three of them had laughed and Bob started calling Norm "Slowhand."

As Norm heads for the beer counter, Eddie shouts after him, "Get three extra glasses, Norm. I feel lucky tonight."

By the time that Norm returns with the pitcher of beer and the glasses, the hall is almost full. The band is doing "The Loveliest Night of the Year" and many couples are dancing. Bob begins to drum his fingers on the table. "It's a quarter past nine. I'm getting restless."

"Easy, Bob. It's early yet." Eddie pours more beer into Bob's glass. "Just hang on fifteen …" Eddie spots Joan, Sandy and Laura at the door. "Oh, oh, oh, would you look at that."

Out of his chair like a shot, Eddie slithers through the crowd, popping up in front of Joan. He looks into her eyes and smiles a genuine, happy smile, thinking, this girl looks like a fuckin' cameo; like Mom's ring. He greets the trio, "I thought you ladies would never get here. I saved you three seats, right down front, near the band. I'm Eddie Flynn and I'd like to be your host for the evening."

Joan finds his brashness refreshing. His black eye intrigues her. "I'm Joan Whitman," she answers. "These are my friends, Sandy and Laura."

Laura is glancing around the hall. "Ohh, look at all the airmen."

"You like airmen?" Eddie waves to his table. Bob waves back. Eddie points. "I've got two of 'em waitin' to meet *you*!" Turning to Joan, he adds, "They're both from California and that's almost as good as bein' from New York City."

"Which is where you're from, I'm sure," Joan responds.

Eddie laughs. "How'd you know that?" He winks. "What do you say? You girls look like you're here to have fun." He offers Joan his arm.

Joan sees Sandy and Laura both smiling and hooks on. Eddie leads the girls to the table, introduces them to the guys and pours beer for all. The girls put their handbags on the table. "Help yourselves to smokes, ladies, compliments of the Rotary Club," Eddie announces. They all take cigarettes. Bob snaps open his Zippo and everyone at the table lights up, except Norm.

Sitting next to Norm, Laura's thinking, "He looks so handsome in his uniform. I just love his military haircut. Wonder why he doesn't smoke?"

Norm feels Laura's leg next to his under the table. "Oh boy. Laura looks like the photos in the photography shop windows. Hope she likes me."

Sandy comments about the car engraved on Bob's lighter. "That's my car," he declares and hands Sandy his Zippo.

"Looks like my Ford," Sandy observes, and she and Bob begin discussing the merits of Fords.

Eddie clicks glasses gently with Joan. "Here's to the mighty perch," he pledges. "From now on it'll always be my favorite fish." Looking into Joan's eyes, he feels like he could dive into them and take a swim. The whites are ivory and the irises are dark as coal. They each drink their beer halfway down.

I wonder why Eddie isn't wearing his uniform. Joan puts her glass on the table. Her fingers gently brush Eddie's.

Look at those long, slender fingers and those red, pointy nails. This is one real fine, first-class honey, Eddie decides.

Laura fingers Norm's airman second class stripes. She looks over at Joan and Eddie. "Eddie," she asks, "How many stripes do you have?" Bob and Eddie burst out laughing.

"Let's just say, I got two less than Norm." Still laughing, Eddie turns to Joan. "Come on, Joan, let's dance."

The Tunetimers start "Be My Love". Eddie puts his right arm around Joan's waist, takes her right hand in his left, and with their hands clasped down by Joan's right hip, they hit the dance floor. Holding Joan close, but not tight, he goes into his version of a foxtrot.

God, this girl fits me just right, he concludes. And she smells like fuckin' gardenias. He shuffles along to the tune, no set steps, a turn, a half a turn, sometimes a pause or a step backward, maybe two steps and a spin. Eddie never knows what he'll do next. It all depends on the flow of the tune.

Joan glides along with Eddie, floating down a dawdling stream in a canoe. She relaxes and notes, No one, two, three-step here. As the song is ending, Eddie deep-dips her. Her hair hits the floor. Eddie holds her there for just a flash—an exciting flash for Joan, her first dip.

While Joan and Eddie are making their way back to their table, the band announces break time, and Ilsa plugs in the jukebox. "Ooo-who-oo-oooo-ooo, sixty-minute man, sixty-minute maa-aaan," wail The Dominoes. Eddie twirls Joan back out onto the dance floor. "We gotta dance to this one. I had it put in the juke special. 'Looka here, girls, I'm a tellin' you now, they call me Lovin' Dan, I'll rock 'em, roll 'em all night long, I'm a sixty-minute man,'" Eddie sings along with the tune, leading Joan in a slightly sanitized variation on the Dirty Boogie.

Don't wanna go completely apeshit with this girl, he admonishes himself. This ain't some back seat of the car, out in the parking lot honey.

Toning down his most blatant pelvic moves, he's rewarded with subtle hip rolls from Joan. She puts a hand on each thigh and grinds gently. Remembering Rita Hayworth dancing in "Gilda", Joan feels free.

Eddie feels hunger. Oh I want some of this, he resolves.

The next tune is the breathy, "I'm In Love Again".

"I'm in love again and the spring is comin', I'm in love again, hear my heart-strings strummin'," April Stevens oozes.

Joan enjoys the feel of her belly pressed up against Eddie. She pushes in a bit more. Icegirl is on the thaw.

"I'm in love again and I can't rise above it, I'm in love again and I love, love, love it," April sighs. Joan and Eddie dance in place, a slow, non-flagrant grind. Joan feels like she is glowing.

Returning to their table after the song ends, Joan does some thinking. Eddie is as different from my father as Roddy is the same. Joan is extremely happy about that fact.

"You're a really great dancer," Eddie declares. "You got natural rhythm."

"You're easy to follow. How'd you get that black eye?"

"That's a long story."

"That's okay," Joan answers, "I've got all night."

CHAPTER 7

▼

At a quarter to two, Bob and Sandy are dancing. Norm and Laura are huddled and Joan and Eddie are discussing which of the four seasons they prefer. Joan takes Eddie's hand, squeezing it gently. "My stomach doesn't feel so good," she whispers.

"Too much brew? You need to get some fresh air. Want to take a walk by the lake?"

"Yes. Please."

Eddie leans over to Norm. "Tell Bob we'll see you guys after the dance, down by the pier."

Leaving the dance, Joan and Eddie walk along Main toward the Tawas pier. The street is still. The pennants on the deserted booths barely flutter in the on-again, off-again breeze.

"I really am feeling woozy. I don't often drink," Joan offers. "A drink at home on a special occasion, maybe two or three beers at a picnic. That's it."

"I'm sorry. I was throwin' beer at you like it was a Democratic Club rally." Eddie checks her out. She does look a little green around the gills, he observes. "Try breathin' in your nose and out your mouth; real deep breaths."

Walking the four blocks to the pier, hand in hand, taking deep breaths, Joan starts feeling better. Arriving at the pier, she declares, "That breathing thing worked. Let's walk out to the end of the pier, Eddie."

Reaching the end of the pier, they sit on one of the benches and gaze out at Lake Huron and the moonless sky. The lake is only slightly rippled, reflecting every star.

Eddie pats and rubs small circles on Joan's back. "Your color's comin' back. You had me worried for a minute, there. You were white as chalk."

"Mmmmmm. It's a beautiful night. Eddie?"

"Yes?"

"I was wondering why you didn't wear your uniform tonight."

"It doesn't look good with my suedes. Just kiddin' … Although actually my suedes do look pretty cool with my blues. I guess I'm just not a uniform kind of guy. It's good for hitch-hikin' but that's about it, for me."

"You don't like the Air Force?"

"No. I like it fine, especially right now. I always look at things down the long trail. Who gives a shit how much KP I pull as long as I wind up meetin' you tonight?"

"Oh, Eddie."

"Well, it's true. I told you plenty about me back there at the dance, and you still haven't told me anything about St. Clair Shores. I go to Detroit a lot, but I never hit that neighborhood."

"You'd know you were there if you suddenly felt like you were about to die of boredom," she jokes.

Eddie laughs.

They talk about some of Joan's high school achievements and her plans to attend Michigan in September. Eddie lets Joan in on a couple more of his Air Force adventures that resulted in KP or restriction to the base. He leaves out the Benzedrine Nurses and Cadillac Baby. Later, Bob comes walking up the pier.

"Hi, Eddie. Hiya, Joan," he greets them. "The girls are hungry. We're going up to Sy and Gert's."

Eddie turns to Joan. "Want somethin' to eat? Just a little tea and toast?"

Joan rolls her eyes. "I don't even want to smell food."

"You guys go ahead. We'll catch you later," Eddie assures him. "Thanks anyway."

"Okay. Later." Bob trots down the pier to his car and takes off, leaving a thirty-foot patch of rubber.

As the sound of Bob's peeling tires dies down, the breeze picks up and turns chilly. Joan can't help shivering. Eddie takes off his shirt and drapes it around Joan's shoulders.

"Won't you be cold in just your T-shirt?"

"Naw. I don't feel cold much. Last winter I pulled two hours of guard duty at twenty-four below." Eddie shows Joan his arm. "Look, no goose pimples."

Eddie circles his arms around her. Joan leans into him and moves her face closer to his. He lays a lingering, rolling kiss on her, lips only, finishing by slightly nibbling her plump lower lip with his lips. Icegirl's thaw turns into a full melt.

They come out of their kiss, sit back and savor the starry, starry sky. I'd like to jump all over you, Joan, he reflects. I'd like to eat you up like a juicy fuckin' plum. But I can't do that. I gotta wait until you're ready to fall off the tree. He remarks, "You know, without the moon, you can really enjoy the stars."

"You'd think with a whole sky full of stars like this, we might see one falling. I'd like to make a wish."

God, this girl is innocent and sweet, Eddie thinks and suggests, "We'd probably have a better chance in November when all those meteors go by, but you never know. Let's take a smoke and watch for one." They light up and talk about the stars and planets. Eddie shows Joan how to flick her cigarette butt with her middle finger. She sails the butt through the air as well as Eddie had done and it drops into Lake Huron. After twenty minutes they still haven't seen a falling star.

"I'm going to make a wish anyway," Joan declares. She closes her eyes, tilting her head skyward. Eddie stares out at the lake.

A moment later, Joan opens her eyes. "Did you make a wish, Eddie?"

Eddie recalls his father's old saying, "Wish in one hand and shit in the other and see which hand gets filled up first," but instead of repeating it to Joan, he answers, "I already got everything I need." He pulls her to him and kisses her. His tongue gently probes its way between her lips and pauses. She lets her tongue sneak out from behind her teeth and touch his. Thrills run through her, her first tongue kiss. Icegirl, already reduced to a mere ice cube, drifts into warmer waters and becomes part of the sea.

Joan feels exhilarated. "Let's go to my car," she invites.

Turning their backs on Lake Huron, they walk down the pier toward Highway 23 with their arms around each other's waists. Behind them, a huge meteor drops from the center of the sky, ripping its way to the eastern horizon.

CHAPTER 8

▼

Sy and Gert's Diner, an old Woodward Avenue trolley car that Sy had trucked up from Detroit in 1945, still has its bells hooked up. The cook uses the one at the kitchen end to signal, "Order up" and the waitresses use the one at the other end of the diner when they need help bussing the tables. Sy kept most of the trolley original. He had to change the doors for safety, but he left the windows as they were. The clock over the door shows 3:30. A red neon ALWAYS OPEN arches over the clock.

The diner, just three miles south of the 646th on Highway 23, is jumping when Bob, Sandy, Norm and Laura slide into the only empty booth. The dishes of the previous diners are still on the table. Mae, Sy and Gert's twenty-five-year-old daughter, is working her tail off. The juke is playing "I Apologize". Billy Eckstine is a favorite of Sandy's.

Bob is bitching. "I only have six thousand miles on my tires and they're already showing signs of wear."

"You left five hundred miles worth back on the highway in Tawas," Norm points out.

Sandy snuggles closer to Bob. "Yeah, but it sure was fun."

Norm's probably right, Laura thinks, but says nothing.

Mae arrives at their booth and starts loading the dirty dishes onto an oversized tray. "Hi, guys. Hi, ladies," she greets them.

"Hiya, Mae. What's new?" Bob asks.

"Your outfit got those eight new scopedopes today." Mae piles the last of the dishes on her tray and scoots. "Back in a sec," she shouts over her shoulder.

Bob laughs. "Mae told us a month ago the new radar ops would be here today."

Norm gets into his serious look. "That's not funny, Bob. If Mae knows about our troop movements, so do the Russians."

Looking up from her menu, Laura exclaims, "Oh Norm, hot tongue."

Norm scans his menu. "Where?"

"Not there, silly." Laura laughs. "Here." She sticks out her tongue and wiggles it.

They all laugh as Norm blushes.

Laura looks at Norm with assessing eyes. The more she listens to him, the more she sees him as a sensible, level-headed guy. She also feels that he hasn't been down the road with the ladies much. She feels challenged.

The four of them take their time over their hamburgers and fries, talking and joking. The diner slowly empties. Hank Snow is on the jukebox doing "I'm Moving On".

Norm checks his watch. "Speaking of moving on, it's four-twenty. I don't think they're going to show up."

"I wonder if they left Tawas yet." Concern is in Sandy's voice.

"Joan's with Eddie. She's safe." Bob gives Sandy a brief reassuring hug. "Eddie's on KP at six. I'll bet they'll be up at the base road at five-thirty."

Laura pulls out her compact mirror, wipes off her old fire engine red coat of lipstick and puts on a fresh coat of an extra lipstick she keeps in her purse, a shade she calls Virgin Pink. She announces, "I'll bet they're making out." She stifles herself from continuing with, "And speaking of making out, is there someplace we can go to park?" substituting, "Gee, we've got an hour to kill. Is there someplace we could go and talk some more?" She flashes Norm a demure, pink smile and he smiles, shyly in return.

Bob and Sandy exchange looks. "Sure there is." Bob throws three bucks on the table. "Grab us some beers on the way out, Norm. We'll meet you guys in the car."

At the cash register, Laura tells Norm, "Just get four beers, Norm. One each is plenty."

CHAPTER 9

▼

Joan's car is parked a quarter mile north of the pier, the only vehicle left in the parking area. It's four AM. Tawas is shut down and all the revelers are gone. "We paid a dollar to park here," Joan remarks.

"It was worth it. We parked almost a mile away, in one of Bob's special parking spots. He don't like to park near other vehicles. He's got a maroon, custom paint job."

They arrive at Joan's Chev. "I'm in basic black." She strikes a pose. She and Eddie laugh.

Joan opens the door and the interior light goes on.

"Man! Zebra skin seat covers."

Joan laughs. "I knew you'd like them."

"How'd you know I'd like them?"

"Easy. No one else likes them. Sandy and Laura think they're too loud. My dad absolutely hates them."

"Most dads are fulla shit. What about your mother? What does she think about them?"

"Oh my mom likes them because I like them. My mom loves me. There's nothing I could do that's so bad that my mom would ever stop loving me."

"That's some great mom."

"Is it private here, Eddie?" The excitement within Joan is palpable. She's hoping that Eddie gets fresh with her. She's looking forward to it.

"Yeah, it's private. That's a cemetery, just north of us. I got no problems with the dead."

In her permissive frame of mind, sitting in the car with Eddie, sharing one cigarette, listening to Detroit's rhythm and blues station turned down low, Joan decides that she'll go along with anything reasonable.

Eddie wants nothing more than the chance to let their tongues get to know each other better. He sets a limit on his hands to above the waist and outside the clothes. I'd like to get under that sweater, though, runs through his mind.

They finish their cigarette and the fun begins. Joan is an eager pupil in the art of soul-kissing. They spend fifteen minutes tasting each other's mouths, licking one another's lips and progress to thirty minutes of heavy petting, ending with Eddie's under-the-sweater thought occurring.

More time passes and after many passionate kisses, with Joan permitting and encouraging moves from Eddie that would get any other boy slapped shitless, she allows Eddie to unhook her bra. He cups one of her breasts and she feels herself floating away; it's ecstasy. She feels faint.

She whispers in Eddie's ear, "I never felt like this before." Her blood is racing. Her eyes are rolling back in her head, behind her closed eyelids. Joan is ready.

Eddie senses that she's going out of control. He has rubbers for times like this, but this doesn't feel like one of those times. Something is different about this girl. Eddie slows the action down, a new experience for him.

He takes a peripheral glance at the dashboard clock and pulls away from Joan. "Holy shit," he exclaims, "it's already twenty after five."

"Soooo?" Joan's eyes are still closed. She's cruising, somewhere between bliss and rapture.

"So I'm on KP at six." Eddie maintains his distance and Joan, regaining some of her composure, starts to straighten her clothing. Her psyche begins its descent to Earth.

"How far is it to your base?"

"We're two miles south of the fighter base. Fifteen miles, I guess."

"We'll be there in time for a long, good night kiss," Joan promises.

She pulls out of the parking area, onto Highway 23, stops, depresses the clutch and slips the shift lever into first gear. Eddie is still wondering why she stopped on the highway, when she stomps on the gas pedal, slides her foot off the clutch and peels out.

Lingering only a blink in first, she power-shifts into second and continues laying a trail of smoke and burning rubber, a forty-foot patch. Shifting smoothly into third, she hums along Highway 23 at seventy.

Eddie looks at her with unabashed admiration. "Where'd you learn to do that?"

Joan smiles broadly. "Did you like that?" she teases.

"Man! That was better than Bob. I'm knocked out."

"Then how about a kiss." Joan turns her head toward Eddie, puckering up, but keeping her eyes on the road.

Eddie kisses her lightly. "Let's get back to the base road, so I can kiss you right."

Fifteen minutes later, they're parked where the base road meets Highway 23. Eddie is going through the glove box. Joan is directing. "There should be a little pen in there and any kind of paper's all right."

Eddie riffles through some maps and finds a film envelope. "Hey, what's this?" He takes out some photos.

"Don't look at those, Eddie. They're old. From last summer. I've got some better ones at home."

Eddie picks out a photo of Joan standing by her Chev. She's wearing a white, two-piece bathing suit. "I like your smile in this one."

"Well, that is my favorite. But I was a year younger."

Eddie laughs. "I won't tell anyone if you don't." He finds the pen and hands it and the photo to Joan.

Joan writes her name, address and phone number on the back, then turns the photo over. She almost writes, "Love" but decides it's too soon. I don't want to seem forward, she thinks and writes, "Sincerely, Joan."

Eddie gets out his wallet, starts to slip the picture into it and Joan blurts out, "I'm going to be eighteen in two weeks and it won't be any kind of a party for me, if you're not there."

"I'll be there," Eddie answers. "Even if I have to break restriction." They laugh together and Eddie kisses her again. Their tongues are now good friends. Bob's car pulling up next to Joan's Chevy interrupts their kiss.

Bob leans out his window and shouts, "Shake it up, Eddie. You're due in the mess hall in ten minutes."

Eddie waves Bob off. "Arbo'll cover for me if I'm late."

Joan pushes Eddie away playfully. "Hit the road. I don't want you getting in more trouble and missing my party."

Eddie gets out of Joan's car. Norm and Laura disentangle and leave Bob's car. Norm is mesmerized by Laura and his good fortune. "I never had a girl kiss me like that before." He asks for and receives one more of Laura's "Special Delivery" kisses, before getting into Bob's car.

Sandy gives Bob a long good-night kiss and gets into Joan's car. Eddie kisses Joan good night and gets into the trunk of Bob's car. The three girls sit and watch Bob's taillights until the Ford reaches the main gate.

Norm manages to mask his nervousness when they pull up to the guard shack. Bob is cool and when the air policeman on duty asks, "Is Flynn on your shift?" his gut tightens for only a moment.

"Yeah," Bob answers warily, "Flynn's on our shift."

"Well, if you guys see him," the A.P. states, "tell him he's off KP. They need him in Radar Ops."

"Okay. I'll tell him if I see him." Bob smiles and drives slowly past the guard shack.

When the lights move through the gate, Joan cranks the Chevy. She eases the car into first and quietly drives to Highway 23, where she heads south.

On the radio, Dinah Washington is singing "I'll Never Be Free". "Am I going crazy?" Joan asks herself, while reviewing the night's events. "I invited Eddie to my birthday party," she announces.

"Then I'm inviting Norm," Laura declares.

"And I'm going to invite Bob," Sandy adds and they all laugh.

Thinking of Eddie, Joan exclaims, "The mighty perch is my favorite fish." She rolls her speedometer up to seventy-five, and sings along with Dinah.

CHAPTER 10

▼

The 646th Aircraft Control & Warning Squadron has four radar crews: Able, Baker, Charlie and Dog. Eddie and the guys are on Dog crew. The crews rotate through a schedule of three-day shifts, three swing shifts and three midnight shifts, followed by three days off.

The Radar Operations building where the airmen work is a square, concrete block set-up. The radar operations room takes up half of the building's area. The crypto room, the radar mechanics room, a hallway, the break room and the latrine take up the rest. Guard duty is pulled in a phone booth-sized, tar-paper shack, a hundred feet in front of the building's main entrance. The guard shack is unheated, but its telephone has been rigged by the crew's radar mechanics to give free long distance calls.

Dog crew is working day shift. The wall clock in the break room reads 8:08. The room is a mess. A table with a large coffee urn at one end is littered with spilled sugar, milk and broken donut parts. The floor that Charlie crew finished mopping at 7:58 looks as bad as the table. Most of Dog crew is in the radar ops room.

A3/c John Davis and A3/c Pete Peterson are sharing a rickety rattan couch with a medium-sized, unkempt, shedding dog. Eddie is standing next to a rusting Coke Machine talking to the new men.

"I'm supposed to tell you how we do things on Dog crew," he states. "First, let's get some coffee. This crew drinks a lot of coffee."

"I saw that," Pete remarks. "It was like a stampede."

Eddie moves to the coffee urn and the new guys follow. He picks up a cup and starts filling it. "Coffee keeps us sharp." Noticing the two new men cherry-picking among the cups, Eddie adds, "Don't bother lookin' for a clean cup. They're all cruddy. When you come on shift, just grab any cup and fill it. Saves time."

John looks like he's smelling a bad egg. "I don't like coffee very much."

Eddie gives him a full cup. "You'll learn to love it, John. You guys got any questions?"

John, the more serious of the two, asks, "When will Sergeant Brown brief us and show us around?"

Eddie takes a drink of coffee. "I'm briefin' you right now and I'll be showin' you around, because Sergeant Brown is in town shacked up with his little Saginaw honey." Smiling broadly, he adds, "We may not see old Brownie for a couple of days. Next question?"

Pointing at the dog, Pete asks, "What about this dog?"

"That's Ma Barker. She kind of attached herself to our crew. She marches to chow with us and to shift." Eddie grabs some donut parts and begins feeding the dog. "Guess someone must have told her this is Dog crew. Watch out for her. She might be knocked up."

Pete moves away from Ma Barker and Eddie explains, "Last time she was in heat, we put her ass-end-up on an empty ammo box and let Captain Ross' German shep take a hit at her. She seemed to like it."

Captain James Ross, a loose, rawboned thirty-three-year-old with a forty-three-year-old face, enters the break room. His eyes, although bloodshot, are alert. He's wearing custom-tailored linen khakis. Pinned on his shirt are senior pilot wings and three rows of campaign ribbons, among them a Purple Heart.

The new men jump to attention. Eddie stops refilling his cup and greets Captain Ross like a brother. "Hiya, Captain. What great timin'! I was just tellin' these guys about the night Major fucked Ma Barker."

Captain Ross laughs, notices the new men at attention, orders, "At ease, guys," and turns back to Eddie. "You made a friend for life out of Major when you found that ammo box for his girlfriend." He leans over and pats Ma Barker's head. "Brownie in ops?" he asks. The question is casual.

Eddie pops a big, knowing grin, makes a pumping motion with his arm and answers, "Brownie's in town, Captain. Ridin' the Saginaw Express. He called in and asked me to brief these guys."

Captain Ross grabs a random cup and starts filling it. Eddie continues, "I heard it was you who got me off of KP. Thanks, Captain."

"I told Becker you're worth a whole lot more to the Air Force in Radar Ops than you are washing fucking dishes." Taking a pair of aspirins out of a pocket tin, Ross tosses them into his mouth, chasing them with a gulp of coffee.

Looking the new radar operators over, Captain Ross states, "Pay attention to whatever Eddie says. He knows this shit. Nice meeting you. We'll get to know each other as we work together." He turns to Eddie. "I'm going to be in the crypto room for a few hours. Don't let anybody wake me unless there's a full fucking wing of Commie bombers heading for Detroit."

"Gotcha, Captain," Eddie responds and Captain Ross heads for the crypto room. His back is only registering a three on his personal pain scale. "A couple of hours lying flat on the crypto table'll fix me right up," he bullshits himself.

Captain Ross earned his Purple Heart on his 23rd bombing mission, horsing his B-17 back to England on two engines, minus half of the plane's tail and a large piece of its left wing. With the aircraft's landing gear destroyed and chunks of flak in his back, Ross pancaked in, sliding down the runway like a duck landing on a frozen pond. He was the last man out and thirty seconds later "The Bearded Clam" exploded. Combat had ended for Captain Ross.

During his hospital stay in England, the doctors did a good job of removing the shrapnel, but the pain remained. Various painkillers produced side effects that Ross considered more of a discomfort than the pain, so he settled for alcohol when off duty and aspirin when on duty. It worked well enough.

He returned to Springfield, Illinois and married the girl he left behind. Sue Ellen doesn't mind him being half-bombed all the time because he's a happy drunk. She enjoys drinking with him and listening to their records of the Big Bands. Artie Shaw's "Frenesi" is their favorite.

Active duty is no financial burden to Ross. He receives his regular monthly salary from the family real estate business. It never occurs to him to bitch about his back because the vivid images of young men he saw at the hospital with injuries far more grave than his own are still too easily recalled.

He considers Eddie as "fucked up as Hogan's goat when off duty and a fucking godsend in Radar Ops."

Watching Captain Ross make his way to the crypto room, Eddie brags, "He's got the best intercept record in the whole Midwest. He's the opposite of Becker. Becker loves brown-nosers. Captain Ross hates 'em. We ain't got one ass-kisser on this whole fuckin' crew."

"Looks to me like the captain has a pretty bad hangover." John shows his disapproval.

Eddie shrugs. "Sure he's got a hangover. He's sober. I never seen him sober, except when he's on duty. But forget that shit. Did you see all the medals on his shirt?"

Pete is enthusiastic. "Yeah, three rows of ribbons."

Eddie continues, "Captain Ross was a real fuckin' hero in World War Two."

"What did he do?" John asks.

"He led some of those bombers on the Dresden raid. They really blew the shit outta that place," Eddie declares proudly. "Captain Ross don't take no shit from Becker."

Pointing to the ops room, John asks, "Will it be like radar school in there, Eddie?"

"I'm glad you brought that up, John. Our first rule on this crew is, forget everything you learned in radar school."

"Everything?" John looks unhappy.

"Well, not everything. You've still got to write backwards when you're on plotter and you'll use the phonetic alphabet, but other than that, forget it. All of that plotter from operator shit, how do you read me and then the plotter is supposed to say, I read you loud and clear, et cetera and back and forth? All bullshit and jive. If you're on scope your headset's on, you're listening to the flow between the guys on other scopes and the plotter, so when you get a new blip on your scope, just fit yourself in and don't say 'Give me an initial plot,' just say, 'Give me an I.P., zero-four-zero degrees at two-two-zero miles.' On this crew, you only do 'over' and shit like that if you're talking to the pilots and you guys won't be doin' that. You guys got that?"

Eddie looks at John and Pete, reading their reactions. John looks crestfallen, Pete seems almost happy. Patting John on the shoulder and heading for the door to the Radar Ops room, Eddie directs, "We might as well go to work. You both look like bright guys. You'll do good with us Dogs."

The Radar Operations room is dark except for the green glow given off by the radar scopes, the tiny lamps on the controller's desk, a couple of small red lights in the Movements and Identification section, and the well-lit plotting board.

The huge Plexiglas plotting board dominates the rear third of the Operations Room. On the board there's a map of Michigan with mile and degree markers, using the 646th Aircraft Control & Warning Squadron's Oscoda location as the bull's-eye. These range and azimuth markings are in light blue so that they're more discernable to the plotter—who's behind the board, hearing things like, "Move Baker Four to three three zero degrees, one niner zero miles"—than they are to the teller who sits in front of the board.

The teller is interested only in the grid squares that are superimposed on the map. The grid squares' borders are in black, designed to be more visible to him than the range and the azimuth markings.

The grid squares each have five units running vertically and five units running horizontally. The squares have pairs of letters assigned to them, like HB, or phonetically, "How Baker". These letters are in the lower left corner of each square. A track moving northeast through How Baker might get successive readings like these, "HB 2020, HB 3535, HB 5050." The teller tells these plots to the Air Defense Control Center down at Selfridge Field.

The guys at the ADCC move little stands called Christmas trees. Each stand tells the number of aircraft in a track, their speed, altitude and whether they're "identified," "unknown" or "hostile." This is done on a horizontal map board that shows all of the Midwest and a large part of Canada.

Ideally, a new blip goes from scope to plotter quickly in miles and degrees and is immediately read by the teller to the ADCC in grid coordinates. This sounds easy, but with forty or more tracks on the board during a mission with Strategic Air Command, every man must know his shit.

Eddie ushers the new men into the Ops Room and up to the dais, where Norm is working "Movements and Identification." Bob is up there with him monitoring the VHF channels. Down on the floor, six scopes are on. Four are being manned, casually. The altitude scope is unmanned, as is the controller's scope. These two are only used when necessary. Two more scopes are down for routine maintenance. Ten tracks are on the board, Beggar Blue, a flight of two F-86's out of Oscoda on Combat Air Patrol, and nine commercial aircraft. All are identified.

"Routine Sunday morning," Eddie comments. He notices that John seems a bit intimidated, rooted, staring at the plotting board. "What'd you like best in school, John? Plotter? Scope?"

"Scope. I guess."

"Okay, you'll start on scope one. And don't worry when you're on plotter. If we see you're gettin' swamped, we'll send the guy on break to help you. Or I'll jump in. So relax."

Pete looks nonchalant. "How'd you like to do some plottin', Pete?"

"Sure thing."

Bob asks, "How'd you get off KP?"

"Captain Ross did it. Arbo told me at mornin' chow. I'll tell you later. Right now I want you and Norm to get these guys off to a good start. Next hour get John on scope one and Pete on plotter. Then work 'em into the rotation. Like they been here forever, but keep an eye on 'em. I'm goin' out and make more cof-fee. This shift's gonna be a long, slow bitch."

Pete asks, "Eddie, if the crew chief is in town and Captain Ross is sacking out, who's running things around here?"

Jerking his thumb in Eddie's direction, Bob pipes up. "Eddie is." Eddie smiles, jumps down off the dais and ducks back out the door to the break room.

CHAPTER 11

▼

Late Sunday night, Joan is sitting cross-legged on her canopy bed kissing the back of a light blue envelope. She's wearing a shortie nightgown set her mother bought for her that afternoon. The phone rings. She picks it up before it can ring a second time. "Eddie."

"How'd you do that?"

Joan laughs. "Only you and the girls have my private number. Sandy just hung up and Laura called earlier. What are you doing?"

God, this girl has the sweetest voice, he reflects. "You mean besides thinkin' about you, right?"

"Oh Eddie."

Jesus Christ, I love it when she says, "Oh Eddie." Aloud he reports, "Guess what? I'm off KP and I'm off shift for your birthday. Officially, I'll still be restricted to the base, but I'll be at your party."

"That's the best birthday present I'm going to get. Oh, by the way, the girls want to invite Bob and Norm."

"Done. I can tell you that without askin' them."

"I'm telling my dad that I met you when you fixed a flat tire for me."

"Good thinkin'." He walks outside the guard shack, stretching the phone cord to the limit, and stands, looking up at the sky. I'm gonna start bein' a better guy, he promises himself. I don't want nothin' keepin' me away from Joan.

Joan gets off her bed and walks to the window. "I'm looking out my window, Eddie."

"You're lookin' at that same little sliver of a moon that I am."

"I miss you already. I was just kissing the back of an envelope. My first letter to you."

"Lucky envelope. I'll be watchin' the mail." He resolves, I'm gonna make a real effort to shape up.

"Eddie?"

"Yes?"

"Do you think we're in love?"

"Well Joan, to tell you the truth, I don't know what love is, exactly. I don't think anyone does. But I do know that you are the one girl I want to be with. And I know that I feel different about you than any girl I ever met and that's no bullshit. What do you think?"

"I feel like I'd like to be on an island with only you, forever."

"Man, that would be somethin'. You and me layin' on the beach, under a tropical moon, knockin' coconuts off of trees. I'd say that we're in love."

"Good, because I signed my letter 'I love you' and I do love you."

"I love you, too, Joan. And you know what? I'm gonna start bein' a better guy."

"You're already good enough for me, Eddie."

Eddie laughs. "Thanks for that, honey. But there's a whole gang of teachers and people like that who'd disagree with you."

"Well, they don't know shit." Joan throws one of Eddie's expressions back at him.

"Thanks again for the vote of confidence but I am definitely turnin' over a new leaf. No more breakin' restriction. Except for real emergencies, like your party. Maybe I'll even get a white sidewall haircut like Norm's."

"Oh no, Eddie."

Eddie laughs. "Hey, take it easy. I was just kiddin' about the haircut."

They laugh and joke for another few minutes. The last words he hears from Joan are, "I love you, Eddie," just as they hang up their phones together.

With fifteen minutes of guard duty remaining, Eddie spends them thinking about becoming a better guy. "Better Guy" bumps up against "Good Boy" in the "Maybe This Could Happen" section of his brain.

"Good boy," that incomprehensible label, always manages to elude Eddie, staying just out of reach like the end of a rainbow. When the four-year-old Eddie was being marched home after a bad scene in the sandbox with a kid who didn't want to return Eddie's pail, he asked, "Will I ever be a good boy, Mom?"

His mother had sighed. She then assured him that he was a good boy from time to time and suggested, "Let's not tell your father about this incident. It will only upset him."

It seemed to Eddie that being a bad boy came to him much easier than being a good boy. Eddie tried traveling down the Good Boy Trail more times than he could count. It always resulted in failure. Something would crop up. Adventure would come calling or some asshole would have to be dealt with or paid back, and out of nowhere the bad boy would appear as if by magic.

Eddie was fascinated by this metamorphosis. It was automatic. He almost enjoyed it and sometimes thought of this occurrence as "My Other Guy." He often wondered, What's bad about stickin' up for yourself when somebody's fuckin' with you?"

Eventually Eddie gave up on the good boy attempts and settled for being himself, good from time to time and bad when necessary.

On his way over to Radar Operations to pull what he calls, "Volunteer Midnight Guard Duty" Monday night, Eddie has Joan on his mind. Oblivious to the rain soaking his field jacket and fatigue cap, he's hearing Joan's honey-coated voice murmur, "I love you, Eddie."

Thirty seconds after taking over the guard post he calls Joan. Once again, she picks up the phone on the first ring.

"Eddie?"

"Who else? It's rainin' straight down and I hardly noticed it because I was so busy thinkin' of you. Are you gettin' wet down in Detroit yet?"

Joan looks out her window. "No. But it looks all murky. Oh Eddie, I feel so awful."

Eddie hears the distress in her voice. "What's wrong, honey? You sick?"

"Not that kind of awful. I feel good, but it's my dad."

Relief courses through Eddie. "Is that all? He don't want me at your party. We'll get together later and have our own party."

"It's not that bad … yet, but could you, would you be able to come to dinner at my house on Sunday?"

"Your old man wants to look me over."

"I think it's an insult."

"Naw. He's just worried about you. He don't mean nothin' by it. I'm on midnight shift Sunday. I'll work somethin' out with Captain Ross."

"Eddie, my dad is just like what you called your Captain Becker. He's an authoritarian asshole." Joan enjoys calling her father an asshole. She smiles to herself.

Eddie laughs. "Well, there's lots of them around. I guess there'll never be a shortage of authoritarian assholes. There must be a factory somewhere workin' full time turnin' 'em out. Like cars."

Joan begins to brighten. "I think we should try our very best. Would you wear your uniform? Just to make a good impression?"

"Sure, honey. Why not? But if your old man is anything like Becker, chances are he ain't gonna like me."

"That's what I'm afraid of."

"Don't worry. I'll put on a good show."

"Oh I feel so much better. I love you, Eddie."

"And I love you. What time do I show for the big dinner?"

"Seven o'clock, okay?"

"I'll see you Sunday at seven, but you gotta do me one big favor."

"Anything, Eddie."

"I want you to say 'I love you, Eddie' just before you hang up and I'll hear it for the rest of the week."

"Oh Eddie, I love you so much." She hangs up.

Eddie puts his phone back in its cradle, looks out at the pelting rain and runs Joan's dinner news through his mind. Another asshole like Becker to contend with. A matched pair of Double A's. He starts figuring out how to get to Joan's on Sunday at seven and then get back to duty by midnight.

CHAPTER 12

▼

Wednesday, following noon chow, Eddie, Bob and Norm go to the orderly room to check their mail. The line is moving slowly and stretches outside the building. They get on line behind Smitty, who immediately starts bitching to Eddie about how Becker is as chickenshit with the air policemen on the base as he is with everyone else. One of Smitty's buddies was restricted to the base for the weekend for failing inspection, due to residues of ashes being found in his ashtray.

"Residues of ashes in his ashtray," Smitty complains. "What did the simple bastard expect to find in an ashtray? Grits?" After adding, "Becker ain't got the brains God gave a pissant," he finishes his denunciation with, "That peckerhead is mean enough to steal a ball of shit from a blind tumblebug."

Hearing the words "tumblebug" and "ball of shit," Norm sees a chance to dispense some knowledge. "I think what you mean by tumblebug, Smitty," Norm volunteers, "is the scarab beetle."

"Scared beetle? What's he scared of," Smitty asks. "Scared someone like Becker's going to steal his little ball of shit?"

Eddie loves it and laughs. "Man, Smitty gotcha there, Norm. The beetle got the shit scared outta him and he's rollin' his turd off the road so the other bugs don't bunk into it."

Smitty, Bob and Eddie laugh.

Norm presses on, "Not scared, Smitty, scarab. The ancient Egyptians considered them sacred."

Bob joins the conversation. "In California, we call them dung beetles."

"We could use 'em in New York, to roll up all of the dog shit," Eddie jokes and then continues, "Tumblebug, dung beetle or scarab, it's all the same. And just because some nutty Egyptians in the olden days thought they were sacred, don't make it so. They're just shit-rollers. And as Shakespeare said, 'A shit-roller by any other name is still a shit-roller!'"

Eddie and Smitty pass the time telling jokes that cover every kind of animal's excrement, from aardvark shit and bat shit to yak shit and zebra shit, and after what seems like an eternity to Norm, they pick up their mail and head back for the barracks.

Norm is feeling miffed at Eddie making a joke session out of his chance to give Smitty a lesson in ancient history. He can't resist a dig. "You know so much about everything, Eddie," he needles, "you'd think you went to college."

"I did go to college, Norm."

Norm knows this is not true because he once heard Eddie brag about getting out of high school with a barely passing grade. "I used to just study the review books of the old tests and rely on the finals to pull up my shitty marks for the year. Sixty-five was passin', so I gave 'em a sixty-six," was the quote that Norm recalled. Figuring that he has Eddie caught in a lie, he prods, "Oh? And just where did you go to college?"

"On the corner. A Hundred and Twenty-Third and Amsterdam Avenue," Eddie retorts and adds, "I graduated cum loudly and I never had to go to class. We were three blocks north of Columbia and downhill from the university. I figure a lot of excess knowledge must've overflowed and run down to our corner. Then me and my buddies just absorbed it. Like osmosis. We all were just automatically smart."

"Smart-asses, you mean," Norm snaps.

"Good one, Norm." Eddie pats him on the back.

Norm smiles.

"Llama shit," Bob states. "You guys didn't do anything about llama shit."

"Smitty made a camel shit joke," Eddie answers, "and that's the same family, so we're covered. But let's see if we can make one up."

Mercifully for Norm, they arrive at the barracks. It's a sunny day, so the guys decide to read their mail while sitting on the barracks' back steps. Eddie and Bob light up. "We can do something about that llama shit later, Bob. First let's see what the postman brought us."

Norm receives a letter from his mother with twenty bucks in it. Bob gets a letter from the State of California. It's the ownership certificate to his Ford. "My pink slip," he shouts, "I'm an owner."

Eddie has two letters. He smells the lipstick on the back of the square, light blue envelope and tucks it into his pocket. He opens the long white one. "From the Air Force. Probably a well-deserved promotion." They all laugh.

Eddie pulls out a check. He scans the letter. Waving the check, he crows, "A hundred and fifty bucks. I got my bread back. My court-martial bounced." He reads more and continues, "The Air Force fucked up my paperwork."

"I wasn't here when you were court-martialed," Norm states. "What did you do?"

"Not much, really." Eddie takes a long drag on his cigarette and blows out a few smoke rings, recalling the incident. "We used to have a medic here named O'Hara."

"They shipped his ass to Greenland," Bob adds.

"And they'd have shipped mine with him, but Greenland already had radar ops comin' outta their ears."

"So what happened?" Norm tucks his twenty-dollar bill into the back of his wallet.

"It was Saint Patrick's Day, a year ago. Me and O'Hara were drinkin' some of his homemade cough medicine. It was full of codeine. This shit was a big jump ahead of your ordinary G.I. gin. Anyway, then we drank some beer and black-berry brandy and got real shitfaced. I mean, we were fuckin' wasted. O'Hara decides he wants to go see his family in Flint. Sounds good to me, so we take the weapons carrier and he crashes it into the fuckin' radio tower." Eddie starts laughing.

Bob laughs. "It took Frenchie and his radio mechanics two days to get us back on the air. Selfridge went apeshit." Bob drops his cigarette butt in the butt can.

"All our plots had to go to ADCC by teletype," Eddie explains. "It was a real pain in the ass." Eddie checks his watch and adds, "O'Hara, the Mad Medic. I gotta drop him a line about this. Let's go to town and put a dent in this thing." He thinks about his resolution to only break restriction in emergencies and rea-sons, if I got to go to town to buy a gift for Joan's birthday, that's an emergency.

Bob leaves the base with Eddie in the trunk as usual. Norm catches a ride with the supply truck on its run to Arbo's favorite butcher shop in Bay City.

By 1:30, they're in Tawas, sitting at the bar of the Huron Hotel. Two old farmers are at the far end of the bar, near the jukebox. "Blue Skirt Waltz" is play-ing. Eddie likes that tune.

The bartender, a bald, heavyset man in his forties, greets them, "Hi guys. What'll it be?"

"Three beers, Lenny, and pour yourself a shot of somethin' good." Eddie is beaming. "And Lenny, send the old guys a couple of shots of peppermint schnapps."

Lenny starts pulling the draft beers. "What'd you do, Eddie, clean out a crap game?"

"Better'n that, Len. I got government bread." He holds up the check. "Can you cash this thing?"

Lenny puts the beers on the bar and studies the check. He slips his bifocals on, looks it over closely a second time and declares, "Good as gold." Eddie endorses the check and Lenny goes into the back room, comes back and lays the money in front of Eddie. He pours himself a shot of peppermint schnapps. "Here's to happy times," he toasts and knocks it down.

"Happy times," Eddie repeats. He chugs his beer, picks up his money and one pack of cigarettes. "That other pack's for you, Bob. I'll be right back." He throws a five on the bar. "Back these guys up, Len." Eddie heads for the door.

Walking down Main, Eddie catches glimpses of himself in some of the store windows and figures, What's the use of wearin' civvies if you're gonna fuck it up with black Air Force shoes and a white sidewall haircut?

He gets a good shot of himself in the window of a furniture store, stops for a moment and checks his reflection. Haircut, cool, he decides. Levis, shirt, okay. Shoes, fuckin' dynamite. Studying his black, suede loafers in the window, he admires the look of the white stitching where the sole meets the upper shoe. The tight fit pleases him. Like a regular shoe, he reflects, not sloppin' around. Eddie gives full approval to his appearance. Others might believe he looks like he'd be right at home on any street corner or pool hall from New York City to Detroit.

At the window of Wilson's Jewelers, he looks over the array of watches, wedding ring sets, necklaces, charm bracelets and birth stone rings. In the far corner of the display, past the pen and pencil sets and the DON'T 4-GET THE GRAD-U-8 sign near the Masonic rings and the silver ID bracelets, an item catches Eddie's eye.

The Wilsons, a middle-aged couple, run a mom and pop operation. The silver bell atop the door jingles as Eddie enters. Mister Wilson, seated at a desk in the rear of the store, looks up from the watch he's repairing. "No getaway car" flashes through his mind and he relaxes.

Mrs. Wilson pops out from behind a display of expandable watch bands. "Good afternoon, young man," she challenges. "Are you looking for anything special?"

Mister Wilson glances up again at Eddie. Eddie reads their thoughts, takes out his cash and smiles a big smile at Mrs. Wilson. "I saw something in your window, down near the strand of pearls, that looks just right for the sweetest girl in the world."

Mrs. Wilson smiles back at Eddie and retrieves the article. She holds it up. "It's the only one we have."

"I like it. How much?"

"That's fifty-five dollars. The price includes the gold chain."

"This is pure gold? Not plated?"

"That's right."

"I'll take it." Eddie starts counting out money. "Can you engrave it?"

"Oh yes." She hands Eddie a slip of paper. He prints a few words on it and returns the paper with his money.

"The engraving is free." Mister Wilson is now smiling. "I do it myself. How's Friday?"

"Friday's fine." Pointing to a sign, Eddie remarks, "I see you give a ten percent discount to servicemen. I knew I shoulda joined up." He laughs and leaves the store whistling.

Back at the bar he has two more beers with Bob and Norm and they head back for the base. When Bob pulls over to let Eddie climb into the trunk, Norm gets out of the car.

"I'll just walk from here," he declares.

Bob closes the trunk. "It's a hot afternoon and a two-mile walk, Norm."

Eddie shouts from inside the trunk, "Norm, if I'm ever caught, I'll swear that I snuck into the trunk without you guys knowin' it."

Bob adds, "I'll just say I picked you up by the highway."

Norm finally relents and gets back into Bob's car. He rolls through the main gate with an asshole so tight that you couldn't pound a mustard seed up it with a ten-pound sledge.

Evening chow on Wednesday is always steak, but the supply truck's transmission died in Bay City, so Arbo substituted creamed chipped beef on toast.

Sitting at one of the four-man tables during their evening chow break, Norm is moaning to Bob and Eddie. "Even if the supply truck is broken down, you'd think Arbo could have come up with something better than S.O.S." He is picking at his food.

With his mouth full, Eddie snorts, "Whoever named this stuff Shit on a Shingle musta been apeshit. I like it better'n Mom's home cookin'."

"Very funny," Norm retorts, "but I happen to miss my mom's cooking. She used to bake Toll House cookies for our Boy Scout meetings."

Bob stops his fork midway to his mouth. "You were a Boy Scout?"

"You weren't?"

"I spent all my time lying on the beach and swimming," Bob answers.

Eddie jams another heaping forkful of S.O.S. into his mouth. "We did all our swimmin' in the Hudson River." Making arm motions he continues, "We hadda do the Hudson Crawl."

Studying Eddie's arm motions, hands in front of his face, back of hand to back of hand, arms then sweeping outward, as if one were walking through heavy foliage, trying to brush it away, Norm remarks, "That looks awkward. Why would anyone choose to swim that way?"

Eddie does a grin, like the one you'd see on an old-time dentist's sign. "You hadda swim like that, Norm." He looks at Norm intently. "To knock the turds and rubbers outta your way. In New York they empty the sewers into the river."

Norm puts his fork down. Bob and Eddie laugh. Enjoying Norm's discomfort, Eddie steps things up. "The Hudson wasn't so bad, once you swam out past the Shit Line."

Norm pushes his tray to the center of the table. "You make me glad I'm from California."

Eddie laughs harder. "We used to call rubbers Hudson Trout, there were so fuckin' many."

Norm proclaims, "You might think it's funny, but you're just lucky that you never caught infantile paralysis."

Mopping up the last of his S.O.S., Eddie stuffs it into his mouth. "Naw. Nobody in my neighborhood ever got sick from swimmin' in the river. In fact, Jimmy Doyle used to soak his boils in the river. It'd dry 'em right up."

Norm looks at his watch and picks up his tray. "Guess we might as well head back to shift." Bob and Eddie pick up their trays and the three of them head for the dirty tray counter. At the garbage can, Eddie reaches in and salvages Norm's S.O.S.-soaked toast. "A little treat for Ma Barker. She's eatin' for six."

CHAPTER 13

▼

Eddie doesn't have to hitch to Joan's for dinner because Bob and Norm are driving down to see Sandy and Laura as part of the deal he presented to Captain Ross on Thursday after evening chow. Eddie's plan allowed the three of them to miss shift from midnight until 0400, the slowest hours of midnight shift. It flowed as naturally as a maple leaf turning red in October.

Leaving the mess hall Thursday after evening chow with Bob and Norm, Eddie spots Arbo in the back of the kitchen. "You guys go ahead. I wanna shoot the shit with Arbo. Tell Captain Ross I'm here if he needs me."

"Hey Arbo!" Eddie shouts as he steps past the serving line. "You workin' overtime?"

Arbo puts down his clipboard. "Fucking inventory. Stupid bullshit drill. The chow's either here or it's been eaten and turned into shit."

"Spoken like a true gourmet."

"So what's going on?"

"Well for one thing, Arbo, I'm in love."

"Jesus Christ, Eddie, you're a pisser. Don't ever change. A stiff dick is not love."

"No, it ain't like that at all, Arbo. No bullshit."

Arbo nods his head. "Okay, maybe I'm a bad guy to talk to about love. The ladies are just trolley cars to me. Ride 'em for a while, then get off and wait for the next one to roll up. Some rides are better than others and some of the rides last longer, but they all come to an end. At least they do for me."

"I know what you mean, Arbo. I'm like that too, but this girl is absolutely different, man. Hard to explain."

Arbo reads Eddie's intensity. "I really can't help you on anything about women, Eddie. They're all fucking wacky, but beyond that I'm no help. You need to talk to some guy who has a few years of marriage under his belt."

"I'm gonna start shapin' up because of this girl."

"Uh-huh. I can see the headlines now. Eddie Flynn shapes up." Arbo laughs at his own joke.

"Anyway, that's my news. Got any liver left? Ma Barker loves it."

"I'm glad somebody does." Arbo gestures toward a deep-dish tray of liver. "Help yourself, Eddie. There's always plenty of liver left over. Take a bag for Captain Ross' dog, too."

"Now there's a headline. Arbo does somethin' nice for a commissioned officer."

"I don't think of Captain Ross as an officer, I think of him as a flyer, like the officers I cooked for in England. They're a different breed of cat from headquarters guys like Becker."

Eddie fills a large bag with slabs of fried liver. "I know what you mean, Arbo. Thanks for the liver. See you."

"Take it easy, Eddie."

Entering Radar Operations, Eddie finds only Captain Ross and Ma Barker in the break room. Ma Barker jumps off the couch and runs to greet Eddie, wagging her tail. Captain Ross continues filling his cup. "Hi, Eddie."

"Hiya, Captain. Wait'll you see what I got for Major." Eddie pats Ma Barker's head, pulls out a large piece of liver and gives it to her. Eddie holds the open bag for Captain Ross' inspection.

"Major will do a good job on that. Thanks, Eddie."

"My pleasure, Captain. Actually, Arbo thought of it. Said take some of that for Captain Ross' dog."

"I've talked with Arbo a couple of times. We were both stationed in England during the war, but we never met. He's an interesting guy."

"I listen to him. He's pretty smart. Captain, I need a really big favor and I need to ask a question about love. You got a couple of minutes?"

"Sure. But let's do the easy one first. What's the big favor?"

"It's like this, Captain. I gotta go to dinner at a very special girl's house on Sunday at seven and be back here at midnight. I need a few hours off, but I've got a good plan."

Ross enjoys watching Eddie work his way around, through, over and under rules. "Obviously, this is a very special young lady. So tell me your plan."

"How's this sound, Captain? Number one, the Saginaw Express pulled outta town, so Brownie's back on duty. Two, for a case of beer McKinny'll stand by for me in the break room from midnight to four. He don't get the beer 'til *after* shift." They both laugh.

Captain Ross likes McKinny. He felt it was a real waste to put a sharp radar operator in the motor pool. "Sounds good so far, especially the timing of the beer delivery."

Eddie laughs. "Number three, Bob and Norm want to see their chicks. What if Brownie just slips 'em outta rotation 'til four and then they work straight through from four 'til eight with no breaks. How's that sound, Captain?"

"Sounds okay to me."

"Man! That's great. Thanks, Captain. I'm shapin' up because of this girl."

"This girl must be something."

"Oh she is, Captain. Like no girl I ever met. Which brings me to my question about love."

"It better be an easy question."

I don't know, maybe it's more like an opinion than a question with an answer. Do you think there's such a thing as love at first sight, like in the movies?"

"I don't know about the movies, but I fell in love at first sight. I spotted my wife at a cocktail party and I couldn't get across the room fast enough. We had three months together before I shipped out. We got married a week after I was sent home."

"So then you think it's possible, Captain? Right?"

"Sure. But don't take my word for it. Shakespeare, Marlowe, and I'm sure plenty of others wrote about it."

"Good. Because that's just what happened to me. And Joan says she feels the same way ... like we were meant to meet."

"Did you tell her much about yourself?"

"We talked until almost six in the morning. I told her enough where she knows I'm not up for sainthood. I told her on the phone that I was gonna shape up and she said I was already good enough for her. Ain't that somethin', Captain?"

"Jesus Christ, Eddie. That's one girl in a million. You'd better bring your best table manners to that dinner."

"My mother taught me all that shit. I'm okay at the table when I have to be. And Joan says her mom is definitely cool. It's just her old man I've got to make a good impression on."

"Yeah? What kind of guy is he?"

"Well, uh, Joan says he's a lot like Becker."

"Becker?!" Captain Ross snort-laughs. "This guy'll toss you out on your ass the minute he sees you."

"I'm wearin' my uniform, Captain. And regulation shoes."

"Oh that'll fool him," Ross quips, and they both laugh.

Ross sips his coffee and heads for the hall. "Tell Brownie I'm in the crypto room. And good luck on that dinner, Eddie. You'll need it."

Eddie finishes running his meeting with Captain Ross through his mind as Bob stops at Joan's driveway. The two-story colonial house, sitting on a huge lot, is surrounded by many mature trees. Two Cadillacs are parked next to Joan's Chevy. Bob asks, "Should I drive in?"

"Fuckin'-A. I'm a dinner guest, ain't I?"

Bob drives up to the front door. Norm asks, "Did Joan tell you she was rich?"

"She said her neighborhood was boring." Eddie gets out of the car. "It does look kind of stiff."

"I'll be back at midnight," Bob promises. He drives quietly out of the driveway.

Joan opens the front door before the sound of the door chimes dies. She's wearing a yellow chiffon dress, splashed with lime and light blue. Her yellow high heels match her dress and, again, a light gardenia scent is in the air.

"You look delicious." Eddie takes her hands and pulls her to him. While hugging and kissing, Eddie cups one cheek of Joan's ass. She opens her mouth slightly, the tips of their tongues touch briefly and they break their kiss.

"You're ten minutes early. Dad'll like that. I can hardly see a trace of your black eye."

"I'm a fast healer."

Joan's excited, eyes glistening, pulse racing and skin tingling. "Come on in. Dad's making martinis. You'll love my mom."

Eddie wipes off his lips on his handkerchief. "Let's go meet the folks."

The large living room, furnished in American Colonial, is warm and comfortable. Bill Whitman, a forty-one-year-old General Motors executive, is refilling his wife's large martini glass.

Jill Whitman, sitting on the couch smoking a long cigarette, strikes Eddie as an adult Joan. "She's gotta be around forty," he figures, "and still a knockout."

Jill's wearing black silk slacks, black pumps, a blouse that matches Joan's shoes and a silver gray blazer. A small gold scorpion is poised on the jacket's lapel.

If there's anything Jill enjoys more than shopping for Joan, it's drinking martinis. She's not a lush, but loves being half in the bag, observing her husband.

Sometimes she visualizes Bill as a giant-sized piece of dry toast. Watching Joan introduce Eddie to her husband, she feels Joan's excitement.

While shaking hands, Bill studies Eddie with a steely eye and distended nostrils. He sees rebellion and smells trouble. "Just call me Bill," he states. "Mister Whitman sounds so old."

"Sure thing, Bill."

Eddie catches Jill smiling, watching him return Bill's overly forceful handshake with equal vigor. He winks at her. Joan's right, he decides, Mom's a winner.

Aware that he's on a journey to nowhere with Bill, Eddie figures, Might as well have some fun with dear old dad tonight.

Joan pulls Eddie away from her father and over to the couch. "And this is my mom, Eddie."

Jill offers her hand. Eddie gives her a firm handshake, his mother's voice, instructing, "Always give a woman a normal handshake. Not one of those wishy-washy, halfbaked, just holding her fingers things. A real woman expects a real hand-shake from a man."

"Thanks for havin' me to dinner, Mrs. Whitman."

"We're happy to have you here, Eddie." Appraising Eddie through the eyes of Joan, Jill sees action and romance.

Bill offers Eddie a martini and Eddie passes. "No thanks, Bill. I'm not of legal age here in Michigan." As Bill starts to withdraw the cocktail, Eddie takes it. "Maybe I'll try just one, since it's a family dinner."

Bill Whitman would have made a great vice-principal at a junior high school, had he not gone into the auto trade. Six feet tall and slender, wearing rimless glasses, looking Anglo-Saxon and dressed as if he just left a board meeting at General Motors, he's more tightly wound than usual. A strict disciplinarian, he tried to spank Joan once, when she was four. Jill came down on him like a shovel on a garden gopher, warning, "If you ever try to touch that girl, I'll take a frying pan and brain you." Knowing that Jill meant what she said, Bill settled for imposing rigid standards on Joan's school performance. Being naturally bright, Joan does this without effort. She doesn't make big waves in any other ways and as Bill sees it, "She's a pretty nice kid. Not a bad catch for a young man with a solid, bankable future." He is not happy that Eddie Flynn is in his living room.

Bill goes straight for the jugular. "Joan tells us you're a radar operator. How come you have no stripes?"

"I don't worry about stripes. Who cares if you lose a couple of stripes because you jump into a lake to save a drownin' kid and it makes you late for duty?" Turning to Jill, Eddie asks, "You know what I mean, Mrs. Whitman?"

Joan swallows hard and looks away, trying not to laugh. Spotting Joan's reaction, Jill quickly replies, "I certainly do, Eddie. What are a couple of silly old stripes compared to a child's life?" She holds up her empty martini glass. "Bill, are you pouring?" She blows a long stream of smoke in Bill's direction.

Bill instantly refills her glass. Interesting, Eddie notes.

"I suppose I should thank you for helping Joan with that flat." Bill looks like he just bit into a lemon. "I don't see why she didn't call the Auto Club. I've been a member since I graduated from Michigan."

Eddie sips his martini. "I was right there. Helpin' seemed like the right thing to do. It was my pleasure."

"I'm sure." Bill polishes off his drink and refills his glass. "Speaking of college. I guess the war interrupted your studies?"

"Yeah and it's just as well. I was havin' a hard time makin' up my mind, tryin' to choose between law and medicine. Now I got four years to think about it," Eddie deadpans.

This kid is great. Jill sips her drink. I don't know where Joan found him, but dinner will be fun for me tonight.

Joan glances at her watch. "Dinner is served." She takes Eddie's elbow and gently steers him toward the dining room, where dinner is on a buffet table next to the dining table. "Come on, Dad," Joan invites, over her shoulder. "Mom and I spent the day in the kitchen. We're having the all-American Sunday dinner—tossed salad, roast chicken with dressing and gravy, mashed potatoes, fresh spring peas and homemade chocolate cake for dessert."

The dining room is also furnished in American Colonial. Eddie sits facing Bill, with Jill on his left. Joan's empty chair is on his right. She's up putting four plates of salad together. After she dishes them out, everyone sits looking at one another.

"Are you in the habit of saying grace, Eddie?"

"Not as a rule, Bill. I'm always thankful. But I'm ready to pray, if that's your custom."

"No. We don't say grace." Bill picks up his fork.

Jill finishes the martini that she carried to the table. "I'll say a grace that we used to say in grammar school," she volunteers. "Now, everyone please bow your heads and close your eyes. Bill, put down your fork." He does. Jill continues, "Ready? Okay. In the name of the Father and of the Son and of the Holy Ghost, the one who eats the fastest gets the most." Everyone but Bill laughs. They start on their salads. Midway through the salad, Bill tries a probe. "What do you think about unions, Eddie?"

"I guess you gotta have unions to keep the bosses from gobblin' up the whole pie, don'tcha?"

"I'm vice-president of labor relations at General Motors. I have to deal with union demands. It's my job to make sure the unions don't steal the stockholders blind."

"Sounds like a tough job. I don't know much about labor problems." Turning toward Jill, he smiles. "But I do know real olive oil and balsamic vinegar when I taste 'em. Am I right, Mrs. Whitman?"

"You're right, Eddie. But the salad was Joan's special project. We did everything else together."

Eddie smiles at Joan. "You've got the magic touch, Joan. That's a killer salad." Joan looks radiant.

Catching the look between them, Bill fumes. He tries another thrust at the unions, but Eddie counters with, "I've still got a lot to learn, but it seems to me happy workers do better work. Kinda common sense." Bill concentrates on finishing his salad and feels compelled to comment on it, after Eddie's praise of it. "That was a nice salad," he tells Joan.

"Thanks, Dad."

Nice. What a weak word, Jill decides. Watching for Bill's reaction, she declares, "Looks like your cooking is a hit with all the men tonight, honey."

He's steaming, Jill deduces and smiles. Jill and Joan broadcast on their own, private network. Twice, Joan catches Jill smiling at Eddie's effortless ripostes. Mom likes Eddie. Dad's going to pick at him, she figures. I may as well relax and enjoy the show.

Joan takes the plates to the buffet table where the rest of the meal waits. She quickly dismantles the chicken, thanks to Home Ec and many years by her mother's knee. She dishes up a plate for her father. "Just the way you like it, Dad. Nothing but white meat with gravy and mashed potatoes with butter."

She puts together two almost identical plates for herself and her mother, small portions of mashed potatoes, dressing and white meat with gravy, a larger portion of peas, a wing for Jill and a leg for Joan. She puts one plate in front of her mom and the other at her spot, then turns to Eddie. "And now for you, Eddie," she almost purrs, "you can have anything you want." Glancing at her mom, she receives a big smile.

"I'll go for the whole shot. White meat, dark meat and a leg. Same as you and your mom on the other portions, but hit me heavy on the peas and just a little more salad, right on my dinner plate."

"Done." Joan dishes up Eddie's meal, slips his plate in front of him and sits down.

Jill takes a forkful of potatoes and begins eating. Bill can't resist talking about his favorite subject, money. He has always pushed for Joan to date "boys of substance."

"It's just as easy to fall in love with a rich boy as it is to fall in love with a nobody," he reminded her when she was going to her Junior Hop. "I'm only sixteen, Dad," she had answered. Her date that night was a boy whose father was a judge, a friend of Bill's. Joan had ripped her party dress fighting him off and had walked home. The kid was drunk and later in the evening he crashed into a police car on Mack Avenue.

Bill winds up his paean to money and Eddie remarks, "I may be wrong, but some of the happiest and most exciting things that have happened to me have had nothin' to do with money."

Not missing a beat, Jill looks at Bill and bubbles, "That's right, Bill, like Joanie's birth."

Bill quiets down a bit and then, just before dessert, he fires another volley. "The way you favor unions, Eddie," he ventures, "makes me feel you may be a Democrat."

"I'm too young to vote, but in my neighborhood when you need a job, you go to the Democratic Club. And the Democrats throw good picnics. Everyone in New York City loves the Democrats. I don't think I ever met a Republican."

Jill stifles a laugh and takes a slow swallow of her water. Joan does the same.

"You've met one now," Bill exclaims, "I'm a Republican."

"Good for you, Bill. We're all in this together. Right? Democrats and Republicans united against the Commies. What do you think, Mrs. Whitman?"

"I don't take politics very seriously, Eddie." She turns to Bill. "But Truman sure did surprise Dewey. Didn't he, Bill?"

"I still don't understand how that happened." He turns to Eddie. "And why wouldn't you go to the Republican Club for a job?"

"I never heard of one. Don't know where a Republican Club would be."

"Probably down on Wall Street," Jill offers, "where the money is." She laughs and Bill harrumphs.

Eddie changes the subject. "One of the best things about this meal, besides the salad," Eddie smiles at Joan and continues, "was using fresh peas instead of canned peas. I like all the different sizes. Don't you hate it when everything is just the same?"

"Canned peas are boring," Jill jokes, and everyone laughs but Bill.

"Those cars rolling off the line better all be the same," he grumps. Pushing back from the table he lights a long, fat cigar.

"That's true, Bill," Eddie agrees, and Joan smiles.

Bill gives Eddie a level look. "I must say, it's been a most informative evening, Eddie … what did you say your last name was?"

"Flynn, Bill." Eddie returns Bill's look. Then, flashing a broad smile, he adds, "Just like Errol Flynn, in the movies."

Bill's face tightens. "Yes. Like Errol Flynn. I'm sure," he answers.

"Speaking of movies," Joan interjects, "we've got to run. Eddie has never seen 'Casablanca'."

"Let me know if he calls Rick a sucker," Bill jabs.

Eddie gets up and goes over to Jill's chair. Leaning over to speak to her, he states, "Thanks for makin' me feel welcome, Mrs. Whitman. It was a deluxe dinner." He adds, softly, "It's easy to see why Joan is such a cutie-pie."

Jill gives him a warm smile.

As they are leaving the room, Joan announces, "We'll be home by midnight. Eddie's on duty early in the morning."

"And it wouldn't do to be late." Bill puffs on his cigar. "You have no more stripes to give back."

"That's right, Bill," Eddie answers. "And thank you for your hospitality." He reaches across the table and receives a much more subdued handshake from Bill. Well, at least I taught the guy how to shake hands, Eddie concludes. But how did an asshole like that ever have a kid like Joan? Good thing she's got her mom.

Outside the front door, Joan and Eddie begin laughing. "What's it going to be, Eddie? Law or medicine?" Joan mimics her father.

"I knew you'd like that one."

Moments later, in Joan's car, Eddie states, "Your dad was right about one thing, though."

Genuinely surprised, Joan asks, "What was that?"

"I've seen 'Casablanca', and Rick *was* a jerk for givin' up the girl he loved. I'd never give you up for nothin' or nobody." They share a long kiss and Joan drives quietly out of the driveway.

At the corner, Joan stops for a red light and Eddie asks, "Where are we headed?"

Joan smiles. "Not to the movies."

She drives a few blocks to the Harbor Lights Country Club and is waved through the gate. Parking down in the farthest corner of the parking lot, overlooking Lake St. Clair, Joan reaches under her seat and comes up with two bottles of beer. "They're a little warm, but I've got colder ones in an ice chest in the trunk."

Eddie opens them with his church key, passes one to Joan and takes a swig of the other. "Tastes fine to me. You know that was real smart tellin' your old man we're goin' to a movie you already seen."

"I love lying to my father." Joan takes a swallow of her beer. "He's such a phony. I knew he wouldn't like you."

"When guys like him and Becker start likin' me, I'll know I'm doin' somethin' wrong."

Joan takes another hit of her beer. "Do you think I'm awful for being such a liar?"

"Naw. Most people don't want the truth anyway. It's too scary for 'em. They'd rather be bullshitted." They clink their bottles together and drink.

"You sure do look beautiful in that dress."

"Thanks. But this strapless bra is digging into my back."

Eddie laughs and puts his beer on the floor. "Slide over here and let's see if I can fix that." Unhooking her bra, he asks, "Are we okay parked here?"

"My dad's on the board at this place and nobody will bother us unless I scream" she answers. "And I will scream, if you don't kiss me."

CHAPTER 14

▼

Artie's Sugar Bowl, the local high school hangout, stands on the corner of Ten Mile Road and Mack Avenue. At 4:20 PM on a Monday during summer vacation, it's almost empty. A couple of young kids are at the counter sipping sodas. A teenage boy and girl in a back booth are kissing, and two girls are looking through the movie magazines. Laura, Sandy and Joan are Artie's only other customers. They're in the booth nearest the jukebox. Johnny Ray is singing, "Cry".

Having just arrived, Joan is being questioned by the other girls, who've been hanging around the ice cream parlor for almost an hour.

"So how was dinner last night?" Sandy swirls the last of her large Coke around with her straw.

"My dad hated Eddie," Joan states matter-of-factly. "I'm sure he doesn't want him at my party."

Sucking up the last of her soda with sounds like a thousand dice tumbling in a cup, Laura swallows, then asks, "How can you be sure? Eddie might say 'beah' instead of 'beer,' but you can't hold that against him."

"I know my dad. Eddie felt it. He said he hit my dad like a blivet." Joan smiles, recalling Eddie's explanation.

Sandy looks puzzled. "A blivet?"

"Ten pounds of shit in a five-pound bag." They all laugh and Joan continues, "How about you guys? You have a good time last night?"

"I sure did." Laura grins devilishly. "When I got home I threw my panties against the wall and they stuck."

Sandy and Joan groan.

"Just a little sorority house humor," Laura adds and laughs.

"Speaking of humor," Sandy remarks. "You just missed Roddy. He said he'll see us at your birthday party."

"Thrill a minute." Joan makes a face. "My dad must've invited him. I sure didn't." She checks her watch. "Better get going."

"What's the rush? You just got here." Laura wants to gossip.

Getting up, Joan pushes her barely-sipped soda toward the others. "Big family meeting. I'm sure it's about Eddie."

"See you later." Laura sticks her straw into Joan's soda.

Sandy pats Joan's hand. "Good luck with your dad."

"Thanks, San." Joan almost frowns. "I'm going to need more than luck."

In the Whitman living room, standing behind the bar, Bill is getting ready to stir his eight-to-one gin and vermouth mix. The bar he stands behind and its four matching stools are Italian leather, with hammered brass brads. The bar set, the top-of-the-line stemware and the sterling silver martini pitcher with matching stirring spoon were Jill's gift to herself when she decided to take up martinis as a hobby. "If I'm going to get half looped every afternoon at tea time, I'm going to do it in style," she reasoned. Bill sulked about the extravagance of the purchase for two months.

Peering into the pitcher, he observes drops of vermouth riding on the ice cubes. "Looks slippery." He dips the spoon into the mixture and begins to stir. "Slippery" triggers "Greasy" in Bill's brain, unleashing a thought; I don't want that greasy kid at *my* birthday party. He nearly stirs the liquid to a froth.

He pours the mix into two oversize martini glasses, adding an olive only to his own, and glances at Jill. She's sitting on the couch looking elegant in a light green shift with silver hummingbirds embroidered on its bodice. Her legs are crossed and she's dangling one dark green alligator pump. "Someday you've got to figure out how much money I save us by not using olives." She blows a stream of smoke into a ray of sunshine, watching it twirl and eddy.

Eddie, she muses, that's what this meeting's all about. That kid really got under Bill's skin. I should've guessed it. If Bill takes a couple of hours off, it's serious.

As newlyweds and through the late thirties and the forties, Jill thought it was "cute" the way Bill worked all those extra hours, slowly climbing the corporate ladder. At General Motors he was recognized as the most tight-fisted employee in the Cost Control Division. "If you let this guy cut corners on a square, he'll turn it into a perfect circle," a boss had written on Bill's 1937 Evaluation Report. In a P.S. the man had added, "I like his reverence for the dollar."

"We save about two dollars a week on olives," he answers and hands Jill her cocktail.

"I was joking, Bill," she remarks, thinking, He's probably wondering how much this outfit cost. I can almost hear his brain clicking up a total.

Wonder how much that dress and those shoes cost, runs through Bill's mind.

A lot less than you imagine, Jill answers mentally. She sips her drink.

Bill takes a long swallow of his cocktail. "So what did you think of last night's prize package?"

"I thought he was kind of cute." Jill smiles at Bill. "How does he get his hair to shine like that?"

"Grease." Bill grimaces. "And that little bastard's as slick as grease. You didn't go for that drowning kid story, did you?"

Of course not, flashes through Jill's mind, the joke was obvious. She takes another, larger sip of her martini. Broadening her smile, she jabs, "It sounded plausible to me. Eddie seems like the kind of boy who would do something like that." She pauses a half a heartbeat and thrusts, "Joan seemed quite taken with him."

Before Bill can sputter in protest, Joan comes sailing into the room. She's decided to do the happy and bouncy routine. "Hi, Dad." She pecks Bill on the cheek. She goes over to the couch and hugs and kisses her mother. "Wasn't Eddie wonderful, Mom?"

"I liked him just fine, dear. He seems like a real gentleman." Jill polishes off her drink, holds out her empty glass and asks, "Are you pouring, Bill?" She blows a stream of smoke into the sunbeam and gets ready to enjoy the show.

Barely able to control his anger, Bill refills his wife's glass. "You liked him just fine? You can't be serious, Jill. Contempt for society was oozing out of him, like the grease in his hair."

"Oh Bill," Jill retorts, "don't you think you're being overly dramatic?"

Breaking in, right behind her mother, Joan demands, "Dad, it's my birthday party. I can invite anyone I want."

"How's Roddy going to react to this interloper? He's planning on giving you his frat pin."

"I don't want Roddy's old frat pin." Joan's eyes narrow. "Roddy's a jerk."

"Some jerk," Bill snorts. "He's set to inherit forty million dollars on his twenty-fifth birthday."

"Roddy isn't very exciting, Bill." Jill smiles a sweet smile. "He's like a large piece of dry toast."

"Not very exciting," Bill almost shouts, the words exploding. "Roddy is forty million dollars worth of excitement. Anyone who can't get excited about forty million dollars has something wrong with them."

Sensing Eddie isn't going to be allowed to attend her party, Joan cranks up the tears. "I know all about Roddy's money," she sobs, the words tumbling out, "and I know he's going to be a big man at Chrysler when he gets out of Yale. I've heard it from you and I heard it from Roddy and I don't care. All I know is that I feel good when I'm with Eddie and if he's not at my party, I'll have an awful, awful time." Dabbing her eyes, Joan turns to Jill. "May I please go up to my room, Mom?"

"Of course, dear." Jill pats Joan's shoulder.

Joan heads upstairs and Bill freshens Jill's drink. "You know, Bill," Jill offers, "Eddie does have a kind of effervescence about him."

"Effervescence, my eye. That kid is a misfit. He'll never make it in the corporate world."

"Not everyone dwells in the corporate world." Jill's voice takes on an edge. "It is Joan's birthday," she declares, "and, her party."

"Yes, but ..." Bill begins.

Jill cuts him off. "And it's *my* mother's trust fund that matures next year when Joanie turns nineteen."

Bill pictures himself as an exhausted runner approaching the eighteen mile marker in a nineteen mile race. Can't quit now, he vows. Visualizing a mound of currency, he encourages himself, Two million American greenbacks, only a year away. He can almost feel the texture of the bills in his hand. He downs his drink and with pain showing on his face, he lets out a loud sigh. "I guess I might as well go up and tell Joan it's all right for that kid to attend the party."

"That's a good idea, Bill," Jill nods. "I'm sure that will make Joan feel much better. I'm surprised she invited Roddy. She told me he was a real drip."

"I invited Roddy," Bill states, heading for the stairs.

CHAPTER 15

▼

Joan's party at the Harbor Lights Country Club is more like a neighborhood block party than a birthday party. Besides Sandy and Laura, Joan invited some of the regulars at Artie's Sugar Bowl and a few friends from her class. Thanks to Joan's liberal attitude of "sure you can bring a friend or two," her invitation list of fifteen resulted in eighty kids showing up, forty of them right at 8 PM when the Oak Room opened its doors. She and Jill had anticipated this from past experiences with birthday parties thrown at the club and they had the refreshment table filled almost to the point of overflow. Many of the girls, Joan included, are wearing their prom gowns, others are wearing cocktail dresses. No color in the rainbow has been neglected. All the guys are wearing dinner jackets.

The Oak Room is a hardworking room used for parties, business meetings, banquets and award ceremonies. It's the smaller of the club's ballrooms. Jill calls the larger ballroom "the mausoleum." She dismissed it as too large, too white and too cold, and chose the Oak Room.

The Oak Room has a permanent stage, a service bar, and oak paneling throughout. One wall is nothing but sliding glass doors that open onto a spacious patio. They are open for the party.

The Oak Room shares this patio with the club's dining room and piano bar. Many of the older club members have dinner at the club and stay on to dance under the stars and Chinese lanterns. They resent it when rowdy young jitterbugs spill onto "their" patio. Whenever loud band music from a party drowns out the mellow tinklings of the Extraordinary Lazlo doing "I'll Be Seeing You" or "I'll Walk Alone", they cluster down at their end of the patio and mutter about the good old days.

At 8:15 the band, a Detroit outfit billed as the Fabulous Seven, featuring drums, bass, guitar, sax, trumpet, trombone, and a piano player with a lot of personality and a loud, if not excellent, voice, are on stage and almost ready to blow. It would have been more honest had they named themselves the Okay Seven or the Pretty Damn Good Seven, but any minor musical imperfections are canceled by the overall loudness of the group and the energy of the piano player.

At 8:16 the Fabulous Seven kick things off with a rollicking version of "Come On A My House" that gets ninety percent of the kids dancing, half of them spilling out onto the patio, sending the old timers scurrying. At 8:30, a light breeze is blowing in from Lake St. Clair and Eddie and the guys have not arrived.

Roddy Calvin, a twenty-two-year-old version of Bill, except for Bill's glasses, is at the service bar with Bill and some of his corporate cronies. Bill defended his invitation of these GM executives to Jill, whining, "Goddammit, Jill, I'm footing the bill for this shindig. I might as well get some good out of it."

Bill, Roddy and the GM bunch opened the bar at seven o'clock, an hour before the other guests started arriving. Bill and Roddy are smoking cigars and drinking large tumblers of Scotch. They're on their fourth round. A shrink would label Bill an interesting case. Eddie and the guys from his old neighborhood would call him a "signifier."

Eddie once defined the meaning of signifier when Norm claimed it wasn't a real word, like this, "Of course it's a real word, Norm. I'm usin' it. Just because you don't know a word doesn't mean it don't exist. I called Thompson a signifier because he was tellin' you a whole lotta shit about McKinny, tryin' to get you and McKinny pissed off at each other when he's the one who don't like McKinny." Norm looked doubtful.

Eddie put his arm around Norm's shoulder. "You know, like in the poem 'The Signifyin' Monkey', about a monkey down in the jungle who wants the lion to get his ass kicked.

"The monkey knows he can't whip the lion, so he signifies the lion into fighting the elephant. From up in his tree the monkey shouts shit like, 'Hey Leo, King of the Jungle and ain't you a bitch, all covered with mange and the seven-year itch? There's a big, gray, hose-nosed motherfucker down the road who talks about your ass in a terrible way, and that ain't all, he got shit about your momma to say.'

"Long story short, Norm, the lion goes to kick the elephant's ass and gets his own ass kicked, which is what the signifyin' monkey wanted. It's a famous poem, Norm. I'm surprised you've been to college and never heard it." Norm shook his head resignedly.

"Norm, Norm, Norm," Eddie grinned. "Let me put it this way. Say we're standin' on the corner and one of the guys says to another, 'You know, Joey, I was drinkin' with Murray and he said your sister's an easy lay.' The guy speakin' is a signifier."

But signifying isn't reserved just for street corners. Peeling Roddy away from the group of executives, Bill finishes up his evening's signifying. He studies his watch and prods, "It's 8:30, son. You'd better get over to the punch bowl and stake your claim with Joan. That greasy interloper I've been telling you about could show up any time now."

Roddy pokes his cigar out in a nearby planter, downs the rest of his drink and asks, "How do I look?"

You look like forty million dollars, flashes through Bill's mind. "You look great, Roddy," he fawns. "Joan's a fortunate young lady."

At the refreshment table, Jill and Laura are telling Joan, Sandy and two of their former classmates about the Tri-Delts. Jill remembers her sorority days fondly. When she excuses herself to go out and mingle, Joan checks her watch.

"It's only 8:30," Sandy soothes. "It's a long drive."

Laura spots Roddy detaching himself from the service bar group. "Don't look now," she warns, "but here comes Roddy."

The band segues from "It's No Sin" to "Too Young". Roddy arrives at the refreshment table. Joan and Sandy are feigning deep conversation, trying to ignore him. He catches Laura's eye and she's forced to acknowledge him. "Hi Roddy. How's Yale?"

"Very stimulating, thanks." He taps Joan on the shoulder.

"Hi Joan. Like to dance?"

Joan glances at the front door. Managing a small smile, she answers, "Okay." They join the other couples on the floor and do a respectable foxtrot.

"I know we only dated a few times ..."

"Twice, Roddy. We dated twice," Joan interrupts.

"Well, twice then. But with summer vacation here, I'll be able to pay a lot more attention to you."

Oh, my cup runneth over, Joan thinks, laughing to herself. "I'm going to be very busy all summer. Getting ready for college and all."

"I was just telling your dad that I feel a strong attraction to you."

Ugh, Joan comments to herself. You told my dad. Geez, what a jerk. This conversation is driving me buggy. Where the hell is Eddie? Joan stares at the door, wishing for Eddie's arrival. The guys appear. Thank God, she almost says aloud.

The guys are wearing their blue uniforms with Ike jackets. Eddie's jacket is open, revealing a pleated-front, white shirt, maroon cummerbund and a matching maroon bow tie. He's wearing his black suede loafers. When Norm reminded him that he was out of uniform, Eddie's answer had been, "I may not be regulation, but I'm one cool motherfucker."

Joan can't take her eyes off Eddie as he and the guys head for the refreshment table. "I'm sorry, Roddy," she asks, "what were you saying?"

"Us. I was talking about this summer and us."

Joan turns Roddy around so she can watch Eddie and the others.

Laura greets Norm with a big kiss. "Have some punch," she coos, "it's really good. If you know what I mean." Bob and Sandy are hugging. Eddie is looking around.

"Where's Joan?" he asks.

"She's dancing," Sandy points her out.

Joan steers Roddy closer to the group, catches Eddie's eye and winks. Eddie smiles and winks back.

By the time the tune ends, Joan has danced Roddy over to the punch bowl. Disengaging herself from Roddy, she turns toward Eddie. "Eddie, I'm so glad you could make it."

Eddie takes Joan's hand, gently pulling her close. "I wouldn't have missed your party for nothin'. You look terrific in that gown."

Roddy is looking on quizzically. Joan turns back to him. "Roddy, I'd like you to meet Eddie," and to Eddie she states, "Roddy's a friend of mine."

With his left arm around Joan's waist, Eddie extends his right hand, saying, "Any friend of Joan's is a friend of mine."

Leaving Eddie's hand hovering, Roddy declares, "I think of myself as more than Joan's friend. Please remove your hand from her waist."

Please remove my hand? This guy's a joker, Eddie thinks. "This could be a real short friendship," he says, half-jokingly.

The band begins to play, "Would I Love You, Love You, Love You". Making a move for the dance floor, Eddie finds Roddy blocking his way.

"I mean what I'm saying," Roddy commands. "Hands off my girl."

Sandy and Laura's mouths drop open. Norm frowns, Bob looks puzzled and Joan blows up. "Are you crazy?" she shouts at Roddy. "I am *not* your girl!"

"Listen to me, Roddy," Eddie snaps, barely able to control his temper, "if Joan ever tells me she's 'your girl,' I'll disappear. But right now me and Joan are dancin', so move it."

Scrutinizing Eddie, Roddy wonders, How could Joan even know such a crude person? Feeling the Scotches, he grows strong. I'm six-foot-one, he figures. This loudmouth isn't more than five-nine or ten. I could jab him senseless. He decides to continue his blockade. "No dancing until we go outside and settle this like gentlemen."

Joan moves between the two of them. "This is stupid."

"Joan's right," Eddie agrees. "Why don't we let this slide?"

"On the patio, right now!" The scotches are really kicking in. "Or are you yellow as well as crude?"

"Roddy, this isn't fair. You're taller than Eddie," Joan scolds, adding, "and you're ruining my party."

Eddie whispers to Joan, "Lemme give this guy what he needs." He steps away from Joan and announces, "Remember, Robbie, this is your idea." The two of them head for the patio.

"The name is Roddy, not Robbie. I feel it's only fair to warn you that at Yale, I'm the intramural champion in my weight division."

"Gee, I never fought a champ before." Eddie mocks admiration. "You gonna take it easy on me, Champ?"

With long strides, Roddy leads the way to a far corner of the patio, a corner partially obscured by large bushes. Watching Roddy, Eddie plans. This asshole has some long arms on him. He knows somethin' about boxin'. I better get inside on this big prick quick. I may have to take a couple of shots in the head.

Arriving at the spot, they remove their ties and jackets. Roddy assumes a Marquis of Queensberry boxing stance. Eddie smiles. This fuckin' fight's over, he says to himself. He approaches Roddy with his thumbs tucked in his cummerbund. He stops a foot and a half away, sticks up his jaw and challenges, "Okay, Champ, let's see you put one right here."

Roddy flicks out a left jab. Eddie whips his right hand up, knocking the jab aside. He jumps inside on Roddy and drives a hard, solid left deep into Roddy's solar plexus. His wind completely knocked out of him, Roddy starts doubling over. Eddie pivots and delivers a right forearm shiver to Roddy's jaw. Roddy's eyes go glassy even before Eddie rabbit-punches him. The fight is over. Roddy lies on the ground. Grabbing his jacket and tie, Eddie heads back for the ballroom. He runs into Joan and the others.

"Are you okay, Eddie?" Joan's voice is full of concern.

"How do I look?" Eddie flashes a big smile. He strikes a boxing pose and says to Bob, "Roddy wanted to box." Catching the eye of an older couple walking by,

Eddie asks, "Could you folks tell someone there's a young man passed out on the patio?"

The man, in his sixties, looks offended that Eddie is even speaking to him. The matron reacts as if he has just announced that there was puke on her gown.

"He may have had too much to drink," Joan volunteers.

"It's a shame," Eddie adds. "He looks like he comes from a good family." They laugh as the couple heads for the corner of the patio.

Turning to Joan, Eddie whispers, "I whacked that jerk pretty good. I gotta get outta here."

"Not without me, you don't." Joan hooks onto his arm.

"You cuttin' out on your own party? What about your mom?"

"This isn't my party. This is my dad's party. I'll call my mom and tell her something. Let's get out of here."

"We're heading for the Greystone Ballroom," Eddie tells Bob. "See you guys there."

Joan and Eddie run from the patio, across the lawn to the parking lot. Five minutes later, they're parked on a quiet residential street.

"I don't see how you beat Roddy up. He's bigger than you."

"The bigger they are, the harder I hit 'em." Eddie smiles broadly. "The champ never laid a glove on me." As an after-thought, he adds, "In a fair fight he might've kicked my ass."

"You didn't fight him fair?"

"Naw. Fair fightin's for suckers or guys in the ring who're getting paid. What's fair about a big, long-armed stiff like him pickin' a fight with a guy my size, anyway?"

Nodding, Joan agrees, "I guess he got what he deserved. He always was kind of a bully."

"I never hurt anyone in my life who didn't have it comin'." Eddie laughs and Joan laughs with him.

He reaches into his jacket pocket, takes out a small package and hands it to Joan. "Let's forget that asshole," he suggests. "Here's a little birthday present."

Joan unwraps her gift, a gold heart, wafer-thin and about the size of a half dollar, on a gold chain. Joan kisses Eddie, then reads the inscription, "Joan Loves Eddie".

"Now read the other side."

"'Eddie Loves Joan'. Oh Eddie, I love you forever." She kisses him again, then holds up her necklace. Eddie takes it and fastens it around her neck.

"Now let's call your mom. Then we'll go dance to some real music. This is your night to do whatever you want."

On their way to the Greystone, they stop at a drug store. Joan comes out of the phone booth smiling. Eddie quits looking through the postcards. "You look happy," he remarks.

"I am. My mom says to enjoy my birthday. I told her how Roddy started it, and that I might stay at Sandy's."

"Next stop, the Greystone Ballroom." A thought cruises through Eddie's head. "What about dear old Dad? How's he taking it?"

"He's running around going apeshit, wanting to call the cops. Mom was laughing about it. I think she likes trouble at the club. She said she'll take care of him and for me not to worry."

"Wow. Your mom's a winner. Just like you."

Joan stops walking and gives Eddie a big kiss. She loves being told that she's like her mother. They get into the car and head for the ballroom.

CHAPTER 16

▼

When Eddie and Joan arrive, the Greystone Ballroom is already packed. The tables around the dance floor are full and the band is ripping through "Lawdy Miss Clawdy". Joan and Eddie hit the floor and dance through the last half of the tune.

Leaving the dance floor, Eddie hears a shrill whistle. It's Bob, waving at him from a corner table. "Look at this," Bob exclaims. On the table are six cupcakes with unlit matches stuck in them. Bob lights the matches and everyone sings "Happy Birthday". A few neighboring couples join in. Joan blows out the matches; everyone claps. The band begins to play "I Only Know" and Joan slow dances with Eddie, wishing the moment would never end.

Out on the sidewalk after the ballroom closes, the three couples walk to Bob's car, talking and laughing. Arriving at the car, Joan announces, "We'll see you guys tomorrow." Taking Eddie's arm, she pulls him away while he's in the middle of a story.

"Uh-oh," Laura whispers to Sandy, "somebody's going get some pie tonight."

The two of them laugh. Joan and Eddie head up the street to her car.

The desk clerk at the Briggs Hotel has a pencil-line mustache and patent-leather hair. He doesn't feel these two are married.

"We need a room for the night," Eddie requests. "Our car was stolen."

"Have you tried Traveler's Aid?" The clerk twitches his mustache.

"They recommended your hotel." Eddie takes out his wallet.

Joan puts a handkerchief to her eyes and a sob into her voice. "It's just that all our luggage was in the car."

It's obvious that Joan is no hooker, not in a ball gown.

Eddie puts his arm around Joan. "That's okay, honey, we'll buy you some new clothes tomorrow."

That's enough for the desk clerk. Reading the registration card, he states, "That'll be twelve dollars, Airman Flynn. Would you prefer twin beds or a double?"

"A double will be just fine, thanks," Joan answers.

Noticing the clerk looking at Joan's gown with a hint of doubt lingering on his face, Eddie offers, "We were at Selfridge. A benefit for a dead flyer, and when we came out, no car."

The man is now a believer. He puts the key to room 303 on the counter and shakes his head. "My sister had her radio stolen from her new Dodge. Detroit's going downhill. Good night, folks."

Opening the door to their room, Eddie is about to usher Joan inside when she stops. "Would you carry me over the threshold?"

Eddie scoops her up and carries her into the well-appointed, clean room. He puts her down on the side of the bed, walks to the window and opens it. It's a balmy night, more like August than June. Joan tunes the radio to their station and joins Eddie at the window. Lonnie Johnson is singing "Tomorrow Night". A soft breeze riffles the curtains. Joan unzips her gown, lets it fall to the floor, kicks off her high heels and stands in her half slip and strapless bra. "Dance with me," she invites.

Lonnie's in mid-tune, "Tomorrow night, will you be with me when the moon is bright? Tomorrow night, will you say those lovely things you said tonight?" They dance, barely shuffling their feet. Joan is thinking of what she's about to do and she's feeling lightheaded. Nice lightheaded, she reassures herself.

"Tomorrow night, will all the thrills be gone?" Lonnie sings. "Tomorrow night, will it be just another memory? Or just another lovely song that's in my heart to linger on?" As the tune ends, Joan sits on the side of the bed and pulls Eddie down next to her.

The DJ talks briefly and puts on "I Need You So". Joan unhooks her bra and lies back on the bed as Ivory Joe begins to sing. They kiss passionately and Joan guides Eddie's hands to parts of her body she wants caressed. She relaxes and floats off with Eddie to places where she's never sailed before.

In the morning Joan awakens with sunlight in her eyes. Eddie's asleep and the radio is still playing. King Pleasure is doing "Moody Mood For Love". Listening intently to the lyrics, Joan begins kissing Eddie all over his face and chest. "Am I insane or do I really see heaven in your eyes?" sings the vocalist. Joan kisses Eddie's eyes. He opens them and smiles.

Joan looks at him mischievously. "I've got something for you," she purrs. She gives Eddie a long kiss.

Later, after showering together, Eddie pats his pockets while they're dressing. "Wallet, comb, handkerchief, cigarettes. I think I got everything."

Joan points to a bedside table where an unrolled condom and a pack with two more in it are laying and asks, "What about those?"

"Those are what we should have used last night and then again this morning." Eddie puts the packet in his pocket, throws the unrolled rubber in the toilet and flushes it.

Joan wraps her arms around his waist. "I know," she agrees. "But I wanted my first time to be just us." Kissing Eddie, she continues, "From now on we'll use them, but right now I just want to get out of this gown. We can go to Sandy's. Her mom and dad are out of town until tonight."

They check out of the Briggs and arrive at Sandy's at ten-thirty. Sandy opens the door with flour on her hands. "You guys are just in time. I'm making pancakes." And to Joan she reports, "Your mom just called fifteen minutes ago."

"I'd better call her."

"No need to. She and your dad are going to a Pontiac dealer's golf match in Toledo. Your mom said she told your dad that you were so upset about Roddy picking a fight that you ran out crying and stayed overnight with me."

"That's my mom." Joan is smiling.

Eddie gives Joan a little squeeze. "Your mom's a woman of her word."

"I need some clothes, San."

"Go up to my room and help yourself. Then come down to the kitchen and tell me *all* about last night." Sandy looks at Eddie and smiles.

Eddie reddens slightly and looks past Sandy into the kitchen. "You got any coffee in there, Sandy?"

"Fresh perked. Cups are in the cupboard over the sink."

Eddie and Sandy head for the kitchen. "Where's Bob?" Eddie asks.

"Asleep on the couch in the living room. Norm and Laura are in the back yard, probably making out." They both laugh.

"Those two have gotta have the cleanest sets of tonsils in Michigan," Eddie jokes, and they both laugh again.

Eddie takes his cup of black coffee into the living room and sits in an overstuffed armchair. Listening to the rhythm of Bob's snoring, he considers the previous night's events. His thoughts are interrupted by Joan coming down the stairs in a lime sundress and matching lime sandals. Watching her walk toward him,

Eddie decides, Joan must be God's way of apologizing for every shitty thing that ever happened to me."

Joan walks up and stands in front of Eddie. "How do I look?"

Eddie gets up out of the chair, pulls Joan into him and lays a long soul kiss on her. "You're the best thing that ever happened to me," he states emphatically. He squeezes her to him. "You're like a beautiful, juicy plum. I'd like to eat you up."

Sandy enters the room. "Okay, you two, break it up. Breakfast is on the table."

After breakfast, Eddie and Joan go out and buy a case of beer, two pounds of ground sirloin, onions and hamburger buns. Eddie has fun shopping with Joan. Ground sirloin is a new thing to him. "I always thought ground beef was just ground beef," he tells her.

The six of them spend the day dancing, drinking and cooking hamburgers on the outdoor grill. The guys head back to the base at sundown and the girls have the house looking spotless long before Sandy's folks return from the Lumber Dealers' Convention in Chicago.

It's after midnight when Joan's parents arrive home from Toledo. Joan is already asleep, looking innocent, dreaming of Eddie. Jill's soft kiss on the cheek awakens her. "Hi Mom," she murmurs. "I love you. I had a wonderful birthday, thanks to you, Mom."

"I'm glad you did, dear. I just want to warn you about Dad. He wants to have one of his family meetings at breakfast, so be prepared to hear a lot of ugly things about Eddie."

Joan sits up in bed. "Oh Mom, what am I going to do?"

Jill sits next to her daughter and puts an arm around her. "We're going to let your father blow off a whole lot of steam and smoke. Then you and I will work things out. One thing is certain. Eddie must stay away from the house."

Joan's eyes fill with tears. Jill pats Joan's hand and kisses her cheek. "You don't think you're in love, do you?"

"Mom, Eddie makes me feel all crazy and jumpy inside, makes my heart beat loud in my ears. Oh yes, Mom, I'm in love with all my heart. I just found the right boy and now I'm going to lose him. It's not fair."

Joan's lament sends Jill back to the summer before she married Bill. For an instant she sees herself seated on her bed being consoled by her mother. Jill hugs and rocks Joan. "Don't worry, dear. It'll all work out. We'll make it work out," she promises.

The following morning Joan and Jill are in the kitchen cooking breakfast when Bill comes in and pours a cup of coffee without his usual, "Good morning, girls."

Turning toward them, Bill launches into his harangue. "Please don't interrupt me because I have a lot of ground to cover and the things I have to say are *not* up for debate …"

"Do you want your eggs scrambled or over easy, Bill?" Jill smiles her sweetest smile.

"Over easy," Bill answers gruffly. "Now to continue," he harrumphs, staring into Joan's eyes. "Number one, you are *never* to see that young thug again."

"Eddie's not a thug."

Bill cuts Joan off. "I said no interruptions, young lady. You are absolutely forbidden from ever seeing that," he searches for the proper word, "… that greasy little son-of-a-bitch. Roddy's jaw is broken. I'll be lucky if the Calvins don't sue us. On the way to the hospital Roddy told me it wasn't a fair fight …"

"Three strips of bacon or four, dear?" Jill asks gently.

Bill looks at Jill and seethes. He controls his urge to yell and instead sips his coffee and answers, "Four please, and now if I may continue. I gave the police a full description of this hoodlum and his name. If he's found anywhere near this house, they'll run him in."

Joan starts to speak. Her father stares into her eyes. "I know what you're about to say. Now that you're eighteen, you can do what you damn well please and you're correct, but if you walk out of this house before you're nineteen, the trust fund that your grandmother set up will go to the Catholic Church."

"But Dad …"

"Don't 'But Dad' me. Go out that door, run away with that misfit and you'll be taking almost two million dollars out of your mother's hands."

"But Dad …" Joan begins again.

"I said don't interrupt. Your grandmother set that trust up when you made your First Communion. I can't help it if she was crazy."

At the word 'crazy' Jill's cheeks redden and her eyes narrow. "My mother wasn't crazy," she challenges loudly. "Mom was nineteen and a virgin when she got married. She just wanted the same thing for Joanie. I remember you grinning like a cat with a mouthful of feathers when I explained that all those churchy words about the snares of Satan, the wiles of the big city and us protecting Joan from the Devil and his minions were only Gran's way of saying she wanted Joan to stay at home and not marry until her nineteenth birthday."

Bill grunts.

"I even recall the exact words of your crude comment to me about the trust fund that day. Do you?"

The words "All Joan has to do is keep her legs crossed until she's nineteen and we hit the jackpot" run through Bill's mind.

Jill slides a plate of bacon and eggs onto the table and, forcing down her anger, urges, "Why don't you eat your breakfast, Bill? I'm sure Joan understands how you feel about Eddie." Looking at Joan, she winks. "Don't you, dear?"

Ignoring the food, Bill insists, "That's not good enough for me." He lays another harsh glare on Joan. Raise your right hand to God," he orders, "and repeat after me. I, Joan Whitman, do solemnly swear before God that I'll never have anything to do with Eddie Flynn. So help me God."

Joan raises her right hand and repeats the vow, choking back tears. This seems to satisfy her father. Sprinkling a sandstorm of salt onto his eggs, he proclaims, "Now, let's enjoy our breakfast."

Joan manages two bites before requesting permission to go to her room. As she's leaving the kitchen, she turns and gives her father a look that would stiffen smoke. "I may not be allowed to see Eddie," she declares, defiance clinging to every word "but I'll never date Roddy, so you'll never get your hands on his forty million."

Bill looks at Jill. "She'll get over it," he mutters. "Do you have any more toast?"

In her bedroom, Joan tunes her radio to what she calls "our station" and falls asleep crying, listening to the Five Keys singing "The Glory of Love".

CHAPTER 17

▼

The next night, Eddie phones Joan and gets the word.

"Oh Eddie, I don't know where to start. There are so many awful things happening at once," she wails. "My dad made me swear an oath never to see you again." She gets a little choke in her voice, almost a sob.

"I'm sorry you're feeling bad, honey, but don't worry. It'll take more than an oath to keep me away from you."

"It's more than that, Eddie. My dad called the cops. He gave them your name and description. They'll arrest you if you come around to see me."

"He must be really pissed off."

"You broke Roddy's jaw. He's afraid the Calvins might sue us. Oh God, I feel terrible."

"It's a good thing you're eighteen ..."

Joan interrupts. "Eddie, that's another thing. If I leave home permanently before my nineteenth birthday, even if I left to be married, my granny's trust fund would go to the church."

"Oh?"

"It's a long story, but if I'm still living at home on my nineteenth birthday, Mom and Dad get a trust fund. If I've married or if I've left home and subjected myself to the wiles of the big city ..."

"The wiles of the big city?"

"That's how Granny talked. She was a sweet, old Irish lady. She always gave me money for no reason at all. When I was a little girl, she'd slip me a five-dollar bill and say, 'Go buy a lot of ice cream, sweetie, and don't tell your father where you got the money.' Then she'd laugh. Anyway, the trust is almost two million dollars. I couldn't take that away from my mom."

Eddie agrees, "No. No, you couldn't do that to your mom. You got to stick it out for her sake. How's your mom feel about me?"

"She knows that I love you and she says that Dad is overly dramatic."

"He's an overly dramatic asshole," Eddie jokes, and Joan laughs.

"That's better," Eddie encourages. "Listen, honey, I gotta sign off, but here's what I'd like to do. I'll work it out so we can talk every night until my next days off. How's that sound?"

"Good."

"And we'll work out a plan so we can spend my three-day break together. How's that?"

"That sounds perfect."

"Good. And most of all, don't forget that I love you."

"And I love you, Eddie."

"You all cheered up?"

"All cheered up."

"Good. Now go to bed and dream about me. I'll call again tomorrow. Let's hang up together."

By juggling his own duties during swing shift and midnight shifts and by doing a couple of hours of volunteer guard duty stints, Eddie's able to keep his promise of calling Joan every night and he succeeds in getting her to feel relaxed and happy.

Eddie's looking at the moon, thinking about his coming three-day break, when Peterson relieves him on guard duty. Eddie goes into the Radar Operations room feeling good. He takes over for Bob, manning the VHF channels. Big Dog Blue, a flight of two F-86's, is flying Combat Air Patrol and a couple of commercial airliners are tracking for Detroit. Other than that, the plotting board is clean. Captain Ross is asleep in his controller's chair. Norm is reading a tech manual and Dog crew's last midnight shift is dragging.

At 0400 Big Dog Red, another flight of F-86's, relieves Big Dog Blue on Combat Air Patrol. Eddie takes care of scrambling Big Dog Red without waking Captain Ross, normal procedure on Dog crew. There's a little excitement at 0430 when Red Two's pilot gets a nosebleed. Eddie gives him a vector for home and he lands without incident. Red Leader continues his CAP mission alone, not an unusual occurrence.

An hour later, Eddie's up on the dais talking with Bob and Norm. "I won't be goin' with you guys this break. Joan's comin' up here. I got to kind of stay away from her house, if you know what I mean."

"Mama Bear, Red leader here. Do you have me on your crystal ball? Over."

Eddie plugs his headset in the VHF jack. "Affirmative, Red Leader. Over."

"My gyro's out. Most of my electrics are out. Over."

Eddie always admired the hint of boredom in the pilots' voices during stressful situations. "Roger, Red Leader. Try squawking Mayday. Over."

"Roger, Mama Bear. Squawking Mayday, *now*. Over."

"We have you showing Mayday, Red Leader. Stand by for a directional. Over."

"Roger, Mama Bear. Red Leader standing by. Out." Eddie pictures the pilot stifling a yawn. He goes over and taps Captain Ross on the shoulder.

Ross awakens alertly. "What's up, Eddie?"

"Red Leader's up alone. His gyro and most of his electrics are out. I've got him squawking Mayday."

Ross glances at the wall clock. "Scramble Big Dog Green." Putting on a head-set, he continues, "Do anything you want with Green, but keep them out of the northeast quadrant."

"Yes sir." Eddie heads for scope three. "Red Leader's on channel two, Cap-tain."

"Thanks. And Eddie, have someone bring me a big black coffee." He plugs in his headset and announces, "Mama Bear here, Red Leader. Let's go home. Over."

The last two hours of Dog crew's midnight shift fly.

Eddie still has a few days to go on his restriction to the base, so he goes through the main gate in Bob's trunk. Bob and Norm drop him off in Tawas and continue on their way to Detroit.

Sitting on a rocking chair on the upstairs back porch of the Edgewater Hotel, Eddie is watching Highway 23. At exactly eleven o'clock he spots Joan's car pull-ing off the highway. He stands up and starts down the back stairs to greet her. By the time he gets to the bottom, she pulls up.

"Nice day for a drive, isn't it?" Joan is smiling. She's wearing a peasant blouse and her gold heart is resting on her cleavage.

"God Joan, you look beautiful," is all Eddie can think of to say.

"Beautiful enough for a kiss?"

Eddie gives her a brief kiss and gets into the car. "So what's the big surprise you've been telling me about?"

"Today I'd like to teach you to drive."

"You really think you can?"

"Sure I can. Is there any big, open space around here?"

"Head north. There's an old abandoned quarry three miles south of the base."

"Sounds perfect." Joan wheels the Chev back onto the highway. Eddie reaches over, cupping her nearest breast. "Feels like a thirty-four B."

"You little rascal," she teases, quickly adding, "but don't stop." They both laugh. Joan continues, "That's one of the reasons I want to teach you to drive. So I can bother you when you're behind the wheel."

"Nobody in New York City drives. We all just ride the subway."

The sun is brilliant. For a couple of moments they drive in silence, enjoying the scenery.

Joan eventually asks, "Is your dad anything like mine?"

Eddie snorts, almost a laugh. "I got lucky. My old man kicked the bucket when I was ten."

"Eddie, that's an awful thing to say." Joan is stunned.

"I'm sorry if I caught you by surprise, honey," he offers gently. "But me and my old man just didn't get along."

"That's sad, Eddie. How come you didn't like him?"

"Mainly because he kept mistakin' my head for a goddamn punchin' bag." Eddie makes some quick punching motions. "Ba-da-boom. Ba-boom."

Joan laughs, a bit uneasily. "I don't mean to laugh," she explains, "but you make it funny, the way you tell it."

"I joke about it," he pauses, "but I remember when I was a kid, I wanted to grow up quick and kick the shit out of him. I felt kind of cheated when he died before I could get him."

"How did he die?"

"Happy and drunk. He worked construction. Got drunk at work one time too often." Eddie slaps his right hand down on his left. "Splat. Ten stories. You fall ten stories, even your hard hat don't help." He laughs at his joke. His smile is genuine. *In a way, I was glad to see him go*, he thinks.

"I didn't mean to stir up memories. I'm sorry, honey."

"That's okay. It's no big deal. I don't even think about him unless someone asks about him."

"How about your mom? Is she nice?"

"Yeah, she's okay. She brought me and my younger brother up. She don't drink at all. Just goes to church and prays that me and Jimmy'll turn into gentlemen and do good in the business world. That's what she calls it—the business world."

"Is Jimmy like you?"

"He just got kicked out of Catholic high school. I guess you could say he's like me. We're both fuckups." They laugh together. "Keep watching on your left, when we pass that old barn. The quarry road's about a mile past there."

Turning onto the gravel road, Joan slows to lessen the noise. She looks over at Eddie. "I feel so good when I'm alone with you."

"Good enough to give me some of that pie?"

"My bakery is always open for you."

They park near a patch of woods bordering the quarry. Joan opens the trunk, takes out a blanket and spreads it on the grass. "Lunch first? Or driving lessons?"

"Pie first. Lunch second. Driving lessons third."

Joan sits down on the blanket. She reaches up, takes Eddie's hands and pulls him down to a kneeling position. She gives him a long kiss and lies back on the blanket. After a generous serving of pie, they lunch on ham and cheese sandwiches, drinking wine out of paper cups.

"How're things at home? Am I still on your old man's Most Wanted list?"

"Least Wanted would be more like it." They laugh and Joan continues. "Dad is still being a jerk, but Mom helped me make this lunch. I think she likes you."

"Your mom's got good taste." Eddie laughs.

Joan gives him a playful shove. "Sure," she quips, and gets to her feet. She throws Eddie her car keys. "Lunch is over. Let's go driving."

She explains how nothing else matters if the clutch pedal is down to the floor. Eddie stalls the car a few times, being too delicate with the gas pedal, and he mashes the gears a couple of times, but after two hours he's at ease with driving. Joan encourages him to be reckless.

Eddie takes them zipping along the edge of the quarry at fifty miles an hour, losing traction a couple of times. Nothing fazes Joan. "Beautiful, honey," she exults, each time Eddie does something daring.

She shows him how to peel out, saying after one long burst, "On pavement, that would have been a forty-foot patch."

They quit driving lessons a half hour after sundown and Eddie drives them to a steak house a few miles south of Tawas.

After dinner, heading south on 23, Eddie announces, "Now for your surprise."

"How about a little hint?"

"It's in Saginaw."

"Tomorrow Night" comes on the radio. "Remember that song from the hotel?" she asks.

"I sure do. Lonnie Johnson. Top rhythm and blues tune for 1948. I'll never hear it again without thinkin' of your birthday and us."

"I think it should be our song."

"Good idea," Eddie agrees. Joan leans over and kisses Eddie's neck.

Passing a road sign that reads "Saginaw—20 Miles" Eddie kicks the car up to seventy.

"I'm so proud of you. I never saw anyone learn to drive so easily."

"I messed up your gears a few times."

"That's normal. Everyone does that when they're first learning to drive, but look at you now."

"And I ain't even got a license. You're some great teacher."

Just outside the city line, Eddie stops for a red light. "Hit it when the light turns green," Joan coaxes. The instant the light changes Eddie gets on it. He peels out, leaving a thirty-foot trail of smoke and rubber.

"That was perfect," Joan tells Eddie.

A few blocks later, Eddie pulls into a dirt lot, parking next to five Harley-Davidsons that are lined up against the side wall of Slim's Blue Light Inn. The motorcycles are '49 and '50 Hogs. There are a dozen cars parked on the club's lot; half of them are de-chromed and a couple are lowered.

Joan looks around the parking lot. "This isn't the Harbor Lights Country Club."

"It's our kind of place." Eddie puts his arm around her waist and gives her a little squeeze. By the time they walk under the small blue neon sign over the entrance, Joan is feeling more relaxed.

The moment she steps inside she loves it. It's a typical roadhouse, with a bar, booths, a large dance floor and a side room with a couple of pool tables and pinball machines. Every light in the place is blue, except for a baby spot that shines on a rotating, mirrored ball. The ball rotates to the tempo of the tune. A half dozen couples are dancing to "Moonrise" by the Royals. Slim has the ball set at its slowest speed.

Joan checks the crowd. Three of the bikers are shooting pool. Two of the others and their ladies are in a booth drinking beer. She sees other couples scattered among the booths and three soldiers and a couple of other guys at the bar. The bartender, a big, hairy forty-five-year-old, looks like a hard case. Joan watches his look of menace melt into a smile when he sees Eddie.

"Hey Slim" Eddie greets the bartender. "I want you to meet Joan. I'm stayin' outta trouble because of her."

Slim laughs. "Sure thing, Eddie." To Joan he remarks, "Eddie's a lucky guy. Nice to meet you, Joan."

Eddie winks at Slim. "Joan forgot her ID."

Slim smiles. "Take a back booth." He gives Eddie a pitcher of beer and two glasses.

After a few sips of beer, Joan and Eddie make their way to the dance floor. Passing the pool-shooting bikers on their route, Eddie exchanges nods with one of them.

A couple of hours later, one of the soldiers from the bar approaches their booth. He's the burliest of the three and looks close to thirty. Eddie and Joan are seated side by side, Eddie nearest the aisle.

Leaning over the table, leering into Joan's blouse, he drawls, "I just thought I'd come by and see if the little lady would like to dance."

Joan recoils as his sour beer breath wafts into her face. "The little lady doesn't want to dance," she snaps, glaring back at him.

"Come on, baby," he insists. He reaches past Eddie to grab Joan's hand. Eddie knocks his hand away and stands up, forcing Burly to straighten up. Chest to chest, Eddie gets his face into Burly's and barks, "The lady told you she don't wanna dance. Get the fuck outta here, *now*. Before you get hurt."

"You heard him," Joan orders. "Get the fuck out of here!" She feels strong talking like this. Get the fuck out of here, she repeats to herself. She'd like to shout that to her dad. Get the fuck out of here. Before she can finish her thought, Slim is on the scene.

"What's the trouble here?" he demands.

"No trouble with me, Slim." Eddie jerks his thumb in the soldier's direction and continues, "Ace here was just getting ready to take a hike."

Drilling the soldier with a tracer-bullet stare, Slim points, "Why don't you head back to the bar and join your buddies?" The soldier hikes. The three finish their beers and leave twenty minutes later.

Joan and Eddie don't leave the Blue Light until two-thirty, a half hour past closing. The parking lot is empty except for Slim's Olds 88, Joan's car, and two Hogs.

Eddie is unlocking the passenger door for Joan when he spots the three soldiers stepping out of the shadows. Pushing Joan behind him, Eddie moves away from the car, spits, and taunts, "What's it gonna be? All at once or one at a time?"

"Just me, greaser." Burly approaches.

Eddie grabs his crotch and shouts, "Fuck your momma, corn-pone!"

The soldier charges Eddie, plowing him into the wall. Eddie gets a good grip on the guy's hair with both hands. He jerks upward fiercely, straightening Burly up enough so that he can deliver a swift, hard knee to the balls. Feeling the guy sag a little, Eddie jerks hard on his hair again, this time pulling the guy's face down into Eddie's rapidly rising knee. Hearing the solid crunch from the guy's nose, Eddie smiles. He locks his left arm around the guy's throat and is able to pump four solid rights into his face before the other two soldiers jump in.

One soldier grabs Eddie's punching arm and the other puts a choke hold on him from behind. Joan jumps on the choker, raking his face with her nails. She also gets in a couple of ineffective punches to the guy's ear before he flings her aside.

Joan is flying off the choker's back when the two bikers spot the action. They're coming out of the alley that connects to Slim's parking lot. The tall, black-haired biker who nodded to Eddie back in the bar drops his gasoline can, whips out his doubled up Harley chain, and takes off for the fight. His partner, a guy carrying a solid two hundred pounds on a five-foot-eight-inch frame, keeps pace.

The two soldiers have Eddie's arms and Burly, bleeding from both nostrils, is trying to get to his feet when the short biker grabs one of the soldiers by the throat. He mashes the guy against the wall and just keeps punching the guy's face, refusing to let him drop until the soldier's face is wrecked. The tall biker sends the other soldier to dreamland with three good whacks on the head with his chain.

Burly, in a crouched position, is leaning on one arm to brace himself and trying to rise. Eddie kicks him in the face with enough force to score a fifty-yard field goal. Joan winces at the kick in the face, but at the same time she feels strangely exhilarated. As she watches, Eddie and the two bikers put the boots to all three of the soldiers.

Standing over the fallen Burly, Eddie spits on him. "Don't you ever bother a lady who don't want to be bothered." Eddie spits on him again. "You got it, you piece of shit? Never bother a lady. Especially if that lady is with me." Eddie kicks him again. "Now get outta here, you dirty motherfucker. If I ever see you again, I'll fuckin' kill you."

Slim comes out right after Eddie's speech. "Looks like I missed a good one," he observes. Turning to Joan, he asks, "Are you all right, Joan?"

"Oh yes. I'm fine, Slim. Just a little jumpy, I guess." Turning to Eddie, she smiles. "I'm going to sit in the car, honey."

"Okay. I'll be right with you."

Dave and Trash are talking with Slim, using lots of body english, describing the fight that Slim missed.

"I'd have liked to kicked a little bit of that one mouthy bastard's ass myself," Slim adds.

They all laugh. Eddie looks over at the car and sees Joan. She looks all fired up with her eyes shining and bright.

"Thanks, guys," Eddie says to Dave and Trash. "It woulda been my ass without you jumpin' in." Offering his hand, Eddie continues, "I'm Eddie Flynn."

"You were going pretty good," the tall guy states. "I'm Dave and this here guy is Trash."

Trash shakes Eddie's hand. "It was a pleasure hammering that prick. I was in the navy. I hate fucking ground pounders."

"That's a tough little momma you got there, man." Dave is impressed.

"She's really somethin', ain't she?" Eddie feels proud. "I better get her outta here though. Thanks again, guys. See you next time, Slim." The soldiers are dragging themselves along into the night. Dave walks over to the driver's side of the Chev with Eddie. "Me and Trash ride with the Cobras, down in Detroit. We hang out at The Cave. Van Dyke and Nine Mile. Look us up if you're ever down our way."

"You can count on it, Dave," Eddie promises. They shake hands again. Eddie gets behind the wheel and pulls out quietly. "No sense disturbin' the cops this late at night," he tells Joan as he eases onto Highway 23 and heads north.

A few miles up the highway, Eddie pulls onto a gravel road and parks on a knoll overlooking the Saginaw River. His right hand is slightly swollen and the fingers on both of his hands are twitching. "Look at my fingers jump. I hate it when I get that crazy."

"Does your hand hurt much?"

"Not as much as that asshole's face." He takes off his right loafer. "You got any Kleenex, honey? I got that jerk's blood all over my suedes."

Joan reaches into the glove box, gets some tissues and gives them to Eddie. "I thought you were going to kill him."

"I wanted to. I'd like to hit him again." Eddie feels his anger rekindling. "The ugly piece of shit had it comin'," he growls, then brightening he adds, "You were really somethin', jumpin' in like that."

Joan smiles. "It wasn't fair. Three against one." She feels herself calming down. "How come those two motorcycle guys helped you out?"

"They knew I needed help." Eddie's fingers are twitching less.

"They acted like they knew you."

"In a way they did know me. Those guys are one-percenters, just like me. It's us guys against the whole rest of the world."

"I want to be a one-percenter."

"Oh honey," Eddie laughs, "you are a one-percenter." He puts his arm around her, pulling her closer. "If you weren't a one-percenter, you wouldn't be hangin' out with me. Dave called you a tough little momma. That's high praise."

Joan lifts Eddie's right hand to her lips, kissing and licking his knuckles.

"Hey, up here," he points to his mouth.

After sharing a long, deep kiss, Joan requests, "Take me somewhere, Eddie."

Back on 23, driving north at a leisurely pace, Eddie asks, "Where does big, bad dad think you are tonight?"

"I'm at a sorority house in Ann Arbor with Sandy and Laura."

They pass a sign, "Rostonkowski's Lodge and Cabins, Five Miles". Eddie looks at Joan. "What do you think?"

"Anywhere you want, Eddie," Joan rubs the inside of his thigh.

"Rostonkowski's Sorority House, comin' up." They both laugh. Eddie punches the car up to seventy.

Mrs. Rostonkowski, assuming they're newlyweds, goes out of her way to make them comfortable. They sleep late, so Mrs. R makes sure that they eat a "good Polish lunch," having missed breakfast.

Later in the afternoon, sitting in their cabin's porch swing, drinking beer and watching the sunshine filter through the jack pines, Eddie remarks, "You know, New Yorkers work all year to spend two weeks' vacation at places like this."

"Don't you like New York? It sounds so exciting."

Eddie takes a drink of beer. "New York is shot. They're tearin' down my neighborhood and buildin' housin' projects. That's the beginnin' of the end."

Joan snuggles closer. "You like Michigan?"

"Yeah, I like Michigan. In fact, when I get out of the Air Force, I wouldn't mind settlin' down around here." He pauses. "If only I could meet a nice girl."

Joan attacks him, tickling his ribs and spilling beer all over them. After showering together, they enjoy a "good Polish dinner."

That night, walking along the narrow beach, they stop to throw small stones out into Lake Huron. Joan looks up at the starry, moonless sky. "Do you remember the night we met?"

"It was a night just like this."

"Remember, I wished on a star that never fell." They laugh.

"Yeah. I liked the idea that you didn't need a shootin' star to make a wish."

"How come you didn't make a wish, Eddie?"

"If you remember, I said that I already had everything I wanted," he answers. "At that time I had my arms around you."

Joan gives Eddie a quick little kiss. "I love you for saying that, but I get the feeling that you don't believe in wishes."

"Well, I don't. My old man didn't teach me much except maybe by bein' a bad example," he states, "but I remember one thing he told me when I was just a tiny little guy. I said somethin' like I wished we lived in Jersey and he said, 'Wish in one hand and shit in the other and see which hand gets filled first.'"

"That's horrible. It sounds so hopeless."

"My old man wasn't much on hope. He used to say, 'Where there's no hope, there's no disappointment.' How'd you make out with your wish?"

"So far, so good. Here we are together."

"That's good enough for me." He smiles. "You keep on doing the wishin' for both of us."

After checking out of Rostonkowski's they hook up with Bob as planned, two hours before Dog crew is back on duty. "Next days off, you'll be seein' me walk through the main gate." Eddie kisses Joan goodbye and gets into Bob's car. "I'll be off restriction," he adds. "Maybe if I stay out of trouble, Becker won't ship my ass to Alaska."

"Alaska?" Joan's face clouds over.

"Don't worry about it, honey. I already turned over a new leaf." Bob peels out.

Joan watches the guys take off and then she heads south. Cruising at sixty, she allows herself to wonder what would become of her if the Air Force ever sent Eddie away. Earl Bostic is playing "Sleep". She turns up the radio and tries not to think about Eddie ever going anywhere without her.

CHAPTER 18

▼

Dog crew's nine-day shift is uneventful and Eddie's restriction dies a natural death. Parked outside the main gate, Joan watches Eddie approach. Sliding over to the passenger side as Eddie gets into the car, she remarks, "It looked so good to see you walk through the gate, Eddie."

"Yeah. It felt kind of funny." He puts his arm around her, pulls her close and lays a brief soul kiss on her.

"We'll have to stay around Detroit so I can check in at night."

"So you can check in, and check right out again," Eddie quips and they both laugh.

"I've been wantin' to show you a couple of Detroit spots anyway." Eddie slips a card out of his pocket and passes it to Joan. "Here's a little present for you, honey." He hands her a Michigan driver's license with her name and address on it. The date of birth makes Joan twenty-one.

"How'd you get this?" Joan is delighted.

Eddie slips the car into gear and heads quietly down the base road. "A buddy of mine made it for me. A guy named George Dennis. He's the same guy who fixed up my ID card. They took him out of stockade and shipped his ass to Texas. It was kind of a goin' away gift."

Joan compares the bogus license with her real one. "You can't tell them apart, Eddie. It's perfect."

"Yeah. George is a real artist. You know what he'll be doin' in Texas?"

"Ten years?"

Eddie laughs. "Ten years. That's great. No, he won't be doin' time. He's gonna be catchin' spies. He's so good at makin' phony ID's and passes, the government is gonna use him in intelligence. They made him a staff sergeant and he's goin' to a special anti-spy school. Ain't that somethin'?"

"Good for him."

"Becker went apeshit when he got the orders. One of my buddies in the orderly room thought they'd have to call the medic."

"Serves Becker right," Joan states emphatically. "That's what he gets for being an authoritarian asshole."

Eddie laughs. "Fuckin'-A, Joanie."

Eddie drives three miles south on Highway 23, then takes the old quarry road to their favorite parking spot. After an hour and a half of what Joan calls "Fun in the bakery," they drive straight through to Detroit. They catch the late afternoon showing of "High Noon" at the Fox Theater, have Polish hot dogs for dinner in Hamtramck and spend the evening at the Flame Show Bar, where Dinah Washington is appearing. Among the tunes in an excellent set are "I Only Know", "Long John Blues" and "Wheel of Fortune". They finish off the night be checking into room 303 at the Briggs Hotel.

Joan calls her mother to check in. "Consider yourself checked," Jill declares. "If your dad wakes up, which I doubt, I'll tell him you're over at Sandy's for the night."

"Thanks, Mom. I love you."

"And I love you. Good night, Joanie."

At the end of their fun-filled three-day break, Joan drops Eddie off at the 646th, cautioning, "It's so nice to see you walk off the base, Eddie. Please try to stay out of trouble."

"Don't worry about me, honey. I'm a brand new guy. Gimme a little bit of tongue to last me 'til next days off."

Joan gives him a long French kiss and doesn't drive away until Eddie is out of sight.

Summer flies so fast.

Eddie stays out of trouble and late in July, he and Joan are able to spend another three-day break together, thanks to a labor dispute that keeps her father in Ohio for a full week. He calls home twice during Joan's absence. One time Jill tells him that Joan's already asleep and the other time she says that Joan is at the movies with Sandy and Laura.

Mildred's Duck Inn, a picturesque, small hotel near Port Austin on the tip of the thumb, is where they share an idyllic interlude. Their room has a brass bed, a quilted spread, red and white checkered curtains with dingle-balls, and a flowered bowl and pitcher set on the dresser. The view of Lake Huron is impeccable and even the geraniums in the window box are thriving.

"If we had a house, I'd like a room like this, wouldn't you, Eddie?"

"Yeah. It's a bright, happy room. Wonder if that old radio works?" Eddie turns the 1937 Philco on, tunes in their station, and they dance to the last few bars of "Sunday Kind of Love". The tune ends and Eddie jokes, "Wonder if that old bed works?"

After checking out the bed and the shower, Joan and Eddie take one of the hotel's rowboats out for a spin. The five-horsepower outboard is all they need to go putting along the shore. They watch a golden sunset, then have a late dinner at the inn. While out in the rowboat, they discover a hidden cove with a skinny, rocky beach. They picnic there twice during their stay and swim there daily, away from the other guests.

Driving away from the hotel, Eddie remarks, "That was the best three days of my life. Except for the coconut trees, it was like bein' on our island together."

"I was just thinking the same thing."

"Great minds think alike." They laugh together.

After dropping Eddie off at the base, Joan rolls along on Highway 23 in a warm blanket of happiness. Lulled by the Joe Morris Orchestra, she listens to Laurie Tate promise, "Well, anytime, anyplace, anywhere. Just say the word. You'll be heard, yes I'll be there." Near the end of the tune, when Laurie sings, "Can't you see, you were meant for me, and that's the way it's gonna be," Joan glances at her speedometer. She's doing a mellow 60.

While Joan and Eddie use their July breaks cruising Detroit spots and visiting Mildred's Duck Inn, Bob and Sandy, with help from Norm and Laura do a first class job of de-chroming Sandy's Ford. The work is sandwiched in with music, dancing and making out.

For their first three-day break in August the three couples get together at Wenona Beach near Bay City for dancing and drinking at the lakeside pavilions. Joan drives back to St. Clair Shores each night because her father is paying strict attention to her comings and goings.

Dog crew's break falls on three weekdays, so each night Joan gets home after her father is asleep, visits with her mother and then sleeps in until her father leaves for work. The sound of him opening her bedroom door to check on her wakes her up each time. She pretends to continue sleeping. In the morning she has breakfast with her mother, makes a picnic lunch and heads back for Wenona Beach and Eddie.

Jill never asks direct questions about Joan's activities. She knows that it's Eddie Joan is spending all her time with and she knows that Joan knows that she knows. She revels in Joan's happiness and abets in Joan's deceits. "I won't let Bill strangle Joan's chance at real love," she vows.

Joan's shuttle-runs to Wenona Beach go flawlessly. The guys go back to pull another shift and all of a sudden it's mid-August.

CHAPTER 19

▼

It's the ninth day of a shift for Dog crew. The girls are at Sandy's house, anticipating the three-day break. Sandy's parents are up at Houghton Lake, guests of
one of her father's best customers, a local home builder. The house will be
Sandy's for three days.

Sitting on the windowsill in the living room, Laura is watching the rain and
painting her toenails. Joan is listening to the radio, dancing by herself to "Blues
for the Red Boy". The saxophone is growling and she's doing what Eddie calls "a
slow grind." She smiles, thinking how Eddie also calls it "dry humpin'."

Despite the shower, it's a hot, humid afternoon and although they're wearing
shorts, halters and sandals, the girls are still uncomfortable. Sandy comes in from
the kitchen with three beers.

Joan takes a bottle and presses it against her bare, sweaty belly. "Oh God," she
exclaims, "that feels so good against my stomach."

"As good as Eddie?" Laura laughs at her own joke. The shower ends as
abruptly as it started.

"This feels good," Joan answers, "but Eddie feels best."

Sandy takes a big hit from her beer. "I'll sure be glad to see Bob."

"It's been a long nine days," Laura complains, "and that itty bitty shower did
nothing to cool me off." She sips her beer and frowns. "I don't think my mom
believed I was going to Ann Arbor again this week."

"My folks don't care what I do," Sandy declares, "as long as I don't disgrace
the family." She pushes her stomach way out and they all laugh.

Joan takes a sip of her beer. "Do you and Bob use anything, San?"

Sandy raises her eyebrows. "I don't even talk to Bob on the phone unless he's got rubbers in his pocket." All three laugh.

"I hate rubbers," Laura states. "Norm and I just count the days."

"Isn't that kind of risky?" Joan is incredulous.

"I don't care." Laura takes a big gulp of her beer and belches loudly. "Anyway, Norm wants to get married."

"Married?" Sandy's jaw goes slack. "You've only known Norm a couple of months."

"Did Norm propose?" Joan can't hide her excitement.

"Not exactly, but he acts like he wants to get married, kind of ..." Laura finishes her beer and belches loudly once again.

"They all act like they want to get married," Sandy jokes, "but all they really want is some of that pie." She wiggles her butt. The three of them howl with laughter.

Later in the afternoon, while they're in the kitchen making burgers and a big salad, the wall phone rings. "Johnson residence," Sandy answers, "to whom do you wish to speak."

Stretching the phone cord full out, she murmurs, "Hi, honey," and takes the phone out into the hallway. A few minutes later she reenters the kitchen and hangs up the phone, looking crestfallen.

Joan knows that look. "What's wrong, San?"

"We can forget about seeing the guys," Sandy reports.

"And I'm all hot to trot," Laura bitches. "I'll go ape if I don't see Norm!"

Joan stifles a frown. "Is it Eddie?"

"No, it's not Eddie." Sandy pats Joan's arm. "The whole base is restricted because of some kind of big maneuver. Bob says they do this a couple of times a year."

"Well I think it stinks." Laura has her "mad face" on.

Sandy looks at Joan. "Bob says he's going to tell Eddie that you're over here. He'll call in about an hour."

"I'm as horny as an old she-bear." Laura stretches. "Why don't we just go up there and see the guys?"

Joan and Sandy look at each other. Joan grins. "Maybe we can get pitchforks, drive up and storm the main gate, like in those knighthood movies." Laura joins in the laughter.

Eddie calls later and tells Joan that if she'll go to the quarry, he'll get the guys through a hole in the fence and down a back trail.

Hanging up the phone, Joan smiles at Laura. "You got your wish, Laura. We're going to see the guys tomorrow."

At the 646th, Operation Wolverine is in full swing. Bombers from Strategic Air Command are trying to penetrate the radar net. Two plotters are behind the board carrying forty tracks of orange, white and yellow. Two tellers sitting in front of the board are calling in track movements to Air Defense Control Center at Selfridge AFB with speed and clarity.

Eddie worked the previous shift with Charlie crew because they didn't have a reliable intercept control tech, but he isn't tired. He always seems to get energized from all the activity whenever a mission is on.

Six radar operators are manning scopes, trying to read targets through electronic countermeasures and tinfoil jamming that the bombers are putting out.

Captain Ross is going from scope to scope conducting intercepts. Eddie is like his shadow, logging all of Ross' radio transmissions, scrambling fresh flights of F-86's and fine-tuning some of the guys' scopes to cope with the jamming. Bob and Norm are barely keeping ahead of things up in the Movements and Identification section.

Captain Ross glances at scope three. He and Eddie plug their headsets into two of the scope's VHF jacks and Ross states, "Mudhen Red, you should have a 'pounce.' Over."

"No joy, Mama Bear. Over."

"Your bogie's at ten o'clock. Over."

Captain Ross smiles. Eddie finishes logging both ends of the controller-to-pilot transmissions. "Good job, Red," Ross says. "Take a one-niner-zero vector for home. Over."

Most controllers work intercepts from their controller scope. Captain Ross prefers moving around from scope to scope, sometimes working two or three intercepts at the same time. He and Eddie are heading for scope three when the crew chief, Staff Sergeant Brown, appears with two mugs of black coffee. "Hot as hell and black as night." He hands them each a mug.

"Thanks, Brownie." Eddie sips his coffee.

Captain Ross nods his thanks and asks, "How's the count, Brownie?"

"We're knocking the dogshit out of them, Captain. Twenty intercepts already."

"Good. Be sure and let the guys know how we're doing." Turning to Eddie, Ross directs, "Get over to scope four, Eddie, and put Skylark Blue on a two-four-five heading."

Plugging into scope four's VHF jack, Eddie announces, "Skylark Blue, Mama Bear here. Over."

"Skylark Blue here. Read you five-square. Over."

"Vector two-four-five. Buster. Over."

"Roger, Mama Bear. Two-four-five. Buster. Skylark Blue, out."

Kicking in their afterburners, Skylark Blue closes quickly on the bomber. Eddie watches them for two minutes, then transmits, "Skylark Blue, you should have a Pounce at two o'clock. Over."

"Roger, Mama Bear. Tally-ho. Splash one bogey. Over."

"Good job, Blue. How's your fuel? Over."

"Fuel right at half, Mama Bear. Over."

"Understand fuel at half," Eddie repeats. "Orbit where you are at thirty angels. Over."

"Skylark Blue, orbiting at thirty angels. Out."

Unplugging his headset, Eddie joins Captain Ross at scope five. "Skylark Blue splashed one. Their fuel's at half. I left 'em orbiting at thirty. It's all logged," Eddie reports. "What'd I miss over here?"

"Good guy." Ross takes a sip of his coffee. "You didn't miss anything. I'm just getting ready to take Skylark Red in for a run."

Supposedly, every officer at the base is a controller, regardless of their other duties, and they are required to log a few hours of controller time each month. This is a pain in the ass to the regular controllers, but it's a regulation so they have to put up with it.

It's sunrise at the 646th. Captain Becker and Second Lieutenant Sumner are drinking coffee in Becker's office. Looking through a folder Becker remarks, "You haven't logged any controller time this month, Harry."

"Haven't had a chance, sir," Sumner explains. "I've been kept busy right here in the orderly room."

"Well, this might be a good time to get up to Radar Ops while this Wolverine mission is on," Becker suggests, scanning a chart. "Dog crew is on 'til oh-eight-hundred. Tell Ross I want you to run some intercepts."

"Thank you, Captain." Sumner jumps out of his chair and salutes.

Becker returns the salute and watches Sumner leave.

Sumner presents himself to Ross and has his enthusiasm dampened when Ross shouts, "Jesus Christ, is Becker fucking crazy? Can't he have you log your controller time on some midnight shift when we're only carrying a couple of fucking tracks?"

"Captain Becker thought this would be a good time for me to run some intercepts." Sumner is blinking more than usual.

"Are you sure he doesn't want you to fly a couple of the fucking planes?"

"You can call the orderly room if you don't believe me, Captain."

"That won't be necessary. Unfortunately for me, I do believe you." Ross turns away and shouts. "Airman Flynn!"

Eddie stops adjusting the trace brilliance on Peterson's scope. "Somethin's up, Pete. Captain Ross never calls me Airman Flynn unless there's assholes in the area."

Spotting Sumner up on the dais with Captain Ross, Eddie goes military. "Airman Flynn here, Captain."

"Captain Becker wants Lieutenant Sumner to run some intercepts," he almost sighs. "I want you to be his intercept control tech. Get Norm to take over for you."

"Yes, sir." Eddie can't hide his surprise. For an instant his eyes get big.

"You and the lieutenant can take scope five. Who's still up in the northwest quadrant?"

"Skylark Red and Circus Blue, sir."

"Send Red home. They're getting low on fuel." Ross jerks his thumb toward Sumner. "Then you and the lieutenant can work Circus Blue."

"Yes, sir." Eddie picks up a spare headset and hands it to Sumner. "Follow me, Lieutenant. Scope five's over by the wall."

Settling in at scope five, Eddie and Sumner plug their headsets into the scope's VHF jacks. Looking at the plotting board and then at the scope, Sumner asks, "Which one is Circus Blue?"

Tapping the scope with his black grease pencil, Eddie answers, "This one, sir."

"Let's get going on that intercept," Sumner urges, keying and unkeying his headset a few times. He looks as happy and excited as a kid with a new cap pistol and six rolls of caps. Eddie shakes his head, knowing Sumner is pissing the pilot off with the keying and unkeying of the headset.

"First we have to give Skylark Red a vector for home," Eddie states. Noticing the birth of a frown on Sumner's brow, he adds, "Captain Ross said they were low on fuel, remember, sir?"

"Of course, Skylark Red." Sumner looks from the scope to the plotting board and back. "Where exactly are they?"

Eddie taps the scope with his pencil. "Right here, sir."

Sumner puts a clear plastic protractor on the scope. Eddie has never seen a real controller use one. "Looks like about oh-one-five." Sumner keys and un-keys his headset three more times.

"I'd make it zero-two-zero myself, sir," Eddie offers.

"Nobody asked you." Sumner keys his headset. "Skylark Red, this is Mama Bear here. How do you read me? Over."

"Red here. Read you five-square and would you please get that idiot to quit keying and un-keying his headset. Over."

Sumner ignores the pilot's remark. "Awwww, Roger," he answers in a drawn-out manner. "Skylark Red, I read you five-by-five, loud and clear. Take a vector of oh-one-five for home. Over."

"Say again on vector? Over." The pilot sounds perturbed.

"Tell him 'zero,' not 'oh,' sir," Eddie directs.

"Vector zero-one-five for home. Over."

"Roger. Zero-one-five. Skylark Red. Out."

Looking at the weather status board, Eddie sees that it's a clear dawn and that Red will be able to make a visual correction from Sumner's vector. He makes a mental note to keep an eye on Skylark Red.

"Now, let's get busy on some intercepts," Sumner orders. Eddie stifles a laugh. Sumner continues, "Where's the bogie?"

Eddie is checking out the weather status board. He's happy to see the rain moving out of the Detroit area. He taps the scope idly in two spots. "Bogie here. Circus Blue here," then adds "sir" as an afterthought. I owe it to Captain Ross to do the best I can with this asshole, he tells himself.

"Circus Blue, Mama Bear here." Sumner is keying and un-keying his headset with one hand and he's holding his little protractor on the face of the scope with the other. Sumner continues, "How do you read me? Over."

"Blue here. Five-square. Over."

"Awww Roger, Circus Blue," Sumner intones, stretching the "awww" to the breaking point. "Understand you read five-by-five, loud and clear. Over."

"Blue here. Do you have a bogie for me? Over." The pilot has annoyance in his voice.

Monitoring and logging all the transmissions, Eddie can't help thinking, the pilots are flying four hundred fifty and five hundred miles an hour and this jack-off talks to them like they're driving tractors.

"Awww Roger, Circus Blue. Vector two-two-five for bogie. Range, fifteen miles. Over."

"Two-two-five at fifteen. Roger. Blue out," the pilot responds, kicking in his afterburners.

Seeing the fighter's blip jump on the next sweep of the scope's trace, Eddie thinks, good thing the pilots had the sense to go balls out, without waiting for this asshole to tell them "Buster." Eddie continues to watch the fighters close on the bogie, thinking, there's got to be some way to keep this guy from fuckin' things up here without pissin' him off. The fighter's blip is almost on the bogie blip.

"Circus Blue, how do you read me? Over."

"Still five-square. Where's my bogie? Over."

"Awww Roger, Circus Blue," Sumner answers, "you should have a 'pounce' right now. Over."

"No joy, Mama Bear. Over," Circus Blue Leader reports.

"Tell him two o'clock, Lieutenant." Eddie taps the scope with his pencil.

"Huh?"

"The bogie's on the pilot's right," Eddie points with his pencil. "You know, like a clock. Two o'clock."

"Oh yes, I know that." Sumner keys his headset and almost shouts, "Your bogie's at two o'clock. Over."

"He's passed the bogie, Lieutenant. He'll have to go around again." Eddie's voice is dispassionate.

Fuming, Sumner snaps, "I don't like your attitude, Flynn."

Before Sumner can say more, Circus Blue breaks in. "I spotted that bogie. We'll have to go around again. Over." Exasperation drips from the pilot's voice.

Eddie gets Sumner through a couple of more intercepts and is in the middle of listening to, "Get this straight, mister, I'm the officer and you're the ..." when Brownie comes by. Handing Eddie another headset, he tells Sumner, "Captain Ross would like to see you, sir." As Sumner leaves, Eddie looks at Brownie and shakes his head. They both laugh.

"Captain Ross wants you to get hooked up with Ground Control Approach." Brownie hands Eddie a fresh mug of coffee.

"I was hoping that was for me. Thanks."

"You and the lieutenant are going to stack six flights over the Initial Point and let them down a minute and a half apart."

Putting the headset on his other ear, Eddie thanks Brownie again for the coffee, plugs his new headset into the GCA jack and transmits, "Mama Bear to Beehive. How do you read? Over."

The guy at Ground Control Approach keys and un-keys his headset without saying Roger, letting the clicks from the keying speak for themselves, a big time-saver during a mission. "Thank God for small favors," Eddie notes. "I'm working with a pro. Wonder if Sumner will ever figure out he's only supposed to hit the fuckin' key when it's time to talk?" He shakes his head. "No point in holding my breath for that."

Sitting alone at the scope with the GCA headset on one ear and the VHF headset on the other, Eddie takes a big swallow of coffee and breaks out a small notepad. Drawing a line down the center of the first page, he writes "Flight" on the left side of the line and "Angels" on the right. Under "Angels" he writes in a column, "5,5.5,6,6.5,7,7.5".

Sumner returns and sits next to Eddie at the scope. "We're going to be stacking aircraft over the I.P." Looking at his sheet of paper, Sumner continues, "I forgot. Exactly where is the I.P …"

Eddie makes a small black X on the radar scope with his grease pencil. "Right here, Lieutenant, fifteen miles northeast of Oscoda, where it always is." Eddie concludes, I can see I'll be handling this one alone.

"You do know you're not supposed to be drinking coffee while on scope duty, don't you?" Sumner remarks.

"That's never been a rule on Dog crew, Lieutenant," Eddie parries. He can't resist thrusting, "Maybe you ought to tell Captain Ross about it."

Sumner ignores Eddie's sarcasm. "How does Captain Ross usually handle these stacking procedures?"

"Just like pancakes, Lieutenant. He takes the flight nearest the I.P., puts 'em at five angels. Then each new flight comes in and orbits five hundred feet higher than the flight before, until you've got 'em all stacked. Then, I give 'em over to GCA a minute and a half apart and everybody's happy." Eddie sees the unhappy, tight look on Sumner's face. He smiles broadly. "There's nothing to it."

With Eddie pointing out the flights' positions, naming them and suggesting vectors, Sumner has three flights orbiting over the Initial Point, Mudhen Green, Mudhen Yellow and Mudhen Blue are at five, five and a half and six angels.

Keying his headset, Sumner states, "Sliphorn Red, you are ten miles from the I.P. Vector two-seven-five and orbit at six angels. Over."

"Vector two-seven-five. Orbit at six angels. Sliphorn Red, out."

Eddie keys his VHF headset. "Sliphorn Red, amend that order. Orbit at six-POINT-FIVE angels. I say again, six-Point-Five angels, over."

"Ah Roger, Mama Bear, six-point-five angels. Sliphorn Red, out."

Sumner turns toward Eddie. He's angry. "Enlisted personnel do not communicate with pilots without—"

Eddie interrupts. "Chew me out later, Lieutenant. Just put the next flight at seven angels and hurry up about it. Two of these flights are gettin' low on fuel."

After stacking the last two flights with Sumner, Eddie and the guy from GCA get everybody down swiftly and safely, each flight touching down exactly a minute and a half apart.

In the break room at five after eight, Lieutenant Sumner and Eddie are alone. "I want you to know that all of your breaches of discipline will be reported to Captain Becker today." Sumner tries to lean into Eddie's face.

"Thanks for the bulletin," Eddie retorts loudly. "There's no one here but you and me, so get this. I don't give a flyin' fuck. Write it in your report, 'Flynn said, quote, I don't give a flyin' fuck, unquote.' Here's somethin' else. I just finished sixteen hours in Radar Ops, two full shifts. I'm loggin' some sack time. I'm on duty again at midnight."

Eddie walks out of the break room. Back at the barracks he takes a quick shower and is asleep by eight-thirty.

CHAPTER 20

▼

While Eddie is dreaming of Joan, she's already up and preparing for their rendez-vous, hoping to get out of her house before her father awakens at nine. She's out by the garage loading things into her car. Jill is digging in a small flower garden next to the garage. She looks up from her work.

"I'm glad you're having such a nice summer, dear."

"Thanks, Mom." Joan puts two Coleman lanterns into the crowded trunk. I really am having a good time. Sometimes I feel like I'm dreaming. Like it's too good to be true."

"Everybody's got a right to be happy, honey—" Jill is interrupted by her hus-band shouting, "What kind of sorority has to see you twice in three weeks?" Bill is striding across the back lawn in their direction, waving Joan's note.

"It's the Tri Delts, Dad," Joan smiles innocently. "Laura says I'm practically in."

"I remember the Tri Delts as pretty much being the party-girl sorority." Bill realizes his mistake a moment too late.

"Wait a minute," Jill snaps. "I was a Delta Delta Delta and I finished third in my class." Turning to Joan she continues, "Is this the tea dance you were telling me about, Joan?"

"That's the one, Mom."

Jill jerks a big weed out of her garden, spraying dirt all over the front of Bill's bathrobe. "You'd think you'd be happy," she prods. "Joan will be mingling with young men from Gompers-Adams Academy, some of the wealthiest boys in the Midwest." Jill knows all of Bill's buttons and she enjoys pushing them. Her mother used to say of Bill, "He's as predictable as cowshit in a dairy farmer's pasture."

"Gompers-Adams, eh?" Bill brightens a bit.

"That's right, Dad." Joan slams the trunk. "Rich guys." Suppressing any show of mirth, she kisses her mom, gets into her car, rolls the window down, starts the engine and waves. "'Bye, Mom, 'bye, Dad."

"Have fun, dear." Jill waves.

"Try and meet some nice boy," Bill shouts.

Picturing Eddie, Joan answers, "Oh, I just know I will, Dad."

At Sandy's house, she picks up the other girls and by two o'clock they're almost to the quarry road turnoff. The sky is clear and blue, marred only by the condensation trails of the high-flying aircraft taking part in Operation Wolverine.

At two o'clock, the guys are going through a hole in the cyclone fence that surrounds the perimeter of the 646th Aircraft Control & Warning Squadron. Dressed in Levis borrowed from Bob and a shirt of Eddie's, Norm is feeling reluctant about the plan. As Eddie holds the hole open, Norm hesitates, "I don't think this is a good idea."

"Relax," Eddie reassures. "Me and O'Hara used to go through here more than the main gate."

"Think about Laura," Bob claps Norm on the shoulder. "Less than three miles from here."

Up in the orderly room, the morning report clerk is getting an earful through the closed door of Captain Becker's office. The wall clock reads 2:05.

Captain Ross is in a bad mood. Becker awakened him with a phone call about an urgent meeting concerning personnel of Dog crew. The meeting among Becker, Sumner, and Captain Ross starts off badly and quickly deteriorates.

"I know you just finished graveyard shift, Jim," Becker starts, "but I felt you should be here because this court-martial concerns one of your men."

"Oh, does it now?" There's a slight edge to Ross' voice. He continues, "Which of my men might that be?"

"Flynn," Becker answers, waving some papers. "Lieutenant Sumner listed four different breeches of discipline and one count of insubordination, namely, telling the lieutenant that he didn't quote give a flying fuck unquote, if the lieutenant reported him or not."

"I think we should be able to get him at least thirty days in the stockade," Sumner almost chortles.

Captain Ross stands up quickly, knocking over the small wooden chair he'd been slouched in. His face reddens. "Just a fucking minute here, before we go throwing anyone's ass in the stockade."

"Now, Jim ..." Becker begins.

"Don't give me that 'Now, Jim' shit, Becker," Ross orders, throwing Dog crew's log on the desk and jerking his thumb in Sumner's direction. "I thought this little prick might be up to something, so there's eighty pages of transmissions from last night.

Flynn was finishing up back-to-back shifts because Charlie crew doesn't have a reliable intercept control tech since *YOU* sent their best man, McKinny, to the fucking motor pool to drive a fucking bus. All McKinny did was bring a little pussy on base for two of his crewmates that you put on restriction. Jesus Christ! No wonder morale's so bad on this fucking base."

"Now, Jim ..." Becker starts.

"'Now, Jim,' my ass," Ross shouts. He's fuming. "You're going to hear this whether you want to or not because it's your fault for sending this asshole up to Ops in the middle of a fucking Strategic Air Command mission in the first place." Becker grins a tight, nervous grin, almost a grimace.

"What in the fuck were you thinking about? Don't answer. I don't want to know." Ross turns from Becker to Sumner and continues, "If a flight of two F-86's are going five hundred miles an hour, how many miles a minute is that?"

"Er, ummm ..." Sumner stares at Ross.

Captain Ross mimics Sumner. "Er, ummm. Try eight miles a fucking minute. I didn't think you knew. But Flynn knew. Only Flynn's an airman basic and isn't supposed to talk to the pilots."

Becker interrupts. "We've got to have discipline."

Grabbing his crotch, Ross roars, "Discipline this. Look at page sixty-four in that fucking log and listen to me, because we're talking about pilots' lives here, and I place pilots' lives a far fucking cut above discipline and procedure."

"But I ..." Sumner whimpers.

"Shut your ass-kissing mouth," Ross commands, sticking his index finger in Sumner's face. "If you try to interrupt me one more time I'm going to throw you out the fucking window." Turning to Becker, he continues, "Read that fucking page. I've got eight flights of fighters under my control and this jackoff sits there with his head ten miles up his ass, telling Sliphorn Fucking Red to orbit at six angels over the I.P. when Mudhen Fucking Blue is already in that airspace."

Captain Ross leans on Becker's desk with both arms. Becker slides his chair back from the desk. "Now, Jim," he wheedles.

Pounding his fist on Becker's desk, Ross shouts, "No more 'Now Jims' or I'll go apeshit. Look at me. Picture this, if you can. You have two aircraft occupying some airspace and then you send two more aircraft into the same airspace, at the same *TIME* … you can't *FUCKING* do that!!!" Ross picks up his overturned chair and throws it right past Sumner's startled, frightened face. The chair crashes into the far wall and splinters.

Captain Ross takes a deep breath and adopts a mellow, cajoling voice. "The second flight is ten miles away. This means they'll reach the I.P. in slightly over ONE minute. Flynn knows this, takes immediate action, and prevents a fucking disaster. He does this without consulting this Second John, who's as useless as tits on a side of salt fucking pork."

"But Jim," Becker pleads.

"But Jim, nothing," Ross continues, heating up again. "When this halfwit first sat down, I monitored his radio telephone procedure. Movie shit. A fucking joke." Ross begins to mimic Sumner again. "'Awww Roger. How do you read me?' The pilot's waiting for a fucking vector. Flynn made three intercepts for this jackoff, who doesn't know the difference between two o'clock high and his prick. Flynn saves this little cocksucker's meat and then this ungrateful son of a bitch starts to chew Flynn out." Captain Ross turns his glare on Sumner, who is slinking down in his chair. "As far as I'm concerned, you little weasel," Ross growls, "you couldn't smell where Flynn pissed four years ago. If you ever show up in that Radar Ops room again during my shift, I'll fucking kill you!"

Directing his fury back at Becker, Ross continues, "I got on the horn to Major Davis, Sliphorn Red Leader, when I heard you wanted this meeting. Davis'll verify every word that's in that fucking log, so you two assholes can court-martial Flynn whenever you're fucking ready, because I'll appear as a witness for Flynn and I'll drill both of you motherfuckers brand new assholes."

Staring intently into Sumner's eyes, Ross threatens, "*YOU* won't have to worry about sending anyone's ass to stockade because you'll be doing twenty years in fucking Leavenworth for criminal stupidity."

Reaching quickly across Becker's desk for his log, Ross notices Becker flinch and proclaims, "Now if you two assholes will excuse me, I'm going home for a good piece of ass, something I don't think either of you jackoffs ever had." Captain Ross blows out of Becker's office like a tornado, slamming the door behind him.

Becker sits staring, stunned. He is shaken. When Ross grabbed for that log, I thought he was going to hit me, he thinks. He feels like he can't get out of his chair. I've got to take a piss, he realizes. He looks over at Sumner, who's blowing his nose. "I think all those bombing runs over Germany did something to Ross' mind," Becker states. "Did you see his eyes, Harry? That guy's nuts!"

Sumner quits blowing his nose and starts wiping sweat from his forehead. "I thought he was going to hit me." He points to the fragments of the wooden chair. "He wanted to hit me with that chair."

"No, Harry. If Ross had wanted to hit you with that chair, he wouldn't have missed."

Becker gets a brand new bottle of Alka-Seltzer out of his desk and starts to open it. "Maybe I can't court-martial Flynn right now," he grouses, "but I'll nail him yet," adding as an afterthought, "Flynn did save your ass though."

CHAPTER 21

▼

Joan, Sandy and Laura arrive at the quarry twenty minutes ahead of the guys. Setting up at Joan's favorite picnic site, the girls spread three large blankets, get the food out of the ice chests, unload a couple of canvas chairs, along with two Coleman lanterns and a pair of flashlights before popping three beers. They even make a big circle of rocks for a campfire.

On the drive up, the three of them had joked about getting to the spot before the guys, getting everything set up and then sitting around looking nonchalant about it. On the portable radio the Clovers are singing "One Mint Julep". The girls adjust their halters, light cigarettes, assume casual poses and wait.

At the same moment that Captain Ross slams Becker's door, Eddie pops out of the woods. "Don't move, ladies," he shouts. "You guys look like a cigarette ad in *The Saturday Evening Post*." He lays a long, passionate kiss on Joan, turning her away from the others so he can cup the cheeks of her ass. Norm gets one of Laura's hot tongue sandwiches and Bob gets an equally enthusiastic greeting from Sandy.

The girls have laid out an impressive array of food—ham and cheese sandwiches, chicken salad, potato salad, bread and butter pickles and dills, big bags of potato chips and two chests full of beer. Eddie fills a paper plate with some of everything. "We slept through noon chow." He takes a beer and sits next to Joan.

"I made that chicken salad from my mom's recipe."

Eddie takes a big forkful of chicken salad. "Then that's where I'm gonna start." Joan snuggles close to him.

After an hour and a half of eating and drinking beer, Eddie looks at the ring of stones. "We're gonna need some wood for a campfire, Joan." He winks. "Want to take a little walk? Hunt for some wood?"

Joan smiles a snapshot smile. Eddie gets to his feet and gently pulls Joan up. "Let's get some firewood," he announces loudly, as he and Joan head off into the woods.

Joan and Eddie find wood. They also find a pond and take a swim. After their swim, drying out in a sunny patch near some bushes, they make love. Returning to the campsite, loaded down with kindling and two medium-sized jack pine branches, they find everyone gone. "Guess they went out looking for wood too," Joan observes. They both laugh.

As the sun is setting, Joan lights up her Coleman lanterns and she and Sandy get a campfire going. "Joan and I were Girl Scouts for a few weeks one summer," Sandy states.

"Girl Scouts?!" Eddie tries to picture the two of them as Girl Scouts.

"It didn't last long," Joan answers. "I'll tell you about it sometime." She giggles and continues, "Look, I even brought hot dogs and marshmallows."

They sit around roasting hot dogs and marshmallows, and talking. Sandy tells the Girl Scout story and Eddie gives Joan a squeeze. "Good for you, for not bein' a squealer. And good for you, Sandy, for quittin' that chickenshit outfit when they blew Joan outta there." Norm just shakes his head. Laura kisses him.

Eddie doesn't tell Joan about his run-in with Sumner. Nothin'll ever come of it, he tells himself. "Those roasted marshmallows go great with beer," he declares, "but I'm so full, I just gotta take a walk."

Joan picks up one of the lanterns and they head into the woods. While Joan and Eddie are walking, the others are talking. Sandy is telling of her reaction to Bob's call. "I've got to admit, the first thing I thought when you said that you guys were restricted was, what did Eddie do? Even Joan asked, 'Is it Eddie?'"

Bob flicks his cigarette into the campfire. "He's a different guy lately. Isn't he, Norm?"

"He's a little more careful about breaking the rules, but he still does things his way." Norm shrugs. "That's Eddie."

"I think Joan is a good influence on Eddie," Laura states, "just like I'm a good influence on you, Normie." She puts the hot dog she's been roasting on a bun, smears it with mustard and hands it to him. "Here you go, honey. Just like mother used to try to make." Everyone laughs.

Sandy lights a cigarette off a burning stick and blows a long stream of smoke into the fire. "I think we're all good for each other. I know I'm a better girl since I met Bob." They all laugh again. Sandy gives Bob a deep kiss.

"Want to take a walk, San?" Sandy stands up, takes Bob's hand in hers and pulls him to his feet. "Let's go."

"Take your time," Laura shouts as they're leaving. "I'll help Norm keep the home fires burning." Bob picks up a flashlight and he and Sandy head into the woods.

On their walk, Joan and Eddie come upon a large clearing. Eddie shows Joan how to find the North Star. Looking at it jogs Joan's thoughts to Alaska. "Why would Captain Becker ever send you to Alaska? Sandy says Bob told her you're one of the best radar operators on the base."

"I pay Bob to say shit like that," Eddie jokes, and they laugh. "Sometimes bein' good at your job ain't enough. Some bosses want you to grovel and kiss ass. I ain't good at neither. But to answer your question, Becker feels if he can ship me to Alaska, it'll be like punishment. It'll make him feel good."

"Well, it would make me feel shitty."

Eddie takes Joan in his arms and kisses her. "Don't worry about it," he assures her. "It'll probably never happen." Seeing the tears in Joan's eyes, he kisses each eye tenderly.

"Let's just sit here and look at the sky," she suggests.

The two of them sit, then lie on their backs on the pine-needle carpet, gazing up at the stars. Abruptly, Joan rolls over on top of Eddie. She starts kissing him all over his face, ending up chewing on Eddie's lips and tongue. She puts her mouth close to Eddie's ear and whispers, "Oh Eddie, I'll lay right down and die, if you're ever sent away."

Returning to the campsite later, Joan reports, "Eddie wanted to show me a big oak tree."

"Is that what they call it now," Laura asks. Everyone laughs.

Dog crew is back on duty at midnight, so at eleven-fifteen everyone says their goodbyes. Eddie and Joan make plans to hit Wenona Beach for at least part of the Labor Day weekend.

CHAPTER 22

▼

Captain Becker is sitting at his desk, watching a pair of Alka-Seltzers dissolve. He turns his desk calendar to September 1, 1952. He drinks his drink while it's still fizzing and reflects, Monday, Labor Day. He remembers Labor Day, summer furniture clearance sales, and heaves a deep, long sigh. Winter's just around the corner, he broods. With his elbow on the desk, he begins massaging the bridge of his nose with his thumb and index finger. I'll never make major, he moans to himself, talk about Blue Monday ...

Becker's depressing thoughts abruptly vanish as Sumner bursts into the office, his little cherub face all lit up. He's blinking like a nearsighted raccoon in a police lineup and clutching a piece of teletype paper. He puts the paper on Becker's desk. "Excuse my excessive enthusiasm, sir," he gurgles, "but read that TWIX and your spirits will soar." As Becker is scanning the paper, Sumner announces, "The Alaskan Air Command wants one radar operator."

Becker looks up from the message. He smiles. His face softens and his heartburn abates. He looks almost pleasant as his habitual scowl melts. He grabs the paper off his desk, springs to his feet and shouts, "Look at this! I don't even need to send anyone with him. One radar operator is all they want." Becker takes a deep breath. "Ahhh," he exhales, feeling relaxed. "This is goodbye Flynn. Adios to that dirty little bastard. I hope they keep him up there in the frozen north for a full two years."

Sumner has never seen Captain Becker look so happy, but he's feeling happy also. The way Flynn looks at me, like I'm a piece of shit, Sumner thinks, and the way he says "sir" as if he's spitting out something distasteful. He asks, "Why don't I have DiNessi cut orders on him right now, Captain?"

"Good idea. The sooner the son of a bitch is off the base, the better." Becker sits down again, rolls his chair back and puts his feet up on the desk, as Sumner leaves. Becker's stomach seems to be at ease. He smiles and pronounces the word slowly, savoring each syllable, "*A-las-ka.*"

Airman First Class Vito DiNessi, the morning report clerk, is a fellow New Yorker and a friend of Eddie's. He passes Eddie the word at noon chow.

"I had to cut your orders this morning and send them down to Selfridge for approval. I'm sorry, man."

The chow line is moving slowly and Vito and Eddie are near the tail end of it. "How much time do you think I got left in Michigan, Veet?"

"If I was a bettin' man, and I am, I'd say you'll be out of here in seven to ten days. More like seven for you. Becker had me type 'expedite these orders' at the top of the page. You'll ship out of Camp Stoneman in California by troopship around the middle of the month."

"Thanks for the info, Veet. This way I'll be ready to deal with Becker when he hits me with his big flash."

"That's why I told you. But keep it to yourself or Becker'll be on my ass. I'll tell you something else," Vito continues, "I was in the orderly room the other day when Becker and Sumner were trying to cook up a court-martial for you. Captain Ross was there and he was pissed off. He chewed them two up and spit 'em out. It was beautiful. Ross said fuck or some form of fuck, twenty-eight times and that ain't countin' a couple of motherfuckers. He even broke a fuckin' chair. He went apeshit. It was a real show."

Eddie laughs, picturing the scene. "Captain Ross is a real guy, Veet. He knows how to treat people."

An airman walks by with macaroni and cheese, salad and apple pie on his tray. I'm gonna miss Arbo's chow, Eddie reflects. Maybe I'll ask him how to break the news to Joan. When he finally makes it to the front of the serving line, he sees Peterson on KP. "Hit me heavy on the macaroni, Pete," he requests, "light on the salad." He gets a piece of pie, a mug of coffee and takes a seat in a far corner of the mess hall, near a window.

He pushes the immediate problem of how to tell Joan about getting shipped to Alaska to the rear of his brain to marinate in his subconscious. He begins sorting through random thoughts while he eats. Considering and disregarding flashes that strobe through his mind, Becker's rant pops up. The part about, "The thing that I hate the most about you, is your I-don't-give-a-shit attitude," appears in bold print.

Eddie takes note. Even assholes can be right now and then, he reasons. He gives thought to his blasé attitude toward life and starts analyzing it. He comes to the conclusion that he really doesn't give a shit what others think is important to or for him. What others think Eddie should consider important, is of no import to Eddie. "Only I know what's good for me," was his stance as a three-year-old and he's seen no reason to change. His mother used to call him a "rugged individualist." Now I'm called a fuckup. He laughs to himself.

How much of bein' me is choice, he wonders, and how much is automatic? Like losin' my temper?

Eddie states his case to himself. You can take me as I am or you leave me the fuck alone. Either way is okay with me. I'm not gonna put on a fuckin' show tryin' to be what I'm not. I don't give a shit if you approve of me or not. I approve of me and I have for a long fuckin' time, and to me that's what counts. And you can put your stripes up in the same place where you can put gold stars on homework, and other jive like that.

Some might question Eddie's outlook on life, but it worked well for him. Why waste time worryin' about how good your cards are? Just play the motherfuckers. Life is just a game and the name of the game is "Eddie wins in the end." He smiles big at his great thought and continues, I don't give a fuck what the score is at halftime. Check with me when the ball game is over. He starts feeling better. I'll come up with somethin' that'll knock Joan out. Maybe she'd like to get engaged?

A scene from the recruiting office intrudes. When Eddie joined the Air Force, the recruiting sergeant assured him that with his background of two years as a member of a Rifle and Pistol team and his National Rifle Association rating of "Expert," he'd be a cinch to be sent to gunnery school in Wyoming.

Eddie, picturing himself knocking enemy fighters out of the sky from his position as a waist gunner on a bomber, like John Garfield in the movies, said, "Cool, Sarge," and signed up for four years.

On the troop train to basic training in San Antonio, while taking a break from playing blackjack, Eddie got into a conversation with two air policemen making their rounds and found out about gunnery school.

"That fucking school's been closed for two years," the older AP stated. "All that stuff is radar-controlled now. No more gunners. Sorry, kid. You've been bullshitted."

"That's okay, Sarge. I don't give a shit," Eddie answered and he meant it. No more gunners. Tough shit. Wonder what else might be fun? were his first thoughts. He can't resist smiling at the memory. He shakes his head and laughs at himself for being so gullible. He recognized this gullibility trait in himself and tried to combat it by developing a keen eye and an acute awareness for the scent of bullshit in the air. He just threw the old recruiter into the bullshit bin of his mind, along with guys selling sweaters out of car trunks. Sweaters that have two arms when shown and somehow lose an arm on the subway ride home. The sarge lands in the bin between the sweater sellers and the Murphy men asking for cash in advance for non-existent pussy, upstairs in apartment 48.

Eddie smiles recalling one Murphy man's pitch. It was just outside the Five Hundred Club on 125th Street. The man told of the wonders upstairs, girls of all colors and cultures, and quoted ten bucks as the price for an hour. "If you want, I'll hold your wallet and watch for you while you're upstairs. It's some fine pussy up there, but some of the girls can't be trusted, if you know what I mean."

Eddie had laughed in the guy's face. "Nice try, Slick. Do I look like I'm from fuckin' Columbia? I'm a neighborhood guy. I don't have to buy pussy. I get all I need just from hangin' out."

Dwelling on the old sergeant bullshitting him, Eddie concludes, I've been bullshitted before and I'll be bullshitted again. A compensating voice counters, if the old sarge didn't bullshit me, I'd have never joined the Air Force. I never would have met Joan. Thanks for that bullshit job, Sarge, from the bottom of my heart. What a lucky break.

"What a lucky break" brings Eddie back to his original thoughts in the chow line when Vito delivered the Alaskan Turd Casserole. Eddie's first thought was not, "Woe is me." It was, I guess I started shapin' up a little too late. I got this comin'. I've sure done enough shit here at the old Six-Four-Six to deserve a trip to Alaska. I could've been sent to Greenland with O'Hara. Then I'd have never met Joan. Man, that was lucky.

Eddie's follow-up thought had also involved luck. If I wasn't a fuckup, I wouldn't be headed for Alaska, he had reasoned. An immediate counter-thought interjected. If I wasn't a fuckup, I wouldn't have broken restriction to go to Tawas. I wouldn't have met Joan. Lucky thing I'm a fuckup.

That's three times I've been thinkin' about luck, Eddie muses. He considers chance meetings, plans changed, altered circumstances and quirks. He thinks about O. Henry and Damon Runyon, two of his favorite writers and how they used twists of fate in their stories. Twists of fate or luck. It's all the same to me, he decides. I may not believe in wishin' or hopin' but I sure as shit believe in luck. Without it, you ain't shit. He checks his good luck pile, a heaping mound versus his almost invisible dusting of bad luck and sees that he has nothing to bitch about. The older I'm gettin' the more I'm believin' in luck. Luck got me this far and like I always say, so far, so good.

Eddie leaves the mess hall smiling. Too bad Arbo wasn't around. I could've asked him a couple of things.

An unbiased reporter would state that Eddie felt that his I-don't-give-a-shit attitude, a good sense of humor and a little bit of luck were enough to smooth any bumps in his journey down the long trail. I'll come through this like a champ, he tells himself and immediately he hears Joan, "Oh Eddie, I'll lay right down and die, if you're ever sent away."

Hmmm. This ain't gonna be easy. He comes up with a good news, bad news scheme. "Hey Joanie, the good news is we're gonna get engaged. And the bad news is, I'm gonna be up in Alaska for a year or two." He immediately rejects this plan.

I'll come up with somethin' good by the time I call tonight, he promises himself. He feels the "Michigan" chapter of his life drawing to a close. He sees the blank page of the next chapter, "Alaska", before him.

It might be a good idea to let Joan's mom in on the engagement, he figures, and lights up a smoke.

Joan is standing in front of her full-length mirror in a blue shortie nightgown. She's checking her stomach. Her phone rings and she picks it up before the first ring has ended. "Oh Eddie," she wails. She fingers her necklace, rubbing the heart between her thumb and index finger.

From the way Joan says "Oh Eddie," he knows that something's up. "What's the matter, sweetie? You don't sound so good."

"Oh Eddie. I didn't get the curse this month."

"The curse?"

"My period, Eddie. I'm a week late, a full week." Joan is close to tears. Eddie can hear it in her voice.

"You can be late, can't you?" He tries to sound reassuring.

"I'm never late. I didn't have a real period last month either. Just spotted a little for a couple of days. I thought it was because we were having sex. Oh, Eddie."

The forlorn sound in Joan's voice causes Eddie deep pain. This is not the time to break the Alaskan news, he tells himself. He concentrates on listening to Joan, trying his best to console her and alleviate her fears.

"How could this have happened to me? We used rubbers all the time, except our first night and morning." Joan chokes up and gets a catch in her throat.

"I've got a special three-day pass for workin' extra shifts during Wolverine," Eddie tells her. "You come up here tomorrow. We'll go to Wenona Beach and make our wedding plans. How's that sound?"

Joan hears no hesitation in Eddie's voice. He means what he says, she decides. "Okay," she answers in a small voice.

"Are you feelin' any better?"

"A little," Joan answers softly. She kisses the little heart.

"A little?" Eddie teases. I just proposed to you and you only feel a little better?"

Joan manages a small laugh. "Okay. I feel a lot better." She stops fiddling with her necklace.

"That's my girl. Remember this, Joan. I love you and I've wanted you to be my wife since that first night we met and that's no bullshit."

"I love you, Eddie. Everything will be all right, won't it?"

"You bet it will, honey. We're gettin' married."

"I'm feeling a lot better."

"Then I'll see you tomorrow morning at the main gate?"

"I'll be there, Eddie."

"Eleven o'clock," Eddie promises, adding, "Lemme hear you smile."

"I'm smiling," Joan laughs a little laugh. "Here's some kisses." Joan makes some kissing sounds and they hang up together.

"Holy fuckin' shit," Eddie exclaims as he hangs up the phone, "I'm gonna be a family man." He figures, me and Joan can handle this. She'll be a great mom. When I get back from Alaska we can live off base. I'll never hit our kid. I'll always listen to his side of the story. If it's a girl, Joan can teach her all that girl shit and they can go shoppin' together. Either way is okay with me.

Wenona Beach is almost deserted. A cold front drifting down from Canada makes it seem more like late October than early September. A moderate wind out of the northwest is whipping up whitecaps on Saginaw Bay. By sundown a cold, steady rain will be falling.

Eddie and Joan sit on a rocky outcrop looking out at the water, discussing their situation. "I just didn't want to *have* to get married," Joan laments. "I don't want to feel like I trapped you."

"Don't talk that kind of shit," Eddie declares. "We're gettin' married because we want to, not because we have to. You'd marry me if you weren't pregnant, wouldn't you?"

"Yes, but …"

"But what?"

"I feel awfully bad about messing up my mom's trust fund."

"I don't think your mom gives a shit about that fund," Eddie offers. "I think your old man's the one who really cares about that money."

"Fuck him," Joan shouts, "fuckim, fuckim, fuckim. He's been so shitty about you. I hate him for that."

"He ain't worth hatin'. He's just a square," Eddie soothes. "It's like havin' a limp. He can't help it. It's like Becker's an asshole. He was probably born that way."

Joan laughs. She finds herself cheering up in spite of her worries.

"I've got a regular shift break comin' up this weekend. I'll line up a Justice of the Peace in Tawas. We're both of legal age. We'll drive down to Rostonkowski's and have a nice, one-day honeymoon."

"One day?" Joan can't hide the disappointment in her voice.

"Well, I've been kind of waitin' for the right time to tell you this." Eddie licks his lips. "Becker's got me on orders for Alaska." He tries to sound unconcerned.

Sagging visibly, Joan repeats Eddie's final word, "Alaska?"

Eddie runs his index finger over his thumbnail. "Yeah."

"You're going to fucking Alaska," Joan exclaims. "And I'm pregnant. Holy Christ, Eddie, what am I going to do?"

Eddie licks his lips again, finds a small piece of chapped skin and nips it between his teeth. "You'll do fine. Number one, we'll be married. Number two, your mom will help you through your pregnancy. Number three, I'll get stationed at one of them bases where the tour is only six months and I'll be back in time to see our kid get born."

"You make it sound so easy." Joan manages another small smile.

"It'll all be okay. Remember, it starts with us gettin' married."

"But Alaska, Eddie?"

"It's just another place," he jokes. "Someday they'll probably make the big son of a bitch a state." He laughs. "That'll sure piss the Texans off."

"How can you joke about it? You going away isn't funny."

"I'm just tryin' to make the best of it. I hate the thought of goin' away. I'm gonna miss you every minute. But there's nothin' we can do. It's still you and me against the world. Right?"

"You and me, Eddie, against the world."

"That's my girl. Say this with me, Joan. 'Fuck the world.'"

"Fuck the world," Joan repeats.

Eddie gets glimpses of himself hanging on the backs of trolleys and trucks, zipping along Broadway and Amsterdam, screaming, "Fuck the world" at groups of people on corners, near newspaper stands or subway exits.

"That's been my motto for a long time," Eddie brags. "Now let's scream it together, real loud."

"Fuck the world," the two of them shout to Saginaw Bay. They break up with laughter.

"Don't that feel great?" Eddie kisses Joan passionately. A warm feeling runs through her. She feels comfortable and relaxed. Eddie senses it. "Let's drop by the pavilion, dance a little and have a few beers. Tomorrow we'll get everything rollin'. How's that sound, Joanie?"

"That sounds perfect. And you know what, Eddie?"

"What's that, honey?"

"We won't be needing rubbers tonight." She smiles a big smile.

After spending the night together, they drive back to the 646th. Joan drops Eddie off at the main gate, agreeing that she'll be back Friday at midnight.

Thursday afternoon Eddie buys a wide yellow-gold wedding band at Wilson's. He leaves the store humming, "Here Comes The Bride".

CHAPTER 23

▼

Friday night Eddie gets down to the main gate at eleven-thirty. Smitty, the air policeman on duty, served an Alaskan tour and Eddie hopes to get some information about Alaska that he hasn't been able to find in the map he's been poring over since his talk with DiNessi.

"What do you know about Alaska, Smitty?"

Smitty pours a cup of coffee from his Thermos, happy for some company. "I spent the longest twelve months of my life at a place called Naknek."

"A year, huh? Don't they have no tours shorter'n that?"

"When I rotated, I flew back to Tacoma with a guy who'd been out on the Aleutian Chain," Smitty answers. "He only did a six-month tour, but he said he never saw the sun because the fog never lifted in the whole six months."

"I don't mind fog. What was the name of the base?"

"I think it was Shemya. But it was just a little weather site—most radar sites like this are twelve-month tours."

"How bad was Naknek?"

Smitty takes a long swallow of his coffee. "I like to went apeshit. No women at all for a year."

"What did the guys do on their off-duty time?"

"Mostly they got drunk a lot and they got into lots of fights. The fishin' was good … but shit, I'd rather fuck than fish."

Eddie laughs, "I sure agree with you there, Smitty. The year went pretty slow, huh?"

"Slower'n whale shit goin' through a blanket."

Eddie takes another drink of his coffee. Smitty empties his Thermos into Eddie's cup. "You gettin' shipped to Alaska?"

"I dunno," Eddie lies, "but you never know." Taking Smitty's Thermos, he offers, "Lemme go up to the mess hall and get you a refill. If Joan shows up, tell her I'll be right back."

"Sure thing. Thanks, Eddie."

As Eddie leaves the building, Smitty shouts after him, "If they do ship your ass to Alaska, you better get you all the poontang you can handle before you go."

"Yeah," Eddie answers absently. He doesn't think of Joan as poontang.

Eddie gets back to the main gate at ten after twelve with Smitty's coffee. He's surprised to find that Joan has not yet arrived.

At eleven-thirty, as Eddie is entering the guard shack, Joan is zipping along on Highway 23. She's wearing a white blouse and a white linen skirt. She has flowers in her hair, and a small white purse is on the seat next to her. The radio is playing "September Song", Earl Bostic is honking and Joan is feeling happy. Easing into a curve ten miles north of Bay City, she's thinking, this time tomorrow I'll be Mrs. Eddie Flynn.

A carload of drunks swings into her lane midway through the curve. Swerving instinctively, Joan runs her right front tire onto the road's shoulder, still sodden from three days of rain. The tire bites deep, pulls the rest of the car off the road, and flips it.

Everything becomes slow motion as she feels herself flung out of her body, dazedly realizing that she has become an observer. She sees herself gripping the wheel tightly, mashing the brakes, sees herself losing her grip, floating out of her seat, tumbling, smashing her head. I hope the car doesn't explode, she thinks and the car tumbles again. Joan flips over again. She sees her purse hovering near her face and flashes on Alice falling down the rabbit hole. "Will I ever reach bottom?" she wonders. The car rolls over two more times and comes to rest on its roof. Joan bangs her head again.

"Will Eddie ever find me?" is her last thought before she slumps unconscious against the car door. The door pops open and Joan slides halfway out with blood trickling from her nose, mouth and scalp.

Her car's headlights are shining up onto Highway 23. The radio is playing. The disc jockey has segued from Earl Bostic's saxophone heroics to Lucky Mill-inder. Annisteen Allen is singing, "I'm waiting just for you," to a deserted Highway 23.

In the carload of drunks careening southbound, one of them speaks up. "I think that car went off the road back there."

"Bullshit," the driver responds. "I didn't see nothing. Crack me another beer."

Smitty's clock shows two o'clock. All of Eddie's calls to Joan's private number have gone unanswered.

Eddie is worried. "This isn't like Joan," he thinks. "Even if her old man tied her to a tree, she'd find a way to get here." He tells Smitty to call him if Joan shows up, and goes back to the barracks. Not much I can do until tomorrow, he tells himself. Might as well get some sleep. He tries, but is unable to fall asleep until just before sunrise.

An hour after Joan's crash, two fishermen headed for Alpena spot the wreck and call the State Police. By 2:30, Joan is in the Bay City Memorial Hospital. Before dawn, her mother and father are in the waiting room, sitting side by side on a couch.

"I wish they'd tell us something," Bill fumes.

Jill dabs her eyes. "The nurse said it would be a few hours. Why don't you try and get some rest?"

"I can't," he answers. "What in the hell was she doing up here in the middle of the night? That Eddie character is stationed around here, isn't he?"

Jesus Christ I don't believe this, Jill thinks. We don't even know if Joanie is going to live and he's worrying about why she was up here. In answer to Bill's question, she states, "I'm sure I don't know, Bill."

An hour later, a young doctor enters the waiting room. Jill is happy to see that he's smiling. After introducing himself, Dr. Sloane reports, "Joan's going to be all right. We removed a small clot near her brain and she has some internal injuries."

"How does she look, Doctor?" Jill asks.

"Not bad for what she's been through. She's got a couple of huge black eyes, but there's no facial damage."

"Oh thank God." Jill relaxes. "And thank you, Doctor, for saving our little girl's life." Her smile is bright.

"Can we see her?" Bill frowns, "I've got to ask her a couple of things."

"She won't wake up until Sunday morning. You might as well check into a hotel and get some rest," Dr. Sloane suggests. Turning to Jill, he adds, "I'm sorry we couldn't save the baby."

"The baby?" Jill's eyes open wide. Her smile dies.

Bill looks stunned. "Her husband never ..."

"Joan's not married, Doctor," Jill interjects.

Bill swallows hard. "How far along would you say she was?"

"Nine, maybe ten weeks would be my guess. Joan's going to be fine." Taking Jill's hand and patting it, he assures, "It was a clean miscarriage. Joan will be quite capable of making you a grandma."

"Thank you, Doctor, for everything. You've been wonderful." Jill feels relief, and gratitude. "We'll be back later."

"Yeah, thank you, Doctor," Bill mumbles. He follows Jill out of the waiting room, looking dazed. He walks to the car like a zombie, gets in, and starts the engine. Jill sits next to him silently while he cruises for a motel. She notices he's gripping the wheel tightly and muttering.

"What was that, dear?" she asks.

"I've been doing some arithmetic. Ten weeks ago would be around Joan's birthday. That greasy little bastard nailed her on her birthday."

Joan's been in a wreck, Jill reflects. A blood clot on her brain, she's in pain, she's had a miscarriage. I thank God she's alive and Bill wants to know when she got pregnant. She notices her fists are clenched and deliberately unclenches them. Jill makes a conscious decision to maintain her blithe attitude, which she knows infuriates Bill. She puts her urge to kill on the back burner of her mental stove and trills, "Oh look, Bill, there's a cute place."

Bill pulls into the parking lot of the Twin Cities Auto Court. "He disgraces me at the country club, sends Roddy to the hospital and knocks up my daughter. Not a bad night's work."

"Isn't it wonderful that Joan's okay?" Jill asks. Without waiting for an answer, she continues, "Try and get us a room on the shady side, would you, dear?"

"So much for effervescence," he mumbles, getting out of the car.

"What was that, Bill?"

"Effervescence," he almost shouts. "You said that kid had a certain effervescence about him."

"Don't forget, a room on the shady side."

In 104, a pleasant room on the inn's shady side, Jill sits in her slip in front of a dresser mirror brushing her hair. Bill, lying fully clothed on one of the twin beds with his hands clenched into fists behind his head, is staring at the ceiling light fixture.

"She must've been up here looking for that outlaw."

"I'll bet they were going to get married." Jill slips in the needle. "Eddie seems like the kind of boy who'd marry a girl if he got her in the family way," she adds, thrusting deeper. "It's kind of romantic, isn't it?" she asks, slamming the needle home.

"Romantic?!" Are you crazy?" He sits up suddenly with a fresh thought. "Jesus Christ, married?! The trust fund. We can't have Joan getting married."

Crossing from the dresser to her bed, grinning in her mind like a shit-eating dog, Jill asks, "Would you be a dear and pull down the shade, Bill?"

"We've got to do something." Bill is off the bed, pacing the floor.

Relishing the moment, Jill grins. "I'm sure you'll think of something." She gets under the covers.

Bill pulls down the shade. "I won't be able to sleep," he complains. "I've got a heavy schedule of labor negotiations all next week in Flint. Why don't I catch a bus for Detroit and pick up your car? You can stay here and check on Joan."

"Tomorrow's Sunday," Jill remarks.

"It's never Sunday for E.J. We're having a strategy meeting at his hunting lodge tomorrow. It's going to be hell with those unions. Bunch of goddamn reds."

All you think about is money, money, money, you lousy bastard, she thinks and agrees, "Okay, just leave your car keys on the dresser." Mentally, she adds, and get the hell out of here. The sooner, the better.

Rummaging in Jill's purse, Bill complains, "No keys."

"They're in the kitchen, between the sugar and the coffee canisters. Good luck in your negotiations," she states, silently adding, I hope the unions shove it up your ass.

"We'll need more than luck. The unions are being more unreasonable than usual, the greedy bastards." He throws his keys on the dresser and pecks Jill on the forehead. "Tell Joan I'll try and see her soon. I've got some plans for her." He closes the door quietly.

Jill looks at the door. If it fits into your schedule or suits your purposes, you'll see Joan. In the "I see this person as ..." file of her brain, Jill replaces her image of Bill as a piece of dry toast and relegates him to the image of a cold fish, much lower on her scale.

I see a divorce on the horizon, she thinks as she drifts into off-and-on periods of sleep. At five PM she goes to the hospital, is told that Joan is sleeping peacefully, returns to the motel and sleeps until Sunday morning.

On his bus trip from Bay City to Detroit, Bill Whitman stares out the window. Ignoring the passing landscape, he watches bits and pieces of his life drift by.

He recalls his father, William Wentworth Whitman IV, a God-fearing, penny-pinching, strict Anglican. He could trace his roots back to early Massachusetts settlers and quote scriptures citing chapter and verse. Unfortunately, WWW

IV's heavy-duty lineage did not bring matching funds, so he spent his life as a toiler. Buried in the bowels of the accounting department at American Midwest Foundry and Iron Works, with only a small, grimy window for ventilation, he went to an early grave. More than one thing sped WWW IV on his way: an oppressive work atmosphere, with many ten-hour days and six-day weeks; a suffocating wife who constantly belittled him for sprouting from the sun-starved branch of the old Whitman oak; fumes from the foundry that drifted in his window daily; and most important, the stock market crash. He lost the meager holdings that he had watched grow over the years, as a result of his frugal habits, vanish in a flurry of numbers. He died a month later, heartbroken and penniless.

Bill sighs. He was a freshman at Michigan when his father checked out. His mother moved to Ann Arbor and rented a cottage. She landed a job at an exclusive restaurant, thanks to her name. Bill took part-time work at the campus book store. Between them, Bill was able to stay in college. During his junior year, his mother started running a word-of-mouth catering service to supplement their income. She did enough business with university clubs, fraternities and sororities to make it a worthwhile venture.

Although he helped his mother at many of the events, his awareness of the social caste system kept Bill quiet when working frat houses or sororities. He considered these people superiors by dint of their wealth. He longed for money to go with his name, William Wentworth Whitman V.

Bill met Jill by accident. Rushing out of the kitchen at the Tri-Delt house with a tray of pastries, he plowed into Jill, bounced off her and landed on his ass covered with ladyfingers, lemon squares and sugar cookies. Jill and the two girls with her laughed and salvaged what they could of Mrs. Whitman's homemade delicacies. The Tri-Delt social tea continued without incident and Bill's apology led to two movie dates, an invitation to a dance at the sorority house and a demand from Jill's father that Bill come to dinner during Easter vacation.

After that dinner, seeing a chance to marry into a rich family, Bill had asked for Jill's hand. Her father had sent Bill on his way, using a barnyard term to describe the value of Bill's forthcoming diploma. Even with his excellent grades it took all summer for Bill to find a job.

September 8th, 1933 was a good day for WWW V. Bill received a call from General Motors and an invitation to dinner from Jill's father.

He remembers his second meeting with Mister Barry. Dinner is finished. Bill is in the study, seated across the desk from Jill's father, listening. "You asked to marry Jill last spring and I sent you packing. Are you still interested?"

Bill's cup overflows. He knows that Barry's Mortuary and Funeral Home is only one of Mister Barry's enterprises. "Oh, yes sir."

"All right then, these are my rules. I checked up on you last spring. Your family, fancy names, all lineage and no money, am I right?"

"Well sir, as I said at dinner, I start work at General Motors on the twenty-fifth. I expect to do well there."

"I'm sure you will, my boy. Jill tells us you're good at pushing figures around."

"I excel at accounting, sir."

"That's all well and good, but right now as of today, just between us gentlemen, if it cost a nickel to shit, you'd have to puke, wouldn't you?"

"Well, sir …"

"That's quite all right. No harm in coming from modest means. I didn't inherit this prosperous business. I started as a grave digger. You might say I dug my way to the top. I don't trust any man who can't handle a shovel with proficiency. How are you with a shovel, Bill?"

"I don't know …"

"That's all right. Just having a little joke. Jill's going to bring enough money to the marriage where you won't have to dig ditches, but we've got a problem."

Bill's high-flying spirits start to descend. "A problem?"

"Yes, the Church of England. You're an Anglican, are you not?"

"That's right, Mister Barry. I worship every Sunday."

"That's not good. Jill is a Catholic. What your kind call a Papist."

"Oh no, sir. I'd never use that term."

"Of course not. It's an ancient taunt. I'm having a bit of a laugh with you. Anyway, with you being a protestant and Jill being a Roman Catholic, you'll have to renounce that Anglican nonsense and take instruction in becoming a Catholic. Is that agreeable to you?"

Bill quickly calculates how much money being an Anglican has made for him and comes up with a goose egg. "Yes that's quite agreeable, Mister Barry."

"Fine. Then, this is my proposal and you can take it or leave it. Number one, you've agreed to a Catholic ceremony. Number two, a brand new Buick and a thousand dollars, my gift to you. And number three, a quick wedding. I'm sure I can fix it with Father Dugan to have you two married on …" He runs his index finger down the Sunday column on his desk calendar. "September seventeenth. How's that?"

Bill is bewildered. "So soon?"

"You could drive to work on the twenty-fifth in your brand new Buick, with a bride at home who knows how to cook, or we can forget it. Take it or leave it."

"Oh, I'll take it, Mister Barry. Yes, sir. Thank you, sir."

"Oh, one more thing. Have you ever been hit in the face with a shovel?"

"No sir. I can't say that I have, sir."

"Believe me, son, it's not a pleasant feeling, but it's one you'll experience if you ever so much as raise a finger in a violent manner toward my darling daughter. I have no use for any man who'd raise his hand to a woman. We understand each other on that?"

"Oh yes, sir. I'd never strike a woman."

"Good. Let's shake on it. Leave everything to me. Come back tomorrow night."

On his way home after that meeting, many thoughts chased each other through Bill's mind. The lead thought, a thousand dollars, evoked the image of a thousand, crisp one dollar bills stacked on his desk. He could almost smell the ink.

Next, Bill watched himself driving his brand new Buick through the main gate of the GM plant. "No more trolley cars," he said aloud and smiled.

Visualizing himself and Jill saying I do, Bill wondered about Mr. Barry's change of heart toward him. Guess he realized how far I'll be going with General Motors. I hope Jill says yes tomorrow night. But the seventeenth is so soon. I wonder why? I don't care; the sooner, the better.

What Bill didn't know anything about was the scene that had unfolded in Barry's kitchen the night before the Bill's latest meeting with Mr. Barry.

Sitting in the kitchen, sharing a pot of tea with his wife, Patrick tells of his fears. "As damaged goods or, God forbid, if she's baking a cake, we must get Jill married quickly."

"But we don't know."

"That's just it. Suppose she goes back to college and starts to show signs of being in the family way. It'll be horrible for Jill. Of course, we'll stand by her and do what we can, but her life will be destroyed with an illegitimate child to raise. We can't let that happen to our little girl."

By the time they finish their pot of tea, they've agreed that a quick marriage to Bill would be best for Jill and that Mary should try to help Jill see things that way.

Later that night, sitting on the side of Jill's bed, Mary asks a few questions and then presents her thoughts, "It seems to me, Jill, that you had a beautiful summer of love with an exciting lad and now here you are with the rest of your life before you. A boy like Mike will not likely come your way again in a lifetime, my sweet child." Mary pulls Jill close, giving her a light hug.

Jill sobs softly.

"I'm sorry, dear," Mary continues, "but life is happiness and disappointment and practicality. I'm thinking that tomorrow night when Bill proposes to you, I'd like you to look at him in a favorable light ... as a refuge from your father's stern ways, if nothing else. After this summer's adventures, he'll be probing into your affairs more than ever. He doesn't want you returning to college if you don't marry."

"Oh, Mom. What'll I do?"

"From what I've seen of Bill, he seems quite harmless. I'm sure you can have your way with him. He doesn't look like he'll be demanding bedroom privileges damn near every night. There's much more to marriage than sex. Think about it and make your own decision tomorrow night. Good night, dear."

Saturday night, Jill is neither delighted or dismayed when Bill proposes. For Jill, her life ended when Mike walked off to Miller's Crossing. It's been sleep-walking time for Jill since then. It's easier for her to let her parents do the thinking. I had love for a summer and that's something, she tells herself and accepts.

Sunday afternoon, following the 12:30 Mass, Patrick visits Father Francis Dugan, the pastor of St. Bernard's. The prospect of a convert to Catholicism, a 500-dollar donation to the parish food fund and a bottle of Jamesons is too much for Father Dugan to resist. He agrees to perform the marriage the following Sunday, in the rectory, with the banns to be announced for the three weeks after the ceremony, rather than before.

Sunday, September 17th, WWW V marries Jill Barry. They drive Bill's new Buick to Niagara Falls for a short honeymoon.

The Jill and Bill hookup wasn't the best marriage recorded in Michigan in 1933, but it was tolerable. Jill had Joan. Bill had General Motors.

Bill fell in love with numbers at a young age, when their rigidity dawned on him. Becoming aware of the unwavering agreement that two plus two always equaled four, never four and a half or three and seven-eights, gave him a good feeling, a feeling of security. He immersed himself in the Cost Control Department of GM, as content as a rabbit in a briar patch. He channeled his energy into climbing corporately and socially, not into the bedroom.

Their bedroom was outfitted with twin beds to accommodate Bill's lower back spasms that hit him two or three times a year. His doctor called it sciatica. He visited Jill's bed about once a week, sometimes letting a week or two slip by. This was quite all right with Jill.

As a freshly married couple Jill had tried to pass along some of the things she'd learned from Mike about making the mating experience more enjoyable for her, but Bill was a disinterested pupil. Not much of a performer, he was usually in and out of Jill's bed in six minutes. Jill would then give herself a rub, recalling her nights under the stars and in the barn.

Time moved along and Jill submerged her sexuality and doted on Joan. While Joan was the core of her happiness, Jill enjoyed her home, the kitchen and martini time. She realized how fortunate she was to have money and a husband with a job. She kept a soft spot in her heart for wayfarers. Any man trekking down the road of life, bouncing from here to there, could knock on Jill's door and receive a cup of coffee, a sandwich and a dollar.

As the years piled up, Mike made his way into the "Special Memories" trunk in the attic of Jill's mind, treasured, but seldom opened. Jill focused her love on Joan.

CHAPTER 24

▼

Early Friday morning at Artie's Sugar Bowl, about fourteen hours before her accident, Joan and Sandy had barely started on their coffee and doughnuts when Joan implored, "Sandy, I'm going to have a special weekend with Eddie and I can't go to Ann Arbor with you and Laura. I need you to sign in for me at the Registrar's and then pick up and sign for my class schedule at Admissions. I know that you'll have to stand on two long, slow lines, once as you and then again as me, and I know Laura will bitch about it, but I'm begging you, Sandy. I need this day. I've got so much to do."

The speed and flow of Joan's words, the urgency in her voice and the desperation in her face had elicited Sandy's immediate agreement. Only then did Joan relax. "Thank you, Sandy. Thank you so much."

Sandy had patted Joan's hand. "Do I get to ask questions?"

"Not today, San." Joan took a swallow of her coffee. Not very hot, she noted, then said, "But ... on Monday I'll tell you a really big secret." Joan finished the rest of her coffee. "Thanks again, San." She bolted for the door. "I've got to get rolling," she shouted back over her shoulder.

Sandy smiled to herself as she watched Joan leave. My Blood sister is about to elope.

On the drive to Ann Arbor, Laura had tried to pick Sandy's brain about Joan's plans, but Sandy maintained that she knew nothing and changed the subject. "There'll be hundreds of custom cars and hotrods at this show. Bob's going to be horny all weekend."

"Cars make Bob horny?"

"Seems that way. And that's okay with me. A car might have a candy apple red paint job, four-barrel carburetor and a chrome engine, but ..." Sandy grinned and looked at Laura.

"No pie!" Laura laughed.

Sandy laughed with her and turned up the radio. James Moody was just starting to play "Moody's Mood for Love".

"Listen to that. Isn't that smooth?"

"Dreamy," Laura answered.

"Saxophones make me horny. How about you?"

"Music's nice, but only Normie gets me hot to trot. Oh Sandy, I want to get married so bad."

"Don't we all. It'll happen, Laura. Just give it a chance."

The lines at Ann Arbor had been long, but moved at a good pace. Sandy took care of Joan's business so easily that Laura never bitched a bit. As soon as they were done, the girls headed off back home to get ready to go to the car show.

The guys spent those same Friday hours on the base, Eddie doing all his laundry in preparation for shipping out, Bob washing his car for the trip to the hot rod show, and Norm taking a test for his Ancient History course.

When Bob tried to talk Eddie into going along to Toledo, Eddie declined. He told Bob and Norm nothing of his real plans, only that Joan would be picking him up at midnight and that she had promised him a big surprise.

After evening chow they shot a little pool in the dayroom and drank a few beers. At ll:30 when Eddie took off for the main gate, Bob and Norm headed for the barracks. So Saturday morning, Bob and Norm are surprised to see Eddie in his bunk.

"I thought Eddie said Joan was picking him up at midnight," Norm remarks.

"Probably changed their plans. Maybe they'll go to the show with us. I'll wake Eddie up after I shower."

When he goes into the latrine, Bob sees a note written in soap on the mirror. "Bob, Wake Me Up. Important. Eddie."

While he's getting dressed, Bob shakes Eddie's shoulder. Eddie's eyes snap open. He was having a violent dream and looks ready to fight.

"Eddie, it's me, Bob. You and Joan want to go to the hot rod show?"

Eddie's brain kicks into overdrive. He decides to tell the guys nothing, thinking, this is between Joan and me. He shakes his head. "Sorry, Bob, Toledo's out, but I do need a lift to Detroit. Gimme a few minutes to get ready."

Walking from the barracks to Bob's car, Eddie is thinking about Joan and feeling edgy.

"How come you're wearing your uniform, Eddie?" Norm asks. "You're not hitchhiking today, you're riding with Bob."

"Who are you? Sherlock fuckin' Holmes?" Eddie regrets snapping at Norm the instant the words pass his lips. "I'm sorry, Norm, I got a lot on my mind," he apologizes. "I'm wearing my khakis because Joan asked me to. I guess it's part of her big surprise."

On the drive to Detroit, Eddie is happy to let Bob do most of the talking. The conversation is mostly about candy apple paint jobs and rods with chrome mills. Eddie encourages the car talk, asking about special cams and hot ignition systems. When the guys drop Eddie off downtown, he has kept his secret.

"Don't forget we're on duty Monday morning," Norm shouts as Bob drives away.

I'll get my orders for Alaska Monday morning, Eddie thinks.

Eddie takes the Gratiot Avenue trolley out to Nine Mile Road, walks a few blocks to Joan's house and checks it out. Looking into the garage, he sees that all three cars are gone. A light from the laundry room catches his eye. He has his face pressed against the window, trying to get a better view, when the prowl car silently pulls up and parks in the driveway.

The two cops exit quickly, the young one pulling his gun. Good thing I'm wearing my uniform, Eddie thinks.

The old cop with the beer gut speaks. "Can I help you, son? Did you misplace your keys?"

"Thanks, Officer, but I don't live here."

"I'd never have guessed it." The old cop is smiling.

"Look at this, Dan." The young cop shows the old cop a paper.

"My girlfriend lives here, Officer," Eddie insists.

Eddie sizes Dan up as a regular guy and the young cop as just another hard-on bucking for promotion. Directing his conversation to Dan, Eddie continues, "I was supposed to take Joan to the movies, but she doesn't seem to be home."

Dan flourishes the piece of paper. "I'm looking at an A.H.C. That's police talk for an Angry Homeowner's Complaint. Dates back to June." Dan's enjoying himself. He sees no threat in this young airman. "This A.H.C. makes a certain Edward Flynn persona non grata around this house. I've also got a very strong feeling that you're Edward Flynn."

"That's me, Officer." Eddie smiles his very best smile.

"You understand persona non grata, Edward?"

"Yes, sir, I used to be an altar boy."

"So was Billy the Kid," Dan responds. He and Eddie laugh.

"I guess I'll be on my way ... if that's okay with you?"

"Just so you stay away from here. You're free as a bird."

Eddie walks down the driveway and the young cop finally puts his gun away. "Was that true about Billy the Kid being an altar boy?"

"Shit, I don't even know if Billy the Kid was a Catholic. Sounded good, though, didn't it?" Dan laughs and when he leaves the driveway, he goes up the street in the opposite direction of Eddie. He's a nice kid. I don't want him to feel like he's being shadowed, he thinks.

Eddie walks a few blocks wondering where Joan could be, gets back to Nine Mile and Gratiot and takes the trolley back downtown. He stops here and there for a beer, going by places that remind him of Joan. At the Greystone Ballroom, he calls from a phone booth in the lobby and lets the phone ring ten times before he hangs up. He stops at a bar near the Fox Theater, orders a beer, and sips it. "I'm in Love Again" comes on the juke. Eddie chugs his beer and leaves. A couple of blocks away, he calls Joan from a booth and lets the phone ring a dozen times. At the Flame Show Bar, he remembers how excited Joan was that her phony ID worked. He calls from across the street and lets the phone ring thirteen times. Just for luck, he tells himself. He gets no answer, drinks his way to the Briggs Hotel and checks in. Half-drunk, he falls into an uneasy sleep, thinking, maybe I'll dream up somethin' like Sittin' Bull.

He wakes up at 11 AM on Sunday. After a shower and no shave, he brushes his teeth with his finger, combs his hair and looks in the mirror. My khakis look fresh. My beard ain't heavy. I'll be okay." He checks out, eats lunch at The Brass Rail and spends the afternoon visiting the spots he hit on Saturday.

At sundown, he takes the Gratiot Avenue streetcar back out to Nine Mile. He gets off and heads for Joan's. He walks past her house on the opposite side of the street, sees no one home and asks himself, why would all three cars be gone? He lights a cigarette, takes a drag and thinks, Bet her old man got wind of our plans. Probably took her to live with some old maiden aunt. He shakes his head. Naw. Mrs. Whitman wouldn't go for that.

He walks back to Nine Mile Road and east to the shore of Lake St. Clair. He sits on a bench, stares out at the lake and orders himself, Okay, Eddie, let's get some logic goin' here. Eddie became a logic fan in fifth grade when he discovered Sherlock Holmes. Deductive reasoning and common sense had helped Eddie survive many visits to the principal's office during grammar school and to the dean of discipline in high school. Waiting to see the dean of discipline for the first time, as a freshman, he reasoned, what's the worst he can do to me? Kick me out?

No. All I did was cut gym. Probably a few days detention. I can do a couple of days of jug like takin' a shit.

Eddie had been almost correct. He received two weeks of detention.

Eddie hated school from the first day of first grade until that glorious June evening at Saint Patrick's Cathedral when he was presented with his ticket to freedom, what some would call an undeserved high school diploma.

Only the Catholic Church could have pounded an education into Eddie. It's a tribute to the dedicated nuns, teaching brothers and priests that he graduated. Eddie considered school an intrusion into his life and liberty. He despised having to sit still and not being allowed to talk with his friends seated nearby. He detested tattle-tales and teachers' pets. In twelve years at four different schools, he never raised his hand in the classroom, except to request permission to go to the bathroom. He was proud of that record and of the fact that ninety percent of the time he knew the answer.

Homework was Eddie's main bane. He considered it school's final insult. "If they can't teach you the shit during school time, why should I have to study it on my own time," he often bitched.

His grammar school years were divided among three institutions of learning. Blessed Child Academy, an ironic name for a school accepting Eddie as a first grader, endured him for a year and a half before projectile-vomiting him into a four year stint at boarding school. His father's death ended boarding school and deposited Eddie in parochial school for seventh and eighth grades. The school had a much more cheerful group of nuns than Eddie had encountered in first grade and they were a huge improvement over the discipline-dispensing brothers of Saint Andrew's.

In first and second grade, homework was not a problem. At boarding school homework was done during a tightly-supervised study period from five to six PM. Eddie could usually finish his assignments during study hall. In parochial school he faked and slid his way by, doing some homework and copying some from cooperative friends. When copying, Eddie always got two or three answers wrong to throw off suspicion.

High school submerged Eddie into a maelstrom of homework. With six teachers assigning homework as if they were the only taskmaster, Eddie found himself scrambling to finish assignments at the last moment, if at all. Some days he'd copy answers for Trigonometry homework during Spanish class and then copy answers for History during Trigonometry.

It was due to homework that Eddie had gone into the finals in senior year failing in Chemistry, American History and English. Uncompleted experiments, assignments not done and unwritten book reports, not lack of knowledge, brought Eddie to the brink of disaster. Once again, Eddie's trusty review books rode in and helped him salvage passing grades. This spared Eddie the ignominy of receiving a Certificate of Completion, a bogus document that could be turned in for a real diploma after attending summer school.

Eddie first found out about a Certificate of Completion from his English teacher, a priest who relied on humor as a teaching tool, rather than hitting. Father Bearey knew that Eddie could take a ribbing, so he was having some fun berating Eddie for having no idea about the previous night's assignment. He declared, "Flynn, it's my most fervent wish that you don't succeed in stealing one of our diplomas."

"Why is that, Father?" Eddie knew something good was coming. He enjoyed Father Bearey's sense of humor.

"Because, Mister Flynn, let's propose you purloin one of our precious passports promising potential prosperity. That's alliteration, Mister Flynn, but I digress. Should you succeed and surreptitiously slip into the silent, Stygian shadows with an undeserved, unearned diploma, you will have *de*-valued every other graduate's diploma. You shouldn't even receive a Certificate of Completion stating that you were here for four years. No, Mister Flynn, what you should be given is a Lunch Certificate stating that Edward Flynn has successfully eaten lunch for the last four years."

Eddie had laughed along with the rest of the class, thinking, you got me there, Father. Good one. However, an impression had been made. That afternoon, Eddie went to the school bookstore and bought review books.

Father Bearey had no trouble with Eddie and gave him failing grades reluctantly. This put the priest on a rarely-traveled road. Most teachers resented Eddie at first sight. Why not? The way he sat in a chair, slouched, with the set of his brow and his mouth almost saying, "I dare you to teach me somethin'" Eddie's I'm-not-happy-to-be-here attitude was batted right back at him by the teachers as, "I'm not happy that you're here, either. So sit still, shut up and learn, or else." For his enrollment in boarding school, Eddie's mother had him decked out like he was in England. He was wearing a navy blue Eton suit with an Eton-collared shirt, short pants and regimental knee socks. Eddie had resisted this idea strenuously and was not happy. The principal studied Eddie for less than a moment and decided, Fifty pounds of pure anger dressed up like Little Lord Fauntleroy. I'm sure I'll be seeing this lad on many a Friday afternoon.

In addition to his demeanor, Eddie's love of gazing out the window dreaming of better things rather than staring at the teacher's face with a look of rapt attention while facts were being read, recited or droned, angered many of his instructors.

In one instance, Eddie was trotting silently through the woods with a Mohawk hunting party when reality crashed into his daydream. "Mister Flynn!" Brother Gabriel was on low simmer. "Can you answer that last question for us?"

"Yes, Brother. Besides the mint in Philadelphia, there's a mint in San Francisco and another one in Denver."

"Why don't you look at me when I'm lecturing, Flynn?"

Unable to resist the impulse to push that old flat rock out over the edge of the cliff just enough to make it teeter, Eddie answered, "I don't have to see you to hear you, Brother Gabriel. I listen with my ears. Blind guys learn stuff all the time without seein' the teacher."

Eddie's glib statement of absolute fact brought a laugh from his classmates and a full-bore slap to the side of his head that rocked him and left his ear ringing. He couldn't help thinking, fuckin' guy hits hard for a skinny prick.

From that day on, in Brother Gabriel's class, Eddie stared right through the teacher and played out his daydream scenes with the blackboard as a backdrop. He'd still steal glances out the window at billowing clouds in the sky and bitch to himself, It ain't fair. I could be down by the river throwin' rocks at rats on a nice day like this and here I am, stuck in this prison listenin' to a whole lot of shit I don't care about. Fuck Archimedes, and the horse he rode in on.

Sometimes a minor transgression would get out of hand and grow into a battle of wills. Eddie had this type of contest as a sophomore in World History. Father Callahan was warning the class about the material that his March test would cover. Eddie didn't care. Mesopotamia, the Tigris River. He's just reviewin' shit we did in September. Eddie glanced out the window. Some of the clouds looked like mashed potatoes. He drifted off into a medieval banquet scene. He was seated with the other knights, a heaping plate of venison and mashed potatoes before him, when Father Callahan demanded, "Flynn!"

Eddie's head snapped around. He went into full alert. "Yes, Father?"

"Maybe you'd be good enough to tell the class what's going on outside that window that's more important than what's going on in here?"

Eddie's quick, "Spring, Father. Ain't it great?" earned some laughter and a penance. "A five-hundred-word composition on 'Spring' due tomorrow, Flynn," the priest ordered, adding, "Don't come to class without it." This took place on a Thursday.

Eddie didn't plan on doing this assignment, so he played hooky on Friday. He spent the day on 125th Street, dividing his time between the public library and

Charlie's Pool Hall, a safe haven for truants. In the morning he read a few O. Henry stories and in the afternoon he won two bucks shooting pool. He walked home figuring, "Callahan'll forget that composition by Monday."

Father Callahan had not forgotten the assignment and when it was not produced, he upped the ante to 1500 words. Eddie played the hook for two more days to no avail and wound up going home on Friday with an ultimatum, "Be here Monday with a two-thousand, five-hundred-word composition or Monday night bring your mother to see the principal for a conference about finding a different school for you to attend. The choice is yours."

Eddie considered his answer of spring being more important than the Mesopotamia area to be correct. He felt he was being fucked and was adamant in his refusal to perform this unjust penalty. Only the thought of his mother's voice grinding in his ears with shit like, "I send you to that lovely school and this is the thanks I get," and the familiar, "I try to be both a mother and a father to you two boys," wore down his resolve. Friday night, he decided to quit resisting. Just before falling asleep, he wondered, maybe I'll dream up some way out.

Saturday morning he awakened with his version of a good idea. He went to the living room, took his loose-leaf notebook out of his canvas gym bag and sat down. He began to write, "One fine spring day, Tom and Tim decided to play for all their marbles. Each boy put 1250 marbles into a giant marble ring that they had drawn in the dirt behind the softball field's backstop. Tom won the coin toss and shot first. His marble hit one of the marbles in the ring and went, 'click.' They hit two other marbles, going, 'click, click.' More and more marbles hit each other until all the marbles had hit each other, going, 'click, click, click, click' …" What followed was 208 lines of clicks, 12 to a line, almost 8 loose-leaf pages of clicks.

That's twenty-four hundred and ninety-six clicks, plus those other words, well over Callahan's assignment, he figured. Let's see how Callahan likes this.

Father Callahan didn't like it, but he swallowed his bile and accepted it, stating, "Watch yourself, Flynn. I'm going to be on you like sweat for the remainder of the year."

Eddie considered this bout with authority a draw. He got his twenty-five hundred words, but he got 'em my way, he told himself.

In spite of his negative feelings toward school, Eddie made the best of things and had fun. He could always find buddies ready to bend, break or shatter the rules with him. At parent-teacher meetings throughout Eddie's school years, Eddie's mother heard a wide variety of comments about her son. Merciful teachers, with pity in their hearts for Mrs. Flynn and what they considered "her burden" or "her cross to bear" offered comments such as, "Edward has a good imagination, Mrs. Flynn," or "He certainly has a lot of energy."

Other more realistic educators suggested, "Your son should be doing better work," or "Have you ever thought of taking Edward to a child psychologist?"

The third and largest group of those who dealt with Eddie in the classroom fell more in line with his second grade nun's assessment, "I'm sorry, Mrs. Flynn, but Edward is just a bad boy," and his sophomore home room teacher who answered Mrs. Flynn's question of "How's my boy doing, Father?" with a plaintive, "Oh Mrs. Flynn, I only wish he were old enough to quit school."

High school had a few bright spots for Eddie, football games and dances to attend, and in the spring, the annual boat ride from Manhattan to Rye Beach Amusement Park. The dayliner came equipped with a live combo, a jukebox and girls from Aquinas and Cathedral High Schools. Aside from those glimpses of sunlight among the boiling, cumulonimbus clouds of school, Eddie felt like he was running for his life, jumping from ice floe to ice floe, one jump ahead of a ravenous polar bear. "I just never have time to do homework," he'd often remark to his buddies. "There's a lot more shit goin' on in the world than fuckin' homework."

Even during his junior and senior years with an after-school job as a messenger, a job that allowed ample time for scribbling homework on the long subway rides to Queens and Brooklyn, he'd misuse that time reading *For Whom The Bell Tolls* or *The Great Gatsby*. Eddie found a copy of *Candide* on the subway and read it three times in a weekend. Although he eschewed homework, he could always find an hour or two to read before falling asleep. Eddie was not anti-knowledge, he was simply anti-regimentation.

Fortunately for Eddie's brain, schools' rules and regulations couldn't destroy his healthy curiosity. That curiosity, along with a decent IQ and a taste for reading instilled in him by his mother, fed his hungry head. Mrs. Flynn read to her son from infancy. She started with nursery rhymes and progressed to stories about puppies, kittens, rabbits and woodland creatures. By Eddie's fourth birthday, she had worked her way up to *Alice's Adventures In Wonderland* and *Through The Looking Glass"*. When Tweedledee recited "The Walrus And The Carpenter," Eddie wondered why the oysters had been so dumb. His mother's answer, "Well really, Eddie, they're only oysters," didn't fully satisfy him, but thanks to his mother and the Sunday funnies, especially "The Katzenjammer Kids", he was reading before he started school.

On his odyssey through school Eddie read many books and short stories, some as required reading, others by choice. No teacher told Eddie to read *Tobacco*

Road, The Jungle, Grapes Of Wrath, Elmer Gantry or *Studs Lonigan*. Eddie identified with Studs, thought Studs was a cool guy. The Studs Lonigan trilogy was
definitely not on the recommended reading list in Catholic school. On the other
hand, Eddie did run into many authors in school that struck a chord with him.
Reading "Gift Of The Magi" in class sent him on a hunt for everything O. Henry
ever wrote. Edgar Allen Poe, Mark Twain, Charles Dickens, Jack London and
many more of Eddie's favorites first came his way as required reading.

Another boon to Eddie's education was his thick, leather dictionary, a gift
from his mother's brother John. Uncle John, a used-car salesman, was a font of
street-level aphorisms. Eddie once asked his uncle if a convertible on the front
row of the lot was a nice car. "They don't trade 'em in because they're nice,
Eddie," he answered and laughed, adding, "They're all just shit-boxes, shined
up."

Eddie once marveled at the smile on the face of a happy buyer rolling off the
lot in an emerald green Dodge with a bright red interior. "There's an ass for every
seat," his uncle declared. After Eddie laughed, John added, "And that applies to a
lot more than just cars, Eddie."

"There's no substitute for money," was another of his uncle's pithy comments
that Eddie committed to memory, along with, "The public's got a taste for shit."
Uncle John went on to explain the public's taste graphically. "You take a great big
bowl of ice cream and you put it next to a big plate of steamin' shit and nine
times out of ten, the public'll go for the shit banquet. I can't explain it. I guess the
public is just dumb." Eddie was inclined to agree with his uncle.

Eddie had fun with his dictionary. Words intrigued him. He was just starting
seventh grade, so the first word he sought was "Hooer." He had no luck finding
it. He knew it concerned girls because the older guys on the corner would sometimes remark about girls strolling by, "She's just a fuckin' hooer." Judging by the
roll of the hips of the strollers and their provocative attire, Eddie figured a hooer
must be something like a prostitute. Looking up "prostitute," he found only
"harlot" and "whore." He knew harlot from Religion class, so he looked up
"whore," saw the pronunciation, [hôr], read the word's definition and wondered.

That night hanging on the corner, he asked one of the older guys, "Hey, Lefty,
how do you spell 'hooer?'"

"Hooer? How do you spell hooer? W-h-o-r-e, hooer. Jesus, I'm surprised you
couldn't spell hooer."

"Well, I can spell it now." Eddie thanked Lefty, thinking, my hunch was correct, hooers are whores. We just talk a little different here in the neighborhood.
Sherlock Holmes woulda been proud of me on this case.

Eddie takes a long drag from his cigarette and figures, Number one, Joan's Catholic, so her folks haven't taken her somewhere for an abortion. Maybe they're lookin' for a place where the girls live away from their neighborhoods until they have their babies and come home from "vacation."

Eddie smiles, remembering how one of the neighborhood girls spent a few months upstate vacationing. The old busybodies loved it, but the joke was on them. Stella met a rich guy from Saratoga and he married her. "And the three of them lived happily ever after," Eddie states. He flicks his cigarette butt into the lake, remembers teaching Joan how to do that, and feels sad.

His emotions shift. He brightens at the glimmer of a thought of a happy ending for Joan and himself. This could work out okay for Joan and me in the long run. Suppose her old man puts her in a place like St. Ann's Home for Wayward Girls ... He laughs at the name of the place and reflects, What about the Wayward Boy who knocked up the Wayward Girl? I'm a Wayward Boy and I want my Wayward Girl. I want to marry my Wayward Girl. What the fuck is wrong with that? Eddie takes out the wedding band, kisses it, puts it back into his pocket and returns to his original thought.

If Joan's in a place like that she'll find a way to get in touch with me. Her mom'll help. Bet I can get emergency leave. Joan's mom thinks I'm okay. We might not get married before I ship out, but we'll damn sure get married.

Eddie stands up, turns his back on the lake and walks slowly along Nine Mile. He doesn't stop walking when he gets to Gratiot and a few blocks later he finds himself at Van Dyke. He hadn't meant for it to happen, but he's outside The Cave.

In the club's parking lot, Eddie counts twelve Hogs, all of them black. The only other vehicles on the lot are a yellow Cadillac, a black pickup and a scattering of beat-up-looking, well-rusted-out sedans and coupes that were once "The Toast of Detroit."

Eddie has semi-accepted the idea that he'll be shipping out without seeing Joan. But he has convinced himself that they'll be married shortly. With that almost happy thought, he pushes the door open. My last night in Detroit, might as well get shitfaced. He fingers the gold wedding band in his pocket, walks up to the bar and orders a beer. No matter how bleak shit looks, he decides, there's always the chance for a little bit of luck. He downs half of his beer.

▼

CHAPTER 25

Sunday morning on his way to Higgins Lake for his meeting with E.J., Bill drops by the hospital.

It's 8:30 and Joan's been awake for fifteen minutes. She's in a private room. Her head is bandaged from her eyebrows to the nape of her neck. Her nose is swollen and she has two huge black eyes. Her necklace is on the night stand between a box of tissues and an empty glass.

Joan used her time from 8:15 to 8:30 bombarding the nurse with the usual salvo of questions asked by the newly conscious. "What happened?" "Where am I?" "What day is this?" and "Does my mother know I'm here?" All of her questions were answered satisfactorily and sympathetically. Impressed with Joan's alertness and her grasp of the situation, the nurse cranks the bed to a 45-degree angle and props a pillow behind Joan's back.

"So you can look out the window, hon. Your mom'll be by soon. She was here yesterday but you were sleeping. Think you could eat a little applesauce?"

"That's sounds good. Thank you, Nurse ..."

"Parker. I'm your day nurse. Always just a buzz away."

Moments later, Nurse Parker returns with a bowl of apple-sauce and Bill.

"Your dad is here, Joan."

"Thank you, Nurse Parker." Joan looks at the man standing before her. She draws a blank. She tastes her applesauce.

He's my dad? She asks herself. Looks like a science or math teacher. I don't think I know this man.

"I'll leave you two alone for awhile." Nurse Parker quietly closes the door behind her.

"Joan, it's me, your father."

I've never seen this man before, she thinks and doesn't answer.

Bill is impatient. Oblivious to Joan's battered face and bandaged head, he continues, "So how are you doing, Joan?"

I have no idea how I'm doing, runs through her head, but she answers, "Okay, I guess. Nurse Parker says you're my dad, huh?"

"That's right. I'm your dad." Bill tries to sound warm. "And I brought you a nice brochure for you to look at." He takes out the old brochure from Our Lady of the Lakes that he fished out of the family album.

Joan looks at the brochure, then back at Bill. "You couldn't say you were my dad if you weren't, could you?" Joan takes a full spoon of applesauce.

"Absolutely not. Now look that over." He begins to sound more dictatorial than warm. "It's where you'll be going to college as soon as you get out of here." Bill is becoming irritated with Joan's manner. "Are you okay?"

Joan is enjoying the coolness of the applesauce in her mouth and the smoothness of it going down her hot, dry throat. She is bewildered by this man. She takes another spoonful of semi-liquid relief. "I guess I'm okay." Joan puts the brochure on her night table and takes another heaping spoon of applesauce. "Mmm, that's so cool on my throat."

"That's good. Well I've got to go. Strategy meeting. The greedy unions are giving us trouble. You read that brochure now." Bill leans over to kiss Joan's cheek.

She pulls away. She stops and looks at Bill. "Are you sure you're my father?" She goes back to her applesauce.

"Yes. I'm sure I'm your father."

"Then prove it. Raise your right hand to God and swear that you're my father."

"This is stupid. I don't have to swear I'm your father. I *am* your father." Bill is growing more agitated.

"Not if you won't raise your right hand and swear to God, you're not." Joan scrapes her spoon around the bowl, scooping up the last of her treat.

Bill raises his right hand. "Okay, okay. I swear to God that I'm your father."

"Well, all right. I believe you, but I don't remember you. You got any ID?"

"This is absurd."

"Don't you at least have a business card?"

Bill digs out a business card and gives it to Joan. She lets him peck her on the cheek and he's off to Higgins Lake.

Jill enters Joan's room at 8:45. Five minutes earlier and she'd have bumped into Bill. She's happy to see Joan sitting up, but her eyes tear up at the sight of her. The only thing that stops Jill from bursting into tears is the big smile Joan is giving her.

"Oh Mom, it's so good to see you."

"Is it all right to hug her?"

"Go right ahead. Joan's doing real well." Nurse Parker leaves the room.

Jill notices the Our Lady of the Lakes brochure and asks about it.

"Some man who said he was my dad came by. He said he was having trouble with greedy labor unions. He left his business card."

"That's your dad, all right."

Fingering the brochure, Joan remarks, "He said I'd be going to school here."

"Only if you choose to. It's a peaceful place. Gran went to college there. You don't remember your dad?"

"Maybe I'll remember him tomorrow." Joan moves her hand from the brochure to her necklace. She picks it up, looks at it and asks, "Mom, who's Eddie?"

"He's a young man you know. You've been seeing a lot of him this past summer."

"Is he nice?"

Jill smiles. "He's got a few rough edges, but I think he's pretty nice."

"Tell me about Eddie, Mom?"

Nurse Parker comes in, takes away the empty bowl and spoon and says to Jill, "If Joan nods off, it's not the company. It's normal with her kind of injury. Buzz if you need me."

"Thanks, Nurse Parker."

"Tell me all about Eddie, Mom," Joan repeats.

"Well, I only met him once. We had him over for Sunday dinner. It was a wonderful dinner, roast chicken. You and I spent all afternoon in the kitchen. You made an excellent salad. Eddie knew that you used balsamic vinegar and real olive oil. I thought he was the perfect dinner guest.

"Did that man who says he's my dad like Eddie?"

"Not really. Eddie got on the wrong side of your dad by saying the unions were necessary to keep bosses from gobbling up the whole pie."

"Oh?" Joan looks perplexed.

"Then when he told your dad money wasn't necessary for happiness that finished it. But your dad didn't like Eddie from the instant he met him. I could feel it."

"Why, Mom? If you and I like Eddie, why would Dad not like Eddie?"

"Eddie isn't the kind of boy your dad likes. Eddie's too …" Jill searches for the right word. "Free," she declares. "I guess free is the right word. Anyway, I like him enough for both your dad and me. And most important, you and Eddie love each other, just like I read on your pendant."

Joan yawns.

"You lie back and sleep and see if you can remember some of the things you and Eddie did this summer. You seemed to be having such a good time. I'll be right here when you wake up." Jill cranks the bed flat.

Joan smiles, puts her head back on the pillow and is asleep within moments.

Joan doesn't awaken until late afternoon. She opens her eyes and sees her mother sitting beside her bed.

"Hi, Mom."

"Hi, sweetie." Jill smiles. "Good sleep?"

Before Joan can answer, Doctor Sloane enters the room. "Good afternoon again, Mrs. Whitman. Hi, Joan." Jill and Joan return his greeting. He takes a clipboard from the foot of Joan's bed.

"Joan fell asleep right after breakfast, Doctor."

"Thank you." He marks his chart and looks at Joan. "And you woke up …"

"Just now, Doctor." Joan smiles.

"About seven hours." He marks his chart again. "Was it a good sleep?"

"I think so, Doctor," Joan answers.

He looks back at Jill. "Did she toss around? Seem restless?"

"She moved a few times, changing her position, but she didn't seem troubled."

"Sounds good. I'd call it a healing sleep."

"What about my memory, Doctor? I seem to have some blank spots."

"That's common with your type of head injury, Joan. In most cases, there's a full return of memory." He looks at Jill. "I look for a complete recovery. Sleep's a big help. With it comes dreaming and remembering."

"That's good news," Jill responds. "Thanks again, Doctor."

He looks at the two smiling faces. "I'm going to leave you two now." He looks at his watch. "Four-twenty," he announces, "I've got sick people to see." He laughs at his own joke, then looks at Jill. "Are you taking care of yourself?"

"Yes, Doctor?"

"Appetite okay?"

"I'm eating. Not much, but I'm eating."

"When you get your appetite back, try Otto's. It's right across the street. See you both tomorrow." He opens the door.

As Jill and Joan say goodbye to Doctor Sloane, cooking aromas drift through the slowly closing door.

After the doctor leaves, Jill asks, "How do you feel, Joanie?"

"Hungry, Mom."

"That's good news." Jill buzzes for the nurse.

The swing shift nurse arrives and Joan tells her that she's hungry.

"Doctor Sloane predicted that. He suggested a small steak, a baked potato and dessert."

"That sounds wonderful."

"I could go for something like that, myself," Jill jokes.

The nurse offers, "I could get you something, Mrs. Whitman." Jill declines and the nurse turns to Joan. "How do you like your steak, Joan?"

Joan looks to Jill, searching for a clue. "Ummm …?"

"I think you usually take rare, don't you, dear?"

"Yes, rare. And thank you, Nurse. What is your name?"

"Penn, dear, Nurse Penn. You can just call me Pennsy. Be right back."

Minutes later Pennsy returns with Joan's meal and Joan hits it like an offensive lineman at a banquet. Jill is happy to see Joan eat with such gusto. After Joan finishes her milk and a slice of chocolate cake, Jill asks, "So are you getting any memories of your dad?"

"No, Mom. I'm sorry, but I just can't recall him at all." She breaks into a broad smile. "But I was dreaming about Eddie," she adds, "I saw Eddie's face."

"Happy dreams?"

"Oh yes, Mom. We're in love."

Jill smiles. "I knew that, dear."

"Mom, we were going to get married."

I wonder if she'll remember being pregnant, Jill thinks. "I know, Joanie," she answers. "I'm sorry you weren't able to get married. I've never seen you happier than this summer." She pauses and then adds, "Can I do anything?"

Jill watches Joan's mouth start to turn downward at the sides. "The Air Force is sending Eddie to Alaska, Mom."

"I'm sorry, honey. I didn't know that."

"Alaska, Mom," Joan wails.

Jill takes Joan's hand and pats it. "People come back, dear," she offers, "even from Alaska."

"If he has to leave thinking I didn't show up for our wedding, he might think I don't love him anymore." Joan's eyes get watery.

"He could never think that. Can we call him at his base?"

Joan thinks. "I sent a couple of letters to Eddie. Oscoda, but I can't think of his squadron numbers ... it's a radar base."

"A radar base in Oscoda. That could be enough. I'll be right back."

"Thanks, Mom."

Jill goes out to the phone booth in the waiting room and starts to brew her magic. "Hi, Operator. I'm Jill Whitman, the Red Cross representative here at Bay City Memorial. I'm hoping that you'll be able to help us get in touch with a young airman whose fiancée was involved in an accident on the way to their wedding. Do you think you can help us, dear?"

"I'll sure try."

"Thank you so much. All we know is the young man is a radar operator at a radar base in Oscoda. We don't know his squadron number."

"Hold on just a second." Within ninety seconds Jill not only has the phone number of the 646th, she's been put through to the orderly room.

In the orderly room, the Officer of the Day sits alone, having sent the squadron clerk to evening chow. The phone rings. He answers, "Six-Four-Six."

Without going into the wedding part of the story, Jill tells the O.D. that the Red Cross wants to contact Edward Flynn concerning a family emergency. The O.D. is friendly and helpful. He explains to Jill that Edward Flynn's crew isn't due back on the base until eight o'clock Monday morning. He offers to take a message and writes down, "Joan in hospital in Bay City. Urgent that you call, Jill." She thanks the O.D. profusely and hangs up, feeling proud of her accomplishment.

She returns to Joan's room and tells her how well things went on her phone call. "And this nice Lieutenant Summers or Sumpter said he'll see to it personally that Eddie gets our message tomorrow morning. Wasn't that sweet?"

In the orderly room, Lieutenant Sumner looks at the paper. Red Cross, my ass. He crumbles the paper into a ball. That was probably Flynn's girlfriend. He throws the paper into the wastebasket. To hell with her, he thinks. Flynn's off to Alaska tomorrow, and good riddance.

Back at the hospital, Jill feels brand new. "I was thinking I might go down to the city tomorrow and pick up a few things. Is there anything special you'd like? One of your nightgowns? Don't worry, I'll pick out a few things for you."

"Thanks, Mom. I wonder ..."

"Whatever it is, is fine. What do you wonder?"

"Well, I'd like to write Eddie a letter."

At the word write, Jill opens her purse and takes out a small pad and a mechanical pencil. She holds her pencil poised, secretary-style, over the pad and asks, "Where do we send this letter? Oscoda?"

"Oh no, I forgot. Eddie will be gone before the letter ever gets to him."

"What about Sandy? Doesn't she date one of Eddie's friends?"

Joan looks at Jill. She's puzzled. Who is Sandy dating? She wonders. Joan sees a face, but no name comes with it. She thinks, it'll come to me.

"Here." Jill hands the pad and pencil to Joan. You write your letter to Eddie. I'll give your letter to Sandy. She can probably get to Eddie through his buddy. Just in case Eddie's message gets fouled up or if they ship him out without him having a chance to call."

"Oh, Mom, that sounds perfect."

"You can say a lot more in a letter, too." Jill smiles.

CHAPTER 26

▼

While Joan is writing her note to him, Eddie is getting the feel of The Cave. The bar has a good smell to it, kind of a combination of motor oil and stale draft beer, with just a hint of wood thrown in.

Scanning the bar, Eddie notices that both pool tables and both pinball machines are busy. "Drinking Wine Spo-Dee-O-Dee" is blaring from the jukebox and three couples in a booth are singing along. A half dozen couples are dancing. Lively joint, Eddie observes, and on a Sunday night, too.

Eddie finishes his beer, orders another and thinks, Joan would love this place. Immediately, an empty feeling goes through him.

He takes his beer and heads for the jukebox. It's a winner. He puts in a quarter and punches up six tunes. On his way back to the bar, he hears, "Hey Eddie!" Turning, he sees that the two pool shooters at the far table are Dave and Trash. Eddie goes over and joins them. They exchange handshakes and Dave comments, "I almost didn't recognize you in uniform, man."

"I'm hitchin'. It's a big help."

"Welcome to The Cave," Dave chalks his cue.

"We call it the Cobra's Den," Trash adds.

"Great place." Eddie smiles. "Even smells good."

"Where's your little momma?" Trash asks.

"Her old man thinks I'm bad company," Eddie states evenly. "He's probably hiding her out with some relatives."

Dave misses a shot on the five ball. "That sounds like it'd make a good blues tune." He can tell Eddie's feeling down.

"That's no bullshit and I'm shippin' out to Alaska tomorrow."

Trash banks the eight ball in the corner pocket.

"This is my last night in Michigan," Eddie declares. "I'm gonna miss this fuckin' state."

"Sounds like we got some drinking to do," Dave puts up his cue and heads for the bar. Trash lays his cue on the table and introduces Eddie to the three pool shooters at the next table.

"This is Spot Shot, Dutch, and Big Bob," he tells Eddie, and to the pool shooters he boasts, "This is Eddie, the guy that was with us up in Saginaw when we did a job on them fucking ground-pounders." Everybody says hi to each other and then Trash and Eddie join Dave in a booth. One of the tunes that Eddie played comes on the jukebox.

"Good Morning Judge," Trash shouts, "the story of my life!" The three of them laugh and Trash leads them singing along …

> *The other night I took a ride,*
> *With little ol' Lucy Brown,*
> *We went to all the honky-tonks,*
> *We really got around.*
> *She's five-foot-two with eyes of blue,*
> *And pretty as a queen.*
> *I didn't know her pop was a city cop*
> *And she was just fifteen.*
> *Good morning, Judge.*

At the chorus of "Good Morning, Judge" it seems like everyone in the bar shouts out the words. I love Joan and she loves me, Eddie thinks. We'll get together. He cheers up a little at this positive thought and chugs his beer.

Trash spots a pretty young girl wearing jeans and a black sweatshirt. Zipping over to the bar, he takes her out onto the dance floor. As he passes by their booth, he grins at Dave and Eddie, shouting, "Hey guys, lookit this—it's little ol' Lucy Brown."

"My name's Rita," the girl corrects, and the guys laugh.

Eddie has a good time hanging out, but at midnight he announces, "I better hit the road. I gotta be back in Oscoda by eight AM or it's the stockade for me."

"Why don't we take you back?" Dave asks.

"It's a hell of a way, man. I couldn't ask you to do that."

"Bullshit," Dave stands up. "We'll make a night of it." Turning to Trash, he asks, "What do you say, Trash? You think your little sweetie pie wants to go riding?"

"We could stop at Slim's," Trash answers, "it's about halfway." He jumps up on the tabletop and shouts, "Who wants to go scrambling?"

Rita is ready to ride. Out in the parking lot she gets on Trash's machine and Eddie gets on behind Dave. Five other bikes fall in behind Trash and Dave. Two of the guys are wearing old leather pilot helmets with goggles and ear-flaps flapping. Three of them are wearing black leather jackets with yellow coiled cobras painted on the back. Three other girls go along, two of them wearing Harley caps with white bills, the other girl wearing a pirate-style bandanna. The Cobras amuse themselves by tossing a bottle of whiskey from bike to bike on their way to Saginaw. They pull into Slim's as he's getting behind the wheel of his Olds. He reopens and everybody dances and drinks until dawn.

At daybreak, the Cobras hit Highway 23, stopping for gas, coffee and doughnuts at an Esso station just north of Bay City. Rolling through Tawas at twenty minutes to eight, Eddie knows he'll be on time.

Captain Becker and his wife live in a small, rented house about eight miles north of Oscoda. Becker's wife, Lurline, loves cleaning house and chases after microbes with relentless diligence. No germ escapes her passionate pursuit of antiseptic perfection. All the rooms smell of Lysol, Clorox or Pine Sol. Every second Wednesday the whole house reeks of ammonia. All the furniture is covered in form-fitting, clear plastic covers. The small lawn and few flowering shrubs are impeccably groomed. This groundskeeping is performed by airmen on Squadron Detail, a clear violation of Air Force regulations.

Awakening with no trace of heartburn, Becker leaves the house without waking his wife and gets into his immaculate Buick Roadmaster. The Buick, Becker's pride and joy, is his only link to the old days in Buffalo. Sitting behind the wheel, he reminisces about the times before the Air Force reactivated him.

Flicking a tiny speck of dirt off his dash, he looks at the dashboard. He looks at the clock. "Seven forty-five," he says aloud. "In fifteen more minutes, I get to send Flynn to Alaska." Smiling, he starts up the car. Easing out of his driveway onto Highway 23 he exults, "I only wish I was sending him to Sing Sing." The Dynaflow transmission responds to his urging and he starts to sing "The Air Force Hymn".

Almost to the base road, relishing the thought of the look on Flynn's face when he gets the Alaska news, Becker sees a bunch of motorcycles approaching from the south. What the hell is that? he wonders. "Noisy bastards," he mutters and gives the Buick a nudge.

Eddie spots Becker's Buick. He leans forward and tells Dave, "That's the prick who's sending me to Alaska." Dave screws it on. His Hog jumps, and the rest of the Cobras do the same. Barely beating Becker to the base road, they churn up a cloud of gravel dust that blows directly onto the Buick. Rolling up his window, Becker curses, "Goddamn clowns." He doesn't notice Eddie in the group. What the hell could be going on? He drives through the slowly-settling gravel dust.

The Cobras pull up to the main gate, blocking the road, while Eddie says his goodbyes. Becker waits behind them, boiling with rage. He blows his horn. One of the guys, wearing a greasy denim jacket with brads on the back spelling JON, shouts, "Hey, Eddie, watch this."

Cranking his handlebars all the way to the right, he lays out his bike and does some doughnuts right in front of the Buick, spraying it with gravel. He then digs out, giving the car another dose of gravel, flips Becker the finger and takes off down the base road toward Highway 23. The rest of the guys tear after him. Gravel is flying like shotgun pellets during duck season.

The dust finally settles and Becker rolls up to the main gate. He shouts at the air policeman on duty, "What the hell was that all about?"

The AP, a former A1/c who had been demoted to an A2/c by Becker the previous month for returning to duty two hours late, is smiling in his heart. He deadpans, "Looks like a motorcycle club to me, sir. They gave one of our men a lift."

"Motorcycle club, my ass," Becker spits, looking up the road where Eddie is walking toward the orderly room. "Don't bother telling me who they dropped off." He drives away abruptly, quickly pulls abreast of Eddie and parks. Leaning over and rolling down his passenger window, he shouts, "Flynn!"

Eddie snaps to attention and salutes smartly. "Airman Basic Edward Flynn, reporting for duty, SIR!" he shouts, standing rigid.

Redness begins to creep up from Becker's neck to his face. Eddie notices its progress with great pleasure. Becker's heartburn comes back with intensity, his temples begin to pound and the vein in his forehead starts wiggling.

I'd love to give this prick a stroke, Eddie thinks.

Becker speaks. "At ease, Flynn. How did I know that it would be you riding with that bunch of outlaws?"

"I'd say it was just a lucky guess, sir." Eddie watches Becker's redness deepen. Come on, stroke, he roots, grinning inwardly.

Becker hates that smug look. "Get up to my office, pronto," he orders. "I've got a big surprise for you."

"Yes sir!" Eddie semi-shouts, snapping to attention, saluting and holding it. Becker returns Eddie's salute, grimaces and drives quickly to his special parking space next to the orderly room. Eddie keeps Becker waiting three minutes, walking to the orderly room at a leisurely pace.

With Flynn at attention in front of his desk for the last time, Becker begins to feel better. "Nothing you do surprises me, Flynn," he preaches. "I'd expect you to return to the base escorted by the one percent of the motorcycle riders who give all the rest a bad name." He pauses for effect. "I just want you to know, Flynn," he continues, "guys like you lose out in the end. Do you know why you're in my office this morning?" Becker picks up Eddie's orders and slaps them against his open hand.

"It'd sure make me happy if those were orders for Alaska, Captain."

In the act of handing the orders across his desk, Becker stops. "What do you mean by that, Flynn?"

"Well, Captain, I've been hopin' to get shipped to Alaska for a couple of months. I was thinkin' of puttin' in a request for transfer, but I figured you'd turn it down, not wantin' to lose a top-notch radar operator like me."

Becker grows impatient. "Get on with it. Why Alaska?"

Eddie pops a broad smile. "*Outdoor Life*, I made some money from them for pictures I took of deer around here. Enough to buy an Argus C-3. They said they'd pay me big money for pictures of moose and caribou. But there's none of them around here. I'd have to be in Alaska to see those kinds of animals. Make me a happy guy, Captain, and tell me these orders are for Alaska."

"Always steal the other fellow's thunder," Eddie's mom used to tell him. Thanks for that one, Mom, he thinks, watching Becker's face re-redden.

Accepting the papers, Eddie intensifies his act. "I can't thank you enough for this, Captain. This is really great. I'm gonna be a full-time photographer after I'm through makin' the world safe for democracy. Is there anything else, sir?"

Studying Eddie's face, Becker's eyes narrow. He's *got* to be bullshitting me, he reasons. This little bastard is trying to deprive me of the pleasure of sending his ass to the frozen North. But a thread of doubt is becoming a string. Flynn does look genuinely happy.

Checking Flynn's face closely for any clue of unhappiness, Becker continues, "You've got to be at Camp Stoneman by Saturday. I hope you fuck up and don't make it. I'd love to see you behind bars. Pack your gear and be off this base by noon."

"It'll be my pleasure, sir, and thanks again." Eddie smiles broadly and salutes.

Becker continues his study of Eddie's features. That goddamn smile looks real, he thinks. This crazy son of a bitch could really want to go to Alaska.

Eddie holds his salute and widens his smile. He pictures himself putting a ring on Joan's finger and his face beams. Becker doesn't return Eddie's salute. "Just get the hell out of here," he almost shouts.

Eddie brings his hand down to his side smartly. He executes a precise left face and exits Becker's office, closing the door quietly behind him. I guess I finally out-militaried him, Eddie figures. He lights up a smoke. Fuck Becker. He ain't my problem, he tells himself and smiles.

Watching Flynn walk out of his life doesn't bring Becker the joy he was anticipating. His heartburn returns with renewed intensity. He gets out his old, reliable Alka-Seltzer bottle and finds it empty; as empty as the emptiness within him.

CHAPTER 27

▼

Eddie packs his duffel bag and drops it at Supply, where the clerk on duty assures him that it will be on a Greyhound that afternoon. Eddie picks up his small canvas travel bag and heads for the Radar Ops building to say his goodbyes. It's ten o'clock. Dog crew have been on duty for two hours.

The break room is unoccupied except for Ma Barker. She's next to the old rusty Coke machine, nursing her litter. Eddie picks up some broken doughnut parts and feeds them to her, saying, "It was a hell of a night, wasn't it?" He pats her on the head and goes into Radar Ops.

It's a normal Monday morning. Only six tracks are on the plotting board, Captain Ross is dozing in his chair and all the guys are manning their positions. Climbing up on the dais, Eddie huddles with Norm and Bob, showing them his map.

"I'm on Highway 23 down through Flint and Ann Arbor," he points out. "Then I pick up Route 12 to the Windy City and from there on it's Route 66."

Norm frowns. "Why are you taking 66? There are more direct routes to San Francisco," he nags. "66 will leave you in L.A. You'll have to go up the coast on 101."

Eddie smiles, thinking, there's no chance of changing this guy, and explains, "I'm taking 66 because I always liked the song and besides, it'll be somethin' I can tell my kids."

When he says, "kids," he thinks of Joan. "Listen, Bob, this is real important. If you hear anything about Joan, let me know. I'll get the Red Cross to get me an emergency leave. Guess I should tell you, me and Joan were gonna get married.

Anyway, it didn't pan out. But the emergency leave will give me a couple of days to get married if Joan turns up before I'm on the boat. Okay?"

"Sure thing, Eddie." Bob's face is serious.

"I thought you were going to get married when you wore your khakis to Detroit," Norm boasts. "You knew you were getting shipped out to Alaska before you got orders, didn't you?"

"Norm, if the Air Force don't make a general out of you, you gotta go on the cops. You'd make a great detective." Eddie laughs. "Nobody told me about the orders for Alaska, but I suspected it and when I told Joan we decided to get married. But I guess her old man found out and hid her out. It's that simple." Eddie claps Norm on the back.

"I gotta say goodbye to the rest of the guys and be off the base by noon." Shaking hands with Bob and Norm he adds, "Anyway, we had a lot of fun here at the old Six Four Six, didn't we?" Looking around he asks, "I don't see Brownie?"

"He's in town," Norm answers.

"The Saginaw Express must be in," Eddie smiles. "Tell Brownie I said so long." Eddie says goodbye to the rest of the crew and finishes by waking Captain Ross.

"I'm off to Alaska," Eddie states, 'and I just wanted to tell you it was great workin' with you, Captain. DiNessi told me you gave Becker and Sumner a good ration of shit. I want to thank you for that."

"They had it coming. I heard you got shafted. It's been good working with you, Eddie. I hope you catch a short tour."

They shake hands and Captain Ross continues, "Don't get in too much trouble in Alaska." They both laugh.

Eddie leaves the Ops Room with his throat feeling like he swallowed a cannonball. Walking through the break room, he looks at Ma Barker and the pups and his eyes fill. I've got time for a last cup of vanilla extract coffee with Arbo, he thinks as he heads for the mess hall.

Eddie walks into the mess hall and is greeted by Arbo. Arbo assumes a cowboy shoot-out pose. "Be off this base by noon, Podnah," he shouts. Eddie laughs. He leaves his small canvas travel bag by the front door and he and Arbo shake hands and pound each other on the back a few times.

"How'd you know about my deadline?"

"You didn't see DiNessi when you left the orderly room, did you?"

"No, I didn't."

"Because he was in the supply closet, listening to you and Becker. He says you did great."

"Well, I shoulda been an actor then, because I got a big bag of shit to contend with. I gotta find out a thing or two."

"Ask away, but let me tell you, your eyes are redder'n Maggie's drawers."

Eddie checks his watch. "I been up twenty-four hours and I've been drinkin', but I got a big, big problem."

Arbo senses Eddie's bad feeling and holds off saying, Of course you got a problem, you're bein' sent to Alaska. Instead he asks, "What's wrong, Eddie?"

"My girlfriend's bein' hid out somewhere by her old man. We were gonna get married before I shipped out. Last Friday, to be exact."

"When do you have to be at Stoneman?"

"Saturday."

"You flying?"

"Hitchin'."

"Stoneman's up near 'Frisco."

"I know. I got it figured out. I'll make it. Arbo, what do you know about emergency leave? Suppose I'm at Camp Stoneman or even up in Alaska? I told Bob I could get a couple of days to get married. I'm right, ain't I?"

"You're half right. A guy could get emergency leave to get married, *but* only if she is 'with child' as they say in the Bible." Eddie smiles. Arbo continues. "How about some chow? I'll whip us up a ham and pepper omelet."

"I am kinda hungry. All I ate for breakfast was a couple of powdered sugar doughnuts. Funny, I drank all night but I never really got shitfaced."

"Sometimes alcohol don't work."

Arbo and Eddie go to the stove. Arbo gets out a bottle of olive oil, six eggs, a slab of ham, a large onion, and a bell pepper. While's he's cooking up his omelet in a big cast iron frying pan, he's talking. "You can't go out drinking all the time without eating. It'll fuck up your liver. As long as you eat, you can drink your ass off without hurting your liver." Arbo gets out his big jug of vanilla extract, pours two mugs half full and adds coffee. He and Eddie clack their mugs together.

"Here's to guys like us," Eddie toasts.

"There ain't enough of us," Arbo adds, and they both laugh.

While they're eating, they drink a second vanilla extract coffee and discuss what Eddie can do about his situation.

"I'd say you're probably right about her father hiding her out, and I'd say all you can do right now is get your ass to Stoneman, ship out and hope for the best. I'm sorry, but unless Joan's pregnant, you're mortally fucked on any emergency leave."

"She is pregnant, Arbo. And that's Joan's kid and my kid, not her father's."

"Her being pregnant changes things a lot. Not only will you be able to get a furlough, but once she starts to show, you'll hear from her folks quick."

Eddie takes heart. "You really think so, Arbo? No bullshit?"

"No bullshit, Eddie. It's like an unwritten law. You got a girl in the family way who wants to get hitched, the Red Cross will get you leave, even from Alaska. A kid in our outfit got an emergency leave back during the Big War. They sent him home from England."

"I guess I gotta go with that. Joan's mom is okay, it's just her old man." Eddie looks at his watch and starts to pick up his tray.

"Leave the fucking trays. I'll walk you." Arbo drapes his right arm over Eddie's shoulder as they walk toward the door. "Your thing to do right now is to get to Stoneman. This is no time to fuck up. You know that. I'm saying it so that I hear myself remind you of it. Maybe you'll have a message waiting for you at Stoneman. Maybe you don't hear nothing until Alaska, but from what you said, I'm sure you and Joan will get married. Let me know how it all turns out. Just drop me a postcard here at the Six Four Six. I ain't getting shipped nowhere. I run the best mess hall in the Midwest."

"In the whole fuckin' U.S., you mean." They laugh.

Eddie and Arbo shake hands. Eddie picks up his bag and starts walking down the mess hall path toward the base road. Airmen are drifting toward the mess hall for noon chow.

"Fuck 'em all, Eddie," Arbo shouts after him.

Eddie turns and waves. "Fuck the world, Arbo," he shouts back, and they laugh again.

Eddie turns off the path, walks down the main base road and shows his orders to the new A.P. on duty at the gate. He's down on Highway 23 with his thumb up a full two minutes before Becker's noon deadline.

CHAPTER 28

▼

Nine o'clock Monday morning, Jill looks in on Joan. Nurse Parker tells Jill that Joan will probably sleep until noon. Jill asks her to take a message for Joan if Airman Eddie Flynn calls and leaves the hospital feeling no urgency about Joan's letter. Eddie'll probably call before I get home, she figures.

After picking up some new clothing and toilet articles for herself and Joan, she drives over to Sandy's and finds no one home. She wedges a note in the front door asking Sandy to call her at the club, and heads for the Harbor Lights.

At the club, she orders a tuna salad sandwich and a martini. She lights a cigarette and sits at her table, looking out at Lake St. Clair. She wonders whatever happened to Mike, that wild boy who passed through her life like a comet the summer before she married Bill.

The waitress brings her order. Jill sips her martini, sips it again and it's September 1, 1933, a date she'll never forget. She recalls that late-night talk with her mother. "I have absolutely forbidden your father from even speaking to you, until the murderous rage within him subsides."

Jill is crying. She is sitting on the side of her bed. Her mother is seated next to her with her arm around Jill, consoling her. "Your father is from the other side. He doesn't understand American ways. Thinks he's still back in Donegal. He's down in the basement punching that big bag of his."

Jill's crying intensifies.

"We must get in touch with that lad you've been seeing. Mike, isn't it?"

"Yes, Mom. Mike," Jill gets out between sobs.

"Your father believes that Mike took advantage of you and he means to beat him within an inch of his life."

"Mike never forced himself on me, Mom. We're in love."

"I'm sure you are. And Mike seems like a fine lad, the little I've seen of him. But he's in serious trouble with your father. What farm is Mike working at?"

"Krajewski's place, by Mill Pond."

"Get dressed, sweetie. You and me are going to sneak out and see Mike." She pauses. "I know you know how to do that." They exchange smiles, although Jill's smile is a small one.

"That's a good girl. I'll tell you my plan on the way to Krajewski's."

Jill leads the way, out her bedroom window, across the porch roof to the apple tree's nearby branch and the short drop to the back yard. The moon is half full, spending its time ducking in and out of large dark clouds.

On the two-mile walk down Mill Pond Road, past fields of beans, sugar beets and hay, Jill's mother explains, "Your father is a big man here in town, owning the funeral parlor and all. He's prosperous because people continue to die and require burial, even in these hard, mean times. He's also in with the local politicians and the sheriff."

Jill breaks into heavy sobs. Her mom stops walking and takes Jill's shoulders in her hands, as if to shake her. "Listen to me, girl. You must be strong." The moon goes behind a cloud. "I'm sure you love Mike, so you must help me." She continues, "After he finishes beating Mike to a pulp, he plans on getting the lad charged with moral turpitude. I heard him on the phone with one of his political connections. He was asking about hypotheticals, as he called them. I call them 'what ifs.'"

Jill wipes her eyes on the back of her hand and listens intently.

"He was asking about prison terms for statutory rape."

"Oh God, Mom. Mike never raped me and I'm twenty-one. We could get married."

"Face it, girl. Mike's a drifter in a nation of drifters. It's almost harvest. He'll soon be gone, jobless, into an ocean of joblessness. Your father will make sure Mike does time in prison. He's going to have the sheriff serve the moral turpitude writ on him right after he beats the hell out of him."

"That's not right."

"Of course it's not right, it's life. If Mike doesn't get out of town tonight, he's going to jail. If you love him, you've got to chase him away."

"I'll never speak to Dad again."

"I'm sure your dad will regret this someday. He came from hard circumstances, one of nine, always hungry. God forgive him, he's a hard man."

At the Krajewski farm, Jill is greeted by Old Shep, the family dog, without a sound, just a friendly lick. Her mom gives the dog a smell of the back of her hand. She looks at Jill and smiles. "The dog seems to like you." Jill smiles another small smile.

Jill enters the barn and awakens Mike. They leave his makeshift bunk next to the horse stalls and join her mom outside.

Out of earshot of Jill, her mom tells Mike the way the big stick floats. She sums up, "The moral turpitude charge, the politicians and the sheriff in cahoots with my husband means you'll be in county jail by this time tomorrow, working on a road gang the day after that. Listen to me, son, you'll be railroaded. You don't have the chance of a fart in a whirlwind against this outfit. You can get out of here tonight, with three hundred dollars in your pocket, or you can stay. Either way, I'll respect you. But remember, if you stay you'll get a court date. Jill's name will be bandied about and her reputation sullied. Anyway, Mike, that's how it looks from my point of view. If you really love Jill, you might think of leaving her behind." The moon comes out and shines on her face. Mike sees no guile in her look.

"Why don't you and Jill go back inside and discuss this. If I see you come out with a travel bag, I'll know you plan on walking up to Miller's Crossing and hopping the four-twenty. Damn thing wakes me up most every morning."

Mike and Jill go back into the barn. It smells of new mown hay. Mike tells Jill he's got to go. "I've got warrants on a couple of breaking and enterings that'll show up from downstate if I'm arrested up here. That'll be the end of me for seven to ten, Jill. I got no choice." They make love one last time, pack Mike's bag and rejoin Jill's mom outside.

"I wish you well, son," Jill's mom hands Mike the money. She hugs him. "It's in twenties. I wish it was a better world."

Mike puts the money in his pocket and turns. He gives Jill a final kiss and embrace and heads down the road to Miller's Crossing and the four-twenty, his shoulders sagging.

Jill and her mother walk down the road in the opposite direction. "Don't look back," Jill's mother tells her. When they arrive home, Jill's dad greets them with a belligerent, "Where the hell were you two?"

"Out having a girl talk. Jill's going to bed."

"Good night, Dad." Jill starts up the stairs. "Good night, Mom."

Her father grunts. Her mother says, "Good night, dear."

"You think she's in the family way?"

"I have no idea."

"I think she ought to drop out of college and marry that bookish kid who wanted to get engaged to her last spring. Just in case she's got a bun in the oven."

"His name was Bill. Bill Whitman."

"That's the one. I checked up on him last spring when he was mooning around here. Good student, modest means. Had to work to get through school. I'll get in touch with him as soon as I settle this other mess. Are you ready for bed, Mary?"

"Yes, Patrick."

They walk upstairs together. Just before falling asleep, Mary thinks, this is one time I won't mind hearing the four-twenty.

In her room, Jill is crying herself to sleep. "Whenever I hear the four-twenty blow its whistle, I'll be thinking of you, Mike."

Patrick sets his alarm for six and falls asleep thinking about beating the shit out of "that dirty little bastard."

Two weeks later, Jill marries Bill. Joan is born the following June.

Mike hops the four-twenty and goes to Mexico, where he spends his money on a few months of tequila, excellent chili rellenos and friendly ladies. He joins the navy to see the world and on December 7th, 1941, Mike is killed at Pearl Harbor.

Jill's waitress jars her from her reverie. "Would you like another martini, Mrs. Whitman?"

Jill looks at her empty glass. "Yes, dear. That would be nice." She laughs. "I haven't touched my sandwich yet. Day-dreaming." She considers calling the Johnsons at work and asking about Sandy's whereabouts, but decides against it. Why stir up conversation? She checks her watch. I'll give Sandy 'til three. She lights another of her long cigarettes and resolves to eat her sandwich as soon as she finishes her second martini.

At nine o'clock, while Jill was checking on Joan, Sandy's parents had already been at work for an hour. Madge is the office manager and accountant at Johnson's Lumber. She has a head for figures and a nose for shenanigans. Employee pilfering does not occur at their firm. Sandy's father, Jerry, handles all the glad-handing, bullshitting and chiseling with the wholesalers and suppliers. The Johnsons love each other and work well together.

Sandy slept until eleven, enjoying one of her last free days before college. Immediately after waking up, she called Joan feeling her hunch about an elopement would be proven correct. Hanging up after six rings, she supposed that Joan was in some honeymoon hotel with Eddie. Sandy showered, dressed, made toast and coffee and cleaned up the kitchen before she left for her 12:30 appointment at Marie's Beauty Salon.

Arriving home from the beauty parlor at a quarter to three, she reads Jill's note, jumps back into her car and lays a trail of smoke and burning rubber a half a block long. She's at the country club in less than ten minutes.

At the club, Jill orders a ham sandwich and a beer for Sandy. She tells Sandy everything that she knows about Joan's accident and her current condition.

"Can we call the hospital, Mrs. Whitman?"

"Good idea, Sandy. I'm sure Joan would love to hear from you. She's really doing very well, considering. I hope Eddie called her this morning."

Jill calls the hospital and gets Nurse Parker. She tells Jill that Joan was awake for awhile, ate a good lunch and is now napping. She also tells Jill there were no calls for Joan other than her own. "She seemed a little sad that her boyfriend hadn't called," Nurse Parker relates. "Maybe this little nap will chirk her up."

"Thank you, Nurse Parker. And when Joan wakes up, please tell her I'm on my way. I'll try and make it for dinner, depending on traffic."

Jill hangs up, dials the 646th and goes into her Red Cross act. Sandy listens at the earpiece with her.

DiNessi answers and when Jill asks to speak to Airman Edward Flynn, he answers, "I'm sorry, ma'am. Airman Flynn is gone. Shipped out at noon."

Sandy whispers to Jill, "Ask if you can speak to Airman Robert Porter."

When Jill asks for Robert Porter, DiNessi feels he may be speaking with a friend of Eddie's. He patches Jill through to Radar Ops. Any friend of Eddie's is okay with me, he thinks.

Sandy gets on the line and tells Bob the whole story. Bob looks at the map of Michigan on the plotting board, trying to answer Sandy's questions about Eddie's whereabouts.

"If he's having any kind of luck hitching, and he usually does, he could be down by Ann Arbor already. I'd say your best bet is to get on Route 12 west."

"Thanks, Bob. I love you." Sandy hangs up.

Jill gives Sandy Joan's letter. This morning I thought this letter was redundant, she reflects. She asks, "Do you think you've got a chance, Sandy, really?"

"Eddie knows my car. I'll drive to Chicago if I have to."

They leave the club and gas up at a Texaco station. By four o'clock Sandy's Ford is nosing its way onto Route 12 and Jill is heading for Bay City.

Eddie's hitch is what he calls a dribs and drabs hitch. It's a typically slow Monday on Highway 23. He doesn't see a southbound vehicle until 12:15. An old guy, running a knife-sharpening business out of his panel truck, takes Eddie to Pinconning. From there a plumber gives him a lift to Bay City.

Eddie's mind isn't really into the hitch. He keeps thinking of Joan. After a coffee at the Bay City depot, he picks up a ride all the way to Flint with a clothing salesman driving a Cadillac. They go sailing right past Slim's Blue light. Eddie sees Slim's Olds parked near the entrance, thinks of the good times there with Joan and feels a chapter of his life slam shut.

It takes three rides to get from Flint to Ann Arbor, one with a guy who wants to know if Eddie has accepted Jesus into his life. The sunny day is turning gray as Eddie gets out of his last ride, a pickup truck. Eddie waves goodbye and watches the driver get back on Highway 23. He walks around the cloverleaf to the Junction Diner, gets a cup of coffee and a piece of pie and at 4:15, he's standing next to a Route 12 West sign with his thumb up.

Five minutes later he's sitting in the cab of a Peterbilt next to a trucker who claims to be a "Million Miler." With the fans of squinting wrinkles radiating from the corners of his eyes, many years of truck-stop chow showing around his waist and hands like old leather gloves, he looks it.

The old trucker's name is Hank and he's fun to listen to. One of the things he tells Eddie is, "You're doing a smart thing hitching Route 66 while it's still there. Thirty or forty years from now it'll probably be gone."

Eddie doesn't quite understand how a highway can disappear but he answers, "Yeah." He sees Joan's face in a passing oak tree.

Ten miles west of Somerset, Hank is rolling at a solid sixty. Five miles behind him, Sandy is doing eighty, thinking about the Michigan speed limit. Maximum speed shall be whatever is deemed safe and sane, except where posted for slower speeds, or something like that. She kicks the Ford up to eighty-five.

Fifteen minutes later, Hank glances from his speedometer to his side view mirror and back again. "Look at this guy go," he states. "Must be Troopers."

In the mirror on his side of the cab, Eddie sees the car. "This guy's flyin'," he comments. The car gets closer. Eddie sees its color in the fading daylight. Electric blue, he thinks. The car goes humming by. "Ford coupe, forty-nine or fifty." He shouts, "Hank, the girl in that car is lookin' for me. Can you give her a blast?"

Hank hits the airhorn and the accelerator at the same time. Sandy looks in her rearview mirror and sees a truck overtaking her, blinking its lights. When the truck is almost nibbling her tail, she sees Eddie next to the driver. She eases off the gas little by little. When she's slowed to sixty, she sticks her hand out the window and makes follow-me gestures. Hank blinks his lights three times and follows her to a rest area three miles down the road.

At the rest area Hank gets out of the truck with Eddie. "I want to meet that gal."

Standing by Sandy's open window, Hank sticks out his hand. "Missy," he states, "you are one hell of a driver."

Sandy shakes Hank's hand. "Thanks." She smiles. "Thanks a lot."

Eddie gets settled, slams his door, and shouts past Sandy, "Thanks again, Hank."

Hank watches Sandy slip into a slot in the highway, accelerate boldly and disappear. "Goddamn," he says out loud and shakes his head.

Heading back east on 12, Sandy levels off at seventy and hands Eddie Joan's note.

"Dearest Eddie," he reads. "I love you. I hope you get this before you take off for Alaska. I had a car wreck on my way to our wedding but I'm okay now. I told Mom about us. She knows we were going to get married. If you can see me before you go, I'd love it, but if not, I'll wait for you forever. All my love, forever, Joan."

"How fast can we get to Bay City, Sandy?"

"Let's see." Sandy urges the car up to eighty.

On their drive to Bay City, Sandy tells Eddie everything that she's been told by Jill. "One thing is certain," she stresses. "Joan's not in danger. Her memory is a little hazy, though."

Eddie looks at his letter. "'I told Mom about us,'" he reads aloud. "I wonder how *much* she told her mom."

"Mrs. Whitman knows that Joan was pregnant. Mr. Whitman too, only he's out of town."

"They know Joan's pregnant?"

"Joan's not pregnant anymore, Eddie. I'm sorry."

"The wreck?"

"Yeah. Mrs. Whitman said the doctor told her not to mention the miscarriage to Joan just yet. She might not even remember being pregnant. She doesn't even recognize her dad."

"Is Joan really okay?"

"Her mom says yes and the doctor says yes."

"Man, it's going to be horrible facing Joan's mom."

"Don't feel that way. I think she likes you. You should have seen all the stuff she did to get that letter to you." Sandy laughs. "She's funny, gets on the phone and says she's with the Red Cross." Sandy goes on to tell Eddie about how Bob was able to track him down.

"Good old Bob. You got a great boyfriend, Sandy."

"I know that."

Sandy tells Eddie that Joan's eating well and keeps Eddie reasonably calm until they arrive at the hospital with chit chat about the hot rod show. Eddie listens and tries to get his brain settled.

When Eddie and Sandy are met by Jill in the visitors' lounge, Eddie is surprised by Jill's upbeat demeanor. She hugs Sandy. "I can't thank you enough for finding this guy."

She takes Eddie's hands in both of hers. "Joan's going to be so happy to see you, Eddie. She was feeling a little down because you didn't call. Didn't you get your message at the base?"

"I never got a message."

"It doesn't matter. You're here." She gives Sandy another squeeze. "Oh, I love you."

"All I can say is I'm genuinely sorry for the pain I've caused Joan and the trouble I've caused you, Mrs. Whitman."

"This accident was not your fault, Eddie. And please call me Jill, not Mrs. Whitman." She looks at Sandy. "You too, Sandy. I'd like you to call me Jill."

"When can we see Joan?" Eddie asks.

"She just nodded off a few minutes ago. The doctor says these are healing sleeps. She remembered her summer with you after one of them, Eddie."

"That's good news." Eddie looks a little embarrassed.

Jill looks at Sandy. "I've got to get a bite to eat." Turning to Eddie, she adds, "Joan won't wake up for a couple of hours."

"I could eat something," Sandy states.

"Come on. There's a nice place across the street. The doctors recommend it," Jill urges.

Eddie smiles at her. "Maybe I'll eat a sandwich."

In a back corner booth at Otto's they have pork sandwiches and beer while Jill tells them more about Joan. "Don't worry about Joan's memory, Eddie. I'm told it's quite normal."

"Okay, Mrs ... Jill." He agrees, "If you and the doc are happy, I'm happy."

"One thing, both of you. Joan looks a lot worse than she feels. Two huge black eyes and they're almost closed. Her nose is swollen, but not broken. Her head is completely bandaged."

"I'll make sure I smile at her," Eddie pledges.

"She'll smile right back." Jill looks at Sandy. "How about you?"

"I'll be okay, Jill."

Jill pats Sandy's hand. "I'm counting on you." She turns to Eddie. "Joan has some blank spots in her memory. The doctor thinks she may be unaware of her miscarriage. It's best if she remembers this on her own, is the thinking."

"Joan's letter said she told you we were going to be married. She remembers that?"

"Oh yes. And personally, I think you and Joan go together like ham and eggs."

Eddie tries to look humble. "Thanks, Jill."

"It's the truth. But we do have a problem."

"Because of losin' the baby? I'll help any way I can. I'm still ready to marry Joan."

"And I'm sure you will. You can talk that over with Joan later, Eddie. Privately." She turns to Sandy. "Sandy, tell us how you found Eddie."

Sandy goes into her story and everyone continues eating and drinking. Sandy finishes eating first and when Jill orders another round of beer, she declines. "I think I'll go back to the waiting room. Just in case Joan wakes up early."

"Okay. We'll be over in a few minutes, Sandy," Jill assures her, adding, "Thanks again for finding the groom." They all laugh.

"She's such a wonderful friend for Joan. I was serious about finding the groom. I'm in favor of you two getting married." Jill sips her beer. "I'm still not sure if Joan knows she was pregnant, let alone had a miscarriage. She doesn't even remember her father." Jill can't resist a small smile at that thought. She continues, "You know about the trust fund?"

"I'm sorry we blew that, but with Joan pregnant ..."

"You felt that you had to marry immediately. Eddie, I like that, and had it occurred, I'd have welcomed you with open arms." Jill takes another sip of her beer and continues. "I really don't give a damn if the church gets that money, even though they'll just waste it on ermine capes and gold chalices."

Eddie laughs. Just knowing that Joan is across the street, doing well, is bringing back his sense of humor.

"My husband wants Joan tucked away at a Catholic all-girl college until she's nineteen. The trust fund is very important to Bill."

Eddie frowns. Jill reads it. "No, it's a lovely place, way out in the Pennsylvania woods. My mother graduated from Our Lady of the Lakes."

Eddie takes a drink of his beer.

"With no baby on the way, there's no need to rush. How long will you be in Alaska?"

"I'm guessin' a tour of about a year."

"Well if you and Joan decide to wait for your return, I'll throw you a wedding you won't forget. And Bill will get his precious trust fund," Jill states, adding silently, and maybe he'll get the hell out of my life.

"What does Joan think about this college?"

"Her father saw her yesterday. She seemed to like the idea. I'm not sure she even knows she was supposed to start at Michigan." Eddie reads distress in Jill's face.

"I'll do whatever you think is best for you and Joan. I'll marry her tonight or next year."

"I know you will, Eddie." Jill takes his hand. "Under that rough exterior lies a true marshmallow ... and that's a compliment." Jill finishes her beer. "Let's just play it by ear."

Eddie empties his glass. "I like that."

Jill allows Eddie to pay, knowing that she's going to slip a pair of twenties into his pocket when she hugs him goodbye.

Back at the hospital, Sandy greets them in the waiting room. "Joan's awake," she reports, "the nurse'll be right back with some applesauce."

Jill turns to Eddie. "I'll go in with the nurse. You stand by the door. At the right moment, I'll pull you into her room like a big gift."

The night nurse comes back with the applesauce and Jill accompanies her into Joan's room. When Joan finishes eating, Jill remarks, "Excuse me, dear. I've got something to show you." She opens the door, grabs Eddie's wrist and pulls him into the room. "Joanie, look what Sandy found down on Route Twelve."

"Edddieee!" Joan almost sings his name.

Eddie sees her beat-up face and knows how she feels. He sees her beautiful smile and feels joy. He looks at Jill. "Is it okay to hug her?"

"She's quite huggable," Jill answers and she leaves the room.

Joan and Eddie share a long kiss. "It's a good thing I didn't injure my tongue, isn't it?" she asks playfully, and they both laugh.

"Oh, how I love you," Eddie hugs her again. "I'm sure glad you remember me."

"You're not easy to forget, Flynn," she states in a mock authoritative voice. "But" she adds, "speaking of remembering, could you ask Mom to come back in?"

Jill enters the room and Joan speaks. "I want you both here. The two people I love most in the world." Jill and Eddie stand on opposite sides of Joan's bed. Jill holds Joan's right hand, Eddie her left.

Joan turns toward Jill. "I had another one of those long, story kind of dreams, Mom."

"Like the dream when you remembered things you and Eddie did during the summer?"

Eddie's eyes flick to the window. He brings them back and looks into Joan's eyes like that first time he saw her at the Perch Festival dance. Her eyes are almost swollen shut but he sees the lamp's reflection in her bright, black pupils.

"Like that one, Mom, but even stranger. Sometimes it was like I was half awake and half remembering. Hard to explain."

"That's all right, dear. Just tell us about the dream."

"It was about us, Eddie." She turns toward Jill. "Mom, in my dream I was pregnant." Joan turns back to Eddie. "Eddie, could you excuse us for a moment, please? Woman talk."

"Sure, honey." Eddie goes over to look out the window.

Joan speaks softly to Jill. "Mom, how could a girl be pregnant and still get the curse? I've got a pad on."

Jill sucks it up. Here I go, she resolves. "It's like this, honey. Yes, you were pregnant. No, you are no longer pregnant."

"Uh-huh."

"When your car rolled over and over ..."

"My baby died."

At the stricken sound in her voice, Eddie goes back to the side of Joan's bed.

"It wasn't a baby yet, Joan. Do you remember two years ago when we had to rush Aunt Flo to the hospital?"

Joan frowns. "We left the fair early ... oh, I do remember. Aunt Flo had a— you told me all about it—a miscarriage."

"That's what Aunt Flo had, a miscarriage, and then last year, she got pregnant again and had her baby."

"Oh Mom, I'm remembering things so well. I was Tommy's godmother at his baptism. You bought him that beautiful pearl teething ring with the little silver bell on it." Joan's happiness with her memory returning fades as she thinks of the miscarriage she has had.

Jill goes into the clinical aspects of the miscarriage, including quoting Dr. Sloane's remark, "It was a clean miscarriage. Joan will be quite capable of making you a grandma." Joan and Eddie smile at that.

"And now I'm going to leave you two alone for awhile."

As the door closes behind Jill, Eddie leans over and plants a tender kiss on Joan. He takes the wedding band and slips it on her finger. He smiles. "We can get married tonight. Your mom says she doesn't care about the church getting your grandmother's trust money."

Joan thinks for a minute, licks her lips and requests, "Eddie, would you get Mom back in here please?"

"Sure thing, honey." Eddie goes out and comes back with Jill.

With Jill on her right side and Eddie on her left, Joan begins to talk. "Mom, facts are flooding into my mind, moment by moment. I'd like to tell you both how things look to me." Joan pauses, gathering her thoughts. "I was pregnant and we were going to get married. That would have sent Gran's trust to the church."

"You understand about the trust?"

"Yes, Mom. And I know that I could marry Eddie right now and you wouldn't care about losing the trust." Joan looks at Eddie. "And I know that you weren't marrying me just because I was pregnant, Eddie. I'd love nothing more than to marry you at this moment, but ..." Joan takes her ring off. "I can't do that to my mom. I'm going to Our Lady of the Lakes for a year, while you're in Alaska. It looks quiet and peaceful there. Is that okay?"

"If that's really what you want, dear."

"It is, Mom." Joan turns to Eddie. "Eddie?"

"If you want to wait, Joan, I'll wait." Eddie gently removes the band from Joan's hand, puts it on the chain with the golden heart and re-fastens it around her neck. "Looks like we'll both be doin' a tour of duty, me in Alaska and you in Pennsylvania." They all laugh. Jill adds, silently, and me in St. Clair Shores. At least until that damn trust fund matures, anyway.

"If you two will excuse me, I'm going to the powder room." She looks back as she leaves the room. "It's so good to see you together."

As the door closes behind Jill, Joan pats the side of her bed. "Come sit by me, Eddie. I'm not delicate."

"No, you sure ain't that." Eddie sits on the side of the bed. They hold hands. They do some nibbling-of-the-lips kisses, and Joan asks, "When do you have to be in Alaska?"

"I don't know exactly. But I've got to be in 'Frisco by midnight, Saturday."

"And you're hitching?" Joan's voice sounds mildly reproving.

"Sure," he answers, reaching into her gown and cupping her breast. "I could probably make it in four days."

"No you don't," she responds. "No more trouble. The sooner you get to Alaska, the sooner you'll be back. She removes Eddie's hand from her breast.

"You know I go all apeshit when you touch me." Joan puckers up. "Kiss me goodbye for awhile."

Eddie lays a deep kiss on Joan, then gives her a tender little kiss. "I guess I better hit the road. I'm sure gonna miss you." He stops at the door before leaving, and grins. "Those eyes look great."

"Get out of here. And get back soon," she shouts after him. Joan is smiling her biggest, best, brightest smile. She feels a tear on her cheek but doesn't feel sad.

In the waiting room, Eddie thanks Jill again for her understanding. Jill hands Eddie a slip of paper. "I wrote down Joan's address at Our Lady of the Lakes. Just in case you want to drop her a line."

Eddie is touched by Jill's thoughtfulness. "I can't thank you enough. Joan's a lucky girl to have you for a mom."

"Thanks, Eddie. That's a lovely thing to say. I was rooting for you the first night I saw you," Jill smiles. "You'll make a much better son-in-law than Roddy. One stuffed shirt in the family is enough." They all laugh.

Eddie turns to Sandy. "Joan's waiting to see you, Sandy. That trucker called you a hell of a driver. I think you're a hell of a friend." He hugs Sandy. "Tell Bob thanks and tell him I said he should marry you."

"He will," Sandy assures. They laugh and she heads for Joan's room.

Sandy opens Joan's door and starts to enter, gingerly. "Sandy." Joan opens her arms wide. "Come here and hug your blood sister. I've got so much to tell you!"

Out in the waiting room, Jill gives Eddie a goodbye hug and slips forty bucks into his pocket, slick as a grifter.

Eddie leaves the hospital and walks the two blocks to Highway 23. Just before midnight, he's standing next to the southbound sign, his thumb up, singing "Tomorrow Night". Counting days in his head, he realizes that it's been three months and one day since he first met Joan. Pausing in mid-song, he exclaims, "Holy fuckin' shit! This summer's been a fuckin' lifetime."

CHAPTER 29

▼

Eddie's first ride comes tearing up the highway one minute into Tuesday. The bright yellow Hudson Hornet starts braking a hundred feet before him and still passes Eddie by two hundred feet.

Eddie sprints to the car. A wiry guy with a buzz cut opens the passenger door and shouts, "Jump in. I'm going to Toledo."

"Great." Eddie gets into the car. "I need to get to Route 12. I'm headin' for 'Frisco."

The guy tells Eddie that he's a test driver for the factory. He runs through the gears, slick and quick, pulling the max out of each, winds the Hornet up to ninety and never stops talking. He tells Eddie how he came home from the war in 1945 to find out that his wife wanted a divorce.

"She'd been fucking the foreman on her shift at Chrysler for two years," he relates. "I dropped her like a dirty shirt, but first I gave her a fat lip. Then I got the prick who'd been banging her out on the employee parking lot. I worked him over pretty good with a baseball bat." The guy laughs at the memory and continues, "I did a year and a half for that. Worth every day of it. Had it easier in the joint than I did fighting in Italy."

Eddie starts to say something, but the driver continues his tale. "It took three operations to fix the bastard's face." He laughs and adds, "He still drools a little."

"He had it comin'," Eddie quickly interjects, adding, "It's too bad you had to do time for bustin' up an asshole."

"That's the way I see it," the guy agrees. "I'm Ernie Rapinski." He offers his hand.

"Nice to meet you," Eddie shakes Ernie's hand. As soon as he utters the words, "I'm Eddie Flynn," Ernie's off and winging again.

"You know what really pisses me off?" he asks rhetorically, "If I would have caught a slug in Italy, that two-timing rat bitch would have got my GI insurance. Anyway, that was seven long years ago. Now Wilma's a big fat-ass sow and I'm shacked up with a little blonde in Toledo who's got a body like a hood ornament, *and ...*" Ernie pauses for effect. He's told this tale before. "... she works in a drugstore. Who says there ain't no fucking God?!?!?" They laugh. Ernie takes an aspirin tin out of his shirt pocket, pops it open, removes a large white pill and breaks it in half. He puts half of it into his mouth and starts chewing, both hands off the wheel, clocking eighty.

Eddie recognizes the Benzedrine. When O'Hara was the medic for the 646th Eddie used to get Bennies for many of his three-day breaks. "I want to enjoy every minute of my off-duty time," Eddie would declare, and O'Hara would laugh.

"I ain't had no real sleep for thirty-six hours," Eddie hints.

Ernie gives Eddie the other half of the Bennie. "This'll keep you going to St. Louie. It's the real goods." He hands the tin to Eddie. "There's two more in there and you can keep 'em. My contribution to the war effort." They laugh.

This guy's a real kick in the ass, Eddie thinks. "Thanks, Ernie." He tosses the pill half into his mouth. Eddie's pushing the aspirin tin deep down into his pants pocket as they speed past Slim's Blue Light. Eddie thinks of Joan and feels happy knowing they'll be back together. Then he resumes listening to Ernie extol the merits of being shacked up with a chick who works in a drugstore.

A little later, humming down a straight stretch of 23 between Saginaw and Flint, Ernie announces, "Watch this." He drops his left hand onto his lap and grips the wheel at twelve o'clock with his right. He suddenly whips the wheel to one o'clock, then back to eleven. He does this three times, stopping after the third time at twelve o'clock. The car rocks gently and stays straight on course. "You should see this baby corner," Ernie crows.

"Rides better'n a cop car," Eddie comments. They laugh and Ernie gets back to talking about cars and women's bodies. He drops Eddie off at the junction of Highway 23 and Route 12. Walking the cloverleaf to the Junction Diner on Route 12 for the second time within twelve hours, Eddie thinks, I feel great. Joan's waitin' for me. I'll go through my Alaska tour like shit through a tin horn. What a difference a few hours can make? He's smiling when he opens the door to the diner. The food aromas are no match for the Benzedrine. Eddie's appetite is as dead as a Tuesday night in Podunk. He drinks coffee, smokes, plays the juke and wonders about Alaska.

At three o'clock a trucker comes in to fill his Thermos. Eddie hears the guy tell the cashier that he's hauling a load of pumpkins to Chicago. Eddie pays his tab and leaves the diner right behind him. Out on the parking lot, Eddie catches up to the trucker. "I heard you tell the cashier you were goin' to Chicago. Any chance of catchin' a ride?"

"Sure, kid. Mack's the name, just like my truck. What's yours?"

"Eddie." He sticks out his hand and they shake.

Climbing up into the cab of the truck, Mack comments, "Okay, let's get these jack-o-lanterns to the Windy City." The truck is idling. Mack releases the emergency brake, eases into gear and they roll slowly out onto Route 12 West.

"So Mack, you been drivin' long?"

The perfect question. Mack tells Eddie how he started driving back in 1920. "I started trucking beer the day after Prohibition," he states. "I bounced around between the Big Apple and the Windy City." He tells Eddie a couple of anecdotes, casually mentioning names like Dutch Schultz, Ownie Madden, and Vinnie Coll.

"I'll never forget my first Scotch run. I'd been running beer for a few years, doing okay, staying out of jail and out of the hospital. Anyway, I got a chance to do a Scotch run, a lot more dough, a step up. I'm the number three truck. The other two drivers had made these runs before.

The stuff came in by boat from Canada to Wisconsin, way up north. From there we're supposed to truck it down to Chi. It's a foggy night. At first the guys are happy. G-men were bagging guys with surprise roadblocks … almost like they had inside info, you know?"

"Uh-huh."

"Anyway, the fog gets worse. You can almost scoop it off the hood and make fogballs. I've seen fog in 'Frisco, Boston and in Ohio, off Lake Erie, but nothing like this." Mack pauses. "You ever been in really thick fog, Eddie?"

"Just once, when I was stationed in Oscoda. I had to walk four miles back to the base. The fog was so thick I couldn't see my shoes. No wind, no traffic on 23. Sometimes I'd have to look down at the blacktop to be sure I was on the highway. I stopped walkin' for a couple of minutes and wondered if bein' dead was like what I was feelin' and then I heard a foghorn from Lake Huron and shaped up, but it was a spooky feelin'."

"That's exactly the kind of fog I was driving in. I lost track of the other two trucks almost as soon as we started. I just kept crawling along, barely able to stay on the road. I'm driving so slow I'd be a menace, but no one else is out. I get a little break in the fog, maybe two minutes. I see I'm still on the road so I keep poking along. I drive a couple more slow miles when I see a faint yellow glow. 'Swamp gas,' I think, but as I get closer, the glow becomes a big Indian.

"He's wearing an almost yellow buckskin jacket with fringe, a yellow cowboy hat, Levis, and cowboy boots. His hat's beaded hatband has a small, white feather in it. He's standing by the road, straight as a stick, smiling and smoking a big cigar. The glow I'm seeing is him, in his jacket and hat. I pull over and stop, glad to see a human being. He's got a small carpetbag on the ground next to him. About the size of that one you're carrying."

Eddie looks down at his canvas bag, then out his window at the flat landscape. He tries to picture the Indian by the side of the road. Mack continues his story.

"The guy's at least six-foot-six, got a long black braid, not a speck of gray in it, but he's an old guy, seventy at least. He's lean but not skinny. Looks like he's waiting for a goddamn bus. All he needs is a newspaper." Eddie laughs, making Mack smile. "He looks like a straight shooter to me, so I open the passenger door and shout at him, 'You look like you're waiting for a bus!'"

"'You're my bus,' he says. His smile gets bigger. He throws his bag into the truck. He sees me looking at the bag, pats it and says, 'Good medicine. You're lost, looking for Chicago.' He climbs in, sits down and makes himself comfortable, then says, 'I know the way. Should we ride together?' He tells me he can help me avoid the ambush my friends ran into. I don't know what the hell he's talking about at first." Mack coughs, then clears his throat. "Throat's getting dry," he croaks. "There's a couple of mugs in that compartment under the glove box, Eddie. Hope you drink your coffee black."

"Sure do." Eddie gets the mugs, takes the Thermos, fills each cup three quarters full and hands one to Mack.

Mack takes a big swallow. "I tell the old guy I'll take him to Chicago. We shake hands. He gives me a big stogie and says, 'First we smoke together, then we go.' I light up and listen.

"He tells me that his name is White Raven. He says that he got his name because a white raven fell to earth outside his lodge at the moment of his birth. He says he's a Chippewa, a medicine man, shows me the feather in his hat and says he can see through fog. I'm willing to believe him about the raven. I figure what the hell, it could've been an albino, but seeing through the fog is a different story."

"That's a pretty big claim," Eddie agrees. He takes a swallow of his coffee.

"That's what I'm thinking. How do I know that feather isn't from some chicken that quit laying and wound up in the stew pot? But I like the old guy and the cigar I'm smoking is first class. I ask him what he meant about an ambush. He tells me the other two trucks were ambushed and captured by men with machine guns and badges. He tells me that I'm lucky I got lost and that he'll take me to Chicago by another route."

Mack stops talking, takes a big swallow of his coffee and laughs. "Excuse me for laughing. Right now I'm getting ahead of myself. Anyway, to shorten this up, White Raven takes me through the fog, saying things like, 'big looping left turn starting now' or 'hard right turn now.' None of that 'kimo sabe' or 'many moons ago' shit for White Raven. What I'm laughing about is the look on Frank's face when we pull into the warehouse. He sees White Raven and starts to reach into his jacket. He sees me. I'm smiling. 'Don't shoot, Frank,' I shout. I watch Frank's face change from his 'you're dead' look to a big grin and I start laughing. White Raven smiles and hands Frank a cigar. Frank gets real happy. He already knew about the other two trucks going down and figured I got caught somewhere too. He's feeling so good he gives me and White Raven five hundred clams each and has one of the guys drop us off downtown. So we're standing on the corner saying goodbye when White Raven starts to rummage around in his medicine bag. He takes out a feather just like his and a business card. 'With this feather,' he says, 'fog and darkness will never dim your eyes and the road you choose will always be the correct road.' With that, he shakes my hand and starts walking down State Street like he's the mayor."

"A real medicine man. That's great. You ever see him again, Mack?" They both sip their coffee.

"Oh yeah, we're still friends. I looked at his business card and I seen 'White Raven Hunting Lodge' and a phone number. Under the phone number it says, 'Guide Services by Appointment'. I give Frank the card, Frank sets up a deal where White Raven lays out all the Wisconsin runs. White Raven makes a lot of dough, builds a bowling alley and a small-time department store for his village on the reservation.

"We never lost another load of Scotch. I'm going to see him again in a couple of weeks. Every autumn we go canoeing. He must be close to a hundred by now."

"You still got the feather?"

Mack points to the visor on Eddie's side of the truck. Eddie looks up and sees a small white feather held to the visor by a rubber band.

"That's the feather. I wouldn't drive without it."

"Like a Saint Christopher's medal." Eddie finishes his coffee.

"Better. Tommy Nolan had a Saint Christopher stuck on his truck's dash the night that hijackers pumped twenty pounds of lead into him. My feather never let me down like that. I believe in it."

"I guess that's as good a thing to believe in as anything. Okay to use this rag on this cup, Mack?"

"Yeah, go ahead." Mack finishes his coffee. Eddie takes his cup, wipes it and puts the two cups back in their compartment.

"What do you believe in, Eddie?"

"I don't know. I was brought up Catholic but I don't go to church. A lot of the shit I was taught don't make sense. I guess I believe mostly in me." Eddie laughs.

"Nothing wrong with that."

Eddie looks out the window and sees the first in a series of Burma Shave signs. SPRING HAS COME, the first small sign reads. THE GRASS HAS RIZ, continues the second. WHERE LAST YEAR'S, states the third sign.

"'Careless Drivers is'," finishes Mack while Eddie is trying to figure out the last line of the rhyme. "I drive this road a lot."

The CARELESS DRIVERS IS sign comes up, and they laugh.

"It sounds like Prohibition was fun."

Those were great years, Eddie." Mack sighs. "And then on December fifth, nineteen thirty-three, like all good things, it came to an end. Prohibition got repealed. With alcohol suddenly declared legal, I became just another truck driver. Lucky for me I didn't blow all my dough. I had enough to buy a rig. Every few years I trade in for a new model. I don't punch a clock. I work when I want and haul what I want."

Mack tells Eddie other stories about the Depression and unemployment during the thirties. He tells Eddie what life was like for a civilian during World War Two.

"I was forty-one when the Japs bombed Pearl Harbor and I had a high mileage face," he relates, "I couldn't enlist so I got a job in a defense plant. I was up to my eyebrows in pussy."

"I was just a little kid when the war was on. I remember almost every guy was in uniform."

"Sure were. And I had a rule. I never dated any woman who had a husband or boyfriend in the service. I would have felt like a traitor, fucking some soldier's wife while he's fighting for our country."

"A guy's got to be a real asshole to do that kind of shit." Eddie tells Mack Ernie's story.

At the conclusion, Mack remarks, "I probably would've done the same thing."

Some papers blow across the highway. Eddie feels the wind gust hit the truck. "Is it always windy in Chicago, Mack?"

"Naw. Calling Chi the Windy City has nothing to do with the weather." Mack laughs. "It's all about bullshit. Whenever guys from Chi and New York would get together, all you'd hear about was how great Chicago was, when everyone knows the Big Apple is top of the heap. I worked 'em both, had good times in both, but when it's four AM in Chicago, it's four AM. In New York, it's just the start of another hour." Eddie laughs.

Mack is an interesting guy. The time passes quickly and at 8:45 AM he drops Eddie off in downtown Chicago. "You can pick up 66 a few blocks from here. Roosevelt and Ogden. It'll take you right through Cicero, Al's old stomping grounds."

"Thanks again, Mack," Eddie shouts as the truck drives off into the morning traffic.

Eddie stops at a drugstore and has toast and coffee at the soda fountain. He's not really hungry, but he figures he should have something on his stomach if he's going to be hitching all day. He buys a couple of postcards and a cheap pen from the cashier, then persuades her to sell him a few stamps. While going through his pockets, trying to come up with the correct change, he finds two twenties in his usually empty left front pocket. "Forty bucks?" he thinks. He takes his wallet out of his back pocket, slips the twenties into the slot behind his ID card and gives the girl a five, still wondering. Then it hits him. "Jill!" he says to himself and smiles. What a mother-in-law she'll make.

He addresses Joan's card, a beautiful shot of Chicago at sunset, and writes:

Dear Joan,

This is the first city on Route 66. I'm sure you're feeling a little bit better each day.

About to write, "All my love, Eddie," he stops himself. Some nun is going to read this long before Joan ever sees it. He signs the card:

Your good friend, Edward.

P.S. Mr. Briggs says hi!

He addresses the second card, a picture of a voluptuous waitress bursting out of her skimpy uniform, to Arbo. She's flashing a big smile, saying, "What'll it be, Big Boy?"

Hey Arbo,

Found what I lost. Great luck in getting shipped to Alaska. The magazine is sending me $200.00 for filters and a zoom lens.

Your buddy,

Eddie.

He pictures Sumner snooping through the mail, like DiNessi told him he does, and laughs. "That's for you, Becker," he declares.

Eddie drops the cards in a mailbox on his way to Ogden and by 9:30 he's standing by the curb with his thumb up.

In Bay City, Dr. Sloane enters Joan's room on his morning rounds. Joan is asleep and Jill is sitting next to the bed. "Good morning, Doctor," Jill says softly.

"Good morning, Mrs. Whitman." The doctor looks thoughtful.

It's amazing how much confidence he inspires, Jill thinks. And he looks like he just got off the campus. She sips her coffee. "Joan's sleeping a little late this morning," she volunteers.

Dr. Sloane notes the slight tone of apprehension in Jill's remark. "It's quite all right for her to sleep late." He smiles. "The night nurse says she was up late. I understand her boyfriend came by."

Jill smiles. "I'm so happy we found Eddie for her. Joan was delighted to see him and so was I."

"I was under the impression that your husband thought Eddie was bad news."

"Bill thinks anyone who's not an executive is bad news." Jill laughs and continues. "Eddie's a little wild, but I like him. He and Joan are in love. He's in the Air Force, on his way to Alaska. Joan was heartbroken until we found him."

"Well, that's two out of three in favor of Eddie," Sloane remarks. Jill raises her eyebrow and gives him a look of affirmation.

He looks at his chart. "Joan still doesn't remember your husband." He marks his chart. "I was hoping he'd be here today."

"Bill's stuck in Flint. Labor negotiations."

"Too bad. I think the more she sees of her father, the sooner she'll remember him."

Jill looks thoughtful. I wish I could forget him passes through her mind, but aloud she asks, "Do you feel Joan's fully recovered, Doctor?"

"Physically, yes, absolutely. However, with her type of head injury, mental recovery can take time. That's why I'm in no hurry to see her hitting the books."

Jill bites her lower lip. "What about her eyes, Doctor? She has no whites in them, just solid red."

Doctor Sloane smiles. "Good news on that. The whites in Joan's eyes will return brighter than ever and in a very short time. Her body just has to carry the old dried blood away."

"What about her bandages? When will they be removed?"

"When Joan leaves later this week, her stitches will have been removed and we'll just have a small gauze pad covering her wound. About three days later, you can remove the bandage and clean the area with a little hydrogen peroxide. There should be no problem."

Jill smiles and Doctor Sloan thinks, "Beautiful smile."

Jill feels reassured. A sensation of complete relaxation courses through her body. She finishes her coffee. "A couple of Joan's close girlfriends will be up to visit," she mentions. "She recognized one of them right away last night."

"That's encouraging, and to be expected. That's why I feel seeing her father will help her remember him."

Jill says nothing. She thinks, "Joan didn't see that much of him before the accident." She frowns again.

Doctor Sloan notices and asks, "Is there any friction between Joan and her father?"

"Yes, Doctor, there is." Jill is relieved to speak of it. "Bill is obsessed with Joan marrying into the country club set. He's done his damnedest to keep Eddie and Joan apart since they met in June."

"Unsuccessfully, obviously," Doctor Sloane quips, smiling at his own little joke.

Joan knows he's referring to the miscarriage. "I did everything I could to help Joan and Eddie see each other and I'd do it again."

Joan begins to stir.

"I understand." Doctor Sloane nods.

Joan's eyelids flutter, then open. "Good morning, Doctor. Oh, Mom, thank you so much for finding Eddie. I feel so good."

"Well, there's nothing for me to do here this morning," Dr. Sloane states. "I'll leave you two to chat. Breakfast is still being served."

Jill walks to the door with the doctor. "Thank you for being so understanding."

"Joan's going to be just fine," he replies. "She's a lucky girl to have a mom like you." He leaves the room.

Jill blushes slightly. Eddie said that too, she thinks. Funny. I feel lucky to have a daughter like Joan.

Ten minutes after putting his thumb up at the corner of Ogden and Roosevelt, Eddie's riding in a pickup truck with an old farmer who looks like Santa Claus in bib overalls. The guy's name is Harlow and he keeps up a steady stream of jokes about tractor salesmen, ministers, and farmers and their daughters while his radio plays tunes like, "Cold, Cold Heart" and "Poison Love".

A few miles south of Lincoln, Harlow pulls into the Pig Hip Restaurant. The Benzedrine is wearing off and Eddie's appetite is back on duty. He orders the hot pork sandwich that Harlow recommends. This is a hell of a lot better sandwich than the one at Otto's, he thinks. "I had one of these last night in Bay City. It was pretty good, but this is the best ever," Eddie remarks.

"I swear by 'em." Harlow laughs and pats his gut.

When Eddie tries to pay the check, Harlow won't allow it. "You've got a long way to go, son. You better watch your money."

Pulling out onto 66, Harlow looks back at the Pig Hip. "Me and the missus used to stop here all the time before she passed on last year."

"I'm sorry," Eddie offers. Noticing Harlow's eyes go watery, he adds, "Were you married long?"

"Forty years. We had lots of fun. Edna used to laugh at every joke I'd tell her."

Thinking about his wife quiets Harlow down, so Eddie looks out the window at the grain elevators, cafes, motels and gas stations. Route 66 is just as Eddie had always pictured it. The troop train that took Eddie from New York City to basic training in San Antonio had passed through this same territory, but Eddie had been too busy playing blackjack to notice the scenery. He smiles, remembering the two hundred dollars he had won.

A Route 66 highway sign catches his eye and "Get Your Kicks on Route 66" begins running through his head:

> It winds from Chicago to L.A.
> More than two thousand miles, all the way
> You go through St. Louie, Joplin, Missouri,
> Oklahoma City is mighty pretty
> You'll see Amarillo, Gallup, New Mexico,
> Flagstaff, Arizona, don't forget Winona,
> Kingman, Barstow, San Bernardino ...

Eddie remembers the first time that he'd heard the tune. He took particular care to memorize the words after that special night with Gloria LaSalle.

Eddie and some of his buddies had taken a few of the neighborhood girls up to Riverside Drive near Grant's Tomb to play "Trust me?"—a local game that involved putting your hand on a girl's knee, gradually working it up under her skirt toward her pussy, prefacing each small advance with the question, "Trust me?"

Gloria and Eddie were sitting on a bench looking across the Hudson at New Jersey and Palisades Amusement Park. Gloria's radio was tuned to a request program. "Near You" was playing. Eddie had smiled inwardly at the significance of the tune, having just been trusted up the inside of Gloria's thigh to within a few inches of his goal.

This is the furthest yet, he had thought. Maybe tonight's the night.

Eddie and Gloria had been dating for three months. She allowed his hands to roam freely from the waist up and she'd given him a few hand-jobs, but Eddie often said to himself, She guards that pussy like it's Fort Knox.

His cock was about to explode, but Eddie held his hand in check, not wanting to end the game. "Trust me?" had only one rule; the game ended the moment a guy advanced without permission. I can feel the heat from her box. Eddie had pictured himself fucking her.

"Our next request," the DJ had announced, "'Get Your Kicks on Route 66', goes out to Gloria, with all my love, from Eddie."

Eddie hadn't called in a request. He didn't even know the station's call letters. It was just a happy coincidence. Somewhere in the greater New York City area, a different Eddie and Gloria were probably dancing to the jump tune. Eddie had more in mind than dancing.

He took full credit for the request, while thinking, I don't even know the jock's name. He kissed Gloria and she nibbled his tongue gently. Finishing their kiss, Eddie asked, "Trust me?"

He felt Gloria's legs relax, spreading a bit wider, before she nodded and answered, "Oh yes, Eddie." He ran his hand up to her crotch. Her panties were moist. They left the bench and ducked into the bushes. The kids hadn't named that stretch of Riverside Drive "Lovers' Lane" on a whim.

"Kingman, Barstow, San Bernardino," sang Nat King Cole, as Eddie slipped into Fort Knox. He was not the first adventurer to breach the gates of the fort and that was what he had expected. Relishing Gloria's enthusiastic, cooperative moves, Eddie patted himself on the back for his first assessment of her four months past, when her family moved into the neighborhood. The first time she walked into the ice cream parlor, Eddie's reaction was, Looks like Little Miss Prissy, but I smell pussy. He kept that opinion to himself and pursued her despite his buddies' comments of, "What are you datin' that fuckin' stiff for?" and "What do you do on a date with her? Play chess?"

I gotta remember to trust my instincts, he promised himself, as the DJ segued into "That's My Desire". While Frankie Laine pleaded, "To spend one night with you, in our old rendezvous," Eddie sent a mental thanks to the jock for the slower tempo tune.

A month later *The New York Times* sent Gloria's father to Paris. Gloria sent Eddie a postcard of the Notre Dame Cathedral, and that was the last Eddie heard from her. Gloria sure was fun while she lasted, Eddie the realist had philosophized to Eddie the romantic.

Harlow's voice breaks into Eddie's reverie. "This is where I turn off." He pulls onto a side road and parks. Eddie thanks him, gets out and watches the truck's dust trail settle before walking the few yards back to Route 66.

It's not a good spot for vehicles to pull over and Eddie feels like stretching his legs, so he walks along the narrow shoulder of the highway, enjoying the beauty of the cornfields. It's mid-afternoon and comfortably warm, with only three wispy clouds on the western horizon.

I hit San Antonio on a day like this. Eddie recalls basic training at Lackland AFB. It wasn't grueling. The Air Force wasn't looking for infantry troops or riflemen. They were in need of radar operators and mechanics, radio operators, aircraft and engine mechanics, cooks, air policemen, heavy equipment operators and other ground support personnel. Part of the Air Force pitch at their recruiting offices was, "It takes seventy men on the ground to keep one pilot in the air."

Although Air Force basic was only thirty days, Eddie went from 135 to 155 pounds, due to "lights out" at 9 PM, reveille at 5 AM and three full meals daily at regular hours. Morning chow in the Air Force inhabited the opposite end of the nutritional spectrum from Eddie's usual on-his-way-to-work breakfast, the Nedick's Special—a cup of coffee, a powdered sugar donut and a small orangeade for fifteen cents.

Basic training asked nothing of Eddie that he couldn't deliver. He knew how to make a tight bunk with hospital corners from his four years at boarding school. He also knew how to march. Although St. Andrew's wasn't a military school, the students had marched once a week, practicing for the school's Field Day, each June. Eddie's day on KP was easier than any he put in at the Pine Hill Camp for Ladies. He sailed through KP with only one, minor incident.

The episode began with Eddie taking a self-appointed smoking break from peeling a huge mound of potatoes. He was far ahead of schedule for the 4 PM completion time ordered by the mess sergeant, so he was surprised when he heard, "Peel them 'taters, Yankee," shouted in his direction by a young airman approaching him.

Eddie checked him out. Motherfucker's got a brand new stripe and he's comin' on like Big Andy. Goofy-lookin' fuck. Teeth hangin' out like Bugs fuckin' Bunny. Wouldn't mind poundin' his fuckin' head in. Eddie scowled at the guy. "What'd you say?"

"I said, 'Peel them 'taters, Yankee.'"

"That's what I thought you said." Eddie held up a potato. "And you're wrong twice, Abner. Number one, this thing is a po-ta-to, not a 'tater. And number two, I'm a New Yorker, not a Yankee. My ancestors were still in Ireland when the Yankees kicked the shit out of the Confederates. It wasn't my fight then and it ain't my fight now, but I'm glad the Yankees won, even though I'm a Giants fan."

"What the hell are you talking about?"

"You'll never know. But let's get back to this po-ta-to." Eddie took a long drag of his cigarette and continued, smoke coming out of his mouth and his nose as he spoke. "I'm talkin' about these potatoes that I'm gonna peel in time for evenin' chow. Believe it or not, I know how to peel potatoes. And someone hoverin' on my shoulder, whinin', 'Peel them 'taters, Yankee,' ain't gonna speed me up even a little bit. In fact, it'll slow me down." Eddie took another hit of his cigarette and blew a few small smoke rings.

The airman looked puzzled. "Well … When I come back here all of them 'taters better be peeled."

"They sure as shit ain't gonna get peeled with you here bullshittin' about it."

"Well … I'll be back."

"Good. I'll throw a party. Thanks for stoppin' by."

Watching the airman walk away, Eddie shook his head. *I'm sure I'll be runnin' into lots more stupidity like that during the next four years.* He dropped his cigarette in the butt can and resumed peeling. By 3:45 all the potatoes were peeled. Watching the airman with the new stripe's face when the mess sergeant said, "Good job, Flynn," tasted as sweet to Eddie as the two large brownies he ate for dessert.

It didn't take long for the next shipment of stupidity to arrive. Eddie stepped into a steaming pile of it the following afternoon.

To prepare the young airmen for their twelve-hour pass on Sunday, their first brush with civilians since their enlistment, the Air Force used Saturday morning to warn the men of the dangers of San Antonio—spies, saboteurs and the temptations of Eve. The training films shown were such 100% pure Iowa corn that Eddie enjoyed them. The first film featured a Hedy Lamarr look-alike in a trench coat, lurking in a seedy, waterfront ginmill, gleaning important military secrets from unsuspecting, wholesome, young troops. The second film had a man who could have been Paul Henreid blowing up a shipyard, armed only with a book of matches and a cigarette.

Then, after assuring the men that San Antonio's venereal disease rate was the second highest in the world, topped only by Shanghai, the Information & Education officer showed three films of guys dating ordinary-looking girls and coming up with rampant cases of gonorrhea, syphilis and rashes with exotic, tropical names. A guy who consorts with a lady he spots leaning against a lamppost winds up with his dick rotting off. The lieutenant finishes up with a few still shots of the guy with the vanishing pecker and the flight is dismissed from class and marched to noon chow, beans and franks. Eddie got a laugh out of that.

After chow, they were marched to a different classroom for "Familiarization with the M-1 Carbine." A well-meaning, but boring second lieutenant told the men a few facts about the rifle and cautioned, "You must always think of any weapon as loaded, and never point it anywhere but downrange." That was the only useful statement of the session.

Marching the five miles from the class to the firing range, digging his heels in, enjoying the "Crump, crump, crump, crump" of the flight's seventy pairs of brogans striking the blacktop, Eddie wondered, When is someone going to tell these guys about shootin'?

Eddie knew from bullshit sessions in the barracks that only a few men in the flight had any experience with rifles. Three deer hunters from Pennsylvania, two Kentucky guys who claimed they hunted squirrels with .22's, one of the squad leaders who was a former marine, a kid from Wisconsin who hunted and himself, were all Eddie could come up with.

Thinking about rifle instruction brought Master Sergeant Roger Miley to mind. Eddie met the sergeant through his mother's youngest brother Tom. Tom was the only one of Mrs. Flynn's four brothers young enough to get into World War Two. He became the type of aircraft and engine mechanic pilots dream about, meticulous. Any B-24 serviced and certified by Tom and his crew would deliver a flight free from any malfunctions. Military life agreed with Tom. He re-enlisted after the war, married and was stationed at Mitchell AFB in Long Island, where he and his wife lived off base.

When her brother told her he belonged to a rifle club that met weekly, Mrs. Flynn saw a tool to aid in her efforts to pry Eddie loose from the corner and "the scruff of Amsterdam Avenue," her favorite term for his friends. During her lectures, Eddie always got a kick out of that one and the idea that somehow his friends were dragging him down to their level. He knew that with his loud mouth, rambunctious behavior and his arsenal of street words for everything from cunnilingus to Oedipus, coupled with his ability to use "fuck" as every part of speech except a conjunction, he was one of the lowest of the scruffs of Amsterdam Avenue.

A trip to a rifle range with his uncle interested Eddie. He used to enjoy plunking cans up on his roof with his Red Ryder BB gun, so when Tom buttoned down his invitation, promising, "If Miley thinks you're worth a shit, he'll probably let you squeeze off a few rounds," Eddie quickly accepted. The following Wednesday, Tom introduced Eddie to Master Sergeant Roger Miley, retired. A man more fully qualified to teach marksmanship has yet to present himself.

Roger Miley was fifteen when Doctor Bob's Carnival of Fun rolled into Sioux Falls. Doctor Bob needed a strong, willing worker and Roger needed a change of scene. When the carnival pulled out of town, young Miley was aboard, happy to be working his way to Florida. He hadn't been looking forward to another South Dakota winter, trapped in the farmhouse listening to his mother and his stepfather, the Reverend Jeremy Jones, praise, thank and glorify Jesus and the Lord for everything from victory over a resistant jelly jar lid to a triumph over sluggish bowels. Roger's stepfather offered no physical threat. Miley could have snapped him like a kitchen match. It was just Jesus and the Lord, jumping out at him all day from various parts of the house that was grinding a groove into his brain.

When Miley's father was crushed to death under a pile of railroad ties, Reverend Jeremy came to minister to the widow. It was Roger's fourteenth birthday. Although the reverend came only to pray, he took a look at the widow's railroad death benefit check and decided to stay. The pint-sized Elmer Gantry injected a megadose of Jesus into the woman's grieving, despairing brain and married her two weeks later. That was the first time Roger heard the call of the open road.

Roger worked on the carnival for two years. In addition to his roustabout duties, he helped an energetic, eighty-year-old run her shooting gallery, Frannie O.'s Dead Duck. Frannie claimed that Annie Oakley was her sister and Roger believed her. Why not? Every night he'd witness her shooting holes in coins, blasting the spots off playing cards, and blowing cigarettes out of the mouths of daring young men.

Miley quit the carnival and went to war the day after German submarines sank the *Lusitania*. He shot nothing but bull's-eyes at the range and the army made him a sniper. During World War One he knocked off some medium-grade German officers and even brought down an enemy plane. After the war he stayed in the army as a weapons instructor. As a member of the division rifle team, he made stripes with ease, and as a non-drinker, he retained them. His eyesight was still keen in 1941, so two months after Pearl Harbor, he was on sniper duty once more, this time in the South Pacific. He finished the war as a Master Sergeant. In 1947, after over 30 years of service, he retired, moved to Hempstead, Long Island and opened the Dead Duck Rifle and Pistol Club.

Miley admired Tom's sense of precision and his shooting ability. He also liked the fact that Tom, like himself, was a career military man, so he decided to look past Eddie's appearance and haircut for the kernel within the boy that could blossom into a good shooter. Eddie's firm handshake and good eye-contact during their introduction got Eddie off to a positive start with the sergeant.

Miley went to the rifle rack and selected one of the dozen Remington .22's. "We're going up on that platform and watch Tom practice. He'll go through the four shooting positions—prone, sitting, kneeling and off-hand. I'll show you the same things up there. Ready?"

"I'm ready, Mister Miley."

"You can drop that 'Mister' shit. Just call me Miley." They climbed the steps to the target-viewing dais. Directing Eddie's attention to the far end of the rifle range, Miley continued, "This is your standard, fifty-foot, small-bore rifle range with two firing lanes. See those targets down there?"

Eddie looked downrange. An 8x11-inch sheet of white paper with five solid black circles on it hung at the end of each lane. The black circles were laid out on the paper in the pattern of the pips on a die showing five. The two sheets with their five-spot layouts made Eddie think of a pair of dice. "I see 'em. Looks like someone just threw a hard ten." Eddie snapped his fingers and grinned. "Pair of sunflowers."

Miley laughed. "It does, doesn't it? You a crap-shooter?"

"Yeah. I'm okay sometimes. Sometimes not."

"We shot crap every payday in the army. I did all right most of the time, betting wrong. A guy makes two or three passes and I bet against him."

"I hardly ever get three straight passes. I just depend on luck. Same thing shootin' pool. I need my luck."

"Well, luck'll help you with a pair of dice or a pool cue, but with a rifle, you're on your own. There's no luck on the firing range. It's all you."

"Uh-huh." Eddie was paying attention. He had his brain wide open.

The sergeant continued, "You can blow on your favorite pair of dice, shake 'em just the right amount looking for your seven, and have 'em come up snake eyes. Pool's a little different. I've seen some guys who can make three-cushion shots, bank shots, everything. Guys who can run the table, but even the best pool shooter can wind up in the shitter if the balls scatter out in the wrong way."

"Shootin' pool, I just bang the shit outta the balls and hope somethin' good falls. I'm pretty lucky around a pool table. Luckier than I deserve."

"Shit, we're all luckier than we deserve." Miley laughed. "But believe me. There's no luck to a bull's-eye. A bull's-eye is about technique and practice."

"There's no luck on the firing range. I'll remember that. No good luck means no bad luck. That's okay with me."

"Good. Now remember what I'm about to tell you because it's the most important thing I'll tell you all night." Miley locked his eyes on Eddie's. "Always treat any weapon as if it's loaded. Even if you just cleaned it, looked down the barrel and the bolt is open. Always keep your rifle pointed downrange."

Miley's earnestness made an impression on Eddie. "I understand, Miley. I won't forget," Eddie assured him.

Miley handed Eddie the rifle and pointed to a polished brass telescope mounted on the platform's railing. "Take a look at those targets through that scope."

Squinting through the telescope, Eddie noticed that the ten-ring was about the same size as the hole you'd expect a .22 slug to make. "Man, that's a small bull's-eye."

"You don't have to hit it dead center. Just nicking the ten-ring is a bull. Same with the others; nick the nine-ring, it's a nine. Let's watch your uncle."

Down on the range, Tom was loosening his rifle's strap. Miley looked at his watch. "We've got thirty minutes before the other guys get here, let's make the most of it. Let me see that rifle a minute. I'll show you what Tom's doing."

Eddie handed the rifle to Miley and watched and listened as Miley loosened the strap. "We call this the Hasty Sling. It's easy to slip into whether you're target-shooting indoors or out hunting." He showed Eddie how to slip his arm through the sling, bring his hand back and snug it to the rifle's stock. He then had Eddie hold the Remington and sight downrange using the sling, and not using the sling. The sling's advantage was clear to Eddie.

Tom got into the prone firing position, adjusted his sling and took aim. "Right now, he's sighting his rifle in," Miley whispered to Eddie. Tom took two shots and Miley checked the scope. He shouted to Tom, "They're almost on top of each other, barely breaking the eight-ring at seven o'clock." After having Eddie observe the two hits through the scope, Miley showed him how to use the elevation and windage knobs on the peep sight, explaining, "Tom is adjusting his windage and elevation. His next shot'll be a bull." Miley's prediction had been correct and after shouting, "Bull, dead center, Tom," the sergeant turned his full attention to Eddie. "Tom'll be okay on his own for awhile. I want to run a few things past you. First, we saw your uncle get comfortable in his firing position and get into his sling. Right?"

"Right."

"Next thing he did wasn't easy to spot from up here."

"Sighting his rifle in?"

"That's good. But no, before he sighted in, he made sure his elbow was directly under his rifle, rigid as a tripod. Only then did he squeeze one off."

Eddie slipped into his sling, taking care to keep the rifle pointed downrange. He stood straight and aimed at the far end of the range.

"Not bad. Good posture. Now let me explain the trigger squeeze." The sergeant became almost conspiratorial. "The trigger squeeze is the heart and soul of shooting. You never pull the trigger. You never jerk the trigger. Guys in cowboy movies jerk the trigger. Guys shooting blanks jerk the trigger."

Eddie had smiled and nodded, not wanting to interrupt the message.

"Real shooters," Miley continued, "squeeze the trigger. And trigger squeeze starts with breathing. You're in position. You're looking through your peep. You've got your target balanced on top of your front sight. Now, you breathe in and out slowly, not deep breaths, just relaxed breaths. Then after a few breaths, while exhaling, you check your breath. You just stop exhaling and start squeezing the trigger with a gentle, steady pressure. BANG! Your shot's off and you keep on squeezing."

"Like follow-through?"

"Exactly."

"Lemme see. I'm breathin'. Nice and relaxed. I'm aimin'. Then I stop exhalin' and begin squeezin' the trigger with a gentle, steady pressure. BANG! And I'm still squeezin' that trigger.

Eddie did well at the Dead Duck and the street corner had to do without him on Wednesday nights. When the flight was called to a halt outside the firing range, Eddie's last thought before filing in, was, maybe there's a guy like Miley in there, waitin' to wise these guys up.

That was not the case. Eddie's flight was greeted by an airman with the attitude of a movie usher. Another one-strike wonder, Eddie decided as he listened to the airman recite his piece. "I know that Lieutenant Snow already told you everything that you need to know about the rifle. And he told you about your various firing positions. So let's get started."

Thinking, these poor fucks ain't gonna shoot no score, Eddie marched out and took his spot on the firing line. Before dropping to prone position as ordered, Eddie started to make a hasty sling. The movie usher became the Children's Saturday Matinee matron. "What do you think you're doing," he demanded.

"Just makin' a hasty sling."

"We don't use a sling in the Air Force."

"Does anyone ever qualify?"

"Never mind the smart stuff. Just get down there and start pulling that trigger. There are two more flights waiting to get in here and fire."

Shots were already being fired before Eddie got into position. Squeezing off his first round, he spoke to himself. Somebody must've yelled "Commence firing!" but I sure didn't hear him. Okay, Miley, here I go firin' for score without a fuckin' hasty. Deprived of his sling, Eddie still managed to bang out a few bulls in prone, sitting and kneeling. Off-hand produced enough fives and sixes to drive his score down to 169, a tie for Best in the Flight with one of the Kentucky squirrel shooters. When the flight chief congratulated him for qualifying as a sharpshooter, Eddie smiled and thanked him, but thought, sharp-shooter. Shit, I'd've made expert if they let me use my hasty. He put the firing range into his stupidity file in the back of his brain and forgot all about it.

One of the guys who had never handled a rifle before that afternoon was feeling unhappy and he showed Eddie his score. "Forty-four," Eddie exclaimed,

"Jesus Christ, Nick, that's what I got in an Intermediate Algebra test once. Second lowest mark in New York State. Anyway, cheer up. Forty-four is damn good for the amount of instruction you got today. You could probably be a pretty good shooter if you had a real instructor. And another thing, you're in the fuckin' Air Force, you ain't gonna be shootin' no one. Let's go to the PX and get a couple of beers."

Eddie's memories of basic training get sidetracked by the clouds. The three have merged into the shape of an automobile. Looks like Joan's car. Wonder how she's doin'?

Back in Bay City Memorial Hospital, Sandy and Laura are visiting. Joan is opening their get-well gift. "A stationery set! Light blue, my favorite ... oh, it's even got a pen and a pencil."

"So you have no excuse for not keeping in touch," Sandy laughs.

"I filled the pen with violet ink for those steamy letters to Eddie," Laura adds.

Sandy shoots Laura a look and Joan catches it. "That's okay. I don't mind talking about Eddie. In fact, I'm trying to remember everything about him. The violet ink will be perfect. Thanks, both of you guys." As an afterthought, Joan asks, "Shouldn't you two be at school?"

"Just familiarization stuff," Laura answers. "No real classes until next week."

"We're going to Ann Arbor tomorrow," Sandy adds. "We're going to get a little place off campus."

"More privacy than the sorority house." Laura flashes a conspiratorial grin. "For when Norm and Bob come visiting." The three of them laugh.

"She doesn't want to have sorority sisters drooling all over her Normie," Sandy chimes in, and they all laugh again.

"How much do you remember about my birthday?" Joan fingers her pendant and ring. Laura sees the ring.

"Oh," she exclaims, "something new has been added."

Joan beams. She unfastens her necklace and hands the wedding band to Laura. Laura puts it next to her own ring finger. "Oh, I want one of these."

"You hear that, Normie?" Sandy asks, and there is another burst of laughter. Laura hands the ring to Sandy.

"It's beautiful, Joan. Have you tried it on yet?"

"Sure did. It's a perfect fit."

Sandy hands the ring back to Joan. Joan puts it back on the chain and refastens her necklace. "Now, about my birthday. I recall most of it, leaving the club, dancing at the Greystone ... and I remember being at a hotel with Eddie."

"You told me it was the Briggs," Sandy volunteers.

"That's it! Thanks, San." Joan smiles. "The Briggs."

With Sandy and Laura helping, Joan throws a few more pieces into the jigsaw puzzle of her mind. She recalls the tune "Tomorrow Night". "I've got to ask Mom to bring my portable. I'll bet if I listen to ..."

"Our station," Sandy finishes for her. "That's all you ever call it." They giggle.

"Well, I'll just bet hearing some of those tunes will help," Joan declares.

"It won't hurt," Laura replies. "You should hear the icky stuff the nurses are listening to."

They look through the brochure for Our Lady of the Lakes and they all agree that it looks like a nice place to wait for Eddie to return.

Eddie walks less than a mile when a black Mercury pulls over. A man in his fifties with a nose W.C. Fields would envy opens the passenger door and asks, "Where you heading, soldier?"

"'Frisco," Eddie answers, getting into the car.

The man is well-dressed and talkative. He's been drinking but is not drunk. "P.J. Clark's the name." He hands Eddie an emerald green business card.

Eddie introduces himself and looks at the card. The lettering is gold and embossed. Under "P.J. Clark" it reads "Advertising and Novelties". The card has a St. Louis address and phone number.

"What do you know about advertising, Eddie?"

"Not much," Eddie admits. "I guess it's about gettin' people to buy your stuff."

"Pretty good." Reaching into his briefcase, P.J. produces a silver flask and hands it to Eddie. It's untarnished and in raised silver on its front there's a 1920's roadster with its top down. A driver wearing goggles is behind the wheel.

"That was one of my presents when I graduated Dartmouth back in '23. Open it up and pour yourself a shot."

Eddie unscrews the cap and is surprised to find that it telescopes open and becomes a small cup. Pouring himself three quarters of a shot, he sniffs it.

"That's bourbon," P.J. tells him. "Smoother than rye."

Eddie tosses it down and his eyes water. He blows his breath out through his mouth to cool his tongue.

P.J. chuckles. "Pour me one, Eddie, and I'll tell you about advertising."

Eddie pours another shot and hands it to him. P.J. knocks it down, smacking his lips. "Ahhh, the nectar of the gods." He hands the empty cup back to Eddie. Eddie closes it, screws it back on and returns the flask.

"I closed a lot of deals with this." P.J. returns it to his briefcase. He goes on, telling Eddie how he drank and golfed his way through twenty-five years in what he calls "the advertising game."

"When the Depression hit and other guys were selling apples on street corners, I was breaking sales records, driving a Lincoln and living in a big apartment on Central Park West. The ad agency encouraged my drinking because I could take care of my accounts better drunk than most guys could sober." He lets out a deep sigh and quits talking.

Eddie wonders if something is wrong. "Are you okay?"

"Yeah, I'm okay, Eddie. I was just remembering the day the agency let me go. My wife left with the kids the same day the doctor told me my liver was shot. I wasn't a drinker anymore, I was a full-time drunk and instead of helping me, the company tied the can to me. I sobered up three weeks later down on Skid Row. I stayed dry six months but I couldn't get a job anywhere. I was too old. So I bought a bus ticket to St. Louis and an old Dartmouth classmate gave me a job selling balloons with messages on them. I never took a drink until he was killed in a wreck up by McLean. That was a sorry day for both of us."

P.J. seems like a nice guy and Eddie can almost feel his sadness. "Did you ever try Alcoholics Anonymous? It worked for my Uncle Frank."

"I tried it twice," P.J. answers, "but each time I sobered up, I'd start thinking about my past and I'd get so goddamned depressed that I'd start drinking again. I don't get drunk anymore anyway. I only drink enough to stay numb. Basically, I'm just waiting to die."

Trying to cheer P.J. up, Eddie asks, "Can you show me some of the stuff you sell?"

It works. P.J. brightens. "Sure thing. Reach into the back seat and get that gray box."

Eddie gets the box and opens it. It's filled with little desk calendars, pens and matchbooks that say things like "Jim's A-1 Plumbing, Rolla, Missouri," and "Ace Towing, Springfield, Illinois." Eddie tells P.J. how colorful some of the things look and P.J. starts telling him how he built the business up after his friend's death.

"I've been my own boss for the past two years. I make a lot less money than I used to in New York, but I'm happier." By the time he drops Eddie off about a mile southwest of St. Louis, P.J. is smiling.

Eddie gets out of the car and thanks P.J. for the lift. P.J. cautions, "You're a good kid, Eddie. Take my advice and don't sacrifice your life on the altar of some corporation."

Eddie smiles broadly. "Don't worry, P.J., there ain't much chance of that."

It's only after sundown, but Eddie is tired and he doesn't want to tap into another Bennie, so he checks into the Coral Court Motel, skips dinner and sleeps until dawn.

After a shower and a shave Eddie goes to the checkout desk and turns in his key. He's happy to find a rack of postcards. Picking one that says "Saint Louis" in big block letters, he writes:

Hi, Joan!

St. Louis, Gateway to the West. Wed. morning.

Your friend,

Edward

He stamps it and leaves it in the outgoing mail basket on the counter.

Eddie walks a half a mile down the highway to the Red Hen Café where he orders pancakes, eggs and sausage. The food is as good as the desk clerk had promised.

Paying his check, he notices a tall guy in line behind him. The man looks about thirty. He's wearing a straw cowboy hat, jeans, boots and a snap button shirt. His sleeves are rolled up to his elbows showing a couple of tattoos—a panther on his left forearm and a bulldog wearing a helmet on his right. Under the bulldog are the letters U.S.M.C.

Out in the parking lot, Eddie watches him get into a gray '49 Ford coupe. The car has Texas plates and shines like new. Eddie decides to hit him up for a ride. He approaches the man and asks, "If you're headin' west, I'd sure appreciate a lift."

The guy looks at Eddie evenly. He has high cheekbones and penetrating blue eyes. "How long you been in the Air Force?"

"Two years, next month. Why?"

"I'm wondering why you ain't got no stripes."

Eddie shrugs. "Nobody's perfect." He starts to walk away.

"That's the truth," the man agrees. "I'm going to Amarillo. If you don't mind riding with a felon, get in."

"Amarillo, that's great." Eddie quickly runs around to the passenger side of the car.

The guy opens the door for Eddie and offers his hand. "I'm Jesse."

Eddie shakes Jesse's extended hand. "I'm Eddie. Nice to meet you."

Jesse and Eddie talk. Eddie finds out that Jesse was wounded in Guadalcanal. "Then I wound up with a Dishonorable Discharge and three years in Leavenworth for punching out an officer. After they took that out of my shoulder," he relates, pointing to a jagged hunk of metal hanging on a string from the car's rearview mirror, "they sent me to San Diego to recuperate. My first night out of the hospital I go to the slop chute, have a few beers and on my way back to the barracks some second looie starts to chew me out for not saluting. My shoulder was still sore as a bitch—I couldn't raise my right arm higher than my shoulder—but he just kept on talking, not even letting me explain. So I dropped him with a straight left to the head. Two swabbies on Shore Patrol duty saw it happen and they were on me like stink on shit." Jesse laughs. "I busted up one of them pretty good and the next thing I knew I was in the joint."

Eddie tells Jesse about Arbo's thoughts on the similarities between officers and seagulls. Jesse laughs. "That's great. Full of shit and government protected. If that ain't the truth, I hope to shit in my mess kit."

Jesse is a fast driver with a high degree of common sense. Falling in behind a semi, he instructs, "I like to trail along about five car lengths behind these big boys. They roll at a good pace and if some asshole coming at us tries to pass at the wrong time, he tangles with a truck instead of me."

They stop for lunch in Joplin at a restaurant that has its own postcards, then gas up at a Phillips 66 station and are cutting through the southeastern tip of Kansas by one o'clock.

At sundown they hit Oklahoma City. Jesse fills up at a Texaco station and they have bowls of chili in a diner next door. Eddie follows Jesse's lead and adds three little yellow peppers to his chili.

"They're hotter'n August in Leavenworth," Jesse comments, "but they're good for your digestion."

Eddie nods as he swirls a mouthful of ice water around and wipes his watering eyes with a napkin. At the souvenir counter he buys a postcard of a cowboy riding a huge jackrabbit. He scribbles, "Still rolling on 66," stamps it and leaves it with the salesgirl, who assures him the card will get an Oklahoma City postmark.

By the time they're back on the road, all the stars are shining. Jesse asks Eddie about the postcards and Eddie tells him about Joan.

"Sounds like she'll wait," Jesse states. "I was lucky. When I was in the Corps, I didn't have a steady girl at home. Lots of the guys who did got 'Dear Johns', even some of the married guys. Same thing in the joint."

"You got someone now?"

"Yeah, in Amarillo. Her name is Linda. That means pretty in Spanish." Jesse reaches into his shirt pocket and pulls out a fat joint. "You ever smoke any reefer?"

"A few times, back in the old neighborhood. I remember the first time I tried it. I was shootin' pool with a couple of my high school buddies. I didn't feel nothin' at first. I thought they were bullshittin' me. Then all of a sudden it hit me. I felt like my cue stick was meltin'. Couldn't shoot worth a shit. It was funny."

Jesse laughs, lights up, takes a big hit and passes the J to Eddie. Eddie hits it and holds it in, the way Juan had taught him that first afternoon. He smiles, recalling how Juan and Luis had laughed and how he had joined in, laughing uncontrollably. He tells Jesse about them while they pass the joint back and forth.

"I was sorry to see Juan get kicked out of school," Eddie recalls. "We were in the same home room. He used to sign detention slips for ten cents apiece. Guys from all over school came to him. He'd only sign twenty a day. First come, first served." Eddie feels like talking. He rambles on. "He'd only do twenty a day so the ranks at detention wouldn't be thinned out too much."

Jesse takes an alligator clip out of his watch pocket and clips it to the short joint. "Smart move. What got him kicked out of school? A squealer?"

"No. It was funny what happened. He was doin' good work. He could sign 'Father B.J. Murphy' better than the old Dean of Discipline himself. What got Juan kicked out was Religion class. Father Burns was explainin' how it's a mortal sin once you decide to commit the deed, even if circumstances prevent you from doing it. You a Catholic, Jesse?"

"I was raised Catholic but it never took," Jesse answers. "Too many rules."

"That's no shit. So where was I? Religion class and then Father Burns asks if anyone's got any questions. Juan raises his hand and says real argumentative, 'Wait a minute, Father. Are you sayin' if me and my buddies go out on Friday night lookin' for it and we don't get nothin', it's a mortal sin?' and the whole class laughs.

"Then Burns says, 'If by "it" you mean ladies of easy virtue for you to release your Lust upon, the answer is yes.'

"Juan goes apeshit, says real loud somethin' like, 'That ain't fair,' then kind of mumbles 'Bullshit.' Burns blows his top, wants Juan to come up in front and get his hands whaled on with an eighteen-inch ruler. Juan says a whole lotta shit in Spanish and splits. Next day he's gone, kicked out.

"Back in the neighborhood, I ask him what he said. He said it again for me in Spanish and then said it means, 'Son of the great white whore. I shit all over your mother.'"

Jesse laughs out loud. "I'll get Linda to teach me that one. Jesse hits the roach and passes it to Eddie.

Eddie takes a hit and passes back a very short roach. Jesse gives it a final toke, then a nose hit, finishing up by putting the alligator clip into his mouth, opening it, swallowing the now tiny roach and returning the pristine clip to his watch pocket. "Nothing in my car ashtray but cigarette butts," he declares.

They roll down their windows and drive along in silence for a moment or two, when Jesse laughs. "The best thing about living in Texas is that it's next to Mexico. Linda's folks still live in Nuevo Laredo. Every couple of months we drive down and visit them. I always bring back a bag or two of this. You know, Eddie, when I was doing time I did some thinking and it seemed to me like every time I got in trouble I was either drunk or had been drinking."

"I know about that," Eddie agrees.

"So I decided that I'd try not drinking when I got out. I figured it would be easy with a three-year head start and it was, but getting a job wasn't. A con with a D.D. ain't in big demand. I knocked around a little and landed in Amarillo where I got a job washing dishes. That's when I met Linda's brother Pablo. He didn't drink either, but he did smoke reefer. He called it 'Mota.' One night I did a pipeful with him and I felt like I was at peace with the world. I tried it again from time to time. It kind of relaxed my hatred for the world. Know what I mean?"

"I think I do. I know I sure hate havin' people fuck with me."

"Do you ever wonder what life's all about?"

"Naw. I just kind of float along. You know, like that old song says, 'Life is just a bowl of cherries. Don't take it serious. It's too mysterious.' I think the guy who wrote that might know somethin'."

Jesse laughs. "Don't take it serious. It's too fucked up. Life's about learning to live through pain, how to rise above disappointment."

"Not lettin' shit get you down. Like gettin' shipped to Alaska."

"Right. But you're already thinking about the day you come back."

"How'd you know that?"

"It's how we are, guys like us. And you'll come back from Alaska, just like I got out of the joint. Life's about getting back on your feet when you get knocked down."

"And quick," Eddie exclaims, "before they can put the boots to you."

Jesse laughs. "Right. Life's about knowing the world's your enemy and having a good time anyway."

"Life's knowin' how to be happy with a hamburger when everyone else in the chow line is gettin' steak."

They talk and laugh all the way to the Texas border. Eddie finds out that Jesse's father was Irish and his mother Comanche.

"There's two kinds of people who shouldn't drink," Jesse states, "Irishmen and Indians. And I'm both. Biggest favor I ever did for myself was quitting drinking."

Eddie thinks about his father and how alcohol destroyed his life. He thinks about how much trouble alcohol has caused for himself, and nods. "This is the best I ever felt smokin' reefer." He laughs. "With a steady supply of this, I can see why you don't mind quittin' drinkin'." Eddie looks out at the starry sky. "What a fuckin' sky. The stars at night really are big and bright deep in the heart of Texas."

"No brighter than in Oklahoma," Jesse jokes. "Texas just got a song written about it." They laugh.

Eddie stares out into the blackness. "You know what's hard for me to understand?"

"What's that?"

"The idea of God … and religion."

An enormous jackrabbit bounds across the road. Jesse taps the brakes, misses the animal and declares, "Never hit one yet." He darts a glance at Eddie and continues, "I did a whole lot of reading in the joint. When I found out how many different kinds of gods man has come up with down through the ages, I said, 'Fuck it. I'll just go through life trying not to be a prick. If anything comes next, that's okay with me.' You follow me?"

"Sure. That's the same way I feel." Reefer is running through Eddie's brain, rummaging through theories of his, turning them into words. "I hope someone's runnin' the fuckin' universe, but I ain't countin' on it. And if nothin' is comin' next, I sure ain't gonna give a shit, Jesse, 'cause I'll be fuckin' dead. I'm not countin' on eternity to make me happy. I'm havin' my good times while I'm alive to enjoy 'em. I sure ain't gonna waste my life worryin' about what happens after I croak. What a goofy idea."

Jesse gives Eddie an encouraging nod, and continues listening. He enjoys reefer-fueled discussions.

Eddie presses on, "You know, if I was God and I gave a guy a life, and the guy spent his whole life bein' afraid of me, prayin' to me for special favors and shit, and bein' scared of what was goin' to happen to him after his life was over, I'd wonder why I gave him a life in the first place. Far as I'm concerned, religion is nothin' but jive, deep, deep jive. Like a kid is a perfect kid and one Sunday he skips Mass to go to a picnic, drowns and goes to hell forever. It's fuckin' crazy."

"That's another bad thing about gods," Jesse adds "They're always punishing someone. If it ain't Hercules or heretics, it's us."

"It don't make sense to me. How can a guy smart enough to invent a whole universe be chickenshit enough to send people into a fuckin' fire for all eternity? It's dumb. It ain't logical."

Jesse laughs and Eddie continues, "And I'll tell you what I think about hell, not that I believe in it for a second, but if I did and if there really was a hell, I'd rather spend eternity there, if there is an eternity, with my own kind, instead of sittin' on a fuckin' cloud, playin' a fuckin' harp with a bunch of brown-nosers and ass-kissers."

Jesse laughs again and declares, "If anything happens after I kick the bucket, it'll be a big surprise to me. Believe me, Eddie, if you can convince some poor, ignorant fuck that your particular brand of bullshit will guarantee him an eternity of bliss after he dies, providing he just follows your rules, lives his life the way he's ordered and accepts everything you tell him as the truth, you own that simple bastard. You can even get him to kill himself or die for your teachings. And if you can get him to believe in hell and the devil, you've got him by the balls on a downhill drag. Way I figure it, religion and bad logic go together like rice and beans."

"Speakin' of rice and beans. I'm starvin' my ass off."

"Reefer does that. We're just a few miles from Shamrock. We can stop at Big Annie's Diner."

"Sounds good." Eddie looks out the window and wonders how Joan's doing.

Feeling stuffed after a turkey dinner, Joan is sitting up in bed, looking through the Our Lady of the Lakes brochure. Pretty. She scans the photos of the dorms, the grounds and the woods. The trees look so beautiful. She's glad they took the pictures in autumn. Focusing on the photo of the chapel, Joan wonders about God and His ways. I wonder if my accident was God's way of punishing me for all the sins I committed with Eddie?

A grammar school scene unfolds. She and Sandy are lined up with the rest of the fifth-grade girls, waiting impatiently for Sister Carmelina to blow the whistle for recess to begin.

The whistle blows. Against the nun's orders not to run and shove, but to act like young ladies, Joan and Sandy take off full speed for the swings. Leaving the playground blacktop, entering the gravel of the swing area, Joan loses traction, falls hard and skins one knee enough to require Sister Carmelina's care.

"This is God's way of punishing you for being a bad girl," the nun scolds, watching for Joan's reaction to the copious amount of iodine she's pouring into the deep scrape. The intense burning that Joan is feeling is increased by the piece of gauze the nun is using to rub the scrape. "We've got to make sure there's no gravel in there," she declares.

Unhappy because Joan sits there with a tight mouth and narrowed eyes instead of squirming, saying "Oww!" or crying, Sister Carmelina rubs the scrape harder. "The pain you're feeling is nothing compared to the pain of the fires of hell. And that's where bad girls go, to hell." She tapes a piece of gauze over Joan's scrape and continues, "All right, you can return to your class. I've got the sixth-grade boys waiting for recess and they're a pack of devils."

As Joan leaves the room, Sister Carmelina shouts after her, "You'd better stop by the chapel after school and pray to Our Blessed Mother to make you a better girl."

Joan wonders about God. "Why is it when I talk to you or pray to you, I never get an answer?" she asks aloud. She listens and gazes out the window. It's a stone, dark night and she gets no answer from God.

She lies back with two pillows under her head and thinks, I'll just close my eyes and wait for an answer. Drifting off to sleep, she feels herself rising through the clouds. She sees herself walking along a white, puffy cumulus cloud road. She's kicking clumps of cloud like piles of fresh snow.

I don't feel dead, she's thinking as she continues walking down the cloud trail. All of a sudden she's at a gold and white guard shack, next to a pair of massive golden gates. She approaches the guard shack. It's empty. A sign on the shack's door says, "Out To Lunch." Joan walks behind the shack and sees her car. She gets into the car and is disappointed to find that it has an automatic transmission and no radio. Noticing the key in the ignition, she starts the car and sits there a moment before popping the Powerglide into drive.

Suddenly, she's cruising down Highway 23. She's feeling extreme desperation, searching for Eddie. Then, she pops up in a phone booth, at a Texaco station, talking with Eddie. "You don't need a radio," he's telling her. "You know how to sing."

"Where are you, Eddie?" she shouts into the phone. She shouts again. "Where are you, Eddie?" Everything disappears, gas station, phone booth, car and highway. Joan is standing by a gravel road, topless, in her half-slip. She opens her arms. "Dance with me, Eddie," she pleads.

Eddie materializes. He dances with her. She holds him close. He feels hot against her. She watches him turn pink, then slightly red, then darkest maroon. She sees him sprouting a pair of horns. She screams.

She finds herself back at Heaven's gate. An old, white-bearded man wearing an amazingly soiled and tattered white sheet, scolds, "Joan Whitman, you're a bad girl. You're not wanted here."

Eddie, looking like himself, pulls up in front of the shack in Joan's Chev. "Hey, Joan," he shouts. She runs to the car and jumps in. Eddie digs out, spewing cloud clumps all over the old guy and his guard shack.

"Get the fuck out of here," the old, holy man shouts.

Watching Eddie go through the gears, Joan exclaims, "Oh Eddie, you got my stick shift back." She clicks on the radio. Lonnie Johnson is singing "Tomorrow Night". "And my radio, too," she continues. "You're a good boy."

"Good enough to get some of that pie?" Eddie is smiling that smile Joan loves so well.

Everything fades. Joan sleeps on, dreamlessly. She awakens a short time later, to see Jill seated by her bed.

"Oh Mom, I'm so glad to see you. Have you been sitting there long?"

"Just a few minutes. I stopped at Otto's for dinner. Did you have a nice after-dinner nap?"

"I had a strange dream. I can't remember it."

"That's okay." Jill takes one of Joan's hands in hers. "I always forget my dreams, dear. Let's turn your radio on. I brought it from home."

"Thanks, Mom." Joan stares at the radio. "Funny. Something in my dream was about a radio."

"Was Eddie in your dream?"

"I think he was, Mom. I'm not sure. I hope he's making good time, hitching."

"I'm sure he's doing just fine, dear."

At Big Annie's Diner, Eddie and Jesse have ham and eggs, fried potatoes, biscuits and coffee. Back on Route 66, Jesse puts on a country and western station and fires up another number.

The Pepsi-Cola commercial ends as Jesse passes the joint to Eddie. He takes a deep toke and the DJ goes into his intro. "I've got a big batch of songs to play so let's start with a little gal who is on the charts for the first time. I'm predicting Kitty Wells will be around for a long, long while. Here she is singing her big hit, 'It Wasn't God Who Made Honky Tonk Angels'."

"As I sit here tonight, the jukebox playin' …" The opening words of the tune transport Eddie to another world. He lets the smoke drift slowly out of his nose and pays attention to the fiddle and the guitar picking. He also feels as if he's inside the car's radio, lying in a hammock with the music flowing over him.

On the dying notes of the song, the jock segues smoothly into "Honky Tonk Blues" and follows up with two more by Hank Williams, "Lost Highway" and "I Can't Help it (If I'm Still In Love With You)."

The joint journeys back and forth. The guys remain silent, listening, not even speaking when the DJ uses Lefty Frizzell to lighten up the set with "If You've Got The Money, I've Got The Time." The J gets short while Kay Starr and Tennessee Ernie Ford are working on "I'll Never Be Free" and Jesse clips it up. While Patti Page sings "Tennessee Waltz", he does a nose hit and performs his roach disposal ritual.

They roll down the windows. "Cold, Cold Heart" is just starting. Jesse turns up the volume. "Listen to this one."

The song ends and Eddie remarks, "I've heard that tune a hundred times. I've always liked it but I never knew it was so long."

Jesse laughs and turns the radio down. The DJ is starting a Lincoln-Mercury commercial. "Yeah," Jesse answers, "the songs always seem longer to me too, after a little mota."

Eddie laughs. "I guess I never gave country music a fair chance before. Man, there was a whole lotta great fiddlin' and guitar work goin' on. You ever listen to any rhythm and blues tunes?"

"That's funny. I'm on my way home from seeing some musicians up in Saint Looie. Colored guys. I always bring them a little reefer whenever I pick some up. Milton, the piano player is a rhythm and blues expert. He says country music is the white folks rhythm and blues."

"I can see that."

Milton told me an old colored man taught Hank Williams to play guitar."

"No shit?"

"No shit. Milton met Hank one time down in New Orleans and Hank told him a man called Tee-Tot taught him everything he ever learned about music."

"Tee-Tot?"

"Milton says the old guy's real name was Rufus Payne. 'Tee-Tot' was just a nickname, I guess."

They are still talking about music when Jesse pulls into Amarillo. He drops Eddie off at Amarillo Boulevard, at the western edge of town. Eddie thanks Jesse for the lift and watches the '49 Ford's taillights, as Jesse heads south on Western Street.

CHAPTER 30

▼

Eddie walks the couple of blocks to the Lazy Z Motel and registers. He has a new respect for Texas, Texans and country and western music. He falls asleep thinking of Joan and doesn't wake up until eight o'clock in the morning.

The room is so bright that Eddie awakens thinking it's much later. He checks his roadmap while he's in the bathroom. Looks like I'm halfway to L.A., he thinks. He has another thought. This is my first shit in two days. I better eat some greens today.

He brushes his teeth, rushes through his shower and shave and decides he can hitch one more day before getting into his second set of khakis. He puts on fresh socks and boxers, rubs the dust off his shoes with toilet paper and is in the lobby of the motel by eight-thirty.

The old man running the desk has a huge, drooping, gray mustache and a leathery face. His blue-gray cowboy hat has a hammered silver hatband with the word "Eddie" spelled out on it in small turquoise stones.

Eddie admires the old guy's hat and they laugh about both being named Eddie. While turning in his key, Eddie asks where he can get a cup of coffee. The old cowboy goes into the adjoining room and comes back with two mugs of coffee. He sees Eddie looking at an old framed photo on the wall which shows four cowboys standing beside their horses. The second man from the left has a big, black mustache.

"That's me when I was a Texas Ranger."

Eddie is surprised to find out that the old guy is a month away from his ninetieth birthday. Eddie asks about a postcard and the cowboy produces one with a picture of the motel on it. He tells Eddie about cattle brands.

"You see how that Z is laying on its side? That's because it's lazy."
Eddie writes on his card.

Dear Joan,

A real Texas Ranger gave me this card!

He stamps it, leaves it in the mail basket, has a second cup of coffee and is out hitching by nine o'clock.

While Eddie is sticking up his thumb down in Texas, Joan is getting ready to leave Bay City Memorial Hospital with her stitches removed and her bandage down to a three-inch-square patch of gauze on the left side of her head.

Jill has done some shopping and she has Joan looking like a beautiful autumn leaf in harmonizing shades of red, orange and yellow. She ties a multicolored bandanna on Joan's head, Carmen Miranda-style, and tops everything off by giving Joan a pair of dark green aviator-style sunglasses.

"Oh Mom," Joan exults, putting on the shades and looking at herself in the full length mirror. "They're beautiful. Just like Eddie's." She hugs Jill. "You think of everything. The whole outfit is gorgeous. Thanks, Mom. I love you so much."

Dr. Sloane enters the room. "Good morning, ladies. Have either of you seen Joan?" he teases.

Joan takes off her dark glasses and smiles. The swelling in her nose is much reduced but her eyes are still purple.

"Oh there you are." Dr. Sloane smiles. "How are you feeling?"

"Good as new," Joan replies, "thanks to you, Doctor."

"That's what I wanted to hear. A couple of the nurses are waiting to say goodbye to you out in reception."

Joan leaves the room and Dr. Sloane turns to Jill. "She's a tough kid, Mrs. Whitman, but she should have a week or ten days of rest before going off to college."

"How about a leisurely drive to Pennsylvania? A few days here and there at nice hotels and resorts?"

"Sounds made to order."

He's in the middle of explaining to Jill that he considers Joan fully recovered in spite of her memory lapses, when Joan pokes her head in the door.

"I'm all set, Mom."

As Jill and Dr. Sloane meet her at the doorway she impulsively hugs the doctor, saying, "Thank you, Doctor, for saving my life."

"You were an excellent patient, Joan," he states. "You've got a fighting spirit."

Jill kisses him on the cheek. "Thank you, Doctor, for everything."

Dr. Sloane watches the two walk down the hallway and out the door. He smiles.

Walking across the parking lot, Joan takes a deep breath. "It's so nice to breathe fresh air."

Jill smiles. She is so happy she feels like hugging Joan. She does, and while hugging her, she plants little kisses all over Joan's face. Jill starts to cry. "I'm just so happy to have you back."

Tears spring from Joan's eyes. Jill looks at her and sobs, "You're beautiful, black eyes and all. You look like a beautiful little raccoon." They giggle between sobs and end up with hearty laughter. They sit in the car, dry their eyes and Jill wipes her lipstick from Joan's face.

Jill smiles, watching as Joan adjusts her sunglasses and smiles into the vanity mirror on the back of the passenger side visor. "Let's roll all the windows down," Jill exclaims, "and enjoy this pretty day." She feels like she's going to a party.

Traffic on Route 66 is light. Eddie has thirty minutes to look around. Not a cloud in the sky. Bet I can see a hundred miles, he's thinking, looking to the west.

The Chevy panel truck is almost stopped before he notices it. The gold lettering—Stan's Express, Amarillo, Albuquerque, Gallup & Flagstaff—stands out boldly on the maroon paint, glittering brightly in the sunlight. The truck's roof is enamel white. Eddie is glad he's wearing his shades.

The driver, a middle-aged, ruddy-faced man with a good-sized gut, is dressed as Jesse had been, including the straw cowboy hat. He pops the passenger door open and asks, "Where you headin', podner?"

Eddie gets into the truck, says, 'Frisco," and sticks out his hand. "I'm Eddie Flynn."

"Stan Williams." The driver shakes Eddie's hand. He asks Eddie how his hitching's been going and when Eddie tells him how quickly he traveled from Chicago to Amarillo, Stan admonishes, "You're about at the halfway mark, but that was the easy half." He goes on to tell of the rigors of Route 66 that await. Stan knows the Amarillo/Flagstaff stretch of road well and he's eager to share his knowledge. He is not boring.

The windows of the truck are rolled down and the stick-on dashboard thermometer reads 75°. Driving through Adrian, Stan taps it with his finger and it jumps to 89°. "It's going to be a hot one," he observes.

Just west of the Texas-New Mexico border, they narrowly miss a deer that jumps out in front of the truck. Stan enjoys Eddie's enthusiastic reaction and comments, "This is a tough stretch of road. A lot of first-time 66 drivers get into big trouble between here and Flagstaff."

Rolling through Tucumcari, Stan tells Eddie how the Comanche used to ambush their enemies and use the town for sending smoke signals. "They were good warriors," he states, "but you can't beat the US government."

"I guess that's true." Eddie tells Stan about Jesse being half Comanche and half Irish.

"I sure wouldn't want to tangle assholes with that old boy," Stan declares, and they laugh. "Especially if he's drunk," Stan adds.

Eddie laughs. "You know, that's funny, you saying that, 'cause Jesse said he quit drinking a few years ago."

"Well, I'm sure most folks who deal with him on a daily basis are happy about that," Stan jokes, and Eddie laughs again. "As well as the world at large," Stan adds, and Eddie laughs harder.

This is a funny guy, Eddie thinks, and good on the local history and geography.

They stop for lunch at the Club Café in Santa Rosa. Eddie has sourdough biscuits and gravy, a bowl of chili and a big salad. "Sure glad I skipped breakfast," he remarks.

"I know all the best eating places." Stan opens his belt up a notch and laughs. Over a second cup of coffee, Stan explains how the Pecos River that runs right through town and down into Texas used to be where the law ended. "West of the Pecos, it was every man for himself," he states.

Leaving the Club Café, Eddie notices that the Dr. Pepper thermometer mounted on the building's brick wall reads 94°.

"And that's just in the shade," Stan warns.

They gas up at a Phillips 66 just outside of town and Stan gets out two small, square canvas bags from behind his seat. The bags have rope handles. He fills them with water and hangs them on the truck's front bumper. "It'll be uphill and hot the rest of the way," he promises as he gets behind the wheel.

While Stan and Eddie are cruising along Route 66 en route to lunch in Santa Rosa, New Mexico, Joan and Jill are between Bay City and Saginaw on Highway 23. Jill notices Joan looking through the Our Lady of the Lakes brochure. "I want you to know, honey, if anything at that place makes you unhappy, just phone. I'll snap you out of there so fast they'll think you're a magic act."

Joan laughs. "I know that, Mom. You don't have to tell me. But I read this with Eddie and looked through it again with Sandy and Laura. It looks kind of nice, kind of peaceful."

"We took Granny there for a visit to her old Alma Mater, just a year before she passed on." Jill pauses. "You know, I did feel quite untroubled there." She laughs and adds, "It was too quiet for your dad. He couldn't wait to get back to Detroit. Back to work." She looks at Joan. "Do you recall him at all?"

Joan thinks for a moment. "No. Sorry, Mom."

"That's okay, honey. The doctor said you'll remember him when you see more of him. When we get to Flint, we'll call and see if he's available. Would you like that?"

"Sure, Mom. How far is it to Erie?"

"I'm not certain. There's a map in the glove box."

Joan gets the map and looks at it. "Could we take 23 to Toledo and then just kind of go along the lakeshore as we go through Ohio?"

"That sounds fine, dear. Dr. Sloane told me to take at least a week on our way to school. You and I can have a little vacation. I packed most of your favorite clothes. Three suitcases."

Joan smiles a big smile. "Just the two of us. This'll be such fun."

They hit the edge of Saginaw and Slim's Blue Light Inn comes into view. Three Hogs, Slim's Olds and six other cars are parked in the lot.

"I remember that place, Mom," Joan exclaims. "Eddie used to take me dancing there!"

"Looks like a rough part of town."

"It is. But could we stop for just a minute? Slim is so nice. He's the owner."

It might be good for Joan to see another familiar face, Jill figures. "It's against my better judgment, but if it'll make you happy, why not?"

Jill eases the Cadillac into the lot and parks next to Slim's Olds. "Your father would have a fit if he saw us going in here." They both laugh.

Walking from the car to the roadhouse entrance, Jill once again thinks of her old summer love. Mike, she thinks and wonders about what might have been.

Joan leads the way in. All the blue lights are lit, but the baby spot is off and the mirrored ball isn't rotating. The smell of beer and frying hamburgers is in the air. Jill feels herself relax in the darkness.

Joan looks around. Two bikers and their girlfriends are sitting in the booth nearest the juke, two couples are in another booth, three guys are shooting pool, a few people are at the bar and a young bartender is on duty. Where's Slim? Joan wonders.

Slim comes out of the kitchen carrying a small brown paper bag. He's all slicked up in freshly-laundered Levis, shined black biker boots, spotless white T-shirt and a lightweight brown suede jacket. "See you tomorrow, Crash." He waves to the bartender. "I'm going to the bank." He turns from the bar and almost bumps into Joan and Jill.

"Hi Slim," Joan greets him.

Slim looks at Joan, darts a look at Jill, then looks at Joan again. Joan's bandanna hides her shorn head and bandage. Slim studies her face, sees only red where the whites of her eyes ought to be, a slightly swollen nose and two of the ripest black eyes he's seen in seven years of owning the Blue Light. Poor kid, he thinks.

"Slim? It's me, Joan. Eddie's girl."

"Joan?" Instinctively, Slim wraps his arms around her. He pats her back tenderly. He's an all bone and muscle six-foot-three and Jill watches Joan get swallowed up in his arms. "What happened? Are you okay?" He glances at Jill. She's smiling.

Slim releases Joan from his hug. "Did Eddie get to see you?"

"Oh yes. I was in a car wreck, but I'm okay now," Joan answers. "Eddie came by the hospital." She notices Slim looking at Jill and adds, "Slim, I'd like you to meet my mom."

"I'm pleased to meet you, ma'am."

"Call me Jill, please." Her smile is warm.

Without leering, Slim drinks Jill in. Her hat is a small yellow basket of autumn flowers, grains and miniature pumpkins. Her black hair, in a pageboy cut, is glistening. She's lightly made up and she's wearing a rust-colored sheath dress that falls to mid-knee, a necklace of marble-sized orange beads, a matching bracelet and maroon suede pumps. This is a high-quality lady, he decides. "It's close to lunch. How about a couple of frosted mugs of beer?"

Joan looks at Jill. Slim looks at Jill. "I'd like to hear about how Joan and Eddie found each other," he asks.

"Mom helped," Joan volunteers. Jill notes Joan's upbeat manner with Slim.

"We can sit right here," Slim gestures toward a nearby empty booth. "We don't have to have beer."

"No, a nice cold beer sounds good. Thanks." Jill slips into the booth.

"Great." Slim tosses his paper bag onto the booth's table and makes a beeline for the bar. Joan slides into the booth next to Jill.

Slim returns with three mugs of beer and sits facing Joan and Jill. He takes a long swallow of beer, looks at Joan and asks, "So how did Eddie find you?"

Joan tells about her accident and how Jill got her note to Sandy for delivery to Eddie. Jill joins the conversation and at Joan's urging does her Red Cross-lady voice. Slim breaks out a pack of Camels and Jill smokes one instead of her regular long cigarettes.

When Joan shows Slim her wedding band, Slim remarks, "Eddie showed me that ring the last night he was here. Some of the Cobras were taking him back to the base."

"He told me," Joan adds. "He said they took him up to the main gate and his commanding officer went ape." Joan drops the "shit" portion of "apeshit" in deference to her mother.

Slim points across the dance floor. "Those guys were with him. You want to say hi?"

Joan looks at Jill.

"Any friends of Eddie are fine with me." Jill means it. Slim takes them over to meet the guys and girls.

After introducing Joan and Jill to Spot-Shot, Joy, Big Bob and Dreamboat, Slim slides a small table up against the Cobras' booth. He sets up three chairs, holding first Joan's then Jill's chair, as they get seated. He goes back to the old booth, gets his paper bag and their three half-finished beers. He sets the beers on the table.

"I'll be right back."

At the bar, Slim gives Crash the bag. "Stash this under the bar. And let me have a pitcher of beer."

"Who's the classy lady?"

"She's okay," Slim answers. "I like her."

He takes the pitcher back to the table and freshens everyone's beer. Joy and Dreamboat are still eating their hamburgers. Big Bob and Spot-Shot's plates are empty.

"God, those hamburgers smell delicious," Jill remarks.

"Crash's momma can really cook," Spot-Shot blurts out, and he gets a look from Slim.

"Rare, medium, or well done, Jill?" Slim asks.

"Rare, please."

"Joan? You hungry?"

"Yes. Thanks, Slim," Joan replies. "Rare for me too."

"Big Bob, I know you can go again," Slim jokes, and everyone laughs. "What about you, Spot-Shot?"

Spot-Shot doesn't answer.

"It's on the house," Slim prompts.

"In that case, yes, thanks. I would like another hamburger. But tell Natalie to hold the French fries. I'm watching my figure." Everybody laughs and Slim heads for the kitchen.

While they're all eating, Slim turns on the baby spot and mirrored ball at Joan's request so Jill can see the effect.

Joan plays some tunes and tells Slim that she's happy to see "Tomorrow Night" in the juke.

"Eddie asked me to put that one in the last time he was by. It's a good tune. Gets a lot of play." Slim looks at Jill. I'd like to dance close and slow with you, he thinks.

At three o'clock, when Joan and Jill are leaving, Joan asks Slim to leave "Tomorrow Night" in the juke until Eddie comes home. "It's our special song, Slim."

"I figured that. Sure it stays. I own that jukebox. It's not a rental."

They stop at the club's front door. Slim hugs Joan gently. "Get well quick and make sure to invite me to your wedding."

"Oh, I will, Slim." Joan stands on her tiptoes and kisses Slim on the cheek.

Slim takes Jill's hand. She feels the warmth of his hand rush up her arm. "It was a genuine pleasure to meet you, Jill."

"The pleasure was all mine." Jill is smiling her best smile. "Your club has a lovely atmosphere, and excellent food and drink. And most important, a charming host."

Slim steps outside the Blue Light and watches the Cadillac head for Highway 23. "Goddamn, that's a woman," he says out loud.

Driving down 23, with Joan by her side, Jill feels mellow. "Why don't we just drive until sunset? Then we can look for a nice auto court."

"Sounds great, Mom. What did you think of Slim and the Cobras?"

"I can't remember the last time I had such fun. Those phonies your dad hangs around with could learn plenty from Eddie and Slim and their friends." They laugh. "And that music," Jill continues. "Such feeling. I'd like to get that song, 'It's Too Soon to Know'."

"It's called rhythm and blues, Mom. Like to hear some more?" Joan turns up the radio and spins the dial. "Eddie and I call this our station." Ruth Brown is singing "Teardrops From My Eyes".

They stop in Flint for gas. Jill calls Bill and has to leave a message because he's in a conference and can't be disturbed. Jill is neither surprised or disappointed.

At sundown they pull into Bartok's Motor Hotel, just north of the Ohio border. After a light dinner, they sit on the porch of their cabin, enjoying the spring-like change in the weather. They go to bed at nine o'clock, sleep late and don't check out until noon Friday.

Thursday afternoon, at about the same time that Jill and Joan are between Flint and Ann Arbor, headed for a good night's sleep at Bartok's, Stan and Eddie are approaching Albuquerque. Stan points to a row of fluffy white clouds lining up on the western horizon.

"Looks like we'll be hitting some weather around Gallup."

The dashboard thermometer is nudging 100°. They motor slowly down Central Avenue with Stan pointing out motels and cafes, then they cross the Rio Grande. Eddie gets his map out and traces the river to its source in Colorado. "This beats the shit out of studying geography in a classroom."

Stan laughs. "Look on your map for the Continental Divide. A little bit east of Gallup."

Eddie finds it quickly. "Got it."

"I'm betting we're in a thunderstorm by the time we cross the Divide. We'll be over seven thousand feet by then."

Eddie looks at the clouds. The ones on the northern edge of the line are already dark gray. "I wouldn't take that bet."

A few miles east of Grants, Stan notices the truck's heat gauge almost pegging itself at the high end. He pulls off the highway as far as possible and pops the hood. "She'll cool down real quick," he states.

He turns the engine off and lets the truck stand for ten minutes. He and Eddie smoke two of Eddie's cigarettes, then Stan starts the engine and pours half of one of the water bags over the radiator. He unscrews the cap without removing it, letting a small amount of steam escape from the relieved radiator. "I've got this down to a gnat's ass," he boasts while he pours a little more water over the radiator. The radiator stops steaming. Stan removes the cap and pours the contents of the second bag into the radiator.

Eddie asks him why he has the engine running and Stan explains, "You never want to add cold water to an overheated engine without the motor running or you could crack the block. Guys who don't know that keep the mechanics around here rich."

Eddie nods and puts that fact into his fairly empty "Automotive Knowledge" bin.

Stan closes the hood. They get back into the truck and Eddie spots a lightning bolt. He counts to eight before he hears a faint rumble of thunder. He guesses, "Eight miles?"

"Sounds just about right," Stan answers. He slips the truck into gear, gets back on 66 and heads into the impending storm.

They're within three miles of the Continental Divide when the gust of cold air hits them. The dashboard thermometer tumbles from 100° to 86° and the sky turns black. Stan turns on the headlights and they roll up the windows. Two minutes later the rain begins to fall. The truck's wipers can barely keep up and after five minutes the rain gets even harder. The drops are coming straight at them and the wind is trying to blow the truck off the road. Stan has to stop.

"It's like being in a waterfall." Eddie is almost shouting in order to be heard over the racket of the raindrops hitting the roof.

Ten, fifteen minutes it should let up," Stan predicts. "I just hope it don't start to hail. I paid a hundred and fifty bucks for this paint job a month ago in Amarillo."

"How bad does the hail get around here?"

"I've seen hailstones damn near the size of baseballs," Stan brags. "Most times they'll range from buckshot to golf balls."

"Holy shit!?! Baseballs."

"Some of the old timers claim they seen hail as big as goddamn grapefruits. Big enough to break branches off of trees."

"Grapefruits," Eddie repeats. "Son of a bitch," he adds reverently.

No hail develops and the rain slows by half. Stan turns the wipers back on. "I can drive through this," he states. "Sometimes hereabouts, old 66 gets slicker'n owl shit on a tin roof."

He puts the truck back into gear and continues down 66, doing twenty miles an hour. By the time they reach Gallup, there are a few clear patches in the sky.

At Wiley's Texaco, they meet a trucker heading east from L.A. He tells them that the road between Gallup and Flagstaff is no problem.

While the attendant is gassing up Stan's truck and Stan is heading for the men's room to "bleed the lizard," as he puts it, Eddie goes next door to Gert's Trading Post. He sends a card to Joan and brings back two barbecue beef sandwiches and a pair of Dr. Peppers. They stand by the truck eating and stretching their legs as the storm continues its eastward journey, leaving some scattered clouds.

"Get ready for a hell of a sunset," Stan promises as they get back into the truck.

A few miles out of Gallup, Eddie sees that Stan wasn't exaggerating. Looking through the window Eddie sees a postcard. The sky runs coral for the full length of the horizon, with long stratus clouds in varying shades, from grayish green to turquoise floating just above the coral strip. Black streaks of rain with silver sprinkles in it, fall from the northernmost cloud.

A medium-sized leftover cumulus cloud, shaped and colored like a scoop of black raspberry ice cream, hides the setting sun. The sun fights back, highlighting the cloud's edges in orange-gold. The edges seem to sparkle.

Other rays from the obscured sun are lighting clusters of alto-cumulus clouds. The high-flying, tightly-rolled clouds look like rows of pink, red, orange and gold pompoms.

Far off, to the north-northwest, a string of small, pure white cumulus clouds hanging in mid-sky are lined up. They look like Spanish galleons, each a bit smaller than the cloud before it. Eddie counts nine of them.

When the sun drops completely, the stratus clouds turn black and the edges of the sun-blocking cumulus cloud vanish, leaving the cloud a dark gray. Everything else turns indigo, except the sailing ships. They are no longer discernable, having blended into a violet patch. Eddie sees Joan's smile in that patch. Moments later, darkness descends and the first couple of stars show themselves dimly.

"I've seen some pretty sunsets," Eddie observes, "but this one was King Shit."

"This area's kind of famous for its sunsets."

"It should be."

"Some folks think that doing them atomic bomb tests causes it."

"Oh? What do you think, Stan?"

"Well, my old granny swears the sunsets around here were pretty damn spectacular long before the government started blowing up all them atoms. And I'm inclined to go along with Granny."

"Granny's good enough for me," Eddie agrees, and they laugh.

During the remainder of the drive to Flagstaff, Stan and Eddie talk about Stan's express business. When Eddie asks exactly how the business works, Stan explains.

"I've got a few regular customers in each town between Amarillo and Flagstaff, mostly auto parts dealers, two guys who make racing accessories, a couple of restaurant supply houses and a handful of trading posts. I get special runs from some small department stores too. Stuff the big companies don't want to be bothered with. I do okay."

Eddie asks him about getting bigger or maybe getting another truck or two. Stan's answer and change of mood surprise Eddie completely.

"Not a chance," Stan declares with vehemence. "The minute you go into business you get the goddamn government for a partner, with their goddamn income tax, and every time you add an employee things get worse. More regulations, more forms. No siree. I'm a one-man show."

He tells Eddie that he considers income tax to be a kind of robbery. "I fuck the government every chance I get," he brags. "Like this run. I had regular stops all the way east, then in Amarillo, a drinking buddy of mine set me up with this shipment." He points with his thumb to the three crates in the back of the truck. "A hundred bucks, cash money up front, no receipts. Far as my records show, I'm deadheading it back from Amarillo. There ain't no way them bastards in Washington can know if I'm empty or not."

"Good for you."

The conviction in Eddie's voice makes Stan smile. "I'm as free as a bird so long as I remain a solo act." Eddie laughs.

The conversation veers from Stan's business to women, when Eddie asks if they can stop in Winona so he can send a card to Joan. He explains about the tune "Get Your Kicks on Route 66" reciting, in part, "'Flagstaff, Arizona, don't forget Winona, Kingman, Barstow, San Bernardino'. I'm sending my girl a card from each of the towns in the tune."

"Hope she saves them cards," Stan comments. "They'll be a nice thing to have." He goes on talking and tells Eddie how he was married once.

"I woke up one morning and Inez was gone. She just got itchy feet. When I found her goodbye note on the kitchen table saying she was never, ever coming back, I felt like I had just took a good shit." Eddie laughs as Stan continues. "Now I got me a couple of lady friends who don't ask for nothing but a night on the town and a good time in bed." They both laugh. "And I know how to do both." They laugh again.

"Sounds like a pretty nice deal," Eddie remarks. "Is it gettin' serious with either of 'em?"

"No siree it ain't," Stan answers. "And I still keep my eye out for the occasional stray." Eddie laughs.

They make a brief coffee stop at Winona and Eddie sends his postcard, a brilliant, colorful sunset. "*This is almost as good as the sunset I just saw,*" he writes on the card. The clerk assures him that the card will get a Winona postmark.

At 11:00 PM Stan drops him off in front of the Black Cat Café in Flagstaff. "You can get a good meal here," Stan states. "I'm going to spend the night with a little gal down in Sedona."

"One of them strays?" Eddie asks, and they laugh. Eddie thanks Stan for the lift, waves goodbye, and watches the truck's taillights disappear down Highway 89.

At the Black Cat, Eddie has a short stack and a side order of bacon. The waitress keeps refilling his coffee cup and he perks up. He decides to hitch through the night.

I've already used up three of my travel days, he thinks. I'd better keep movin'. He pays his check, leaves a postcard of a giant Saguaro cactus with the cashier, goes to the men's room, pops half a Bennie and is out on Route 66 with his thumb up by 11:45.

Just before midnight a trucker comes out of the Black Cat carrying a large canvas-covered canteen on a strap. He's climbing into the cab of his Kenworth when he spots Eddie and shouts, "I'm going to Barstow."

Eddie runs over to the truck and starts to climb aboard. The driver, a skinny guy with forearms like Popeye the Sailor, continues, "But you've got to talk to me. Keep me awake. I've been humping this load of sunglasses from Saint Louie and my clock is winding down."

"I'm a born bullshitter," Eddie states, taking his seat. Eddie introduces himself and the driver responds, "I'm Gary Gibson. Everyone calls me Gearbox."

Gearbox pulls out onto Route 66 and begins living up to his nickname, with many gear changes and minimum braking. Passing the canteen of black coffee back and forth, Eddie regales Gearbox with accounts of some of his best Air Force adventures.

"No wonder you don't have any stripes," Gearbox observes, and they laugh.

Between Williams and Seligman, Gearbox can't fight off a long hard yawn. "It's not the stories, Eddie. I'm just running out of steam."

Happy with the driver's reactions to his Air Force tales, Eddie decides that Gearbox is an all right guy. He takes out his aspirin tin, opens it and asks, "Want some help stayin' awake?"

Gearbox smiles broadly. "You, my young friend, are a true fucking lifesaver." He reaches into the tin, takes the half, puts it in his mouth and chews it up, chasing it with a mouthful of coffee. "I feel better already." He grins at Eddie and shouts, "Happy motoring!"

They both laugh and Gearbox's foot gets just a bit heavier.

Going through Seligman, Gearbox slows down to the speed limit. "Most of these little pissant towns make good money off of guys like me, so I give 'em what they want and then speed like hell in between."

"Kind of like a compromise?"

"Yeah, kind of. But it still pisses me off, so I run without baffles in my muffler and rattle their windows when I downshift." He shouts, "Fuck 'em all, big and small." They grin at each other.

After passing through Hackberry, they come into a curve a few miles down the road that Gearbox describes as "the longest fucking curve I've ever drove."

Coming out of the curve, Eddie remarks, "That was really something. You sure we ain't headed back east?"

At Kingman, while Gearbox refills his big canteen, Eddie sends Joan a postcard. The card is a photograph of the natural bridge in the Grand Canyon. He pulls out his pen and writes across the back, *"Still under construction."*

From Kingman to Needles they drop from over 3,300 feet above sea level to 480 feet, and Gearbox takes full advantage of it. Eddie thinks, Man, I'm sure glad I had a Bennie for this guy.

"Any asshole can ride his brakes along here," Gearbox boasts. "Real drivers go through the gears."

Eddie relaxes, sits back and enjoys the ride.

They rip through California from Needles to Barstow, rumbling through little towns like Amboy and Ludlow with Gearbox and his gutted muffler showing the sleeping residents no mercy as dawn breaks behind them. At 7:45 they pull up in front of Lupe's Cantina, and Gearbox drops Eddie off. Eddie waves goodbye, and Gearbox gives him a couple of blasts on the air horn as he heads down 247 for the truck depot.

Opening the door to Lupe's, Eddie inhales deeply. His appetite returns. He has huevos rancheros, rice and beans and two large glasses of fresh orange juice. The owner, an attractive, older Mexican lady, is running the cash register. When Eddie pays his check, he asks for and receives permission to clean up, shave and change clothes in the men's room. He leaves the immaculate restroom as he found it, goes next door to a souvenir shop and sends a postcard with a picture of a sign that reads Welcome to California. He buys a pair of turquoise earrings, and the girl who packs them tells him they'll be mailed free of charge. Eddie looks at the wall clock. Nine AM Friday morning and I feel fine, he thinks and counts backward: nine Pacific, ten Mountain, eleven Central. It's noon in Joan Time. He walks outside into the bright California sunshine.

After checking out of the Bartok Motor Hotel at noon, Jill stays on 23 until it junctions with Ohio State Route 2, just west of Toledo. She then takes Route 2 to downtown, where she and Joan linger over lunch at a family-owned Italian restaurant before getting back on the road.

Later in the day, near Port Clinton, Jill finds the perfect spot. The Sail Inn. Like most of the lake resorts, it's been buttoned down since the Labor Day weekend. All ten of its little sailboats are wearing canvas covers, bobbing in their slips along the dock. Only one of the blue and white cabins has a car parked next to it.

Jill books a cabin and she and Joan then go to a local grocer for supplies. They buy two small steaks, a pound of ground sirloin, four baking potatoes, two onions, a small head of lettuce, two large, fully-ripe tomatoes, a bag of hard rolls, ketchup, bacon, eggs, butter, sugar, two cans of evaporated milk, a jar of George Washington instant coffee powder, pickles, olives, potato chips, cookies and a case of beer. The old guy who owns the place is so happy they came by, he gives them a small chocolate cake. "It's on the house, ladies," he announces.

Back at the cabin, they bring in their luggage, put the groceries and their clothing away, open a couple of beers and walk out onto the dock to enjoy the sunset together before starting dinner.

The cabin's kitchen is small, but stocked with all the proper utensils, and it's clean. Joan turns the radio on and gets her Detroit station. She finds another station from Cleveland that's also broadcasting an R&B format.

Jill and Joan have dinner by the yellow light of an insect-repellent bulb, drink two more beers each and fall asleep listening to the radio.

As Jill and Joan are driving away from Bartok's, Eddie is walking down 66 toward a Shell station. Looks like a good place to set up, he thinks. He buys a Coke and consults his map. He's facing a decision.

If I get off 66 and hitch 58 to Bakersfield, I can save miles and a hitch through L.A., he figures. Then, "Kingman, Barstow, San Bernardino," runs through his head. He says to himself, the song doesn't say, "Kingman, Barstow, Bakersfield." Then another part of Eddie's brain kicks in, the practical part. You promised Joan. No fuckin' up, it nags.

This shortcut could be the difference between being on time or being late to Camp Stoneman, the practical part insists, but the romantic part wins by default when the white Cadillac pulls up.

The driver is so sleepy that he stumbles getting out of the car. Eddie watches him head for the men's room, while the attendant starts pumping gas. When the guy comes back to the car, Eddie asks him for a lift. "Okay," he answers, "if you'll do the driving."

"Sure. Where to?" Mentally, Eddie thanks Joan for her driving lessons.

"Santa Monica, I've got to be there today or I lose my fifty-dollar deposit." He explains to Eddie that he's on a drive away delivery from Detroit to a restaurant owner in Santa Monica and introduces himself as Chad.

Eddie shakes his hand. "I'm Eddie. Nice to meet you."

Chad is a good-looking guy in his early twenties. He volunteers, "This was the cheapest way I could think of to get to Hollywood. I'm going to get into the movies."

"I wish you luck." Eddie means it.

Chad pays for the gas and gives Eddie the keys. Then he crawls into the backseat and falls asleep before Eddie drives a mile.

The Cadillac has an automatic transmission, power steering, a power seat, power windows and a red leather interior. Smells like a good piece of luggage, Eddie reflects, familiarizing him-self with the dash. After thirty minutes behind the wheel, he feels as relaxed as he does when he's driving Joan's Chevy.

He doesn't need to stop for gas in San Bernardino, but stops anyway so he can send Joan a card. The man running the station is friendly and gives Eddie a California roadmap that shows the Los Angeles area in a blowup.

"Just stay on 66 and you'll end up in Santa Monica." He traces the route with his finger.

Eddie thanks him and gets back on 66. Chad doesn't stir. Route 66 is well marked and Eddie, driving without a license, pays meticulous attention to the speedometer. He easily makes his way through Cucamonga, Azusa, Pasadena and Los Angeles, then stays on Santa Monica Boulevard, looking for the Pacific Ocean. At 2 PM Eddie parks the car across from the Santa Monica Pier and awakens a grateful Chad.

After saying goodbye to Chad and telling him that he'll be watching for him in a movie, Eddie walks out to the end of the pier and spits into the ocean, adding it to his mental list of "Notable Bodies of Water I've Spit In."

The Pacific, he thinks, looking out at the ocean, I'll never spit in nothin' bigger. The smell of potatoes deep-frying in grease makes him think about getting something to eat. He gets a big bag of French fries, a hot dog and, using his phony ID, two beers.

He takes a ride on the merry-go-round before getting Joan a card showing an air view of the Santa Monica beach, including the pier. "*It's 85° here,*" he writes, adding, "*This is where Route 66 ends, or begins.*" He signs it, "*Your very good friend, Edward.*" He yawns and thinks, I haven't slept since Amarillo. I got until tomorrow night at midnight to get to Stoneman. He leaves the pier, walks a couple of blocks and registers at the Wind and Sea Motel. He leaves his card to be mailed and is asleep by three-thirty.

It's a warm morning at the Sail Inn. Jill and Joan sleep late, make a bacon and egg breakfast and then walk out on the dock. Mrs. Kirby, the widow who owns the place, uncovers one of the boats, and Jill and Joan spend the early part of the day sailing.

While they're making hamburgers and lettuce and tomato salad for lunch, Jill comments, "I can't believe we didn't get any mayonnaise. I'd better get some salt, too. There's only a little bit left in that shaker and I don't see any around. I'll be right back."

At the grocery store, Jill discovers a small general merchandise section. Most of the things are seasonal items—sunglasses, sun hats, suntan oil, shorts, swimsuits and first-aid kits.

Back at the cabin, she shows Joan her purchases. Salt, mayonnaise, a first-aid kit and ..."

"Bathing suits!" Joan finishes.

"That water felt so warm. And Pops gave me a fifty-percent off-season discount." She laughs.

"Pops?"

"Well, he's old enough to be a Pop." Jill puts on one of the sunhats.

"Very stylish," Joan jokes, and they laugh. "Let's eat. These hamburgers are ready."

After lunch they put on their bathing suits. Jill dives off the end of the dock and swims in to shore, where Joan is waiting. "It's been quite awhile since I've been swimming in real water. I hate that old chlorine crap at the country club pool. It burns the eyes right out of your head."

Joan laughs. "I don't like it because I think everyone pees in it." They laugh together and Joan wades into the lake up to her shoulders.

After dinner, Jill tries calling Bill at home and is half surprised when he answers. She gives him a complete report on what Dr. Sloane told her about Joan's recovery. She also tells him that she and Joan are going to stay at The Sail Inn for a week before heading to the college.

"It's just as well," he grumps. "Those greedy union bastards are really giving us a hard time. I'll be back and forth between here and Flint for at least another week."

"I'm sure you'll do a good job, dear," Jill smiles at Joan and thinks, I'm sure you'll grind the workers' requests down to the bone.

Bill notes the lack of enthusiasm in Jill's voice, thinks, As if you care, and changes the subject. "I can't cook anything here at home but bacon and eggs."

Quit whining, she thinks. You've got an injured daughter and you're worried about your stomach. She rolls her eyes. "You should pick up some nice frozen foods … and some canned tuna. You know how you like tuna salad. A little bit of mayonnaise, a chopped-up onion, a little celery and you're all set. Here, talk to Joan." Jill hands the phone to Joan.

Joan tells Bill that she's starting to "kind of remember him." Winking at Jill and covering the mouthpiece she whispers, "I might as well try to make him feel good."

Jill gets back on the phone and Bill bitches about being out of vermouth. Jill suggests he have dinner at the club and do his shopping at Steve's Grocers on Mack Avenue. "They're open 'til ten, even on weekends. And they're right next to the liquor store."

"Maybe I'll go out later," he moans. "For right now, straight gin is good enough. See you soon."

"Good night, Bill." They both hang up.

Jill feels relieved. She goes to the sink, gets a cup of soapy water and a saucer of hydrogen peroxide from her new first-aid kit.

"Now let's see what's under there." She starts soaking the adhesive tape around the edges of Joan's bandage. "There's no sense pulling out any more hair than we have to."

"Let me help, Mom." Joan works her fingernail under one corner of the softened tape. "It's almost loose." She gives it a quick tug. The bandage comes off neatly and Jill is happy to find a clean, L-shaped scab an inch and a half by an inch. She soaks a Q-tip in the hydrogen peroxide and dabs at the scab. "How does that feel, honey?"

"I don't feel anything," Joan answers. "It's just numb."

Jill puts the first-aid kit away. "Fifty percent off," she declares, imitating a sales lady, and they laugh.

"All I have to do now is grow some hair."

"You'll do that," Jill promises. "Feel like a little walk?"

"Sure do. Let's go."

They walk along the lakeshore and Jill tells Joan about her old love.

"I had a boyfriend like Eddie," Jill blurts out. She pauses. "A lifetime ago." She closes her eyes for a moment. "Mike was …" She stops, opens her eyes and continues, "It was the summer before you were born."

Joan watches her mother's eyes begin to glisten. Jill's face takes on a peaceful look. "I was twenty-one, ready for love. A junior at Michigan and a Tri-Delt. I had as much fun as a girl with Gramps for a dad could have."

"I remember Gramps, Mom. Those big bushy eyebrows. How red he'd get when he laughed."

"And when he was angry. You were the bright spot in his life, honey. Anyway, you know how strict your father was about dating? Well, compared to Gramps your father is permissive. I had fun at parties and dances, but I was too scared of my dad to, as he used to put it, 'let any boy take liberties' with me. And besides, most of those frat boys were drippy ... kind of like your dad and Roddy."

"Stiffs," Joan suggests, and they both laugh heartily.

"Stiffs," Jill repeats, still half laughing. "Oh, Joanie. What a perfect word choice. That's what Gramps used to call the dead people, stiffs. He used to say he liked working with the stiffs because they didn't give him any guff. Mom hated the business, couldn't sell it quick enough when he died. 'It was our bread and butter through hard times, but I'm done with it,' she said when she set up the trust." Jill sighs deeply.

"What about Mike, Mom?"

"Mike was ... he was a beautiful spirit, but he was what he called himself—'a knock-around kind of guy.' He'd work at anything, when there was anything available. It was 1933, no one had jobs. Mike gained fifteen pounds working that summer at Krajewski's farm just from eating regular. 'It seems like I'm always hungry,' he used to say. He knocked me for a loop. I snuck out of the house four or five times a week. We'd make love in the hayfield on pretty nights and in the barn on rainy nights. Sometimes it was so romantic I felt like I was in a movie."

"Oh, Mom, that's so beautiful."

"Yes, it was, but like all good things it came to an end. Dad found out about us and made plans to beat the hell out of Mike and have him arrested."

"Oh no, Mom." Joan's eyes narrow and she tightens her mouth.

"I know. I felt pretty bad, thought of running away with him. But I knew Dad would track us down. And Mike had two burglary warrants. Times were hard, and he had stolen food. What could I do? Things were different then. Gran and I got Mike out of town a couple of hours before Gramps and the sheriff came to Krajewski's looking for him."

Mom, that's awful."

"Life's funny. Two weeks later, with my Dad's blessing, almost his order, really, I married your father. I think my dad gave him a car. Bill was a year ahead of me at school, already graduated, so I never went back for my senior year."

"How'd you know Dad?"

I'd dated your dad maybe three or four times at school and he had dinner with us during Easter vacation. I think he must've asked my dad if we could get engaged or something like that."

"Dad asked Gramps if he could marry you? How corny."

"I thought so too. I heard my folks talking about it in the kitchen after Bill left that Easter break." Jill imitates her father's loud bray. "'I told him his college diploma wasn't worth a handful of goat shit and to come back when he had a real job,' he said. I laughed when I heard him. A few weeks later I met Mike. I thought that was the last I'd see of Bill. I never dreamed we'd get married a few months later. Life sure doesn't have a roadmap."

"Did you ever see Mike again?"

"No. And in a way, I'm glad. I don't know how I'd have reacted. It's just as well, I guess. I hope he's happy."

"No wonder you were so good about Eddie." Joan puts her arm around Jill's waist and gives her a squeeze. "Thanks, Mom."

"You're quite welcome, my dear," Jill says kiddingly. "Now why don't you tell me how you spent *your* summer?"

Joan tells Jill about the Briggs Hotel and some of her other happy times with Eddie. Back at the cabin they have two more beers and Joan shows Jill her phony ID. They fall asleep with the radio playing "Sitting by the Window" and don't wake up until ten o'clock Sunday morning.

Saturday morning for Eddie starts at six. He wakes up fully rested, gets ready at a leisurely pace, checks out, and eats breakfast down the street at a place that has outdoor tables. He looks over his map while he's drinking his second cup of coffee and sees that Route 1, a block away, hooks into 101 up near the town of Oxnard. It's Saturday, he figures. Should be lots of people driving up the coast on a day like this. He kills his coffee, pays his check and walks briskly up the highway.

Before Eddie has time to watch twenty waves break, a young guy driving a red 1950 Chevy convertible pulls over and asks, "Where you headin'?"

"'Frisco," Eddie answers.

The driver opens the passenger door. He's wearing Levis and a T-shirt. Eddie sees a set of Air Force khakis on the car's back seat. The shirt has staff sergeant stripes. "I'm goin' to Mill Valley," the driver states.

Eddie gets in. "Is that near 'Frisco?"

The driver pulls smoothly back into traffic. "Sure is, but up there they like you to call it San Francisco. I'm Bobby Howser." He sticks out his hand and Eddie shakes it.

"Hiya, Bobby, I'm Eddie Flynn. What do you call it, 'Frisco or San Francisco?"

"I go with 'Frisco, but it drives my girlfriend apeshit."

Eddie laughs. He points to the backseat. "Your uniform?"

"Yeah. I'm a radar op."

"Holy shit," Eddie exclaims, "me too."

They start talking and by the time they hit Santa Barbara they find out quite a few things about each other. Bobby is from Jersey City. He joined the Air Force two months before Eddie. While attending radar operator school at Keesler AFB, they had frequented many of the same Biloxi bars and clubs. Bobby had dated a cocktail waitress from the Beachwater Club and Eddie had dated a girl who dealt blackjack at the Famous Door Bar, a place where the door opened automatically with an electric eye setup.

At one point in their conversation, Eddie laughs. "We sound so much alike. How'd you ever make staff?"

"It's a funny story. I didn't do dick at Keesler. I was hungover every fuckin' day. I finished next to last in my class. I didn't even know all the words in the phonetic alphabet when I graduated but I got my airman third class stripe, just like everybody else. But and this is a big 'but,' they shipped the bottom third of our class straight to Alaska."

"That's where I'm goin'. How was it?"

"Not so good. I never seen so many fuckups in one place since I left the old neighborhood." He and Eddie laugh.

"Compared to some of the guys I was stationed with up there, I looked like 'Airman of the Month.' Guys were goin' apeshit left and right. Our fuckin' mess sergeant used to dribble an imaginary basketball everywhere he went and they still wouldn't ship him home 'til his tour was up." Bobby laughs. "The last month he was there, he served shit on a shingle three times a day and at midnight chow."

"Jesus Christ. How long was your tour?"

"One full year. We were out on a cape, where the wind never dropped below twenty knots and it always blew from the northwest."

"Goddamn." Eddie whistles softly between his teeth.

"You can see how I made rank. I fucked off as much as anyone, but I always showed up for duty. In two months I made airman second. Six months later, airman first. And believe me, I didn't know shit."

"Did the year go slow?"

"Slow enough that I used to X out the days on my calendar. Most of us did. Sometimes I wouldn't X 'em out for a few days and then I'd get to X out four or five days at once. It was almost like gettin' laid. All anyone thinks about in Alaska is finishing their tour and gettin' the fuck outta there."

"Goddamn," Eddie repeats.

"When do you sail?"

"My orders say the fifteenth."

"That's tomorrow. No fuckin' way, man. You'll be at Stoneman at least five days, processin'. How bad's your 201 file?"

"Not bad. A couple of old 104's and two Article 15's," Eddie totes. "One summary court-martial, but it bounced. Bad paperwork."

"It'll still be in your 201," Bobby states. "But that's good. All the real fuckups get outpost duty. They don't want 'em around Anchorage. The guys who get stationed in Anchorage serve a two-year tour."

"Nice to see that bein' a fuckup pays off sometimes," Eddie comments, and they both laugh.

As they continue north on Highway 101, they talk about officers, women, cars and towns. Bobby tells Eddie how he made enough money playing poker to pay cash for his car when he returned from Alaska. "I had over three grand when I rotated for two reasons. I never drank when I played cards and I never stayed around in seven card stud unless I had a pair of nines or better by my third card."

"I'm more of a crap-shooter," Eddie states. "But I'm gonna remember that about nines or better in seven card. Makes sense."

They stop for hamburgers and beer in Paso Robles and when they get back into the car, Eddie asks about Mill Valley.

"Well, if you think of Alaska as hell, then Mill Valley is heaven. I been there almost a year, a few miles north of the Golden Gate, on top of a fuckin' mountain. Mount Tamalpais. I can see 'Frisco from my room. Sometimes, when the fog is in, all you can see are the towers of the Golden Gate Bridge.

"Sounds nice."

"It's better than nice. On my off-duty time, I can take a back road to Stinson Beach. It's empty most of the time. Or, if I want, I can go to 'Frisco. Last week I seen Flip Phillips at the Blackhawk. The week before I caught Sarah Vaughan at the Downbeat. Good local pussy, too, and if you can't get laid in 'Frisco, you ain't tryin'."

"That sure makes up for Alaska."

Bobby grins. "That's no shit. If I knew it was gonna turn out like this, I'd do Alaska all over again … but just for one year."

Eddie looks at his map, finds Mill Valley and asks, "What's all this green area, a big park?"

"Kind of," Bobby replies. "It's called Muir Woods. It's fulla fuckin' redwood trees bigger around than this car."

"No shit?"

"No shit, man. They got a big stump there with one of its rings marked for when Columbus landed."

"Too bad they cut down an old tree like that."

"They can't cut 'em down no more. At least not there."

"Good." Eddie tries to picture trees that size.

At 4:30 Bobby drops Eddie off in downtown San Francisco at the Greyhound bus depot. "There's no sense tryin' to hitch from here to Stoneman," he advises. "The bus'll only cost a buck and it'll take you right to the main gate."

Eddie thanks Bobby for the lift. Bobby wishes Eddie good luck and a quick tour, then drives away.

At 6 PM Eddie checks in at Camp Stoneman, six hours ahead of his midnight deadline. Having missed chow, he goes to the PX and has a grilled cheese sandwich and a chocolate shake. After eating, he calls his mother. She picks up on the fourth ring with a weary, "Hello?"

"Hi, Mom. It's Eddie."

"Eddie?"

"C'mon, Mom, quit kiddin'."

"Oh, Eddie. My *son*," she says with mock surprise. "I almost forgot about you, it's been so long since you've written."

"I know, Mom. I'm callin' about that. I'm sorry. August kind of got away from me, we had a big mission back in Michigan. Now I'm in California, gettin' ready to go to Alaska."

"Alaska? What did you do to get sent to Alaska? Hit someone?"

"It's not like that. Only the best guys get sent to Alaska. It's our first line of defense in case the Commies send their bombers over the North Pole. I wanted to let you know I'll be writin' you when I get my new address."

"Are you behaving yourself?"

"I was up for Airman of the Month back at the 646th but I got shipped out."

"Um-hmm. I had another call from the truant officer about Jimmy. He's playing a lot of hooky."

"You know what a pain in the ass school is, Mom. I barely got out of high school with a passin' grade and look how swell I turned out."

"I see you still have your sense of humor. I've given up on you, but I still have a chance with Jimmy."

"Jimmy's a smart kid. There's lots of places to learn things besides school."

"It seems he's learned to do the mambo from some of his hooky-playing friends."

"You see that, Mom? Just like I said."

"You're not funny, Eddie. One of the men down at our place, a big exec, says with the length of time you've been in the Air Force you should be at least an airman first class. His boy Stanley is a second lieutenant, so he should know."

"I know, Mom, but I say, what the hell do I care about stripes as long as I'm keepin' my country safe? I feel good just doin' my job. And speakin' about doin' my job, I gotta go now. I'm due back in the barracks for inspection."

"You never helped clean up around home here, Eddie."

"Right, Mom. Look, I gotta go now. Tell Jimmy I said to be cool."

"I love you, Eddie."

"I know that, Mom, and I love you too." Eddie hangs up the phone. "Whew."

On the other coast, Eddie's mother hangs up the phone and sighs. She looks at her 8x10 of Eddie in his Air Force blues, shakes her head and smiles.

Eddie starts to walk away from the phone, then stops, thinking about Joan. She's probably out of the hospital by now, probably on the road with her mom. No sense trying her number, but still, you never know. It'd be funny if she was home packin' for college. What the hell.

He pumps in enough coins for a station to station call. Just hearing Joan's phone ring makes him feel happy. He counts the rings. "One, two, three, four, five …"

It's 9:30 PM in St. Clair Shores. Bill Whitman, carrying two bags of groceries, is halfway between the garage and his front door when he hears Joan's phone ring.

Joan's phone. It's him.

Bill counts three more rings as he double-times to the door. He doesn't have to fumble for his keys. He kept them in his hand after turning off the car's ignition, but it costs him five more rings while he puts down the bags of groceries and fights with the front door lock, which always resists him. Son of a bitch. I'm calling the goddamn locksmith tomorrow, he vows, and shouts, "Stay on the phone, you greasy little bastard. I'm on my way."

The tenth, eleventh and twelfth rings sound as Bill is taking the stairs two at a time, running down the hall and bursting into Joan's bedroom. He hears the thirteenth ring while he's in mid-air, diving over Joan's bed to grab her phone. He puts the instrument to his ear. No one is on the line.

Bill rolls over on his back and loosens his tie. His head is pounding. His heart is thumping. He puts one hand on his heart and the other on his forehead. "I know it was that son of a bitch," he confides to the bed's canopy.

In the phone booth, in the PX at Camp Stoneman, a smiling Eddie hangs up the phone after the thirteenth ring. While scooping his coins out of the coin return, he figures, if Joan ain't home, she must be havin' fun with her mom. Probably already on her way to school. Guess I'll hit the sack early.

The days at The Sail Inn are heaven for Jill. The weather cooperates and the water remains warm. She buys bright red nail polish and she and Joan paint their fingernails and toenails. They read movie magazines and listen to the R&B radio station together. They buy red beans and chili powder to go with their ground sirloin and onions and make some decent chili con carne. Their fudge turns out so well that they make a second batch for Joan to take to Our Lady of the Lakes.

Friday morning, a week after checking in, Jill and Joan hit the road as a cold front is sliding down from Canada, feeling as much like girlfriends as mother and daughter. They do some shopping in Cleveland and after spending the night in Fairport Harbor, they arrive at Our Lady of the Lakes late Saturday afternoon.

CHAPTER 31

▼

The College of Our Lady of the Lakes, about thirty miles southeast of Erie, Pennsylvania, covers fifty acres of meadows and woods. The school's academic standards are high and enrollment is limited to two hundred young ladies of "high moral character."

The students are housed in three-story dormitories. Only the top two floors of each dorm house students. The first floor of Dorm One is the library. Dorm Two's first floor is the recreation room and Dorm Three's ground floor is the gym.

The dorms and the administration building are laid out to form the school's quadrangle. Dead center in the quad is a large statue of the Blessed Virgin with a circular brick sidewalk around it. From this circle four paths radiate. The north path goes to Dorm Two, the east path to Dorm Three, the west path to Dorm One, and the south path to the "Quad Entrance" of the administration building.

The administration building, in addition to the school's offices, includes the classrooms, the kitchen, the refectory, the laundry and the infirmary. It, too, is a three-story structure.

An entrance on the west side of the administration building leads to a meditation garden, which separates the convent from the main building. The convent is a two-story building that's home to thirty of the nuns who run the college and the two or three girls who decide to enter the order as novitiates each year. Six other nuns have rooms in the dorms for supervisory duties. The administration building's east entrance opens to the path that runs behind Dorm Three and up the hill to the chapel.

The chapel, with its spire and its stained glass windows of female saints, all with hands clasped in prayer and blissful eyes cast heavenward, looks down on the quad like a beacon.

All the buildings are made of gray stones that were quarried when the school was built just after the end of the Civil War. An eight-foot-high wall of the same stone, topped with broken glass set in cement, surrounds the fifteen acres that comprise the quadrangle. A cyclone fence topped with three strands of barbed wire encloses the entire perimeter of the college's grounds. No Trespassing and Posted signs are prominently displayed at random points along the fence.

The only other structures on the grounds are a brick powerhouse that includes a sixty-foot smokestack and incinerator, and a large red barn that's home to the small herd of cows tended by Sister Angelica and the novitiates. Adjacent to the barn are fifteen acres of cultivated land where the nuns grow vegetables, hay and cow corn. An athletic field next to the farmland has a softball diamond and a small cinder track.

Jill parks in the dirt parking lot across the county road from the main gate. The only other vehicle on the lot is a black '49 Ford station wagon. Jill takes the large leather suitcase from the trunk, Joan takes the two smaller bags and they head for the main gate.

Joan notices the no trespassing and posted signs and thinks, It looks so peaceful ... and they've got the fences and signs to keep it that way. Peaceful *and* secure. Eddie would call that a good combo.

The gate is the old fashioned kind, with rows of sharp, eight-foot spears set six inches apart. Just inside and to the right of the gate there's a phone booth-sized gatehouse in among some shrubs. It looks unused. Eddie would have a hard time breaking restriction at this place, she thinks as she watches her mother ring the bell. She doesn't know that a pang is going through Jill's soul as she pushes the button.

Sister Maria Dolores, the Mother Superior, sees them from her office on the second floor. She hits her gate control. There's a loud clank from the gatehouse and the gate to Our Lady of the Lakes swings open.

When they reach the front door of the administration building, Sister Maria Dolores is standing there with the door open. She greets them cordially, ushers them into her office, and quickly dispenses with the paperwork.

"I called Sister Cecilia at Dorm Three when I saw you at the gate," Sister Maria Dolores states. "She'll be ..." A knock on the door interrupts her. "Come in, Sister," she shouts to the door.

The door opens and a tall, slender nun glides in. Jill and Joan rise to greet her. The Mother Superior makes introductions and Sister Cecilia, Jill and Joan head for Dorm Three.

Sister Cecelia has a warm, genuine smile. As a model she had done well, including a cover on Vogue, but she chose the religious life. Her devout mother was happy with her decision and in ten years of teaching, Sister Cecelia's enthusiasm has never waned. She insists on carrying one of the suitcases. She's upbeat and chatty as the three of them walk through the quad.

"You'll feel right at home with Barbara and Mary Elizabeth. They're two of the most down-to-earth girls in the dorm. They're sophomores, and they'll be able to help you adapt."

"You don't keep freshmen by themselves, Sister?"

"No, Joan. We sprinkle you freshmen in with the sophomores and juniors."

"Sounds like a good idea," Jill observes.

"We used to keep the freshmen apart, but we found that the news girls assimilate more quickly mingling with the upper grades." She turns to Joan. "The seniors, of course, insist on being left alone." They all laugh.

They enter the dorm and Sister Cecelia leads the way to the second floor. The dorm halls are well lit and clean. The smell of floor wax is in the air. Halfway down the hall, Sister Cecelia stops at a door and knocks. "No answer." She looks at her watch. "Benediction's over. Maybe the girls stopped at the library or rec hall." She opens the door and hits the light switch.

It's a large room, but homey. A peach-colored shade softens the glare from the ceiling's white bulb. Jill sees two maple beds along the wall to her right and a third bed along the wall to her left. All the beds have blue and white checkered bed-spreads. "Small beds," she thinks, "but the mattresses look nice and thick." She glances at Joan and sees that she's smiling.

The wall facing Jill has a large window in the center of it. Light blue curtains, Jill thinks. Joan will like that. On one side of the window, a large roll top desk is open, with a typewriter and a gooseneck lamp on its deck and a wooden chair in front of it. A small square table is on the other side of the window. It has a chair tucked under it and a Princeton pennant tacked on the wall above it. The only other things on the wall are a watercolor of Mary holding a baby Jesus and a calendar. September's picture is a New England autumn scene.

Jill looks at the radiator under the window and the large wardrobe next to the solo bed. She feels good about the room. It looks so cozy, she thinks. Turning to Joan, she asks, "You like it, dear?"

"I think it's just perfect, Mom," Joan answers. Which is my bed, Sister?"

"That one is yours, Joan." Sister Cecilia points to the bed next to the ward-robe. "There are two large pull-out drawers under your bed and lots of room in the wardrobe." The three of them put the suitcases down next to Joan's bed.

Voices from down the hall turn into Barbara Andrews and Mary Elizabeth "Beth" Ferguson. Barbara has straight, shoulder-length light brown hair and dark eyes. She wears no makeup other than lipstick. She likes light colors and wears her skirts, sweaters and blouses as sets. She's wearing light green and carrying a folding chair.

Beth, who is called Mary Elizabeth only by Sister Cecilia, has short, curly orange hair and a few small freckles. She's thin, but robust. In the 8th grade the boys used to call her Pipelegs. She dresses casually, with no sense of color, but in quality clothing. Beth has a lamp similar to the one on the desk. "Good after-noon, Sister," they say in unison.

"Good afternoon, ladies," Sister Cecilia replies. She makes all the introduc-tions, then turns to Jill. "Would you like a cup of tea?"

I'd rather have a double martini, Jill thinks. Aloud, she answers, "Yes, Sister. I'd love a cup of tea."

"We'll be back in twenty minutes," Sister Cecilia states. "You girls can get acquainted." She looks at her watch. "The refectory opens for dinner in thirty-five minutes."

"And not a minute too soon, Sister," Beth jokes. They all laugh.

"Mary Elizabeth must have a tapeworm," Sister Cecilia comments, after she and Jill leave the room. "She eats like a longshoreman and doesn't gain an ounce."

"Find out her secret," Jill quips, and they laugh.

In a sitting room at the end of the hall, Sister Cecilia takes a kettle off a hot plate, pours hot water into two cups, apologizes for using tea bags and offers Jill her choice of cream, lemon, honey or sugar. They both take lemon and honey.

Sister Cecilia mentions all the postcards. They laugh about the "your good friend, Edward" signatures and Jill assures Sister Cecilia that Eddie has a good heart under his rough exterior.

"My brother was a wild one." Sister Cecilia smiles. "Now he's a fireman, a fine husband and father of three. All girls."

After their tea session, Jill feels better about Joan being away at school. At least she's in good hands, she reasons.

Heading back down the hall to Joan's room, Jill declines Sister Cecilia's invita-tion to stay for dinner. "I'd rather say goodbye to Joan before dinner. Make a clean break. Easier for me."

"I understand."

Approaching Joan's room, Jill hears laughter. That's a good sign, she tells her-self.

Joan opens the door to Sister Cecelia's knock. "Beth and Barbara are helping me get settled," she announces. Two of the suitcases are open on her bed. The new lamp is on the corner table and the folding chair is next to the wooden one.

"We can finish this later, Sister," Beth suggests. "If it's time to head for the refectory."

"It's time, Mary Elizabeth."

The five of them walk back to the administration building together. At the entrance, Sister Cecelia tells Beth and Barbara, "You two might as well go inside and hover by the refectory door. Dinner's in seven minutes." To Joan she instructs, "When you come inside, Joan, the refectory is on your left."

"Just follow your nose, Joan," Beth adds, and they all laugh.

"Nice meeting you, Mrs. Whitman," the girls say, almost together.

Opening the door, Barbara turns. "We'll save you a seat with us, Joan."

"Thanks, Barbara. I'll be right in."

Sister Cecilia smiles. "I really enjoyed having tea with you, Mrs. Whitman."

"The pleasure was all mine, Sister. I'm sure Joan will be happy here." Jill's head feels light. She offers her hand.

Sister Cecilia takes Jill's hand in both of hers. "We'll do our very best. Now I'm going up to the Mother Superior's office. We'll see you when you get to the gate and we'll open it for you." She enters the building, leaving Jill and Joan look-ing at each other.

"Let's get out of the way." Jill guides Joan away from the entrance. Small groups of students are starting to become a steady stream. Jill and Joan walk toward the east end of the building, step off the path, and watch the girls empty out of the dorms.

"Must be good food," Joan remarks, trying to cheer Jill up.

"Well, I guess I won't be seeing you for awhile." Jill's mouth feels dry.

"Beth says we get Thanksgiving vacation, Mom. That's just a few weeks."

Jill takes Joan in her arms, hugs her tight and smiles. "That's true. Just a few weeks. You feel okay?"

"I do." Joan smiles a big smile. "I really do, Mom. How about you?"

Not wanting to put a damper on Joan's good mood, Jill smiles. "I'm fine, dear. I'll miss you, of course, but you've got to get on with your life." Jill steps back from the hug, takes Joan's shoulders, one in each hand, and kisses Joan's forehead. "Call me anytime. Drop me a note. You know how much I love you."

"I love you too, Mom. You know I'll be in close touch."

Together, they turn from each other and walk in opposite directions. Neither looks back. Jill's path takes her around the east end of the building and across the front lawn to the gate.

Joan takes a few steps toward the entrance, steps off the walkway and leans against an old maple tree. It's going to be awful for Mom without me around, she thinks. I'll make sure and call home every weekend.

She spots some quality tweed jackets, a short camel's hair topcoat, a stylish suede jacket and some good-looking pleated skirts. My stuff will fit right in.

When the flow of students slows to a dribble, Joan enters the building. She smells roast turkey, turns left and easily finds the refectory.

There's no path from the east end of the administration building through the front lawn to the gate. Jill's high heels dig into the lawn and she stumbles. She takes off her heels and continues walking through the lawn in her stocking feet. Oh God, that feels good, she thinks. At the gate she waves to the Mother Superior's window. She slips her shoes back on while the gate is opening.

Jill is almost across the road when she hears the gate clang shut. A quick, short breath catches in her throat at the finality of the sound. Her eyes fill and she feels the mixed emotions of missing Joan, yet knowing that Joan's in the right place. The right place for the time being, she tells herself. She doesn't allow herself to cry until she gets behind the wheel.

After a heavy sobbing, draining cry, Jill pulls herself together. She looks across the road at the school. It looks peaceful in the fading twilight, she thinks as she wipes her eyes and fixes her makeup. Thanksgiving vacation, Christmas vacation, Easter vacation. Then in June, you'll turn nineteen, sign Bill's goddamn papers and come home for the summer. You won't have to go back to school if you'd rather stay home with me and wait for Eddie. If Bill doesn't like it, he can go to hell. Eddie seems to like Michigan. I think I'll buy them a house for a wedding present. Jill smiles, starting to feel happy. She cranks the engine, turns on her lights and begins her journey back to St. Clair Shores without her best friend.

Joan pushes the heavy door open and sees the quintessential refectory. It's a huge room with a high ceiling. Four large, wrought iron chandeliers, along with rows of windows on two sides of the room, keep everything bright.

Twenty-one tables are set up in three rows of seven. Each row is assigned to a dorm. Four more tables, used by the nuns and novitiates, are half hidden behind two long, wide serving tables.

The refectory functions nothing like the mess hall at the 646th or the high school cafeteria where Joan ate lunch for four years. Sister Veronica, a female version of Friar Tuck, including the taste for fine wine, runs a smooth operation. Every year the students vote Sister Veronica "Our Favorite" in their yearbook. She's an excellent cook, meal planner and diplomat, keeping peace among the five salaried women who help with the cooking, the dishes and all the kitchen chores.

Sister Veronica, always slightly buzzed but never drunk, likes to think of herself as a chef at a fancy restaurant. She sees mealtimes not as a mass feeding of two hundred students and forty nuns and novitiates, but as "dinner for ten, done twenty-four times."

Nice that they all order the same dish, she often thinks with a laugh.

Putting all the food out on the huge serving tables and having the students eat boarding house-style was her idea. It was also her idea to have employees for kitchen help instead of students. "I want professionals in my kitchen, not students," she once told Sister Maria Delores when the Mother Superior wanted to cut costs. Sister Maria Delores acquiesced to Sister Veronica on that issue for the same reason that she overlooked the nun's wine consumption—the consistently delicious, never repetitious meals.

The dining rules at Our Lady of the Lakes are not rigid. Except for respecting your table assignments, things are loose. Students may skip breakfast, although few do. Lunch is handled in two sessions, early or late, depending on class schedules. Dinner finds students filtering in anytime between 5 PM and 6:30.

Joan looks all around. The room is three quarters full and noisy with chatter and dining sounds. She heads for the first serving table, where she sees stacks of dishes, bowl, cups and bins of utensils.

"Joan!"

She turns in the direction of the shout and sees Barbara coming her way. "Just grab a plate and some silverware," Barbara directs. "The food's already on the table."

Joan takes a plate, cup and utensils. She follows Barbara to a table where Beth is sitting opposite three girls. As Barbara and Joan slide onto the bench beside her, Beth points with her fork. "Rita, Mary and Catherine, meet our new roommate, Joan."

"Hi everyone," Joan smiles and makes eye contact with each girl.

The three girls smile and acknowledge Joan. Gesturing toward the table, Beth urges, "Dig in."

Joan looks at the drumstick on Beth's plate, gnawed almost to the marrow. I guess I can be myself, she thinks. She looks at the array of food: a platter of roast turkey and dressing; a large bowl of creamy mashed potatoes that's about half full; a gravy boat; a big bowl of peas; and French bread. She fills her plate.

During dinner Joan finds out a couple of things about how mealtimes work. "This is our regular table," Barbara informs her. "Whoever gets here first starts bringing the food to the table."

"Usually, that's me," Beth adds, and everyone laughs.

When more coffee is needed, Joan goes with Rita to refill their pitcher. "We may as well bring back some dessert," Rita suggests. They pick up a spice cake with vanilla frosting.

Joan sips her strong black coffee and thinks, Eddie would love this.

As Joan is leaving the refectory with Beth and Barbara, she sees four girls seating themselves with Rita, Mary and Catherine. Beth and Barbara wave at them. "They're from down the hall," Barbara tells Joan. "We'll introduce you later."

At the dorm, the three of them talk about boyfriends while they finish with Joan's unpacking.

"Back in high school they called Wesley 'The Mad Scientist.' He blew up the lab once," Beth relates. "They wanted to kick him out of school."

"You mean he did it on purpose?" Joan asks.

"Oh no. It was an accident. Wesley's not an anarchist or anything like that. But the school was unhappy with his apology. Said it showed no true remorse."

"His apology wasn't good enough?" Joan looks surprised. "Was somebody killed?"

"No, he was working alone, after school." Beth laughs. "When we went to the Senior Prom his eyebrows still hadn't grown back."

"Well if he apologized what more did they want?" Joan frowns.

Barbara grins. "Tell her what the apology said, Beth."

"It was something like, 'I'm sorry about the damage to the laboratory. An experiment went wrong. That's what happens sometimes. That's why they call them experiments.'"

Joan and Barbara laugh.

"Anyway, his marks were so high they had to graduate him. Even after the zero for his final quarter, due to the little explosion, his year's average was seventy-five because he got a hundred in each of the first three quarters."

"That's great. The joke's on them." Joan smiles.

"They love him at Princeton. Because of the seventy-five he had to take a special test. He finished a three-hour test in forty-five minutes. His buddies tease him and call him 'The Wizard,' but I'll tell you something. I started dating Wesley when I was a junior and I never had trouble with math again."

Beth raves on about Wesley, ending with, "I've got a feeling he's going to propose to me during Thanksgiving vacation."

"The only proposals I heard all summer were invitations to commit mortal sins," Barbara states, and they all laugh. She then goes into a version of "How I Spent My Summer." She keeps Joan and Beth laughing as she relates how she fought off "Spoiled Prep School Brats" and "Country Club Snots" while vacationing with her family at Saratoga. "They expect every girl to let their hands roam all over the place," she declares with indignation.

"I only let Wesley's hands roam on special occasions," Beth admits. "But I never let him into the Garden of Eden." They all laugh.

"What about you, Joan?" Barbara asks. "Anyone special?"

"Eddie's on his way to Alaska," Joan replies. "He's in the Air Force."

"Oh how nice," Beth squeals. "He's a flyer."

"No, he's a radar operator. An enlisted man."

"My older brother's an enlisted man," Barbara remarks. "He's sergeant. He hates officers."

Joan laughs. "Eddie would get along great with your brother."

Joan tells them a sketchy tale of herself and Eddie, leaving out the lurid details of their summer's adventures—no Briggs Hotel, no weekends at Rostonkowski's and nothing about hanging out at Slim's Blue Light Inn. She gives the impression that Eddie's a great dancer and a perfect gentleman. Joan is nervous about getting more questions and is relieved when Barbara looks at her watch and announces, "It's almost seven-thirty."

"On Saturdays we say the rosary with Sister Cecelia," Beth explains. "She's so nice about food in the rooms and overlooking smoking, as long as it's done outdoors, that we all go. Sister says it's for the conversion of Russia. I don't think that'll ever happen, but it makes Sister happy, so what the hell."

Joan gets her First Communion rosary out of the drawer where she had just put it with her socks, and the three of them head for the sitting room.

When they finish saying the rosary, the students disperse, some to the rec hall, some to the library and some back to their rooms. Sister Cecelia invites Joan into her quarters for a brief meeting about the school's rules and policies.

Handing Joan the stack of Eddie's postcards, she comments, "We don't encourage or discourage boyfriends, but we do limit correspondence with male friends or acquaintances to one letter every two weeks." She delivers the message matter-of-factly and adds, "Do you think you'll find this a hardship?"

"I don't think so, Sister. Can it be a long letter?"

Sister Cecelia smiles that cover-girl smile and Joan thinks, She's pretty. Not at all like the old nuns I had in grade school. Why did a pretty lady like that become a nun?

"You may write as long a letter as you choose." Sister Cecilia hands Joan a daily/weekly schedule of events and a card with Joan's classes typed on it. "As you can see, we'll keep you quite busy here at Our Lady of the Lakes."

Joan looks at her class card. "Latin?"

"Yes, you'll have Sister Ignatia," Sister Cecelia's voice is reassuring. "She's a really gifted teacher, very low-key. You'll like her. I'm your home room teacher and you have me for English Literature and Religion as well."

"I went to public high school, Sister. Some of my subjects were kind of easy. I like to cook, took Home Ec for two years and Typing my senior year."

"I don't think you'll have any problems, Joan," Sister Cecelia replies. "I saw your transcripts. Straight A's. Some of our courses will be more demanding than Home Ec, but I'm sure you'll do well."

"I'll do my best, Sister."

"That's all God asks of you." She stands. "And Joan, if you have any difficulties or questions, my door is always open. I mean that. You can go now."

"Thank you, Sister." Joan stands and leaves the room.

When Joan reenters her dorm room, Beth and Barbara go over her class assignments with her and decide that only Sister Anne in World History is tough. Joan shows them her postcards and they trace Eddie's trip on Route 66 in Beth's atlas.

Joan tells the girls more about herself, mentioning her accident, saying only that she was driving to see Eddie. She says nothing about being on her way to get married and nothing at all about being pregnant.

At one point in the conversation, Barbara shows them a book she's reading about the life of Saint Barbara and mentions casually, "It wouldn't be a bad life being a nun, you know."

"Wesley wouldn't like it if I become one." Beth giggles.

By lights out at 10:30, Joan is ready for sleep. She tucks her postcards under her pillow, thinking that she's been fortunate in her room assignment. Beth and Barbara, she thinks. They're not Sandy and Laura, and they're sure not one-per-centers, but they're not snobs. She falls into a deep, untroubled sleep.

Sunday morning, Joan gets a big surprise. She's awakened at seven o'clock. While they're getting dressed for eight o'clock Mass, Beth and Barbara take turns explaining weekends at Our Lady of the Lakes, or as Beth calls it, O.L.L.

"On Saturday, one of the priests from Saint Jerome's up in Erie drives down to hear confessions," Beth relates. "Then we have Benediction."

"It's on your event schedule," Barbara adds. "You got here after Benediction yesterday. See?" She points to a line in the schedule Joan is scanning.

"Saturday, 1 PM—3:30 PM … Confessions," the card reads and underneath that, "3:45 PM … Benediction."

Joan tries to remember the last time she went to Confession. It must've been just before Easter, she thinks. I sure haven't been to Confession, or Mass for that matter, since I met Eddie.

"Then on Sunday," Barbara finishes, "we have eight o'clock Mass."

"After that, the rest of the day is ours." Beth looks at her watch. "We'd better get going."

Walking the path from the dorm to the chapel, Joan is happy to see the girls streaming along at their own pace rather than marching in twos like in grade school. She can't help thinking of some of her grade school catechism. "I was made to know God, to love Him and serve Him," runs through her mind.

In the chapel, Joan is relieved to see Barbara and Beth slip into a rear pew. "Barbara says sitting in the back shows humility," Beth whispers to Joan. "I like it because the priest can't see you back here in the dark."

Joan follows the lead of Beth and Barbara and kneels down. She bows her head as they do and tries to think holy thoughts.

The Mass begins and quickly progresses to the Gospel, with Joan making all the appropriate moves—kneel, stand, sit. It's just like swimming, she thinks, you never forget it.

After the Gospel, Father Quinn, a wiry, spry seventy-year-old, heads for the pulpit. Beth whispers to Joan, "Four priests from Erie take turns coming down here on Sundays. Father Quinn's the best." Before Beth can add, "Nobody falls asleep during his sermons," Father Quinn, born in Galway, is bounding up the steps of the pulpit.

"Good mornin' to you all!" he nearly shouts, his voice a happy bellow. "This mornin', ladies, I'm here to warn ya about the Divil and those that I call Pawns of the Divil … livin' in sin, causin' ithirs to sin.

"You must be strong and resist sin," his voice picks up in volume and intensity, "as the Archangel Michael was when he cast Lucifer down into hell." During the words, "Lucifer down into hell," the little priest jumps straight up in the pulpit, raises his right arm in mid-jump and brings it down in a stabbing motion on the sound of the word "hell."

"Take that, you piece of filth," he shouts, looking down on the imaginary, vanquished foe. "Down, down into the eternal agonies of hell's flames," he shouts again. He pauses. He looks all around the chapel. Very quietly he continues in an almost conspiratorial tone, "But the Divil is out of hell. He's all around us. He takes many forms. We live in a permissive age—suggestive songs, ads that tell you to be sexy, impure dances and foreign films. There's no end to the list of the wiles of the Divil. Satan may be that nice boy from next door, who wants you to sit in his car with him and have a few beers after a football game or a dance."

Beth moves around in her seat. Barbara is motionless. Joan makes a conscious effort not to slink down in her seat. She sits up more erect, pressing her back into the pew.

Father Quinn goes on punching and jumping, praising purity and punishing Satan, warning of the dangers of sacrificing your immortal soul to the torments of hell for all eternity for just a few moments of Lust.

Listening to Father Quinn Lacing into Lust as the fastest road to eternal damnation, Joan thinks, I know one thing. All those things I've been doing with Eddie are mortal sins. I knew that when I did them. I knew they were big sins and I did them anyway. I can't receive Communion. I'll bet I'm the only girl who doesn't go to the altar. Oh, this is awful. What'll I do? Or say? How about, "I didn't want to receive because I can't remember when my last Confession was. Because of my accident, I guess." No, I won't go for sympathy. If anyone asks, I'll just say I woke up and ate some of my fudge after midnight. I forgot about it being Sunday. I like that. A good, simple, straight-forward lie. Eddie would like that. He loves the way I lie. A jump from Father Quinn and a thump from his fist hitting the edge of the pulpit, along with a shout of "Resist Lucifer and his snares!" jolts Joan back from her thoughts.

"The easiest way to keep the Divil out of your house," he continues, "is to not let him loiter in your front yard. Avoid the occasions of sin." He leaps at least two feet in the air and lands, bringing his arm down in a punching motion. "Back to hell with the Divil," he shouts and after a brief pause, resumes in his normal voice, "Now, let's get on with the Mass."

At Communion time, Joan is the only girl who doesn't go to the altar. I'll bet everyone in the chapel thinks I'm a sinner, she imagines. Like that lady in *The Scarlet Letter*. Then she remembers her lie and feels secure in it. She relaxes slightly. No one notices that she doesn't receive Communion, other than Beth and Barbara, and they don't seem to care. All of Joan's guilt-fueled paranoia was a wasted effort.

Back at the dorm after breakfast, Joan looks through her postcards, putting them in order from Chicago to San Francisco. She looks at the "Mr. Briggs says hi!" postscript on the Chicago card and thinks, That night was a mortal sin. Then she shakes her head, dismissing the thoughts. She smiles at the "so far, so good" message on the San Francisco card and pictures Eddie at various diners, standing next to the highway with his thumb up.

Beth starts writing a letter to Wesley and Barbara begins to read a book. Joan decides against writing Eddie, she thinks it will be better to wait until she receives his new address. Instead, she goes for a walk around the school's grounds.

She walks away from the dorm past the barn and out into the woods. The cold front that accompanied her from Ohio is keeping the temperature at fifty and the sky gray. A beautiful fall day, Joan thinks as she walks among the huge old maple trees and the smaller white birches, enjoying the smell of the woods. She feels comfortable in her warm sweater. She wonders where Eddie is and what he's doing. She looks at her watch. It's ten AM.

CHAPTER 32

▼

Eddie is walking the deck of a troopship bound for Alaska. He looks at his watch. Sunday morning. Wonder if Joan's at her school yet? Mom probably dragged Jimmy to the nine. And after Mass, the regular Sunday mornin' crap game on 122nd. Then, shootin' pool all afternoon down at Charlie's, home for dinner at six, maybe leg of lamb. Then take a chick to the movies. He laughs as he remembers telling his mother, "There's just no time for homework."

His brain jumps back to a partly sunny day in 1945. On the south side of 122nd Street, between Broadway and Amsterdam, a crap game involving twenty young men is in progress. All of them are dressed in their Sunday suits. Most of them have just come from attending ten o'clock Mass.

It's the regular, Sunday Morning Delivery Boys Crap Game, so named because most of the participants, like Eddie, have after-school jobs as delivery boys for grocery stores, butcher shops, cleaners and dyers, florists and drugstores. The game is twenty minutes old. It started at 11 AM when the guys asked the two little kids who were playing Chinese handball against the crap game's potential wall to go play "Chickee." For fifty cents each the little guys were happy to watch for cops; one kid on the corner at Amsterdam Avenue, the other down on Broadway. As a two-way street, 122nd allows the cops to take a run at the game from either the east or the west. Lookouts are important and even the youngest kids know the unmarked cop cars.

The dice are as chilly as the spring morning. The side-bettors offering "Two to one, no ten," and "five bucks says he don't eight" are smiling. None of the first six shooters have made more than two passes. Eddie's on his first roll. His point is six.

While clacking the dice in his right hand, with his left hand Eddie throws down five bucks. "Here's a pound says I hit that six."

His side bet covered, Eddie releases the shiny, red cubes from his hand smoothly, almost gently, with just enough force to bounce them off the wall. "Lookin' for a six, baby," he implores. The dice come to rest, a five and a four.

"Nina Ross, the fartin' hoss," Big John announces. "Here's two bucks says Eddie sixes." Jerry Casey takes Big John's bet, but before Eddie can scoop up the dice and continue working to make his six, a piercing whistle from the nine-year-old on duty at Amsterdam sends the crapshooters scrambling. Some duck into nearby apartment house basements and hallways, others run up to Broadway and three daring runners go speeding right past the approaching car-load of cops and vanish into Morningside Park.

By the time the four members of the "Flying Squad" jump out of their unmarked prowl car, all that's left of the game are cigarette butts and two singles that one of the players dropped.

In twos and threes, the guys drift to their previously-selected standby location on the roof of 540 West 123rd Street. The crapshooters have many venues. As delivery boys their knowledge of the neighborhood, its basements, its interconnecting backyards and various quick-exit routes yield many sites for their games. Each week they put out the word of the A and B spots, anywhere from Cherry Park up near Grant's Tomb, to the old fort in Morningside Park.

Eddie likes shooting crap up on the roof. He enjoys the view at "five-forty." Waiting for the last of the players to straggle back to the game, he looks north. The elevated station at 125th Street is in shadow, but the medical center's white building cluster up at 168th is sunlit. Looking beyond the George Washington Bridge, he takes a deep breath and gazes up the Hudson. He wonders how things used to be. He sees himself dressed in buckskins, showing some Mohawks how to shoot crap. He takes another deep breath and slips into a zone.

The last three guys come huffing up to the game. Eddie shakes the dice. "Now, where were we before we were so rudely interrupted?" Some of the guys laugh. "Oh yeah. I remember. I was about to make my six." He throws down the money that he grabbed and resumes shaking the dice. "Everybody got your bets all straight? Okay then, no more fuckin' around. Here comes my six." He watches the dice jump out of his hand and dance their way to the roof's brick wall. Bouncing off the wall, the first die comes to rest with a three up, while the second die spins on its corner like a top.

"Oh be there, baby," Eddie urges. The spinning die answers Eddie's plea and matches its partner's three.

"Two rows of rabbit shit." Eddie pushes his side bet money into the middle of the pot. "Shoot it all. Twenty bucks.

"Come on babies, be good to me." Eddie kisses the dice and starts shaking them. He's one of those crapshooters who talks to the dice and all the bettors when he's the shooter. He throws a five.

"Fever. I ain't takin' no bets on that." He shakes the dice and tosses them, shouting, "Fever in the funk house. Run, Kitty, run." Up pops a four and a one.

"Right back. Would you look at that." Eddie takes another deep breath and looks at the medical center, white as a wedding cake, and the slightly out-of-body feeling he's experiencing heightens. "I feel like I'm watchin' myself." He starts shaking the dice. "Shoot that fuckin' forty."

His bet gets covered and he releases the dice. "Gimme an ee-ho-Leven, baby." He gets a six and a four.

"That's close. Big Dick from Boston." Jerry laughs. "I'm layin' two to one, no ten."

Eddie has a long hard roll looking for his ten. Hitting every number but his own keeps the side-bet guys betting, "Five bucks, no ten or four," and "Ten bucks says he don't ten or eleven."

Eddie hits his ten, drags seventy bucks out of his winnings and shoots ten dollars. He gets eight for a point and seven's out before anyone can goad him into a side bet. He doesn't wind up the big winner, Jerry and Big John each quit the game with over a hundred, but Eddie's happy to go home with his fifteen-dollar stake pumped up to eighty bucks.

As the troopship rocks him back to the present, he thinks, Hope Jimmy's havin' a lucky Sunday. Jimmy is having a lucky Sunday up at 140th Street, getting special, private mambo lessons from Nadia Garcia on her couch.

Eddie's thought run on. Man, I blew through that week at Stoneman like a champ. He feels a surge of pride. Thanks to my stay away from the barracks modus operandi, I pulled no KP, latrine duty or any work details. I'm three for three, battin' a thousand. He grins, remembering Keesler AFB and Selfridge. He had hatched his plan at Keesler while waiting to ship out after finishing radar operator school. He used it again at Selfridge while waiting for orders to the 646th.

Eddie's plan is simple, as he once told Norm when Norm bitched about getting KP three times in ten days while waiting for orders to the 646th. "When I'm assigned to a casual barracks at one of them big bases, I just pull a 'Mandrake' and fuckin' disappear," he'd boasted.

He laughs, recalling his week at Camp Stoneman. After his call to his mother and his attempted call to Joan, Eddie had left the PX, walked over to Headquarters and turned in his orders and records to a disinterested staff sergeant. He was assigned to a casual barracks.

In Air Force terminology, a casual is an airman not assigned to a particular unit, usually a guy waiting to ship out. Sergeants look at a barracks full of casuals the same way that lions view the veldt. Where lions see zebra, wildebeest and impala, sergeants see KP's, latrine cleaners, posthole diggers and garbage-duty personnel.

Early Sunday morning, Eddie left the barracks, had breakfast at the PX and wandered around Camp Stoneman. Probably as big as Keesler, he had thought. Twenty, twenty-five thousand. He checked the supply building. It's huge and it's closed. My duffel bag's in there, he thought. I'll pick it up tomorrow.

He walked by the base movie. A sign in the box office said "Open at 12:30" and there was a poster on the door for "King Solomon's Mines". Shit. Saw that in basic, he thought. It was pretty good though. What the fuck. I'll see it again.

Eddie continued wandering the base. He found the bowling alley open and practically empty. He bowled a few lines then hit the movie. After the movie, he ate at the PX then went to the Airman's Club, had a few beers and returned to the barracks, where he found that the two guys in the bunks next to his spent the day on KP.

"You'll probably catch KP tomorrow," one of them had said.

"Yeah, probably." Eddie got undressed and hit the sack.

Monday morning, Eddie awoke early, got out of the barracks and went over to the orderly room, complaining of a toothache. He signed up for sick call and got his dental records. After a brief visit at the dental clinic, he went to the PX and hung out until the movie opened with its new feature, "Singing in the Rain". After the movie, he picked up his duffel bag at supply. He stowed it by his bunk, skipped evening chow and went to the Airman's Club. He won ten bucks shooting pool and didn't sack out until midnight.

Eddie had spent Tuesday, Wednesday and Thursday bouncing around the base. He visited the library and read up on Alaska, found a second movie house and still took care of his processing. He got his tetanus booster shot, verified his payroll records and received his September pay that he didn't get at the 646th. He returned his dental records on Friday, the same day he received his new Alaskan mailing address, an Army Post Office number.

Friday night Eddie wrote Joan a long letter detailing his Route 66 hitch and the characters he met. He signed it, "Loving you with all my heart and soul, Eddie."

No more of that "Your good friend, Edward" bullshit, he had thought as he laughed.

Saturday afternoon the troopship sailed for Alaska and before they cleared the Golden Gate Bridge guys were already puking their guts out. Must be psychosomatic, Eddie thought. This ain't no worse than walkin' from car to car on the A train when it's really rollin' from Fifty-Ninth to a Hundred and Twenty-Fifth.

After evening chow, which less than half of the troops attended, Eddie went below to his assigned bunk. He found that he had a bottom rack with two bunks above him, each with a seasick airman. When a load of puke hit the deck and almost splattered him, he went to the staff sergeant in charge of his group and said he wanted to spend the night up on deck. The guy was too sick to say yes or no.

It was a warm night and Eddie slept comfortably on a rolled-up tarp. He wakes up Sunday morning just a little bit stiff and starts walking the deck, sorting through sections of his life.

The ship takes a sudden pitch and roll, jarring Eddie back to reality. He reacts automatically, shifting his weight to keep his balance. That's more like it, he thinks as he upgrades the ride from ridin' the A train to walkin' through the rotatin' barrel at Coney Island.

Eddie takes a few deep breaths. I'm starvin', he thinks. Must be the salt air. With Joan, his mother and brother and Camp Stoneman sorted out he says, "So far, so good," and heads for the galley.

The galley has many breakfast choices—honeydew melon, grapefruit halves, sausage, bacon or ham, pancakes or eggs, and two kinds of hot cereals as well as little packages of various Kellogg's cold cereals. The coffee is steaming and strong. This is like a fuckin' diner, he thinks as he fills his tray.

For the remainder of the voyage, Eddie stays away from his bunk and avoids all work details.

Joan receives Eddie's letter on Tuesday afternoon, after class. She kisses it and slips it into her jacket pocket. Back at the dorm, she kicks off her loafers, hangs up her jacket and gets comfortable on her bed, with her knees tucked up under her chin and her back pressed against the wall.

I can hardly make my fingers work, she thinks, opening the envelope carefully to preserve the return address. She reads:

Eddie has something to say about everyone from Ernie to Chad to Bobby Howser. He devotes the last page and a half to memories of Rostonkowski's and the Briggs Hotel. "I'll never listen to 'Tomorrow Night' without remembering our beautiful night together on your birthday."

While reading the last page, Joan has some vivid images of herself and Eddie at the Briggs Hotel and at the quarry. She feels some stirrings within her and thinks, Lust. I'm getting lustful thoughts.

Barbara and Beth burst into the room. Just in time, Joan thinks.

After dinner, while Beth and Barbara go to the library, Joan stays behind to write Eddie a long letter. She gets out her stationery, sits at the roll top desk and turns on the lamp. She opens a sliding door behind the typewriter and turns on Beth's radio. She smiles, remembering Beth showing her the radio and saying, "Radios are allowed at O.L.L. but they must be played at a ladylike volume." Beth had said this in a prissy voice that made Joan laugh. She leaves the radio on Beth's Buffalo station. Guy Mitchell is singing, "My Heart Cries for You".

Eddie would call this a square station, she thinks and she begins to write her letter.

As pop stations go, it's not that bad. While she's telling Eddie about her visit to the Blue Light and her trip with her mother, she hears Al Martino sing "Here in My Heart" and Jo Stafford do "You Belong to Me".

During "Wish You Were Here", when Eddie Fisher sings "Someone's painting the leaves all wrong this year, wish you were here," her eyes fill. She continues writing, telling Eddie all about her life at O.L.L. and the two-weeks-between-letters rule. As she's putting the finishing touches on her letter, "It's No Sin" comes on. Eddy Howard sings, "Is it a sin, to love you so? To hold you close and know you are leaving. Though you take away my heart, dear, still the beating there within. I'll keep loving you forever, for it's no sin."

Joan pauses, frowning at the word sin. She decides against signing her letter "Your Eternal Love Slave" and settles for "I love you, forever." She signs her name and admires her excellent penmanship. That violet ink on the pale blue paper looks sharp, she thinks and she puts a big red kiss next to her signature.

On her walk to the mailbox in the administration building, she smokes a cigarette. The smell of the smoke jogs her memory. She thinks of her first night with Eddie in her car, sharing a cigarette with him and encouraging him to do things with her that she'd never done with any other boy. I wonder if it's lust if you're just remembering something that happened?

On her walk back to the dorm, Joan thinks about some of the many things she learned in grammar school, and decides that she'll go to Confession on Saturday and make a fresh start. She thinks about hell and hears Father Quinn saying, "Pawns of the Divil." Eddie flashes through her mind for an instant.

I hope I don't dream tonight, she says to herself just before drifting off to sleep. She has a couple of brief dreams and awakens rested and happy.

I dreamed something, but I can't remember if it was bad or good. Oh well, if I can't remember it, that's as good as not dreaming. She has a pleasant day at class and decides that learning still comes her way with minimum effort.

Eddie and the other airmen arrive at Elmendorf AFB in Anchorage on Saturday and are billeted in Quonset huts in a remote corner of the base.

The first sergeant, a tall skinny, hyper-as-a-ferret, carnival barker kind of guy who considers himself a comedian, goes into his "Welcome to Alaska" rap for Eddie and the other thirty guys in Quonset 2C.

"I'm Sergeant King and I'm here to welcome you to Alaska. I know all of you guys are volunteers …" He's interrupted by hoots and groans.

"Oh? No shit? You guys didn't volunteer? Well, what the fuck, since you're here I might as well clue you in. Your assignments will be on the bulletin board in a couple of days. Most of you will stay here at Elmendorf for two years. Some of you will go to remote sites for one year.

"One of these sites has its landing strip on the side of a mountain. Nothing larger than a C-47 can land there. And they only get in when the wind is right. Our little L-20's can usually get in a couple of times a week with the mail. Another site is out on a cape where anytime the wind drops below twenty-five knots, it's news. A couple of sites are near fighter bases and get regular mail, but all these sites have a few things in common." He makes a couple of quick neck moves, rolls his shoulders and throws them back. "They're all cold as a bitch in winter, and come spring every fucking bug with a pair of wings will rise up out of the tundra in search of your blood."

He steps to the left, then back a step and rubs his hands past his face as if brushing away insects. He crouches, then straightens up and continues, "You will not leave the barracks without a mosquito net hanging from your helmet liner or your face will be eaten. You'll look like poor Yorick." Eddie and three others laugh.

Sergeant King laughs at his own joke and continues, "Some of these things are so small the Eskimos call 'em no-see-ums. You may not see 'em but you'll fucking well feel 'em. They hit you like starving horseflies. They don't really bite, it's more like they just tear off a hunk of meat and go looking for some bread. Other spring friends are the blue tailed fly and the Alaskan mosquito, big gray and black striped bastards about the size of small dogs. They will be after your ass. Seriously. Some are really big. Down at one of the fighter bases guys started fueling one up … thought he was an F-86 … got a hundred gallons of jet fuel in him before they found out." A few guys laugh politely and King continues, "Oh yeah, and one other thing these sites all have in common. There are no women of any kind at or near them. Your only girlfriend for the next twelve months will be Mary Fist.

"On the other hand, no pun intended, you lucky guys who stay here at Elmendorf for two years will be able to enjoy Anchorage and the many bars and gin mills of Fourth Avenue, as well as the hookers who frequent them.

"I see that most of you are airman basics. Your eighty-two bucks a month will go a long way here, where pussy costs twenty bucks for a short time and all the hookers drive Cadillacs." He darts a quick look left and jumps forward.

"I see some of you thinking, 'I don't pay for pussy. I get all I want free.' Free pussy in Alaska? That's a nice idea. Me, I'm looking for a rainbow at midnight. Our chances are about the same. No. That's not true. My chances are better of seeing that midnight rainbow." He shudders like the Scarecrow when Dorothy cut him loose and continues, "My advice to those of you who stay at Elmendorf is, learn to bowl." He does a quick bowling motion. "Go to the base movie, read some good books, do your drinking at the PX or the Airman's Club and most important, make friends with Rosy Palm and her five daughters." He makes a funny face and does a big jack-off motion. Everybody laughs.

"In conclusion, let me say, don't expect much while you're up here. Try not to kill each other and most of all," he pauses for effect, "do not fuck up during the few days that you're in my outfit. I'm short. I go stateside in thirty-nine days and I don't want no fucking paperwork. You can get drunk and fight all you want, but don't destroy any government property."

Eddie spends little time at Elmendorf. Joan's letter arrives on Tuesday and on Wednesday he's on a C-47 with seven other guys heading for Naknek.

Besides the men and the duffel bags, the plane is loaded with sacks of mail, cartons of boots, crates of oranges, boxes of apples, cases of beer and soda, along with cigarettes and candy. Everything is lashed down properly.

Eddie is thinking about Joan's letter. One letter every two weeks is okay, he thinks. Twenty-six letters and I'm back with Joan. Her roommates sound okay. What the hell, things could be worse. He stops daydreaming and reads the sign on the plane's door. In red letters on a white background, it states simply and honestly, ALASKA HAS BEEN ROUGH ON ME. Eddie laughs and says to the guy sitting in the bucket seat next to his, "It was rough on Dangerous Dan McGrew." He sticks out his hand and says, "I'm Eddie Flynn."

The guy shakes Eddie's hand. "Don Reeves. Nice to know you. Who's Dan McGrew?"

"A guy in a poem we had to read in high school," Eddie answers. "He came up here or to the Yukon. Anyway, he got himself shot dead in a card game."

Don is pudgy and talkative. As Eddie listens to him talk about his folks and his girlfriend of many years, Eddie finds himself thinking of Don as a nice kid, the same way he used to think of Norm. At one point in the conversation, Don is lamenting about being sent to Alaska. "I guess I just went AWOL one time too many."

Eddie points out the rugged mountain terrain, visible from all the plane's windows. "It don't look like you'll be goin' anywhere up here." They laugh.

Naknek, Eddie thinks as he steps out of the plane after a smooth landing. This is the place that Smitty told me about. He looks around. It's a gray, windless day. To the southwest he can see water, but on most other points of the compass mountain peaks are visible on the horizon.

My home for a year, he says to himself. He slings his duffel back over his shoulder and heads for the truck that takes him to the 901st Aircraft Control and Warning Squadron. The 901st has the same function as the 646th, another link in the Distant Early Warning network. It's just a little bit farther north on the DEW line, Eddie thinks as he and the others climb aboard the truck.

The base layout is similar to the 646th except the barracks are single-story, two-men-to-a-room buildings, rather than the two-story structures of the 646th, and every building on the base is connected by long, enclosed walkways. The only building that's not attached is the radio shack. It's on a hill, a mile away from the Radar Ops building.

The truck drops them off outside the orderly room. Eddie is the last of the new arrivals to report to the first sergeant.

The first sergeant is sitting behind his desk, looking through Eddie's 201 file. He's wearing crisp khakis. Eddie notices a Purple Heart among the sergeant's campaign ribbons. He looks at the hash marks on the guy's sleeve and thinks, He was in before Pearl Harbor.

The first sergeant closes Eddie's 201 file and looks him in the eye. The sergeant has hunter's eyes and a hawk's nose, but he's almost smiling. "According to this, you're a pretty good radar operator," he states. "I can forget about the rest of this crap if you can."

"I sure can, Sergeant." Eddie smiles.

The first sergeant hands him a map of the base. "You're on Able crew. Deke Mizell is your crew chief. Follow that walkway outside my office all the way down to the end, then turn left and keep going."

Eddie takes the piece of paper. "Thanks, Sergeant. I don't have to report to the C.O.?"

"No. He's up in Anchorage getting a couple of teeth pulled." The sergeant smiles. "You probably won't ever see him unless you fuck up."

"I don't plan on fuckin' up."

The first sergeant smiles broader. "That's what they all say," he replies, and they both laugh.

Eddie steps outside the orderly room and consults his map. The walkway he's standing on runs east for about a mile to the Radar Operations building, with a southbound branch going to the mess hall and a northbound branch leading to the PX, the main squadron dayroom and the Information and Education room. Movies and informative Air Force lectures are given in the I & E room. A new movie each week and lectures hardly ever.

The same walkway, if taken west, ends in a T where a left turn will take you to Able Crew Bay and a right turn brings you to Baker Crew Bay. The map shows many walkways connecting other barracks, the powerhouse, the motor pool and the NCO club. Looks like we're at the southwestern edge of the base, he thinks and heads west down the walkway.

Halfway down the walkway, Eddie is overtaken by an airman carrying a case of beer. It's A2/c Johnny Beeman. Johnny was released from reform school in Connecticut with the proviso that he join the military. He's on his second hitch and it's the third time he's been an airman second class. His sleeves are rolled up, showing what authorities call "multiple tattoos"—a yellow and black bumblebee wearing a top hat with the word "Beeman" under it, a duck with a surprised look on its face and "Who, me?" tattooed above its head, and a seagull sitting on a rock with "Johnson Island" printed beneath it.

On his left bicep he has what he calls his "piece of resistance," a big red heart with an arrow piercing it and drops of blood pooling underneath. The heart has a blank banner across it. When guys ask about the banner, he tells them, "I use it on chicks. I tell 'em, if you play your cards right, your name could go in there. Dollies love it." Johnny shows as much respect for pronunciation and grammar as Eddie.

Beeman falls in step with Eddie. "Lookin' for Able crew?" he asks.

"Yeah."

"You found it." Beeman sticks out his hand. "Johnny Beeman."

Eddie switches his grip on his duffel bag to his left hand and shakes hands. "Eddie Flynn."

"You got good timin'. We just began our three-day break."

"Well, that's a good start," Eddie comments and they laugh. Eddie continues, "First thing I gotta do is check in with the crew chief."

"Don't worry about it. Deke's playin' poker at the NCO club," Beeman replies. "You can hang out in the dayroom. We're shootin' pool and drinkin' beer."

"I like doin' both."

"You a good pool shooter?"

"Not really." Eddie shakes his head. "Hit 'em hard and wish 'em well is my motto." Beeman laughs.

At the end of the walkway, Beeman shouts, "Double to the rear, by the left flank, March!" They execute the maneuver and laugh, then walk down the bay toward the dayroom, stopping at the last room on their left. Its door is open and there's a large speaker in the doorway. The speaker is pointing toward the dayroom door across the hall. Joe Liggins is singing, "I've got a right to cry, I've got a right to cry. You left me all alone, come back where you belong."

In that room, A3/c T.J. Jones is sitting on the side of his bunk, shuffling through a dozen 45 rpm records. Opposite him, an empty cot with a three-foot by five-foot sheet of plywood laid on it, holds a record turntable, a leatherette reel-to-reel tape recorder, six spools of tape, a pile of multi-colored wires, a stack of 78 rpm records, all in their paper sleeves, and a few record albums. Three records are on the spindle, waiting for their turn on the turntable. An open pack of Luckies, a Zippo, an ashtray, a church key and an almost-full bottle of cognac are on his dresser.

T.J. from East Saint Louis, "That's Illinois, not Bumfuck, Missouri," he's quick to point out, likes to think he looks like Billy Eckstine. He has over forty rhythm and blues records, "Tomorrow Night" among them. He wants to be a disc jockey when he gets discharged. T.J. borrows country tunes from Jesse Joe, jazz from Prez, pop songs from Scarpa, mixes in some of his R&B numbers and cooks up what he calls his "All Star, All American Revue." He spends much of his off-duty time in the Armed Forces Radio Services studio, taping practice radio shows. He's almost twenty-three and never discusses his past, except to comment, "All the really fine, Saint Looie women call me Mister Bee."

Beeman opens the case of beer, pulls out a can and tosses it to T.J. "Think fast," he shouts while the can is in mid-flight. T.J. drops his stack of records into his lap, catching the can without looking up. "Thanks, Beeman."

"Eddie Flynn, T.J. Jones," Beeman announces. T.J. finally looks up. Eddie leans over the speaker and shakes T.J.'s hand. "Nice tune."

"You like rhythm and blues?"

"Who don't?"

"Come by after you get settled. You can look through these."

"Thanks, T.J., I will."

Beeman and Eddie enter the dayroom. A pool table is set up in the middle of the room. A rack holding a pair of cue sticks and a bridge is mounted on the wall. The lighting fixture, shining brightly on the table, looks like it might have been stolen from any first class pool hall in the USA.

A card table and four chairs are in one corner and a half-size refrigerator is in another. Beside the refrigerator is a large stainless steel garbage can. A table with a coffee urn, a dozen mess hall coffee mugs and a sugar dispenser on it is next to the can.

A long black leather couch runs along one wall. It faces three tall stools that are lined up against the wall on the other side of the pool table.

The stools are excellent seats for watching the pool shooters. Frequent comments are made about the players' prowess.

The three airmen at the far end of the pool table, busy flipping and matching coins, don't notice Beeman and Eddie enter the room. Only A1/c Anthony "Don't call me Tony" Scarpa, sitting on the middle stool drinking a beer, catches sight of them.

A1/c Scarpa is the only short-timer on the crew. Like all the guys of the 901st with less than ninety days to go, he has a large laundry bag safety pin fastened on the front of his fatigue cap and answers any requests that he take part in work details with the standard reply of, "Shit. I'm short!"

Anthony is from Philly and he shows the same high regard for grammar and pronunciation that Eddie and Beeman show. He played high school football and basketball. He still wears his hair in a short crewcut. He's the assistant crew chief.

Beeman stops by Anthony's stool on his way to the refrigerator. Anthony kills his beer and lofts the empty can over the pool table's light fixture and across the room into the garbage can.

"Good shootin'," Eddie comments.

"He don't miss," Beeman brags. "Eddie, I'd like you to meet Anthony 'Don't call me Tony' Scarpa. Anthony, Eddie Flynn."

"Good to meet you, Eddie."

"You too, Anthony." They shake hands.

"Be right back," Beeman says. He hands Anthony a can of beer and he and Eddie take off. Eddie puts his duffel bag down next to the garbage can and helps Beeman load the refrigerator with beer. Beeman and Eddie open beers for themselves and Beeman introduces Eddie to the pool shooters.

Getting ready to break is A3/c Jesse Joe Lee from near Lubbock, Texas. He's a country music fan and has records by Hank Snow, Ernest Tubb and Hank Williams. Jesse Joe's in love with a girl back home but she doesn't know it. He has a beat-up old guitar that still manages to be in tune. When he gets drunk he writes songs for his secret love, Ermaline Rae. "I may write a song about Alaska," he often states. "Wait'll after I rotate," Scarpa always adds.

Midway down the table, chalking his cue, is A/B Joseph "Red" McClain from Portland, Oregon. He never went to Radar Operator school but has become an average scopedope through "on the job training." He was shipped to Alaska for running a forklift into an F-86 during a drunken escapade. Red receives master sergeant pay each month, with a deduction to cover "government statement of charges." The deduction brings his real pay down to the eighty bucks a month airman basics are paid. Red explains, "It's the only way the government can make things look good on paper. And I don't give a fuck because eighty bucks a month is enough to keep me drinking."

Red got engaged the day before he shipped out. His fiancée works at the Dairy Queen just outside of San Antonio, where Red had been stationed. He knew Lulubelle for three weeks before they got engaged.

Standing down at the end of the table is A2/c Hollis James from Tennessee. Most of the guys on Able crew range in age from nineteen to twenty-two. Hollis is twenty-five and he was worldly at twelve. He drove carloads of moonshine before joining the Air Force. "I can make a U-turn doing sixty with a load of mule," he claims. "Been driving since I was thirteen. Guess my family's been hauling mule long as there's been cars."

Telling about his father driving moonshine, Hollis relates, "My old man only drove at night and never on Sunday. Daytime and Sundays he was a preacher. He might drive a load up to Red Jacket, West by God Virginia. I never heard him say 'West Virginia' in my life. It was always, West by God Virginia for my old man.

"Anyway, he'd preach his way back from Red jacket or Coal City. Everyone called him 'The Rev.' He could say 'Gawd' and make it sound like the crack of doom. He liked his own product and always took a nip or two, or three, before preaching. He loved preaching. He got drunk one night and told me he didn't give a shit about saving nobody's soul. I guess I was about sixteen at the time. He said he just liked putting the fear of God into folks and riling them up against Satan. He called it riling the rubes. He told me he'd been searching for Satan all his life and had never seen hide nor hair of him. 'I can scare the shit out of any-one who believes in the Devil,' he told me. 'Don't waste your time worrying about Satan. It's all in your mind. You got a better chance of running into Santa Claus than the Devil.'

"My old man got his ticket punched three years ago. Raced a freight train to a crossing near Cumberland Gap. It was a tie. The Rev was hauling a full load of moon. An old farmer who was a mile from the crossing said the whole sky lit up. The old man would've liked that. We buried what we could find of him and the next day I joined up."

Hollis has no one in particular waiting for him.

Jesse Joe rockets the cue ball into the pack. The balls scatter, nothing falls.

Eddie and Beeman join Anthony. "Hollis is the only shooter in this game," Anthony confides. "Red gets lucky from time to time. And Jesse Joe should stick to ropin' fuckin' cows."

Red misses a straight-in shot on the one ball and before Anthony can hoot, "Fuckin' guy missed the ace." A3/c Thomas "Prez" Jefferson enters the dayroom. He's a Lester Young fan. He calls everyone Prez and everyone calls him Prez in return. He's wearing his non-regulation, two-piece fatigues, his yellow-tinted shades and walking his shuffle walk, his left hand tucked in his waistband and his right hand carrying a slender cane with an ivory wolf's head handle.

He walks up to Anthony and declares, "Prez, I'm back from supply. I'm happy to say our sides will arrive by next Tuesday." He laughs. "Goddamn, I'm cool. I didn't even mean to make that rhyme." Prez gets a beat going. "I'm back from supply and happy to say, our sides will arrive by Tuesday." He takes note of Eddie enjoying the show. Beeman, his best audience, is breaking up.

Anthony jumps off his stool and puts his arm around Jefferson's back, half hugging him. "I love this fuckin' guy," he exclaims. "He found the first song me and Loretta ever danced to."

"Dick Fuckin' Haymes, nineteen forty-nine." Prez grins. "'Maybe It's Because'."

Hollis sinks the ace, deuce and trey quickly and cleanly while the conversation continues. "Eddie Flynn, meet Prez. Official name, Thomas Jefferson," Anthony states. "This man can get you anything. Old records, comic books and past issues of *Popular Mechanics*, anything."

"I can get you anything but pussy," Prez corrects him. Everyone laughs and Beeman almost falls off his stool.

Prez gets a beer and joins the onlookers.

Hollis is not one of those guys who needs quiet and concentration to shoot pool. He sees the shot he needs to make, sees where he wants the cue ball to end up and makes his shot. Most times he sinks the shot. A circus parade could go marching past within three feet of the table and he'll still bank the eight ball in the side pocket.

The guys are playing Moneyball. The five, eight, ten and fifteen are each worth a buck. Total score is also worth a buck. You start by making the ace and following the balls in rotation. Sometimes you can't see the ball you're supposed to hit; it may be blocked by one or more balls. You may have to use a cushion or two to get at it. Other times you may not care if the ball you're after falls. If the five ball is hanging on the lip of a pocket and the ten ball is hanging on the lip of another, a guy like Hollis might be playing the three ball and knock it into the five ball, have the cue ball hit a couple of cushions and come back and drop the ten ball. Two moneyballs drop and fifteen points of score is racked up.

"Skill and luck dukin' it out," is the way Eddie describes Moneyball. "I respect skill in all things," Eddie preaches, "but in an ass-kickin' contest between skill and luck, I'll bet on luck every fuckin' time. There's absolutely no substitute for luck."

Jesse Joe is lining up a shot on the eight ball when A/B Donald Reeves wanders into the dayroom from outdoors. The door is near the refrigerator. Don puts his duffel bag down by Eddie's and looks around.

Eddie breaks away from the guys and walks over to Don.

"I got lost," Reeves states.

"Are you assigned to Able crew?"

"Yeah, but I lost my map."

"Don't worry about it. This is Able crew," Eddie tells him. "And you can have my map."

Eddie introduces Don all around and during the afternoon, Eddie gets answers to two questions he thought of asking but didn't.

Don asks Scarpa, "So Anthony, how come you don't want to be called Tony?"

Eddie catches a faint, brief, almost-smile on Scarpa's face before Anthony starts, "I'm named after a fuckin' saint, for Chrissakes!" Beeman and Prez are looking away so Don can't see them grinning. Anthony sees Eddie smiling and continues, faking umbrage. "People should show some fuckin' respect for holy things. My mother, God rest her soul," Anthony crosses himself, "named me Anthony Francis after her two brothers. You know what my uncles are called? Tony and Frank. Tony and fuckin' Frank. One's named after the saint who helps you find lost shit, Anthony, and the other one's named after a guy who was always kind to fuckin' animals, Saint Francis. Jesus fuckin' Christ …"

Beeman loses it, laughing uproariously. He jumps off his stool and stomps his feet. Eddie catches Don's eye, nods and winks. Don's dazed expression changes to a smile.

"Fuckin' Beeman," Anthony laughs. "I was just gettin' goin'."

A bit later, with a spindle full of tunes and another stack on standby, T.J. leaves his room and joins the group just as Don is commenting to Prez, "I guess they call you Prez because you're named after Thomas Jefferson?"

"Named after?!" Prez looks amazed. "I'm descended from the motherfucker. Old Tom used to come to the slave quarters and fuck the shit out of my great-great-great grandmother."

"No shit?" T.J. asks, like he's never been down this trail before.

"He got that 'all men are created equal' shit from my great-great-great grandmaw. Used it in the Declaration of Independence."

"No shit?" T.J. asks again. He's looking for some fun.

"Well, that's a fact. Old Tom fucked quite a few of the slave ladies." He looks at T.J. "Including this motherfucker's great-great-great grandmomma."

"No shit?" T.J. repeats.

Prez cocks a thumb at T.J. "His momma wanted to name him Thomas Jefferson, but she wasn't sure how to spell Thomas and she sure as fuck couldn't spell Jefferson, so she had to go for T.J."

T.J. loves it and hoots right along with Beeman and Anthony. "You just thought of that one right now, didn't you?" T.J. slings an arm around Prez. "Damn, you're good, Prez." He pauses. "But not as good as your momma."

More hoots from all, including Prez. Eddie smiles, recalling the days on the corner of 123rd Street and Amsterdam, "Playing the Dozens" with his buddies.

"Playing the Dozens," also called "Slippin" or "Cappin," usually was about each other's mothers, though it could include other family members and their genitalia. One of Eddie's old favorites, and he had many, was "Don't play the dozens. The dozens is a game. But the way I fuck your mother is a goddamn shame."

It's like bein' back in the old neighborhood, Eddie thinks. If I gotta spend a year away from Joan, at least I'm in good company.

Eddie and Don go to supply and check out bedding before evening chow. Deke left room assignments. Flynn to Hollis' room. Reeves to McClain's room.

At 0315, when the whole crew is sleeping, Staff Sergeant Deke Mizell returns from the poker game a hundred and twenty-dollar winner. Deke is Barracks Chief as well as Crew Chief. He's a self-described Missouri farm boy who doesn't care what Able crew does on their off-duty time as long as they're sober and skillful in the Radar Ops room.

He runs the barracks with a lax hand, tolerating mess, but not filth. The dayroom looks like a big wind just blew through it, but the latrine is always spotless. Able crew always passes inspections, which are rare. Beer and whiskey may be brought to the rooms. The crew has a gang-like tightness. I hope these two new guys aren't too fucked up, he thinks just before he falls asleep.

CHAPTER 33

▼

October and November pass quickly for Joan. She goes to Confession and becomes a regular Sunday Mass communicant. She does well in her studies and is third in her class when she goes home for her Thanksgiving break. While she's home she tells her dad that she "almost, sort of" remembers him. Counting Thanks-giving dinner, she sees Bill three times.

The first day of Joan's break, Jill takes her to a portrait studio. For her photo session Joan wears a light-blue sweater and matching kerchief tied into a bow. A small spit curl in front of each ear gives her a Latin look. Her eyes are fully healed and sparkling. She wears her gold necklace and the turquoise earrings that Eddie sent her from Barstow. Before returning to school, she mails an eight-by-ten color photograph in a silver frame to Eddie for a Christmas present. She signs it, "All my love, forever, Joan."

Eddie's package arrives two days before Christmas. He immediately writes Joan, telling her it was the best Christmas present he ever received. He also tells her he's been staying out of trouble and that he's been promoted to airman third class. "Like we give a shit," he puts in parenthesis.

Joan's Christmas present from Eddie, a silver bracelet with opals, is waiting for her when she arrives back at O.L.L.

In her mid-January letter, Joan writes:

My dearest, darling Eddie,

First let me tell you how much I love my bracelet. I wear it to class every day. You have such good taste. Now here's some big news. I hope you're sitting down. Sandy is now Mrs. Bob Porter. They got married while I was home on Christmas vacation. Isn't that wonderful? I'm so happy for them. It was a small beautiful ceremony at Sandy's house. I was the Maid of Honor and Norm was the Best Man. Bob and Sandy are going to be living in Tawas. During the wedding I thought about us and I cried (just a little) but I know our chance will come.

More news. At the wedding Bob told me to be sure to tell you that Becker got sent to Greenland. Bob said the Inspector General came up to Oscoda for a surprise inspection, and the morale at the 646th was so bad that a week later Becker was gone. Your friend Captain Ross got promoted to major and was made the commanding officer. Isn't that great news?

Joan's letter goes on for two more pages, telling Eddie about her studies, her thoughts and how happy she'll be to be reunited with him. She signs her letter, *"Counting the days (258) 'til your return. All my love, Always, Joan."*

The following week, Able crew has a "going home" party for Captain Miller. No one gets too drunk and nobody gets into trouble. The C-54, with Captain Miller on board, takes off an hour before sundown and Eddie doesn't feel like drinking anymore, so he hits the sack. He wakes up at 11:30, hungry.

Able crew is on their three-day break, so Eddie goes to midnight chow with Baker crew, signing the chow list as A3/C Dick Tracy. He gets lucky; the meal is chipped beef on toast. Eddie loads his tray, gets a big mug of coffee and sits down next to Staff Sergeant McCabe, Baker's crew chief.

McCabe looks at Eddie's tray, shakes his head and smiles. "You really go for that S.O.S."

"Mack," Eddie replies, "shit on a shingle, or steak, it's all the same to me. Just sumpthin' to make a turd." Eddie looks across the mess hall. "Don't look right now," he continues, "but there's a second looie near the door starin' daggers at my ass."

Mack laughs, "I don't have to look. He's got a crewcut and his Garrison cap is too big."

"That's the guy," Eddie nods. "His cap's pushin' his ears out like trophy handles.

"He's probably wondering if you're in the Air Force," Mack comments, laughing. "Look at you, for Chrissakes, black suede loafers and sweat socks, paratrooper fatigue pants and your fucking fatigue jacket is bleached almost white. I'm not even going to talk about your hair."

Eddie takes a big slug of his coffee. "Yeah," he agrees, "I guess to him I look a little bit out of uniform. Good thing he's on your crew."

Mack smiles a big smile. "Only 'til your crew goes back on duty. You're looking at your new controller, Captain Miller's replacement."

"Tell me you're shittin' me, Mack."

"I shit you not," Mack replies. "This guy just got out of OCS and he's chickenshit to the bone. It's our third night with him and the whole crew's sick of him. Even Lieutenant Russell thinks he's a pain in the ass. Russell is showing him how we do things here and this guy's writing it all down in a notebook."

"Thanks for the good news." Eddie stares back at the officer and thinks, Holy shit. Here we go again. Another Double-A."

The next night, Able crew is at chow before going on midnight shift. Beeman, Hollis and Eddie are sitting at a table watching the new officer go through the serving line.

"Lookit here," Hollis starts, nodding his head toward the officer. "That old boy walks like he's got a broomstick up his ass."

"That's our new controller," Eddie smirks.

"Shit. I'm glad I'm short," Hollis shoots back.

Beeman frowns, "You ain't short. You got a hundred and fifty-five days to go. I keep the tally board in the dayroom, remember?"

"Well, I only got sixty-five days to go 'til I'm short," Hollis brags.

"So you see, Beeman, Hollis is short toward bein' short," Eddie returns, and they all laugh.

"Anyway," Beeman joins in, "that guy looks like a real hard-on."

"Able crew'll soften him up," Eddie replies, and they all laugh again.

Second Lieutenant John Knox, a six-foot-one, 160 pound washout from Flight School, takes his tray of French toast, sits next to Deke, introduces himself and gets right down to business. "I spent the afternoon in Colonel Gunderson's office going through the personnel records of this crew, Sergeant," he snorts. "They're a pretty sorry lot."

Deke takes a big swallow of coffee. "Some of them don't look too good on paper," he responds, "but they're okay on duty."

Lieutenant Knox cuts a precise square of his French toast, puts it in his mouth and makes a face. "I don't see a single man in this mess hall who's in uniform," he continues with contempt.

Deke spears a forkful of French toast into his mouth and grunts.

"Including you, Sergeant," Knox adds. Deke is wearing a green turtleneck sweater under his fatigues, instead of a white T-shirt.

"Just getting over a stiff neck, sir," Deke lies.

The lieutenant takes a small pad and a mechanical pencil out of his shirt pocket. "Who's the airman with his sleeves rolled up?" He points with his fork toward Eddie's table. "The one with all the tattoos."

"That's Beeman, Lieutenant," Deke answers. "He's our Movements and Identification tech. A really good man."

Knox opens his pad and writes Beeman's name down. "I don't like tattoos," he states sourly. "Why is he wearing sneakers?"

"He injured his foot," Deke lies again. "Dropped a big crate on it unloading the supply barges last summer."

Knox looks around the mess hall, checks his watch, pushes his tray with the remains of his breakfast aside and prepares to leave the table. "It's almost time to march the men to duty," he states.

"We don't march, sir," Deke starts to reply as he runs the last forkful of his French toast around his tray, soaking up the remaining syrup. "It's too—"

Lieutenant Knox interrupts him sharply. "We *do* march, Sergeant. Starting tonight and from now on. Get the men assembled out in the hallway.

"Yes sir." Deke gets up, downs the last of his coffee and puts his tray, cup and utensils on the checkout counter. We'll march tonight, he thinks, but we damn sure won't march from now on. He smiles and starts getting the guys together. Three minutes later he has Able crew lined up at attention, in two rows, out in the hallway under Knox's scrutiny.

"Left face!" Deke barks. "Forward! Harch!"

All of the guys except Eddie and Beeman are wearing their heavy brogans and Eddie's loafers have full horseshoe taps on the leather heels, so Beeman's sneakers are the only quiet pieces of footwear in the bunch. They all dig their heels in. Their heels striking the wooden floor give off a loud, deep, snapping sound that rebounds and echoes off the plasterboard walls.

The crew has only marched twelve steps when Knox realizes his mistake. He resists covering his ears, falls back a few paces and observes the Frankenstein that he turned loose. Smart-asses, he thinks.

The word, "incredible," flashes in Knox's brain when he hears Deke counting cadence. "Hut, two, hut, four. Hut, hoop, haireep, haw." Deke bellows. Able crew's enthusiasm goes up a notch and the crescendo begins at 6 on the volume knob.

Sergeant Mizell isn't going to be much help, Knox thinks.

"Hut, two, hut, four. Hut, hoop, haireep, *haw!*" Deke hits the "haw" with his country baritone like a muleskinner. The crew responds, cranking up the zest level. They bang their heels into the floorboards harder, thundering down the hallway like a herd of buffalo in a thunderstorm. The volume level jumps to 9.

A hundred yards from the Radar Operations building, two guys on Dog crew stick their heads out the door to see what's coming. At the entrance to Radar Ops, Deke halts the march with an old "Monkey Drill" command.

"Double to the rear, with a slight hesitation, by the left flank, right flank, halt!" he shouts.

Able crew responds with gusto. The volume knob hits 10, when they slam their heels into the floor with such vigor on the last two beats that Red McClain breaks through one of the floor-boards.

Deke dismisses the men and Able crew herds loudly into the break room. Knox calls Deke aside and orders sharply, "Tell the men there'll be a crew meeting at oh-eight-hundred, Sergeant."

"Yes sir, Lieutenant," Deke responds, grinning. Knox makes another notation in his pad.

It's a boring shift with nothing more than Combat Air Patrol flights, bush pilots doing 130 knots and the usual Northwest Orient flights coming in from the Pacific. Lieutenant Knox spends the night going from position to position, introducing himself to the men and making more notations in his pad.

Eddie is working scope number three when Lieutenant Knox sits down next to him and introduces himself. Scope three is set up for long distance pickups ranging from 150 to 300 miles. Eddie has the range and azimuth markers turned down so low that they're invisible. With this method, he has picked up flights 280 miles out.

Eddie's carrying two tracks, commercial aircraft heading for Anchorage, both identified and on course. Eddie keys his headset, "Love Nine, two-one-zero at one-seven-five miles. Love Ten, two-one-zero at two-two-zero miles. Time, one-eight."

Hollis keys and un-keys his headset and puts the two moves on the plotting board. Knox reaches past Eddie, turns up the range and azimuth markers to full brilliance and spins in his chair to face Eddie.

The scope's sweep line hits 270° and the first azimuth marker flashes a thick line, while the range markers start making thick circles at every ten miles of range. Eddie rolls his chair back from the scope as if he'd been scalded when the 300° azimuth line flashes thickly, and shouts, "Jesus Christ, Lieutenant! What'd you do that for? I can't look at a scope all lit up like that, I'll go fuckin' blind." Eddie squints his eyes like he's driving into a blazing desert sunset. The sweep line hits 330° and is continuing to flash at every thirty degrees.

Eddie decides to enjoy himself. I'm goin' nowhere with this guy, he thinks, I was right. He's a Double A, just like Becker and Joan's old man. "Lieutenant," he continues, "my scope's gonna look like a fuckin' wagon wheel. Between that and the range markers startin' to look like a target, I'll go apeshit."

"You can't be guessing at range and azimuth, Airman," Knox states with an authoritative tone as the sweep line passes 210°. Track Love Nine is now partially obscured by the thick 210° marker, and Love Ten, being on the thick 220-mile range marker, as well as the 210° azimuth marker, is completely buried.

"Who's guessin'?" Eddie turns the range and azimuth markers back down to his original setting, points to the scope and argues, "There's Love Nine and there's Love Ten. They're both under that two hundred and ten degree marker, like I called in, only now you can hardly see 'em." Eddie taps his black grease pencil on the scope. "Zero-nine-zero, one-eight-zero, two-seven-zero. Who needs markers? It's just a fuckin' circle, Lieutenant."

"I don't need to be told about circles by you"—Knox darts a glance into his open pad—"Flynn," he adds after a brief pause.

Knox stands up, preparing to head for the next name in his book. "What's that drawing on the back of your fatigue jacket?"

"Yosemite Sam. Anthony Scarpa drew it for me before he rotated."

"It's not regulation."

"I know that, Lieutenant," Eddie smiles. "Looks good though, don't it?"

Knox shakes his head and makes another notation before he heads for the plotting board.

Eddie keys his headset as soon as Knox is on his way. "Look out, Hollis, here comes an asshole at one-eight-zero," he warns.

At 8:01 AM, Charlie crew comes on duty. Their two crew members on first hour break are sitting at a wobbly card table in the corner of the break room getting ready to play Casino. They're wondering why Able crew is hanging around the break room instead of heading for the mess hall.

At 8:02, Deke and Lieutenant Knox enter the room. Deke asks the Charlie crew guys if they'd take their card game to the radar mechanic's room and Knox starts his meeting, "Gentlemen."

Hollis, T.J. and McClain are grousing about being hungry. Beeman whispers to Eddie, "This is bullshit."

"Gentlemen," Knox continues, almost shouting with irritation. The guys quiet down. He opens his pad. "Last night, I made a few observations of this radar crew on duty. I didn't like what I saw."

Eddie raises his hand. "Lieutenant?" he asks.

Knox looks impatient. "Yes?"

"Is this goin' to be a long meetin', sir," Eddie continues, "because they stop servin' mornin' chow at eight-thirty and it's almost five after eight."

"This meeting will be as long as necessary." He glances at his pad. "You're Flynn, aren't you?"

"That's me, Lieutenant."

"I'll get to you later," Knox replies. "First on my list is Airman Basic John Burroughs." Burroughs replaced Scarpa when Anthony rotated. He was a medic stationed in Florida … great duty. He was an airman first class, then a whole bunch of amphetamines couldn't be accounted for, now he's training on the job as a radar operator on Able crew. He fits right in and is doing well thanks to Hollis and Eddie.

"Burroughs, here, sir," Burroughs acknowledges while raising his hand.

"I have you down for sloppy radio telephone procedure and for poor scope viewing habits."

Burroughs says nothing. What do I care what you think, asshole, he thinks. Eddie says I'm a natural.

From Burroughs, Knox moves on to Reeves, another two-infraction man. Bad scope habits and non-regulation haircut are his transgressions.

McClain, Beeman, Prez and Eddie are all cited for non-regulation two-piece fatigues. "Regulation one-piece fatigues will be issued and you'll have the cost deducted from your next pay."

Beeman mumbles, "Chickenshit son of a bitch," to Eddie.

"What was that, Airman?" Knox looks right at Beeman.

Eddie interrupts. "He said he's got a pair of one-piece fatigues back in his room."

Beeman chimes in. "Would it be okay if I didn't order new ones, since I got a pair?"

"You're supposed to have two sets of one-piece fatigues. Therefore, if you only have one set, you'll have to order a second set, and …" He refers to his notepad. "Beeman, order brogans. No more sneakers." He looks at his notepad again. "And Flynn, you order brogans also. No more loafers."

"I have brogans, Lieutenant," Eddie replies, "I just like my suedes better." Some of the guys laugh.

"You can like them on your off-duty time," Knox quickly snaps back. "If you have brogans … wear them! If not, order a pair … and Air Force issue socks! And get a haircut!" He consults his notepad once more before continuing. "And you're down for bad scope habits!"

I'm not even goin' to try to talk to this clown, Eddie decides. He says a quiet, "Yessir," and lets Knox get on with his business. He glances at Deke and sees the faint hint of a smile.

Knox goes on for a few more minutes about sloppy scope viewing, lax attitudes, the necessity of uniforms for morale, discipline, bad radio/telephone procedure and military haircuts. He stops to take a breath and Deke looks at his watch.

"It's eight twenty-five, Lieutenant," Deke remarks. "Should I march the men to the mess hall?"

The look on Knox's face as he answers, "That won't be necessary, Sergeant," makes up for all the aggravation that Deke and the guys endured during the shift and the meeting.

At morning chow, the crew gets the leavings of what had been breakfast—almost-warm scrambled eggs, toast as stiff as a dead squirrel on a Vermont road in January and bacon that's more petrified than the toast. Able crew spends breakfast saying unkind things about Lieutenant Knox and the lieutenant's mother and father.

After chow, while the guys are sacking out, Deke stops by to see First Sergeant Matthews. "You got a few minutes, Amos? I got a problem."

Amos Matthews is an "old soldier" and a fellow Missourian. He joined the Army Air Force in 1941. He runs the 901st for Colonel Gunderson.

Colonel Gunderson, a West Point graduate who fully understands the importance of non-commissioned officers, relies heavily on his first sergeant's suggestions. It's Colonel Gunderson's combination of intelligence and common sense, along with his willingness to listen to his NCO's that keeps the 901st, an outfit saturated with fuckups, running smoothly.

After laughing about farm chores, manure and second lieutenants for about thirty minutes, Deke leaves the first sergeant's office knowing that in a day or two there'll be a couple of memos on the bulletin board stating that because of a lack of clothing supplies, fatigue regulations will be relaxed and that since the base has no barber, haircuts need only be "reasonable."

"As far as your new second John not liking the way your troops do their radar jobs," Amos advises, "I'm leaving that up to you, Deke, but I can tell you that Elmendorf's happy as a pig in shit about our outfit's performance and the colonel's got a couple of letters from ADCC to prove it. I suggest you tell that shavetail that it don't matter how you pull the old cow's titty, just so the milk goes in the bucket."

It's still snowing when Deke falls asleep at 10:30 and the temperature never rises above zero during the rest of the day. The snow stops during the afternoon and by the time Able crew goes on duty at midnight the temperature has dropped to twenty below zero. The skies are clear and a twenty-knot wind is blowing from the northwest. It's not an ideal night for guard duty.

The unheated, black tar-paper guard shack is located a hundred yards from the Radar Operations building's back door, near the radome, a huge balloon-like, thick rubber dome that protects the radar antenna from the weather. The shack, although unheated, does keep the wind off the man on post.

When Able crew goes on duty, Eddie consults the roster on the break room's bulletin board and finds that he's on guard duty for the first hour of the shift. He goes to the cloak room, where the foul-weather gear is stored, gets into a pair of fleece-lined flight pants, puts on a pile jacket and a parka. He finds a size ten pair of white felt "bunny boots with their felt boot-liners still in them. He gets them laced up quickly. He pulls a woolen watch cap down over his ears, wraps a scarf across his face and ties the parka's hood tight, leaving only his eyes exposed. He puts on a pair of woolen gloves, slips a pair of leather gloves over them and is outdoors relieving the guy on Dog crew at the stroke of midnight. Eddie's luck kicks in and the twenty-knot wind drops to three knots five minutes after he goes on duty.

A daydreamer by nature, Eddie enjoys guard duty. The solitude agrees with him. He puts his senses on alert and then runs tunes through his head, while picturing things like lying on a blanket at Wenona Beach with Joan or imagining the two of them dancing together at Slim's Blue Light.

Guard duty is Eddie's favorite hour of shift. It always speeds by. He takes pride in never looking at his watch to see when his hour is up and he'd never walk the hundred yards from his post to see where his relief was if the guy relieving him was five minutes late, no matter how cold, wet or windy it might be. Whenever Eddie hears a guy knocking on the Ops door, he thinks, what a fuckin' pussy. But tonight is different.

Eddie looks at the half-moon and figures, I must've been out here at least an hour and a half. He is neither uncomfortable or cold. The carbine slung across his shoulder seems weightless and he has thermal underwear on under all of his other clothing.

Funny, Eddie thinks, even though the wind is down to next to nothin', facin' into it still makes my eyes water like faucets.

Keeping his back to the light wind as much as possible, Eddie starts to stamp out a dance floor the size of the one at Slim's Blue Light. I might as well have some fun. I couldn't look at my watch if I wanted to. He starts counting cadence out loud, "Hut, two, hut four. Hut hoop, haireep, haw."

Goddamn, these bunny boots work great. I could stay out here all night if I had some coffee. He starts counting once more, "Your eyes are right and your pants are tight and your balls are swingin' from left to right. Sound off. One, two. Once more. Three, four. Cadence count. One, two, three, four. One, two. *Three, four!*"

The duty sheet that Deke posted had a break scheduled after guard duty, so Eddie isn't missed until five minutes into the third hour, when no one relieves McClain on Scope Three.

Deke goes into the break room to see what the foul-up is and notices that the duty sheet on the bulletin board isn't in his handwriting. He's reading the duty positions to himself when Lieutenant Knox enters the room and comments, "I made up that duty list this afternoon, Sergeant. How do you like it?"

"Captain Miller always had me make up the duty sheet, sir," Deke replies, "but if you'd rather do it, that's okay with me."

"Glad you see it that way," Knox smiles a tight little smile.

Deke continues looking at the list. "Wait a minute," he exclaims. "When did you post this, Lieutenant?"

"About fifteen minutes after we went on shift. Why?"

"Where's my sheet?"

Knox points to the wastebasket. Deke picks out a piece of crumpled paper and straightens it out.

"Guard duty," he almost shouts. "You don't have guard duty posted on your list. It's twenty below out there. Flynn's been on guard duty over two hours."

Deke goes to the other side of the break room, where T.J. and Hollis are playing cards.

"Hollis, get some gear on quick. Flynn's been on guard duty since midnight." Deke glances in Knox's direction. "I sure hope Flynn's not frostbitten, Lieutenant."

Five minutes later, Eddie comes into the break room smiling. "Two hours and twelve minutes at twenty below," he announces. "That's gotta be a record. What the fuck happened, Deke? I felt like the Lone Ranger out there."

Deke tells Eddie what happened while Eddie is getting out of his parka. Lieutenant Knox comes by, visibly upset.

"You're not frostbitten are you?" Knox's face is whiter than new snow.

Eddie picks up Deke's wink, takes off one of his bunny boots and checks his toes. "I don't know," he replies, "but I sure could use a cup of black coffee."

Knox goes to get Eddie a coffee and Deke whispers, "I told him it would be his ass if you had frostbite. I told him to relax and let the crew run itself."

Knox gives Eddie a mug of coffee. "Thanks, Lieutenant. I think I'm gettin' some feelin' back in my toes." He rolls his eyes and turns his head left, then right. "I was startin' to feel almost sleepy out there," he deadpans. "I guess I had a close call."

"How are your toes, Flynn?" Knox is still concerned.

"A lot better, Lieutenant. They're stingin'. That must be the blood comin' back."

"I'm glad to hear that," Knox replies and goes back into the Ops room.

Eddie takes a swallow of coffee. "So what do you think, Deke?"

"I think he's got the fear of God in him, now," Deke answers, "and I talked with the first stud this morning. I think things are going to settle down on this crew."

Things did settle down on Able crew and Knox became what Eddie would call "a fairly reasonable seagull."

CHAPTER 34

▼

Lent looms over Our Lady of the Lakes. It's the Saturday afternoon before Ash Wednesday.

Joan goes to Confession and confesses that she had some "impure thoughts" that she took pleasure in during the past week.

Father Norton is more subdued in his manner than Father Quinn but he is just as vigorously anti-lust. "You must learn to resist these lustful thoughts," he advises. "Think of Our Lady. Think of her purity whenever these thoughts occur, my child." For penance, he gives Joan twenty Hail Marys, along with the gentle admonition, "Don't say them like a machine gun or like you're counting to a hundred playing hide and go seek. Think about the beauty of the prayer. God bless you."

Joan leaves the confessional booth, kneels in a back pew and starts saying her first Hail Mary. She recites it slowly, "Hail Mary, full of grace. The Lord is with Thee …"

When she gets near the end and is saying, "Pray for us sinners, now and at the hour of our death. Amen," she gets a fraction of a second flash of herself, weightless and tumbling during her car wreck.

She has no recollection of the accident but knows that she was close to death. She thinks, if I had died in that wreck, it would have been straight to hell for me. She sees Eddie's face for a moment and thinks, I'm a sinner and Eddie's an occasion of sin.

Joan got to Confession just under the 3:30 deadline. The chapel is only about one-third full with most of the girls in the front half. She finishes Hail Mary number twenty, sits back in the pew and thinks, it's so quiet and dark back here. I think I'll hang around a few more minutes for Benediction.

During the service, while the girls are singing "Tantum Ergo", Joan closes her eyes and lets the smell of the burning candles and the incense transport her to another time. She sees Jesus at the Pharisee's house telling Mary Magdalene that she's forgiven for being a sinner. "Me too, Jesus," she pleads, "Can I have a second chance?"

After Benediction, with the smell of incense and candles still in her nose, Joan is seated on her bed, talking with Beth and Barbara. Beth is sitting at the roll top, Barbara is sitting at the table.

Barbara, who was at the Benediction, though unseen by Joan, is talking about Lent. "I think Lent should be about doing something. Not just giving something up," she states.

"Doing what?" Beth asks. She was out running laps while Benediction was on. Saturday night rosary and Mass on Sunday is praying enough for me, she thinks. I wonder what Barbara wants to do? Hope it's not more praying.

"Well ..." Barbara hesitates. "I'm thinking of doing the Stations every day."

Joan recalls some of the Stations of the Cross—Jesus gets crowned with thorns, he falls down carrying his heavy cross ... all on the way to getting crucified. She comments, "The Stations of the Cross are so sad."

"Yes," Barbara agrees, "that's true. But it all leads up to Easter Sunday."

"And Easter vacation," Beth adds. "Speaking of Easter, I think I'll give up candy. I don't like it much, anyway. What about you, Joan?"

"Oh, I don't know. I like candy," Joan answers. "And the Stations are just so ... so depressing. Maybe I could give up candy ..." She sees Barbara looking pensive and adds, "... and do the Stations, twice a week."

Beth feigns awe. "What a girl," she exclaims, and they all laugh.

I've got plenty to atone for, Joan thinks. She looks at her watch. "I've got a Progress Meeting with Sister Cecelia." She leaves the room and heads for the dayroom.

Joan enters the dayroom and sees Sister Cecelia sitting by the window, reading a book. "Sister," Joan says softly.

Sister Cecelia closes her book, stands and greets Joan. "Come in, dear. The water's boiling." She hands Joan the book. "I thought you might enjoy reading this."

Joan takes the book. "Thank you, Sister." She looks at it. "Joan of Arc," she reads. "Kind of thin for a biography, isn't it?"

Sister Cecelia, half-laughs. "Joan had a brief but glorious life. The English burned her at a stake when she was nineteen or twenty."

A fleeting look of sadness sweeps across Joan's face. Sister Cecelia sees it and comments, "Tough way to get into Heaven, isn't it?" They laugh together.

Joan watches Sister Cecelia pour water into two small teacups and pop tea bags into them. She likes Sister Cecelia and sees many of her mother's qualities in the nun. She's fair, undemanding and likes me as I am, Joan thinks. She has a sense of humor and even calls me "dear" like Mom.

Sister Cecelia offers a cup to Joan. They both put honey and lemon in the tea. Joan stirs her tea and sips it. "Mmmmm. This is good," she states and her first Progress Meeting begins.

Sister Cecelia pulls a sheet out of a brown envelope and hands it to Joan. "No one sees this report other than Sister Maria Delores and your parents, Joan."

Joan starts reading and Sister Cecelia continues talking. "This report is purely from my point of view. My observations of you as a student and a Catholic young lady." She takes a smell of her tea and then a big sip as Joan scans the three-paragraph report.

Joan is smiling. "Strong sense of self-worth," she reads. "Sensitive, but not soft. Better than average student, doing the best work she's capable of doing." In the last paragraph she sees, "Considerate of others, friendly and outgoing."

"Anything you want to discuss or change?" Sister Cecelia takes another big swallow of her tea.

"Oh no, Sister." Joan is elated. "Such a glowing report. Thank you."

"Thank yourself, Joan. You wrote that report with your actions and your good nature. I just document what I see and sign it. Sister Maria Dolores will mail this to your folks on Monday." They sip their tea.

"We still have fifteen minutes," Sister Cecelia remarks. "Do you have any questions or problems?" She finishes her tea.

"Not a problem, really, but I sometimes wonder about ..." She stops. She realizes that she doesn't want to tell Sister Cecelia how afraid of the devil and hell she's becoming and says instead, "Barbara said that she told you that she wants to join the order." Joan finishes her tea.

"That's true," Sister Cecelia agrees. "Let's have another. These cups are pretty but small." She pours water over the old tea bags. "There's plenty of life left in these." They add honey and squeeze more juice out of the lemon slices.

"Sister," Joan asks, "would it be rude to ask how you decided to become a nun? Did you hear a voice?"

"No, to both," she replies. "No, it's not rude to ask and, no, I didn't hear a voice." She smiles, points to Joan's book, and states, "But that girl did. Nowadays they'd say she suffered from dementia or schizophrenia." She does a little half-laugh and sips her tea.

"What do you think, Sister? Did Joan hear God or was she crazy?"

Sister Cecelia needs time to think. She sips her tea again. "I'm giving up tea for Lent and it seems I just can't get enough of it. I'm probably storing up caffeine for Lent, like a bear stores fat for the winter." Joan laughs.

Sister Cecelia continues, "But about your question, "Did Joan hear God, or was she crazy? Who knows? Who's to judge?" She smiles. "Why don't you tell me which you think after you read the book?"

Joan sips her tea and wonders. I've read about people hearing voices, she thinks. As far as I'm concerned people who hear voices are crazy.

Sister Cecelia interrupts Joan's thought. "Would you do that for me, Joan? Not a book report, or an assignment. Just what you think. I've been teaching for ten years and I learn more every year." Sister Cecelia finishes her tea, puts the cup on the tray and proclaims, "That's it for today on tea for me."

"What about your own vocation, Sister?"

"My own vocation," she thinks for a moment and continues, "was as natural as breathing. I just drifted into it. I was working as a model ... doing well." She smiles and pauses. "It was a couple of years before the war. Anyway, it's a long story."

"Oh, please, Sister." Joan finishes her tea and puts her cup on the tray.

"Well, the whole world was ready to explode. My brother was in the army. Japan was rolling through China. Hitler was flexing his muscles and I, with a good college education behind me, was busy running all around town, getting my picture taken in pretty hats. I was having fun, but I wanted to do something. I thought about being a nurse, but I could never handle all that blood and gore. I'm far too squeamish."

"I don't think I'd be a good nurse either, Sister, but I think I'd be a good ambulance driver."

"You still like driving?"

"You mean, even after my accident, Sister? Sure, I drove Mom's car a couple of times on our way here. I had a wreck and now it's over, but please continue, Sister. You couldn't be a nurse."

"No, but I'd see newsreels at the movies of nuns in China helping children and teaching them to sing hymns. I talked to my mother about it. We lived together. Went to Mass and Communion every week to pray for my dad. He died young, heart attack."

"Oh, I'm sorry, Sister."

"That's all right, Joan. I was only two when he died. I have no memory of him. But I still pray for him. He gave me life. Anyway, one night my mother and I were sitting at the kitchen table having tea and I told her that since the first vows were temporary, I was going to give the religious life a try."

"Lucky for Our Lady of the Lakes," Joan interjects, and they both laugh.

"Naturally, my mother was delighted," Sister Cecelia continues, "and I'm happy. I never got to China but I love teaching and I feel close to Our Savior." She pauses, then continues, "All I can tell you about having a vocation is this, Joan. People choose the religious life for many reasons. Most don't hear voices. I'd say the only voice to pay attention to is your own voice with which you speak to yourself. Does that make sense?"

"Oh yes, Sister. My inner voice. I have that." Joan smiles. "Mine asks more questions than it gives answers," Joan continues. "Barbara says you can choose any saint's name you want when you take your vows?"

"That's true."

"How did you decide on Saint Cecelia?"

"Right off the religious calendar on our kitchen wall." Sister Cecelia smiles. "We had one of those calendars that shows all the feast days and the fast days. I looked up my dad's birthday, November twenty-second, and there was Saint Cecelia."

"I'm afraid I don't know anything about her, Sister."

"Neither did I at the time. So I made it a point to read about her. She had a tragic life. She grew up as a Christian, in a well-to-do family, back when Rome was Pagan. Even though Cecelia had taken a vow of virginity, her father made her marry a young Roman who was a Pagan."

"Even back then, the fathers tried to run the daughters' lives," Joan remarks. "What a sad story."

"That's only the beginning, Joan. The young Pagan, Valerian, turned out to be a very nice young man. Cecilia told him about her vow and he became a Christian. His brother Tiburtius also converted. Then they made a big mistake. They buried some Christian martyrs. They were beheaded for this."

"So Cecelia became a widow."

"Only for a short time. Cecelia had Valerian and Tiburtius buried at her villa. Then she, herself, was beheaded."

"That's so sad, Sister," Joan shakes her head.

"It was sad, Joan. Many early Christians died for their faith. Things are a lot easier, nowadays."

"I guess so, Sister."

Sister Cecelia rises and picks up her tea tray.

"Sister," Joan asks, "is Mary Magdalene a saint?" Joan stands up and the two of them head for the door.

"A saint of the first order, a repentant sinner. Jesus loves sinners best of all. All a sinner has to do is ask to be forgiven."

Sister Cecelia checks her watch. "Almost time for dinner," she states. "You coming to rosary tonight?"

"Yes, Sister. I'll be there."

"I enjoyed our tea, Joan."

"Me too, Sister. Thanks for the book." Joan watches as Sister Cecelia seems to float down the hall.

Sister Cecelia heads for her room. "Is Mary Magdalene a saint?" I hope Joan's as happy as she seems. I wish I were a child psychologist.

Joan joins Beth and Barbara back at her room.

"How'd it go," Beth asks.

"Pretty nice. I got a good report. We had tea. Sister told me how Saint Cecelia was a martyr."

"She was beheaded," Barbara states.

"You know what," Beth comments, "I was named after Mary, Queen of Scots, and she was beheaded." Beth puts on a serious, thoughtful face. "You know what all this talk about beheading makes me think about, Barbara?" Without waiting for an answer, Beth jumps up out of her chair and shouts, "It makes me think we ought to BE HEADING for the refectory." Joan and Barbara groan, all three laugh and leave the room.

Easter Sunday, Jill is surprised to see Joan receive Communion. Returning to her pew, Joan reflects, I'm starting a brand new life, completely forgiven for all my sins with Eddie.

Slipping into her spot next to Jill, Joan kneels. If I died right now I'd go to heaven, she tells herself. She smiles, thinking, I'd get there after a few centuries in purgatory atoning. At least I didn't dream about the Devil last night.

During Easter vacation, Joan talks with Sandy a few times on the phone, but they can't get together for a visit. Laura's in Miami with her folks, so two shopping trips downtown with her mom are socially it for Joan, other than Easter dinner.

Joan tells her father that she remembers him, and Bill, with visions of Joan's rapidlyapproaching birthday and the trust fund's maturity dancing in his head, takes Jill and Joan to a fancy French restaurant. During dessert when Bill loudly declares, "Nothing's too good for my girls," Jill thinks, Jesus Christ!? What's Bill trying to do? Make me gag? She smiles sweetly, tells the hovering waiter, "Bring us a bottle of your very best champagne," and watches Bill wince.

On the way back to O.L.L., Jill's attempts to bring the conversation around to Eddie are met with transparent parries. One of them, "Mom, did you know that Joan of Arc was burned at the stake when she was just about my age?" prompts Jill to ask, "Is everything okay at school? You want me to get you out of there?"

"Oh no, Mom. I love it at O.L.L. It's so peaceful there."

Joan's enthusiastic answer gives Jill some happiness but she can't shake a vague feeling that something has changed in her daughter. Thinking about the situation on her way back to St. Clair Shores gives her no clear answer.

Back at Our Lady of the Lakes, Joan starts making visits to the chapel. Kneeling before the statue of the Blessed Virgin, she thinks, I feel so peaceful here ... and so *safe* from the Devil.

April moves along, taking its showers with it and leaving flowers blooming in its wake, just the way a good April should.

May first is warm and sunny, a perfect day for the May Day services honoring Our Lady of the Lakes. After the outdoor services, Joan goes to the chapel, kneels before the statue and prays, "Oh blessed Mother of Jesus, if I'm to have a vocation and serve your Beloved Son, please give me a sign."

That night while she's writing her "End of April" letter to Eddie, she recalls part of one of Father Quinn's sermons. "If we are to save our immortal souls, if we want to avoid sinning, we must avoid the temptations that lead us into sin. We must avoid the occasions of sin." She signs her letter, simply, "Love, Joan."

One warm afternoon, Joan is sitting under a tree reading when the nuns begin heading for the chapel in groups of two or three for Vespers. On a nearby branch, a meadowlark is singing. The feeling of tranquility almost swallows her. She writes to Eddie that night. After finishing her letter, she goes to bed and dreams that she's Joan of Arc. She kills the devil in a sword fight while a group of nuns cheer her on. She recalls the dream when she first awakens and decides, the devil would never show up here at Our Lady of the Lakes.

At O.L.L., May is designated "Mary's Month." Many devotions honoring The Blessed Virgin, and Our Lady of the Lakes in particular, are held. Every afternoon the rosary is recited in the quad, or in the chapel if it's raining. Mother

Superior Maria Delores leads the rosaries and she always offers them up for the conversion of godless Russia.

On the last Saturday of the month, May devotions end with the rosary being said in the chapel, following Benediction. On Monday, while walking in the woods, Joan finds a small, sunny, grassy clearing. The new grass sprouts feel soothing to her knees, as she kneels and prays to The Blessed Virgin, asking for a sign, if she is to have a vocation. She does this daily, and on June tenth, a day of unsettled weather with a murky, overcast sky, the sun breaks through a tiny hole in the clouds and shines a narrow sunbeam directly on her. In the boiling clouds next to the hole, for just an instant, Joan sees The Blessed Virgin, standing, holding a rosary. The clouds quickly shift and Joan's vision is gone. I'd better tell Sister Cecelia about this, Joan decides as she heads back to the dorm.

Joan doesn't get a chance to talk to Sister Cecelia until after dinner. On their way back to the dorm, Joan breaks away from Barbara and Beth, catches up to Sister Cecelia and asks her to take a walk with her. Sister Cecelia agrees.

As they head for Joan's clearing, she tells Sister Cecelia about her experience. At the clearing things are different. The morning clouds that participated in Joan's vision are far away and the sun is now behind her, hanging low in the western sky.

"The lighting is different now, Sister," Joan points to the sky. "Just above those two maples, the big ones. It was The Blessed Virgin ... and she was even holding a rosary, Sister. And the sunbeam shined right on me. Do you think I'm crazy?"

Sister Cecelia laughs. "Oh no, Joan. You're not crazy. Not at all."

"Do you think I really saw The Blessed Virgin?"

"Perhaps ..." Sister Cecelia pauses. "Perhaps not. It seems to me there's some kind of quirk or bend in the human mind that tries to make order out of chaos. We spill ink on a desk blotter and then think, 'Gee that looks like Florida' or we see faces in trees, clouds or knotty pine boards. As a child I had a board in my bedroom wall and the knots and wood grain looked like a tiger's face."

Joan is looking thoughtful. Sister Cecelia continues, "Haven't you ever seen anything in the clouds like cowboys herding cattle? Castles?"

"Oh yes," Joan answers, "lots of times. One time I saw a fox and then he became a bear as the clouds moved around. Another time I saw a big bearded face, like Santa Claus." She stops, thinks, and says, "You think maybe ... it was just my imagination." Joan sounds disappointed.

"Maybe. Sometimes we see what we want to see. Almost like wishful thinking." She smiles. "Anyway, Joan, you didn't hear any voices."

"No. Just Father Quinn saying we must avoid the occasions of sin." She smiles. "You know, Sister, I feel very peaceful in the chapel ... and out here."

"It's a peaceful place." Sister Cecelia exhales slowly. "I love it here."

"Barbara says I could stay here during the summer and take temporary vows in September."

"If you really have a vocation, Joan."

"Well, I think I might have a vocation, Sister. I'd like to stay for the summer and find out."

"Have you spoken with your mother about this?"

"Not yet, Sister."

"She may have made some other plans for the summer."

"Mom hasn't mentioned anything."

"You two seem very close."

"We are, Sister, but ..." Joan hesitates, thinks of hell, sees Satan's face and remarks, "When I tell Mom how peaceful and safe I feel here, she'll understand." Sister Cecelia notices a quick frown flit across Joan's face. I'm safe from the Devil, here, Joan tells herself. I feel like I dreamed about him again last night. Wish I could remember.

Sister Cecelia's voice interrupts Joan's thought. "What was that, Sister?" she asks.

"Edward," the nun repeats. "How will Edward feel?"

"Are you trying to talk me out of this, Sister?" Joan smiles big, trying to keep things light.

"No," Sister Cecelia replies, "but these are things you must think about. Have you considered Edward's feelings?"

"I have, Sister. Eddie should understand. He's a Catholic. Used to be an altar boy."

"An altar boy." Sister Cecelia recalls her parochial school days. The worst boys in school, them and the choir boys, she remembers. I think Father Kelly assigned the worst to altar and choir duty so he could keep an eye on them.

"Hmmm, hmmm." She asks, "You're going to write Edward about your plan?"

"Yes, I'm going to write him after I tell my mom, next week. So what do you think about my decision, Sister?"

"I think it would be all right for you to spend the summer," she answers, "if it's okay with your mother."

"Oh, thank you, Sister." Joan is smiling. She's tempted to hug Sister Cecelia, but controls herself. You can't just hug a nun, she thinks.

"One other thing, Joan. What about your father? What will he think?"

"Oh him? What he thinks doesn't matter." Joan smiles knowingly. "I'm going to sign a piece of paper for him next week and after that he won't care if I fly to the moon." She half-laughs. "But what I meant was, what do you think of my decision to become a nun?"

"First spend the summer here in prayer, as you plan. Then see how you feel in September, when it's time to take your temporary vows."

"I'll feel the same, Sister. I'm sure I will."

"That's good, but remember, your first vows are temporary. Jesus likes to be sure that you're doing what you really want." She smiles. "Should we head back for the dorm?"

The two of them walk back to the dorm in silence, side by side. Joan pictures herself in a habit, walking with Sister Cecelia. This is the place for me, she resolves. The Devil is helpless against all this prayer. Eddie crosses through her thoughts. I'd better write Eddie, tell him about my new life and cut things off clean. A clean break is best. Just like Mary Magdalene, I've closed the door on sin. Eddie's going to become a part of my past life, like the men who sinned with Mary Magdalene became part of her past. Jesus is my new life.

Friday, June nineteenth is graduation day, final report card day for the undergraduates and going home for the summer day for all. The Whitmans arrive at noon. The parking lot is nearly full. Bill finds a spot in a far corner, but he doesn't bitch about it. Bill is happy. Bill is smiling. Bill has the trust deed papers in his jacket pocket. Joan will be nineteen tomorrow, she'll sign the papers and we'll head home, he's planning. Sending Joan to this place was the best idea I ever came up with.

Jill doesn't mind walking through the dirt parking lot; she's thinking about having Joan back home for the summer. Then Eddie will be back and we can see what kind of wedding they'd like to have, she reflects. Whatever they want, a big church wedding or a little ceremony with a Justice of the Peace like they were going to do … just so I'm there.

Undergraduates and parents who choose can stay for the graduation ceremony. Joan saved good seats on the shady side and Jill is enjoying herself until the Mother Superior names six girls who will be taking their temporary vows and Joan whispers to her, "Isn't that wonderful, Mom?"

Jill gets a fluttery feeling in her stomach and manages a, "Yes, dear," then spends the remainder of the ceremony stringing thoughts together, reviewing Easter vacation.

Joan did seem a bit quiet, she thinks, a little distant … reading herself to sleep instead of listening to her radio. A sudden, electrifying thought bursts. It unnerves her. Jesus Christ! Jill almost says the words aloud. No wonder Joan showed no interest in those cute outfits we looked at. She wants to become a nun.

Jill sighs, murmurs, "Oh God, let me be wrong," under her breath and steals a glance at Bill. He's wearing a vacant, happy smile, thinking about tomorrow. Jill looks away.

Most of the students and their parents head home right after the ceremony. Those who stay enjoy an excellent outdoor buffet. Bill doesn't like driving at night, so he and Jill are booked into a rustic motel a few miles from the college.

Feeling great about what Saturday morning holds in store, Bill heaps food onto his plate. Joan takes a little of every-thing. Jill takes a small portion of tossed green salad and a piece of bread. She only picks at it. She's thinking of when she was briefly introduced to Barbara's mother. "Isn't it nice that our daughters have so much in common?" Barbara's mother had said in a confidential tone.

After eating, on their walk to the main gate, Jill asks, "Isn't Barbara the girl you said was going to become a nun?"

"That's right, Mom. Why?"

"Just something her mother said. Nothing serious. Oh and don't forget, please be packed and ready to go by eight, dear. Jill puts her arm around Joan's waist, pulls her close and states, "You know how Dad hates to drive at night."

"I heard that," Bill jokes from two steps behind where he's following along, happy as a bank robber finding an open vault. They all laugh and hug and kiss.

"See you in the morning," Jill shouts from the open car window as they drive off the lot.

On the drive back to the motel, Jill remarks, "I've got a feeling Joan is holding back some kind of bad news."

Bill laughs. "Joan's bad news is in the deep freeze, up in Alaska."

Oh God, I wish I had someone sensible to talk to about this, she thinks. Slim comes to mind. She gets mad at herself for having only Bill. Old, cold, insensitive Bill, she says to herself.

She raises her voice, "Listen, Bill! I'm not kidding. I think Joan wants to stay there and become a nun."

Bill laughs again, louder. "Joan, a nun. And I'm going to be the Pope," he quips. "That'll be the day."

"Let's just not talk about it," Jill orders and they drive back to the motel in silence.

That night just before he falls asleep, Bill declares, "Joan, a nun. That's a hot one." He falls immediately asleep and smiles all night, dreaming of signed trust deed papers in his pocket.

Jill has a horrible night. She's jarred awake at 2 AM by a bad dream. In her dream, she's watching Joan being tied to a stake with a mound of kindling at her feet. Jill sees herself in current attire, trapped in a crowd of Puritans. The crowd is watching the main Puritan set the firewood ablaze.

The main Puritan turns around after lighting the fire and it's Bill. He shouts to the crowd, "That's a hot one!"

"You dirty son of a bitch," Jill screams. She tries to break away from the herd and succeeds after a scuffle, while all the time she sees the flames grow higher. She loses one of her high heels in the action, picks it up and hobbles toward Bill. She starts hitting him in the face with her spike heel, shouting, "That's my daughter. You son of a bitch."

She sits straight up in bed. She's sweaty. Bill stirs. "Everything okay?" he mumbles.

"Yeah. Everything's just fine," Jill answers, and thinks, sarcasm is a waste of time with Bill.

Bill falls right back to sleep. Jill turns, tosses and tries to sleep. At 4:30 she finally drifts off. She awakens at 7 AM in an unrested, agitated state. She shakes Bill awake, saying, "Let's get out there and take Joan home."

Under her prodding, Bill showers, shaves, dresses and skips breakfast. They arrive at Our Lady of the Lakes at 7:55. Only a handful of cars are in the lot and the school's front gate is open. Joan is standing inside the gate talking with a nun.

"Hi, Mom, hi, Dad." Joan looks serious. "Mom, you remember Sister Cecelia."

"Of course. Good to see you again, Sister." Jill shakes Sister Cecelia's hand. "This is my husband, Bill."

"It's a pleasure to meet you, ma'am." Bill shakes the nun's hand. He pats his jacket pocket, says, "Happy birthday, Joan," and gives her a peck on the cheek.

Jill gives Joan a hug and a kiss. "Happy birthday, dear. I thought we could stop off in Cleveland on the way home and get you a nice summer outfit for a present."

Sister Cecelia excuses herself and Jill continues, "Let's go get your bags, dear."

Jill gets an ominous feeling when Joan answers, "Why don't we take a little walk first? I'd like to show you something." She walks her parents toward the woods. Arriving at her clearing, she turns to Jill. Mom, I've done a whole lot of thinking and praying right here and in the chapel. I feel that I have a vocation.

Jill's knees go weak. She swallows hard and says nothing.

Well, I'll be Goddamned, Bill says to himself. Then he realizes, this is a bad development. I'll have to wait for just the right time. He pats his pocket and comments, "This is quite a surprise. I never thought of you as nun material."

"What do you mean by that?" Jill doesn't try to take the edge off her tone.

"I mean, Joan's always seemed like such an ..." he hesitates. I'd better choose the correct word, he thinks, or I'm dead in the water. He blurts out, "An individualist." Smiling, he says to Jill, "I'm trying to help."

Joan ignores her father. "I'd like to stay here at the school for the summer. And in September, I can take my temporary vows and start my novitiate."

Bill looks at Joan blankly.

Jill's whole body is light. She feels as if she's floating away but she musters up a small smile. "That's a very big decision, dear," she offers, taking Joan's elbow and guiding her away from Bill. She asks softly, "Have you told Eddie?"

"I'm going to write him on Monday, Mom. He'll understand."

Jill feels crushed. Her best friend is vanishing from her life. She feels as if she's watching the scene through a telescope, helpless to intervene. "I wouldn't be too sure of that," she hears herself say.

"He'll have to understand." Joan is adamant. "It's about the devil and hell. My soul and eternity."

The three of them walk back to Joan's room in silence. Entering the room, Jill sees Joan's packed bags and her knees go weak. She sits in the chair at the roll top desk and holds her head in her cupped hands, elbows on the desk. She's feeling hopeless.

Bill is laying out his papers on the other table, droning, "There's plenty of discipline required in a religious order. Many rules and regulations ..."

Jill tunes him out. Her dazed gaze stops on an envelope. She sees Joan's name on it and in the corner A3/c Edward Flynn. I've got to talk with someone, she says to herself as she opens her purse. She gets her pen out and copies down Eddie's address in her address book. Neither Bill or Joan see a thing. She clicks her purse closed, thinking, Eddie, you're my only hope."

Joan signs the papers and Bill's heart sails away to the land of perfect martinis and no unions. He hardly feels the weight of the two suitcases on their way to the car. Joan is carrying the third suitcase and Jill is feeling sorry for herself. I feel so empty. She sighs. I don't even have a bag to carry.

"I had to keep my underwear, raincoat and one outfit, in case I get sent home for illness or something," Joan tells Jill.

If only you were still pregnant, Jill wishes. "Let's hope you don't get sick," she replies.

At the car, Joan pecks her dad on the cheek, hugs and kisses Jill, and watches her folks get into the car. This is the beginning of a new chapter in my life, she's thinking, feeling strong. She waves goodbye.

Bill looks at her, waves back and has to fight off the urge to break into song. "I've got close to two million good old American dollars in my pocket," he gloats. "Where do you want to stop for lunch, honey?"

"I'm not hungry. Just drive and let me think." The radio is playing, "Powder Your Face With Sunshine". "And turn off that goddamned radio!" Jill is too bewildered to cry. She lights up one of her long cigarettes, takes a deep drag and blows a plume of smoke toward the windshield.

At Our Lady of the Lakes, Joan brings her few belongings over to the convent building, where Barbara, so happy with Joan's choice of the religious life, already has a room set up for them. Barbara brought the blue curtains from their old room, as well as her watercolor of The Blessed Virgin. It's a sunny room on the second floor and it looks out onto the meditation garden. "It looks beautiful, Barbara," she praises, and thinks, safe and secure from Satan.

On Monday, only Joan, Barbara and eight other girls comprise the student body. The quiet atmosphere gives Joan such a feeling of peace that it takes her all afternoon to write Eddie's letter.

She sits at her desk, calm and resolute in her decision. She decides it's the only way to save her soul, and writes. "Dear Eddie."

Back in Saint Clair Shores, earlier in the day, right after Bill left for work, Jill, sitting at her kitchen table watching her cigarette smoke work its way toward the open window, had picked up her pen. Listening to Dinah Washington sing, "I Only Know", Jill decided to quit feeling sorry for herself and take action. "Dear Eddie," she wrote.

CHAPTER 35

▼

June starts out with a bang for Eddie. He wins $160 in the payday crap game in the Airman's Club. Walking back to the barracks, many thoughts buzz in his brain. Man, I love it when I'm smart enough to quit a winner, instead of blowin' all my bread back tryin' to bust the game. What great timin'. Joan's birthday's comin' up. Her letters have been gettin' different. I'll get her somethin' real sharp. T.J. rotates next week. Maybe he'll sell me some of his tunes. Better pick up a half a case of beer at the PX and find out.

At the PX, Eddie buys a light blue satin warm-up jacket for Joan. A silver and white map of Alaska is embroidered on its back. The message, "America's Last Frontier" arches above the map in small gold letters. Beer and a large bag of potato chips complete his shopping.

Continuing his walk to the barracks, he recalls his first visit with T.J. It was following evening chow, which T.J. had not attended, the day after Eddie and Reeves had joined Able crew. He sees himself with an open can of beer in each hand, knocking on T.J.'s door with the side of his shoe.

"Thirty seconds," T.J. shouts through the closed door. Eddie sips his beer and waits.

The door opens. T.J. is smiling. "Come on in, man. I'm just getting ready to check a show I put together. Almost three hours."

"Here you go, T.J." Eddie hands T.J. a beer. "Didn't see you at chow."

T.J. checks his watch. "Did it again. God damn." He opens the bottom drawer of his dresser and pulls out a large bag of potato chips. "No harm done." He points to the cognac bottle, two-thirds full. "I've been nipping. Want a taste?"

"A little after-dinner brandy? Thanks, T.J."

T.J. hands Eddie the bottle and gestures toward a folding chair leaning against the wall. "Take a seat. Have a nip. I'll play this show back thirty minutes at a time. We can listen and shoot the shit."

"Sounds like a good plan." Eddie takes a sip of the cognac, hands the bottle back, opens the chair and sits down.

T.J. sips his beer, puts it and the cognac bottle on his dresser, crosses the room and stands next to a large map tacked on the wall. "Before I start that tape, maybe you could help me. Yesterday you said you were from New York."

"I'm proud to admit, I'm a born New Yorker."

"Then take a look at this. Would you?"

Eddie gets up, walks across the room and looks over the layout of New York City. "Nice map. Better than a road map."

"It's a tourist map. Prez got it for me." T.J. points to the northern boundary of Central Park. "I'm heading for Harlem, when I get out. Going to be a disc jockey."

"You played some great stuff yesterday."

"Thanks. But that was just spur of the moment. Wait'll you check this tape out. You know anything about Harlem?"

Eddie puts his index finger on the map. "This is my neighborhood. There's Harlem, over there. I know a little."

"All I know is Harlem starts at a Hundred and Tenth Street," T.J. states. "I know that Lenox Avenue and Seventh Avenue are main stems, but that's it."

"Don't forget a Hundred and Twenty-Fifth Street. You got the Apollo, the Theresa Hotel, the Baby Grand."

T.J. realizes he's struck a small vein of Harlem information. "Do you know how far east and west Harlem goes?"

"Well, T.J., the furthest east I've been in Harlem is a Hundred and Sixteenth and Fifth Avenue, an after-hours joint called the Abraham Lincoln Lodge. You had to have a card to get in. The guy on the door would give you one if he thought you were cool. I'd guess Harlem ends around Park Avenue on the east. You got Spanish Harlem down here and an old Italian neighborhood out here and all around Pleasant Avenue. So Park Avenue, north to the Harlem River would be my best guess for Harlem's eastern boundary."

Eddie takes a swallow of his beer. He continues, "The west side of Harlem starts down here at a Hundred and Tenth and Morningside Park. The park ends at a Hundred and Twenty-Third and Amsterdam. Me and my friends hang out on that corner. See a Hundred and Twenty-Fifth and Amsterdam? That's where the Five Hundred Club is. That's where I first started listenin' to rhythm and blues. A Hundred and Twenty-fifth is cool. Drinkin' age is eighteen in New York but if you're sixteen and hip you can get served in the bars on a Hundred and Twenty-Fifth, startin' at The Seven-Twelve, down here by the Hudson."

"Is Amsterdam Avenue Harlem's western boundary?"

"Kind of. But there's no real boundary. It's kind of blurry. It's mostly Convent Avenue. See, just east of Amsterdam, up to a Hundred and Forty-Fifth. Right around here is Sugar Hill, Edgecombe Avenue, Hamilton Terrace, all kinds of rich colored people, boxers, singers, band leaders, entertainers. It's a pretty nice neighborhood. Goes back to the olden days. Washington and Hamilton times. Then I guess it's Amsterdam up to around a Hundred and Sixty-Eighth. Maybe up to around Highbridge, maybe a little further. I'd only be guessin' after that."

Eddie stops talking and they both take drinks of their beer. T.J. gets a pencil out of the top drawer of his dresser and starts marking Harlem's perimeter. "What about over here? Park Avenue, Madison, Lenox, Seventh and Eighth. Looks like they end up in the Harlem River?"

"Yeah. That's all colored up there." Eddie finishes his can of beer. T.J. finishes with his map, then downs the rest of his beer. Eddie gets two more beers out of the dayroom's refrigerator. They light up two of T.J.'s Luckies, each take another hit at the cognac and T.J. rolls the tape.

The unwinding tape reveals a musically knowledgeable T.J. with a snappy, relaxed line of patter. "This is Tee Jay, your midnight Dee Jay," he announces. "Listen for Lester Young on this side. This is the Prez back in nineteen thirty-seven. The tune? "A Sailboat In The Moonlight". The vocalist? The incomparable, Billie Holiday."

T.J.'s All Star, All American Revue lives up to its name, touching all the musical bases with tunes by Billie Holiday, Ernest Tubb, Roy Milton and His Solid Senders, Anita O'Day, Lester Young, Hank Williams, Duke Ellington, Frankie Laine, The Clovers, Dick Haymes, Big Joe Turner, Ruth Brown, Hank Snow, Percy Mayfield, Patti Page, Flip Phillips, Louis Armstrong, Ivory Joe Hunter, Nat Cole, Moon Mullican, Stan Kenton, Lonnie Johnson, Peggy Lee, Lefty Frizzell, The Ravens, Earl Bostic, Hank Thompson, Todd Rhodes, Camille Howard, Kay Starr, Lucky Millinder with Annisteen Allen, The Four Aces, Doris Day, Roy Byrd and His Blues Jumpers, Wynonie Harris, Billy Ward and The Dominoes, Tony Bennett, Dinah Washington, Jumpin' Joe Williams with Red Saunders and His Orchestra, as well as Maurice King and His Wolverines, with Bea Baker (later to be known as LaVern Baker) on vocals doing "I Want A Lavender Cadillac".

T.J. weaves the musical genres together smoothly, sometimes working themes into the play list. In one case, Hank Snow sings, "I'm Movin' On", right after Wynonie Harris scolds his girl-friend, singing, "Don't Roll Those Bloodshot Eyes At Me" and just before "Travellin' Man". Coming out of that set, T.J. back-announces Hank and Wynonie and their songs, tagging it with, "That was Anita O'Day with Stan Kenton's crew doing "Travellin' Man". The First Lady of Swing gave Stan Kenton his first hit record with "And Her Tears Flowed Like Wine". Anita O'Day also had a hit with Gene Krupa, "Let Me Off Uptown". And what better way to get uptown than on the A train. Duke Ellington jumps into "Take The A Train" within a breath of T.J.'s voice fading. Another set in the All Star, All American Revue is launched.

With most of the crew watching "The Thing" at the Information and Education Center or drinking at the Airman's Club, Eddie and T.J. have three uninterrupted hours to exchange musical and cultural knowledge, some of it trivial, some practical and some philosophical.

T.J. has a theory that music can help bring people together. He keeps a composition notebook labeled "Race Relations." Some of the observations in his journal are personal. "I know I have colored and white blood in my veins. I refuse to hate either half of myself. I'm sepia. And I'm a handsome motherfucker." He had written that in his notebook the day that he had an eight by ten portrait taken down in Biloxi. Other notations are general. "Colored and white musicians get along. Maybe music is a bridge between the races."

T.J. considers his All Star, All American Revue a step in the right direction toward harmony. Eddie's reaction to what folks back home called "Race Music," prompts T.J. to comment, after Frankie Laine's soulful "Black And Blue", I thought the man was colored when I first heard him.

"Me Too. He's in the juke down at the Five Hundred Club, right along with Lonnie Johnson, The Ravens and Ivory Joe."

Eddie's enthusiastic comment fortifies T.J.'s theory.

By the time that Prez, Scarpa, Hollis and Beeman return from the movie and knock on T.J.'s door requesting pool-shooting music, Eddie has received a good deal of musical enlightenment and T.J. has learned Harlem's boundaries and picked up some ammo for his journal; a fair exchange.

Eddie gets out of the way, joining the guys in the dayroom while T.J. sets up the music. Before joining the others, T.J. writes in his notebook, "FACT: Hank Williams learned to play guitar from an old, colored musician, Rufus 'Tee-Tot' Payne." Just below that item, he enters, "I'm not the only one who thought Frankie Laine was colored the first time I heard him."

During the eight months they served together on Able crew T.J. and Eddie had more than one conversation that provided grist for T.J.'s journal. One time, up at the A.F.R.S. studio, helping T.J. put a new revue on tape, Eddie handed T.J. "Love Will Make You A Slave" and the issue of slavery arose when T.J. remarked, "I'm sure glad slavery's over."

"Slavery ain't over, T.J. My chick's old man thinks he's a big shit executive. He don't know it but he's just a slave to General Motors."

"A damn well paid slave, I'll bet," T.J. quipped. They both laughed and the conversation veered toward the value of slaves. This resulted in an anecdote for the notebook, when Eddie declared, "You know, T.J., I hate to sound like a fuckin' Commie, especially when we're havin' a war with the motherfuckers. But it's pure fact, you got the very, very fuckin' rich and you got the rest of us, just scramblin' our asses off like slaves. Slaves to big companies.

"I'm not sure if what I'm gonna tell you is true. My Uncle Frank told it to me, so it could be bullshit. But down on the Mississippi during slavery times, sometimes a big bale of cotton would get away and go tumblin' down the levee into the river. This would cost the cotton company a lot of money, so they'd put a couple of guys at the bottom of the levee to stop these runaways from goin' in the drink."

"Slaves, huh?"

"Nope. The death rate on these bale-catchin' motherfuckers was way too high to use slaves. Slaves were worth a lot of bread. So the company used Irish guys. It made good business sense. Losin' one or two Irishmen was a hell of a lot cheaper than losin' a good, expensive slave. Big Business. Fuck them."

"Bet Old Tom wouldn't have put my great-great-great grandmomma down at the bottom of a levee," T.J. remarks, killing the frown that thinking about Joan's father and General Motors had put on Eddie's face.

That night T.J. was able to enter the short tale in his notebook almost verbatim.

Another time, pulling KP, T.J. and Eddie were peeling potatoes when a dispute broke out between one of the cooks and one of the KP's. The words, "Fuck you, nigger," and "Fuck me? You nigger motherfucker. Fuck your momma and everybody else on the corner where she works," were exchanged, before the mess sergeant calmed things down.

"That shit could have got ugly," Eddie commented.

"It was ugly. I hate that word. You ever use the word nigger, Eddie?"

"Not as much as you guys." Eddie got a small smile, not the laugh he was expecting. He added, "I quit usin' 'nigger' in high school when I started knowin' colored guys better. It made my mother happy when I started sayin' 'colored peo-ple.' She considered herself Lace Curtain Irish. Anyone who used 'nigger' or other racial slurs was Shanty Irish in her book. 'Slurs,' that's what she called words like spic, mick, guinea, kike … she was even against 'hillbilly' or 'queer.'"

"Your mother sounds like a good person."

"She is. She's got a good heart. She was so happy when we had to study race relations in eighth grade after the Harlem riot in the summer. Right now we bet-ter finish up these spuds. Wilcox is lookin' our way."

Back in the barracks after KP, with the rest of the crew on radar duty until midnight, T.J. and Eddie have the dayroom to themselves. Playing Eightball for fifty cents a game, Eddie's up a buck fifty. He banks the eight ball in the side pocket and T.J. announces, "I owe you a deuce."

They lay their cues on the table, get fresh cans of beer and T.J. continues, "In sixty days, I'm home for thirty days leave. Three months later, I'm discharged and off to Harlem."

"Here's to Harlem, T.J." Eddie clinks his beer can against T.J.'s and takes a drink. "You better get there before they tear the motherfucker down. The do-gooders are tearin' down neighborhoods all over the city, buildin' housin' projects." Eddie takes a sip of his beer.

"What's the matter with tearing down slums?"

"They're not slums, T.J. These fuckin' Civic Sams think any building without an elevator is a slum. They've never been in the apartments of any of the build-ings they're wrecking. You know what's funny, T.J.?"

"What's that?"

"What's funny is they say it's to prevent crime, so they tear down a bunch of five and six-story buildings with thirty or forty apartments per building full of families and you replace them with twenty-story housing projects, each building with hundreds of families who have to prove that they're scufflin' just to get by. Projects ain't gonna do nothin' but fuck things up worse than they are. Anyway, I'm sorry to get all carried away, but they're tearin' down my neighborhood and I take that personal."

"I understand, man. I'm sorry. Can I ask you about that riot in Harlem you talked about in the mess hall? When was that?"

"Back in nineteen forty-three. Why?"

T.J. decides to tell Eddie about his Race Relations notebook. "Back in a sec-ond." He returns with his map and his journal. He spreads the map on the pool table and explains his idea about music and racial harmony, flipping through the pages, pointing out some of the entries. He leaves his notebook open to a fresh page and asks, "Could you tell me anything about the Harlem riot?"

"Not really. We were out at my aunt's place in Jersey for a week. We missed the riot."

"Oh, too bad." T.J. sips his beer.

"Yeah." Eddie brightens. "How about a secondhand story. Guaranteed to be true?"

"Sure."

"One of my buddies told me this when we got back from the lake. Jerry's old man has a grocery store." Eddie puts his finger on the map. "See Manhattan Avenue and a Hundred and Seventeenth?"

"In Harlem."

"Yep. That's where the Shamrock Grocery is. Left over from when that area was Irish, I guess. Anyway, the riot broke out and everybody was goin' apeshit up on a Hundred Twenty-Fifth, bustin' in windows in the big furniture and clothing stores, cartin' off couches, big radios, suits and dresses, settin' fire to shit. I'll tell you, T.J., I'd have liked to have been there." T.J. laughs.

"Anyway, while all this shit was goin' on, Mister Casey kept his grocery store open. All his regular customers, colored families, stood guard outside the Shamrock, sayin' shit like, 'No one's going to bother the Shamrock. This is our store, Mister Casey is a gentleman.' Pretty good story?"

"Just what I need. Let me make a couple of notes."

"Be sure and include Mister Casey used to give people credit 'til payday and he didn't fuck people on prices like the big stores up on a Hundred and Twenty-Fifth. I figure people don't forget."

"This is great stuff, Eddie." They both sip their beer.

"Did any of the riot spill over into your neighborhood?"

"Not a chance." Eddie laughs. "'Too many Irish.' That's what Bones, the bartender at the Five Hundred Club used to say."

"Bones? What was he? A crap-shooter?"

"I'm sure he shot crap. Everyone in our neighborhood shot crap, but he got his name because he's the tallest, skinniest guy in the world. He's the guy who took me, Joey and Dave to the Abraham Lincoln Lodge. Introduced us as three of The Ink Spots. He was a funny guy. You'd like him. Maybe you could use some of his stuff."

"Maybe."

"Well, Bones is about forty, remembers the thirties, remembers the Irish Dukes and other Irish 'social clubs,' as he calls them. And he once told me that lookin' for trouble in an Irish neighborhood is like lookin' for sand at the beach. There's plenty of it and you can have as much as you want."

"I'm writing that one down."

"I told you Bones was funny. Used to call bricks 'Irish Confetti.'" Eddie sips his beer while T.J. scribbles.

"Bones said throwin' rocks at Irish guys is like gettin' into a shittin' contest with King Kong after the King just ate a fig tree. Claims he was nineteen before he found out that 'white motherfucker' wasn't all one word. His last name is O'Grady. When he intros himself to someone he says, 'I'm not a Negro, I'm Smoked Irish.'"

That had been a fecund day for T.J.'s notebook.

Eddie drops Joan's jacket off at his room and heads for T.J.'s with his beer and potato chips.

While Eddie had been walking from the Airman's Club to the PX and from there to Able crew's barracks, T.J. had been making a cold-hearted appraisal of his possessions.

Listening to one of his tapes, nipping at his brand new, payday bottle of cognac, he's talking to himself. "I've got too much stuff. If I ship all of this shit home, I won't have nothing left to spend playing with the ladies." Looking at his record collection, now numbering over fifty, mostly fragile 78's, his twenty-four large spools of practice radio shows, the bulky tape recorder, the turntable and the wooden, two-foot speaker, he shakes his head. "The speaker will have to stay."

Eddie's knock interrupts T.J.'s calculating. He opens the door.

"Just call me Lucky." Eddie tosses the bag of chips to T.J. "Just in case you missed chow, like me."

"I was there. You missed steak."

"Fuck a steak. I can buy a cow. I won a hundred sixty bucks. I'm a crap-shoo-tin' motherfucker from Crap City."

"You are one lucky motherfucker." T.J. hands Eddie the bottle of cognac and takes the half case of beer. Eddie takes a drink, swishes it around his mouth and swallows. "Just cleansin' the old palate."

T.J. opens two cans of beer and hands one to Eddie. "Part of luck," Eddie continues, "is knowin' when to quit." He puts the cognac bottle on T.J.'s dresser and sips his beer. "I don't always win, T.J. One time back in Oscoda I had the worst crap-shootin' day of my whole goddamned crap-shootin' career. It was pay-day. I took my eighty bucks to the crap game behind the motor pool and blew it on three rolls of the dice. I shot twenty and crapped out, ace deuce. Shot another twenty and hit fuckin' snake eyes. Shot forty and threw boxcars. I couldn't fuckin' believe it. I'm a pretty lucky shooter and I didn't even get a point."

"Man, a month's pay. That's an unlucky day."

"I sure thought so. I borrowed twenty bucks and went to town to do some drinkin' and my luck changed like a shot."

"You won your bread back?"

"A whole lot better than that, T.J. Me and my buddy met a couple of European chicks right out of nursin' school down in Flint. They had a big bottle of Bennies and they were as horny as fuckin' minks."

"Lady Luck is on the mend."

"In a heavy-duty manner. The one I got, a big Swede, grabbed a'hold of my dick the minute she got in the back seat with me and never let go 'til we dropped them off at the airport down in Detroit two days later. When my cock wasn't in her hand, it was in her mouth or her box."

"Man!" T.J. sips his beer.

"I'm tellin' you, T.J., it was the highlight of my summer." Eddie takes a long swallow of beer.

"I'd call that a lucky day," T.J. remarks. "Seems to me you got a hell of a lot more than eighty dollars worth of pussy."

"I think of it as a lucky day. But that was a year before I met Joan. Which brings me to why I'm here. I got all of this extra money and you're rotatin' next week, goin' back to the land of plentiful pussy. I was wonderin' if you'd sell me some of your tunes. 'Tomorrow Night', 'Bald Head', ones you can replace, none of your special real old shit."

T.J. points to the speaker. "How about this big beauty?"

"Huh?"

T.J. explains his situation and Eddie eagerly buys twenty records, including "Tomorrow Night". T.J. throws in a special phonograph record shipping box.

Over two more beers and nips of cognac, T.J. decides he can ship his remaining records and his tapes for a reasonable sum and carry his tape recorder by its handle like a suitcase.

Eddie agrees to buy the turntable and the speaker, figuring, When I rotate, I'll ship the tunes back to Jimmy for safekeepin' and donate the turntable and the speaker to the crew for the dayroom. Somethin' to remember me by. He offers T.J. a hundred bucks, a better-than-fair deal.

T.J. accepts the deal and tells Eddie it's too much. "Don't worry about it," Eddie replies, "when it rains on me, it rains on everybody." He gives T.J. the money and says "Good night." He puts the sense of apprehension that he's been feeling since Joan started signing her letters "Love" instead of "All My Love, Forever" to rest on the way back to his room.

This time next month, I'll be short, he thinks, just before he drops off to sleep.

"Dear Eddie," Joan stares at the words on the sheet of paper and wonders, how am I going to do this without making Eddie feel bad? She frowns. It's not like Eddie *is* the Devil. He's just what Father Quinn calls one of Satan's wiles or snares. She thinks of Eddie's hands on her and feels a pleasant rush course through her. Lust, she thinks. Better say a Hail Mary.

Joan stands up, reciting the Hail Mary to herself as she walks over to the almost-empty wardrobe that she shares with Barbara. She takes Eddie's birthday present out and lays it on her bed. She runs her hand over the satin and embroidery. She looks at the map of Alaska and decides, first, I'll have to thank Eddie for this lovely jacket.

She returns to her seat and writes, "First let me thank you for my lovely jacket. I'm sitting here admiring it. Pale blue is my favorite color, but you know that. I'll always cherish it and whenever I wear it I'll think of you."

Joan watches her hand start the second paragraph. "This is not a Dear John letter, like you told me your friend Red got," the hand writes, "but ..."

June 26th, Eddie wakes up feeling rested and ready for work. He goes to his wall calendar and x's out the 23rd, 24th and 25th.

"Ninety-seven days, Hollis. That puts you down to nine days. How's it feel to be that short?"

Hollis sits up in his cot. "It feels great. This'll be my last shift in Alaska." He jumps out of bed. "Goddamn, look out, all you little Tennessee babes, Hollis is coming home."

At four o'clock when Eddie gets off shift, he heads for the mail room. He usually hears from Joan with her mid-month letter by the 19th or 20th of the month. When he still hadn't received a letter by the 22nd, he told himself, Joan's probably out of school for the summer. She'll write from home, I guess, and with that he thought no more of it on a conscious level, but every now and then a question would drift into his mind. A question like, Why didn't Joan tell me when school's out for the summer? or How are we goin' to write each other without her old man gettin' wise ... maybe through Laura? or I wonder what's goin' on with Joan? Her letters are gettin' different and she didn't kiss the last letter.

The mail clerk gives Eddie two letters. "You ought to check the squadron bulletin board, Eddie. There's two new Dear Johns posted. One guy's wife is leaving him for another woman."

Eddie laughs. "That's different. Maybe I'll check it out. Thanks, Tommy."

Eddie looks at the two letters. One has Jill's name and address embossed in the upper left hand corner. He considers opening it first, but opens Joan's letter instead. He starts reading it on the way to his room. He smiles, reading the first paragraph about how Joan liked her jacket.

"This is not a Dear John letter, like you told me your friend Red got, but it is the end of us as lovers and the beginning of us as friends," Eddie reads. He stops almost in mid-step. "There is no other guy," the letter continues. "You'll always be the only love of my life, but I won't be writing to you anymore."

Eddie walks a couple of steps, stops under one of the walkway ceiling bulbs, leans against the wall and continues reading. "All those things we did together were mortal sins and if I would have died in my accident, I'd be burning in hell right now for all eternity."

"Holy fuckin' shit," Eddie exclaims. "Joan's got religion."

He reads on in a stupor. Phrases like "praying for spiritual guidance" and "remorse for past sins," blow through his mind along with words like "atonement," "eternal damnation," "the devil" and "hell." But the thing that knocks the wind out of him as effectively as a hard swift kick to the solar plexus is the ending.

"By the time you get this letter, I'll be living in the convent building and by the time you return, I'll have taken my temporary novitiate vows. You'll always have a special place in my heart. I'll be praying for you. Your friend, Joan. P.S. I won't be able to receive mail here at the convent. I know you'll understand. God bless you."

Eddie re-reads the letter. He can't reconcile the letter with the Joan that he knows. He jams the letter down into his pocket, takes a deep breath and decides to skip evening chow. He doesn't feel like talking to anyone, so he goes to the Airman's Club, sits at a corner table by himself and starts drinking beer. He's half-drunk at ten o'clock when he remembers Jill's letter.

He pulls it out of his pocket, opens it and reads.

Dear Eddie,

I'm assuming that you received or will receive a letter from Joan telling you of her decision to become a nun. I'm sure that you're as heart-broken as I am. I know that you're due back in a few months. Please write and let me know what I can do to help you and Joan get back together. I'll do anything. I'm devastated by this news.

Eddie, this is a plea for help. Bill is useless. He's got the trust money and Joan could be going to work in a coal mine for all he cares. Please write to me soon.

You know I'm your friend.

Jill Whitman

Jill's letter includes her home address and a P.S. *"Don't worry about writing me here. Bill is always off to work long before the mail arrives."*

Just the act of writing the letter cheered Jill up enough that she added a P.P.S. *"I can't stand the idea of Joan wasting her life in some convent, dressed in black. She's too stylish for that (ha-ha)."*

The following day, Eddie writes to Joan. He feels funny about writing to Jill. I'll just put that off for a few days, he figures. First I'll see if Joan answers my letter.

Dear Joan,

I don't know what they did to you at O.L.L., but believe me, you don't have to worry about going to hell because there's no such place. All of that hell and devil stuff is just jive to keep the squares in line.

You went to public high school. I went to Catholic high school. We studied religion one period a day, just like algebra or science. I did that for four years. I've been bull-shitted by experts. One time in religion class, the priest was telling us how you couldn't get into heaven unless you were baptized so I raised my hand and asked him, "What if a tribe on a remote island never get visited by missionaries, but they all live good, happy lives, never getting drunk and beating their wives and kids, never picking on smaller, weaker people, never being mean to small, defenseless animals, and what if— (I tried real hard to get these people into heaven, honey) — they have a big feast every spring to thank whatever Great Spirit or Wonderful Force created the world, the stars and everything. Could they get into heaven?" I asked him and the guy said, "No." That didn't sound fair to me, or logical, but I just kept my mouth shut.

Another time in religion class, I asked one of the priests, "What if a kid is a really perfect kid, never gets in fights or steals stuff, goes to Mass every Sunday and always receives Holy Communion, goes to Benediction, says his rosary, never eats meat on Friday and besides that he's a choir boy." (I used to love making up these questions for religion class even though I always knew what the answer would be). "So what if one Sunday, he skips Mass, goes to a picnic and drowns?" I asked him, "Does he go to hell for all eternity for just one mistake?" And the priest says something like, "Well, the boy knew that missing Sunday Mass was a grievous matter, so if he gave it sufficient reflection and then went ahead and with the full consent of his free will he missed Mass, he fulfilled the three things required for a mortal sin—a grievous matter, sufficient reflection and full consent of the will. The boy did not die in the state of grace." So I said, "Then I guess it's hell for him?" And the priest said, "I guess it is."

By the time I got out of high school, I knew that religion was about controlling people and punishment. I'm not talking about just Catholics, I mean all religions—Puritans, Jews, Moslems——burning witches, stoning women and chopping hands off and then, in case that's not enough, they've got hell waiting for you. And that's another load of crap—the devil. I didn't believe that one, even when I was a tiny little guy. I'd do something bad and my mother would yell, "Eddie, you're a devil from hell, sent to torment me." I knew better than that. I knew that I loved my mother and I knew that whatever kind of jackpot I'd gotten myself into it wasn't done to torment her and I damn sure knew that I wasn't a devil sent from hell. So whenever my mother would say that to me, I'd just chalk it up to old Irish sayings; like my Aunt Aggie saying, "Jesus, Mary and Saint Joseph," if she'd drop a cup or dish in the kitchen.

When I was around ten, I asked my uncle if there was such a thing as the devil and Frank laughed. He was my funniest uncle. He said, "Of course there's no devil. If there was he would have appeared to you, to tell you what a great job you're doing raising hell!" Then we went to the ice cream parlor where he worked and we got ice cream cones. You know what I think the devil is? I think the devil is an excuse that yellowbellies use when they don't want to own up to something they've done.

Anyway, Joan, I'm going to cut this short. It's Saturday morning up here and I want to get this on the plane for Anchorage before noon. Don't take any vows until you see me. PLEASE!!! If you wait for me, we'll get married by a priest and I'll go to Mass every Sunday, if that's what it takes to prove that I love you.

All my love, forever,

Eddie

Eight days later, Eddie's letter is returned, rubber-stamped 'Refused. Return to Sender."

That night, Eddie goes to the Airman's Club. Hollis is gone, leaving behind only his empty cot, his radio and an autographed, 8x10 glossy of Gloria Grahame taped on the wall.

Red McClain and Reeves are in the club when Eddie gets there. He buys three bottles of beer and pulls a chair up to their table. Reeves is talking about his two-day-old Dear John letter.

"To tell you the truth," he declares, "I felt kind of good when I got my D.J."

Red crushes his cigarette in the ashtray. "How can you feel good about getting a Dear John?"

Eddie lights up a cigarette and smiles. He takes a hit off his beer.

"Thanks, Eddie," Don takes a big slug of his new beer.

"Yeah, Eddie, thanks." Red takes a swallow of his beer.

"I never told anyone this," Don begins, "but Becky was more trouble than she was worth. I took her to the movies when we were in eighth grade and she's been on me like a tattoo ever since."

"What's so bad about steady pussy?" Red asks. He and Eddie laugh.

"You guys can laugh all you want," Don replies, "but after seven years, I'm free ... *and,* I didn't have to be the one to break it off. Whenever I'd try to break up, she'd get all depressed. She jumped in the lake one time, took a whole bunch of aspirins another, they had to pump her stomach, tried to hang herself but the knot came undone, jumped out of a hotel window but an awning broke her fall." He looks at Eddie. "I didn't tell you on the plane, Eddie, but the reason I was always going AWOL to see Becky was to visit her in the hospital."

"Do you know who she's going with now?" Red asks.

Eddie laughs. "Yeah? Who's the lucky stiff?" Eddie can see that Don is truly happy about this chick dumping him, so he adds, "He must be a doctor." They all laugh.

"No. He's not a doctor but you're close," Don answers. "He's one of the attendants at the nut house where Becky's staying."

"What'd she do to wind up in the bug house?" Eddie takes a deep drag on his cigarette.

"Tried to gas herself, I guess." Don shakes his head. "All she did was blow up the kitchen, and blow her folks out of bed."

"And blow herself into Loon City," Eddie adds, and they all laugh.

"How do you know she's really in the nut house?" Red demands. "Most women would rather lie than breathe. She might be bullshitting you."

"Don't care if she is," Don declares. "She's gone ... and anyway, she wrote me on hospital stationary. Right across the top of the page it said, 'Serene Acres Sanitarium and Convalescence Hospital.'"

"Yep. That sounds like what rich people call the looney bin," Eddie agrees. "Serene Acres. That'd be a great name for a boneyard. You ever see anything more peaceful than a dead motherfucker?" Eddie closes his eyes and rolls his head way back. They all laugh. All three take drinks of their beer.

"So let's see the letter," Red prods.

"It's already on the bulletin board."

"You posted your D.J.?"

"Sure, Eddie. Why not?"

"I dunno." Eddie puts his cigarette out. He has trouble finding an empty spot in the overflowing ashtray. He finishes the rest of his beer, takes the ashtray and some empty bottles that accumulated before his arrival and says, "Be right back."

Five minutes later, he's back with six beers and a clean ashtray. He puts the ashtray and beers on the table and states, "Let's get fuckin' wasted tonight."

"Why not?" Don finishes the beer in front of him.

"That was my original idea," Red shouts, and they all laugh.

Red kills his old beer. "You know what I'm going to do when I rotate. I'm going down to Texas and punch the shit out of the asshole who stole Lulubelle."

"Why bother?" Don asks. "You said you only knew her for three weeks."

Eddie lights up a cigarette and tunes in. He enjoys listening to these two.

"I said I knew Lulubelle three weeks before we got engaged." Red takes a drink of his beer.

"How long were you engaged?" Don asks.

"We got engaged a day or two before I shipped out." Red lights up and takes a deep drag.

"So you knew Lulubelle three weeks and two days?" Don takes a swallow of beer.

"Almost a month," Red declares. "What do you think, Eddie?"

"What I think isn't important, Red. You got to do what feels right for you. As for me, I got a problem of my own."

"Don't tell me you got a Dear John, Eddie?" Don looks stunned.

"Not exactly," Eddie answers, "it's more like a Dear Jesus. Joan wants to become a fuckin' nun." Eddie finishes his sentence with a huge slug of his beer.

The three of them spend the next few hours drinking, smoking and seeing how many guys they can name who received Dear Johns. The ashtray rises once again to flood level and many bottles of beer are emptied, while they discuss the perfidiousness of women in general.

While they talk and drink, the jukebox inexorably grinds out tunes of heartbreak and separation. Pop tunes, "Auf Wiederseh'n Sweetheart", "Wish You Were Here" and Joni James' "Why Don't You Believe Me" are played more than once.

Hank Williams gets a heavy workout with "Long Gone, Lonesome Blues", "I can't Help It (If I'm Still In Love With you)", and "Your Cheatin' Heart". During one stretch of the evening, the three tunes pop up in a row.

"These Foolish Things Remind Me of You" by Billy Ward and His Dominoes, and a new Johnny Ace tune, "The Clock", are played along with Ernest Tubb doing "(Remember Me) I'm The One Who Loves You."

Hank Snow is singing, "Now and then there's a fool such as I am over you, you taught me how to love and now, you say that we're through ..." Eddie listens and reflects while Don and Red dominate the conversation.

Eddie doesn't think of Joan in the category of "rat-bitches" to which he's relegated all the Dear John writers and he tells the guys, "I won't be posting Joan's letter. Number one, because she's not with some other guy and number two, I'm markin' this down as unfinished business."

They stay until the club closes and return to their barracks in a drunk and rowdy condition, singing "Old Soldiers Never Die". They stop outside Eddie's room. He opens the door and turns on the light.

"Turn that fucking light out," the large body occupying Hollis' bunk bellows.

Thinking he opened the wrong door, Eddie hits the light switch and starts to close the door when he sees, "Flynn, Edward P. A3/c" on the door's nameplate.

Eddie opens the door wide and switches the light back on. The body in the cot sits up. "I said put that fucking light out, Airman," the body shouts.

Eddie looks at the guy, a beefy-faced fucker with little pig eyes, short brownish hair and a big beer gut. Eddie's been feeling cheated all night because all the guys who got Dear Johns have someone to go punch the shit out of, but he has only

Jesus to be pissed off at. Suddenly, here's this fat, loud-mouthed prick to focus on. He feels almost happy.

"Fuck you, asshole," Eddie shouts, "you're in my room. I undress at night with the light on."

Red McClain comes to the doorway and shouts, "What the fuck are you doing in Flynn's room anyway, asshole?"

Doors are popping open all along the hall. Beeman, Prez, Jesse Joe and two strangers spill out into the hallway.

"I'm Master Sergeant Baker," the guy says, getting out of the cot and standing up. "Down here with the Elmendorf inspection team. I'm ordering you to turn that fucking light out!"

Eddie looks at the guy standing there in his boxer shorts with his belly hanging down. A flash of his father shoots through his mind. "I'm Airman Third Class Flynn. This is my fuckin' room. The light goes out when I'm ready to hit the sack," he shouts. Eddie feels the blood beginning to pull away from his skin, a familiar feeling to him. He thinks of his father again. "And if you want some of my ass, come and get it, you fat-bellied motherfucker!"

Baker comes roaring at him, driving his shoulder into Eddie's chest, pushing him through the doorway and smashing Eddie against the hallway's wall.

Eddie knees Baker in the balls, half-effectively, punches him twice in the ear and jumps away.

McClain picks off one of the strangers and punches him in the face. "Let's kick these assholes out of our barracks," he shouts.

Beeman pushes past Reeves and jumps the other stranger. Don is happy to be pushed aside. I wouldn't be much help in this, he thinks. Beeman and the guy are scuffling and rolling on the floor, with Beeman getting in some good licks.

Eddie is up and bouncing. He pops a left jab into Baker's face. "Come on, fatboy," he snarls. "Let's see how good you go." He pops Baker with another left, steps in and buries his right fist in the sergeant's gut. Baker grabs Eddie in a clumsy bear hug.

Deke comes out of his room at the dayroom end of the bay, at the same time that the Officer of the Day and two air policemen enter the bay from the walkway end on their regular nightly patrol.

Eddie has his left arm locked around Baker's neck, still pummeling him with his right when the A.P.'s pull him away.

Eddie, McClain and Beeman spend the night in the guardhouse.

CHAPTER 36

▼

Colonel Gunderson at fifty years of age, his black hair sprinkled with gray, looks like a judge seated behind his desk. Eddie is standing at parade rest in front of the colonel's desk listening as Gunderson reads the officer of the Day's report.

He finishes and states, "Captain Wharton's official charge against you is 'Inciting Federal Troops to Riot' as well as 'Striking a Non-Commissioned Officer.' Either of these charges, if they are upheld in a court-martial, will result in stockade time or possibly time in a federal prison." He pauses. "Do you understand that?"

"Yes sir, I do, but I'd sure like to tell my side, Colonel."

"That's why you're here," Gunderson replies. "Although, as your Commanding Officer I won't be sitting on the court-martial, I do review the facts of the case with the court-martial board before they convene. I can make recommendations if I think the charges are excessive. What do your friends call you?"

"Eddie, sir."

Colonel Gunderson opens Eddie's 201 file. "Well, Eddie." He smiles. "I see we're both short-timers."

"Yes, sir. Eighty-six days."

"I'm going home in six weeks," Gunderson states flatly. "Why don't you tell me about yesterday and what led up to all of this trouble? You can stand at ease, Eddie."

Eddie relaxes and tells his tale, showing the colonel his returned letter and mentioning how his room was empty when he went to the Airman's Club. He tells of his surprise at finding someone in Hollis' vacated bunk. At one point he relates, "About that striking an NCO, sir, he started the physical shit. I was just fightin' back. He was just a big, fat, loudmouthed bully like ..." Eddie stops.

"Like who, Eddie?"

Eddie hesitates. "Like a bully ... you know, sir."

"The way you said, 'like,'" the colonel remarks, "I almost thought you were going to say he looked like your father." Eddie's eyebrows go up, just a bit. "Maybe, sir, a little. I guess I just went apeshit, Colonel."

"You and your dad get along okay?"

"He died when I was ten."

"Sorry. You miss him much?"

"Not really, Colonel."

"I see." He looks at Eddie's personnel file again and smiles. "These personnel files are interesting," the colonel continues. "You've got a higher score on your Air Force Qualification Test than most of the officers on this base."

Eddie resists shrugging. Suspicions verified, he thinks, suppressing a smile.

"That's a big part of the problem," Gunderson continues. "You're smart enough to know stupidity when you see it and dumb enough to tackle it head-on." He laughs. "That's a mighty bad combination."

Eddie smiles. "I think I see what you mean, sir. I know good combinations when I see 'em. I gotta pay more attention to bad combos."

The colonel looks at Eddie's 201 file and shakes his head. "Not much point in sending you to the stockade. Stockade time would only worsen your already-strong feelings of negativity toward authority ... But more important than that is the fact that Airman Donald Reeves was here to see me, first thing this morning. He told me that Sergeant Baker rushed you into a wall, starting the brawl ... and I believed Reeves."

Eddie lets a big breath whoosh out of his mouth. "I'm sure glad to hear that, sir. Because it's the truth."

"'Inciting Federal Troops to Riot' is a ridiculous charge." Gunderson snorts. "Captain Wharton tends to get melodramatic."

Eddie smiles and the colonel scribbles a note on Captain Wharton's report. "That inspection team will be gone back to Anchorage day after tomorrow," the colonel continues, "I've got them billeted over on the other side of the base in the Bachelor Officer's Quarters. You probably won't see them again. I'm recommending squadron punishment instead of a court-martial. I'm going to take one stripe away from each of you."

Colonel Gunderson watches Eddie. He sees the look of relief and happiness brighten Eddie's face. He's always happy when he can lessen the punishment that one of his men is expecting. He opens McClain and Beeman's files.

"And there'll be no forfeiture of pay."

"Yes, sir," Eddie smiles broadly.

Glancing at the open files, Gunderson comments, "McClain, Beeman and yourself have been up and down the rank ladder like yo-yos anyway."

They both laugh. Eddie suggests, "You know, sir, me and McClain don't care about stripes but this is the third time Beeman's been airman second, he's on his second hitch and he's real short."

Colonel Gunderson looks at Beeman's file. "Three weeks. He's damn short."

"Beeman's the best Movements and Identification tech I've worked with, sir," Eddie declares. "He wasn't even drinkin' with us. He probably only jumped in because he thought I was gettin' beat up." Eddie pauses a second. "Maybe latrine duty 'til he rotates, Colonel? In lieu of a stripe. Just a suggestion, sir."

"You think three weeks in the shithouse is a fair trade instead of a stripe?"

"I do, sir," Eddie agrees. "And if Beeman's as good cleaning the latrine as he is workin' M and I, that shithouse will sparkle." They both laugh.

"From the looks of this two oh one file, you're not going to make the Air Force a career. I'd suggest you think about becoming a lawyer."

"Thank you, sir." Eddie smiles.

"Okay, I'll go for that. You're dismissed."

Eddie snaps to attention and salutes. The colonel returns Eddie's salute smartly. "You're a hell of a guy, sir."

"Thanks, Eddie. On your way out, send in Beeman." Taking another look at Beeman's records, Gunderson says loud enough for Eddie to hear, "Jesus Christ, this guy's been in more shit than a barnyard pitchfork."

Eddie leaves the colonel's office smiling. Beeman and McClain look at him like he's crazy.

"You're next," he tells Beeman. "You're gonna like this guy."

The next day, Eddie sends away to San Francisco for some books. Then he writes a letter to Jill, telling her about his letter to Joan coming back to him unopened. He tells Jill that he'll be in the Detroit area sometime in early October and that he'll call her.

The following day, Able crew gets lucky while working barge detail. Eddie and Burroughs are on one of the barges, loading drums of fuel oil, gasoline and light-weight motor oil into slings. A crane swings the slings over to a pier, where the slings are being unloaded and the drums are being stacked in the back of a truck by Reeves and McClain.

Burroughs taps Eddie. "You see the numbers on that drum? That's one-nine-zero. Wonder how it got in with this shit?"

"What's that?"

"Hundred ninety proof alcohol that hasn't been denatured," Burroughs states. "We used to drink that shit down at my last base."

"You sure about that?"

"Sure am," Burroughs insists. "See those numbers right after the U-S-A-F? Zero, zero, zero, one, nine, zero? There's no 'D' after the last zero. Denatured alcohol would have a 'D.' This shit is definitely drinkable."

"Be right back." Eddie jumps from the barge to the pier. He runs to the end where the truck is being loaded. He climbs up into the truck's bed and whispers to Red.

On the trip from the dock to the 901st, McClain and Reeves kick the drum of alcohol off the back of the truck into the tundra, a half-mile from the main gate.

That night, Able crew has a barracks party with Burroughs as the guest of honor. A little hit of one-nine-zero and some grapefruit juice make a smooth drink. Deke even drinks half a cup of it straight. Nobody gets too drunk and nobody gets in trouble.

A few days later, Eddie gets a letter from Jill. While waiting to hear from Eddie, the practical part of her mind was at work. The letter that Eddie receives tells of her plan to rescue Joan. It's a letter that surely brought a smile to the face of Machiavelli's spirit, as it hovered over her shoulder while she wrote it.

Dear Eddie,

Thank you for your most welcome letter. While I'm sorry that your letter to Joan was returned, I'm not surprised. Sandy called and told me she had the same results. It seems that I'm the only person Joan will write to. Eddie, I think that between the two of us we can find a way to pry Joan loose from the clutches of Holy Mother Church. I'm not giving up. Since I last wrote you, I've been doing some thinking about our situation. Here are my thoughts.

We have two big problems. The first is to get Joan to agree to see you. I feel I can accomplish this by appealing to Joan's sense of fairness. I'll arrange a meeting. Our other problem seemed tough at first. How to get the Mother Superior to let you and Joan meet? The answer came to me almost instantly. Sister Maria Dolores has never laid eyes on you. I'll just tell her that you're Joan's cousin James, and that you were always like an older brother to her, very protective, and that you're being shipped overseas for two years.

I've already doubled as a Red Cross volunteer, after all. I can get you past Mother Superior. The rest will be up to you and I feel good about that.

Your friend and co-conspirator,

Jill

P.S. Sandy said to tell you that your buddy Norm was promoted to Airman first class and sent down to Biloxi to be an instructor in radar school. Laura's quitting college to go down and be near him. Sandy said that Arlene (Laura's mother) told Laura to follow her heart. I always liked Arlene.

Eddie drinks and reads his way through the summer. Beeman rotates. Deke rotates. New guys slide into the crew like grease and Eddie keeps X-ing out those days on his calendar.

A few days after Labor Day, Eddie gets a letter from Jill.

Dear Eddie,

Wonderful news. Joan has agreed to meet you. It's almost magical, the way it came about. Bill moved out a month ago. I was happy to see him go. I cut that trust fund money right down the middle, just to speed him on his way. In a perverse way, I sort of miss him. I miss him the way you might miss an ugly weathervane. You don't really like looking at it, but it does show you which way the wind is blowing. I don't have him around to react to anymore.

Having him around did make my life easy. If he thought some GM executive was hot stuff, I'd know that the guy was a blowhard. Bill was always impressed with the wrong people, for the wrong reasons. I'll never forget the look on his face when Joan introduced you to us. He looked like he just found a big, crawly bug in his salad. I knew right away that you were O.K.

Anyway, Bill and I had some happy times bring ing up Joanie, even a couple of vacations when Bill could get away from General Motors. That was *always Bill's big love, General Motors, and that was quite alright with me. Bill wasn't the big love of my life either, but that's another story for another time.*

Back to Joan agreeing to see you. When I wrote her, telling her that Bill and I were getting a "friendly divorce," Joan wrote back and said that she'd pray for us. I quickly wrote back telling her that it was O.K. if she prayed for us as long as she didn't pray for us to get back together. Joan wrote back, saying she laughed about that. Then in another letter I reminded her about a story I told her while we were on our way to Our Lady of the Lakes of how I had to say goodbye to the boy I loved. I'm so glad that I let my hair down on that drive to school with Joan.

Anyway, our letters got better and better, and now with some gentle hints from me, Joan feels that the right thing for her to do is to tell you of her decision face to face. I think she's kind of enjoying the intrigue of meeting you as her cousin James. I'm starting to see a faint glimmer on the horizon. I think we've got a fighting chance. I'll be waiting for your call.

Your future mother-in-law, (ha-ha)

Jill

P.S. Joan says she's not dreaming anymore. For quite a few months, she was dreaming frequently. I'd call them nightmares. I'm glad they're over.

September slips away and on October first, Eddie is aboard a C-47 looking down on Naknek for the last time. The drum of one-nine-zero sounded hollow at Eddie and Reeves' "Going Home" party the previous night.

At Elmendorf, Eddie, Reeves and the others from the 901st who are rotating are billeted in a Quonset hut with some other "casuals" for a few days while awaiting a flight to McChord AFB near Tacoma. Eddie shows Don how to avoid getting tagged for KP and other work details.

On their first afternoon in Anchorage, Eddie and Don go drinking in a few of the bars along Fourth Avenue. At the Ten Forty Two Club, a good-looking blonde at the end of the bar crosses her legs. Reeves heads her way. Eddie says to the bartender, "Goddamn, I could swear I saw her snatch. Looks like Don might get lucky."

The bartender continues drying a glass. "He will if he's got twenty bucks to spend for a short time."

"Twenty bucks?" Eddie whistles softly. "No free pussy driftin' around?"

"Free pussy never drifts north of Seattle," the bartender answers, and they both laugh. The bartender continues, "I had to marry a hooker just to get some steady ass without going broke!"

"You married a hookin' chick?"

"Why not?" The bartender laughs. "When I go back to Portland next year, I'll just blow her off. You can get a divorce in Reno in six weeks. You looking for any action?"

"Naw. I ain't been laid in a year. I can wait a few more days," Eddie says. "Where's the nearest tattoo parlor?"

A few days later when a C-54 drops him off at McChord, Eddie picks up his orders and is happy to see that he's been assigned to Selfridge, for dispersal from there to any of a half dozen radar sites in the Midwest, as he had requested. He takes his orders over to the Military Air Transport Service and signs up for a flight to Selfridge. The MATS terminal is almost empty, so Eddie uses his small canvas travel bag as a pillow, stretches out on a bench and goes to sleep.

At 0200, a staff/sergeant wakes him. Eddie's booked on a C-54 that's stopping at Selfridge on its way to Mitchell AFB in New York.

At 11:30 AM Eddie is on the phone to Jill. "I'm calling from a bar called The Hanger. It's right outside the main gate at Selfridge."

"Welcome home, Eddie." Jill's happiness comes right over the phone.

God, she sounds just like Joan, he thinks.

"You're only twenty minutes away," Jill exclaims. "I'll be right over."

When Jill comes walking into the bar, all heads turn. She's wearing a yellow dress, black alligator high heels and a string of black beads.

"Man, you look great." Eddie gets up from his stool to greet her.

Jill laughs, "You've been in Alaska way too long." She gives Eddie a big hug and takes the stool next to his.

Jill declines Eddie's offer of a martini and has a beer instead. "I quit martinis right after I quit Bill." They both laugh.

Jill sips her beer. "Eddie, I'm so glad you're back."

"Me too," Eddie agrees. "Maybe even gladder than you."

Jill laughs. She's feeling almost giddy. "You ready to rescue Joan from the convent?"

Eddie laughs. "I've read so much about religion the last couple of months. I could debate a bishop!"

They sip their beer. Eddie decides to inquire, "What did you mean in your letter about Joan not dreamin' anymore?"

"Until about a month ago, Joan was having dreams that were bad enough to wake her up. Nightmares, I guess."

"From the accident?"

"Maybe. Or, maybe that damn school. All that praying. All that religion."

"Joan never wrote me about any dreams."

Jill sips her beer. "I only found out recently. I knew she had a couple in the hospital but I thought that was it. Sandy told me about Joan's dreams at school."

"Sandy?"

"She called when her letter came back. She told me things Joan had never let on to me about. How she felt safe from the devil at Our Lady of the Lakes, and about the bad dreams."

"But she's not dreamin' anymore? Right?"

Jill smiles. "Right. I wrote and asked Joan about the dreams and I got back the happiest, upbeat letter. She even mentioned that she's looking forward to her visit with her cousin to tell him about her decision."

Eddie smiles. "Sounds like she's still got her sense of humor."

Jill takes note of the growing number of airmen straggling in. "Looks like the regular lunch crowd."

"Yeah." Eddie finishes his beer.

"How about a really good steak?"

"In this joint?"

"Hell no." Jill finishes her beer. "Let's get out of here," she offers. She opens up her purse and gives Eddie her keys.

Out in the parking lot, three young lieutenants watch Eddie slide behind the wheel of the red Cadillac. Jill waves to them from the passenger window and they shake their heads in wonder as Eddie drives off the lot.

At the Harbor Lights, when Eddie comments on the filet mignon, Jill explains some of the intricacies of her divorce. "Bill wanted to join a more expensive, more prestigious club downtown. All male, secret handshake stuff." Jill laughs. "So I bought out our membership here. Here, where Andre has run this kitchen for twelve years. And Bill is now a member of his fancy club."

"Tastes like you got the best of the deal."

"We each got what we wanted." Jill smiles. She takes a small piece of steak and bites into it. "But it does taste like I got the best of it. Besides, Eddie, Madge, Arlene and some of the other girls are my friends, not Bill's. He never used the club, except for the bar to make deals. He was on the board strictly for business reasons. I play tennis here with my friends, and cards. Bill never set foot on the tennis court." She sighs a long sigh and smiles. "You know, Eddie," she continues, "it cost me almost a million dollars to get rid of that stiff. But it was worth every penny. I feel so free."

"Well, you sure sound happy to me, Jill."

Throughout the rest of the meal, Jill tells Eddie the story of how she had to say goodbye to her old boyfriend, and with what she feels are a couple of casual questions, finds out that Slim is not married.

After dessert, Jill excuses herself to go to the ladies room. On her way back, Bucky Simmons falls in step with her. Bucky sees himself as a blend of Don Juan, Casanova and Charles Boyer. He's a thirty-year-old General Motors executive, who spends more time at the club playing golf, drinking Scotch and exercising his overactive libido than he spends at his office. He gets away with his lax business attitude thanks to his forty-five-year-old wife's huge General Motors stock holdings.

"I heard that you and Bill split up," Bucky begins. "If you need a shoulder to cry on, I'm available."

Jesus, that's original, Jill laughs to herself and returns, "That's nice to know."

"You know, Jill, I've had my eye on you. With Bill gone, I'll bet a date with a younger man might spice up your life." They are nearing Jill's table where Eddie is sitting blowing smoke rings into a sunbeam and sipping coffee.

"Maybe you're right, Bucky."

They arrive at the table. Eddie looks up at them. Jill gives Eddie a broad wink. "Eddie," she begins, "I'd like you to meet Bucky."

Eddie stands and shakes Bucky's hand. "Nice to meet you."

Jill turns to Bucky. "Eddie's been helping me forget all about Bill." She puts one arm around Eddie's waist, pulls herself up against him and brushes a kiss onto his cheek. "Haven't you, sweetie?"

Eddie puts his arm around Jill's waist and smiles a big smile. "Well, I've been doin' my very best."

"Speaking of doing your very best, honey," Jill coaxes, "why don't we go over to my place?"

Eddie puts on his super cool look. "Sure thing, baby," he replies. "Why not?" To Bucky, he says, "Nice meetin' you, Bucky."

Jill and Eddie leave the room, walking with their arms around each other's waists, laughing and chatting, leaving a slack-jawed Bucky Simmons in their wake.

"Nice going, Eddie," Jill laughs, "I know his wife. Believe me, Alicia deserves better than that."

On the way to Jill's they stop and pick up a dozen beers.

At Jill's they put the beer in the refrigerator and Jill shows Eddie up to Joan's room. "You can sleep here tonight. Get up bright and early tomorrow and head for O.L.L." She notices Eddie checking out the canopy bed. "This room is really Joan, isn't it?"

"It smells almost like Joan's here." Eddie closes his eyes, breathes in softly, slowly and continues, "I'm smellin' gardenias. I'm seein' Joan at the front door, huggin' me." He opens his eyes. "That time I came to dinner. She was wearin' a dress with lots of bright colors, yellows, blues, light greens and yellow high heels."

"Smells are funny," Jill agrees, "I can never smell new-mown hay without thinking about Mike leaving my life that morning on the four-twenty." She adds, "So long ago." Jill swings open the bathroom door and continues. "You've got your own bath. Blue and white, of course." They both laugh.

"I'm going to get into some slacks and flats. I'll bring Joan's letters and meet you down in the kitchen." She closes the door behind her.

Eddie takes his travel bag into the bathroom, zips it open and puts his toiletries on the counter, next to the sink. He looks at himself in the mirror, takes off his tie, hangs it over the doorknob, takes Joan's letters and his own returned letter out of the bag and heads downstairs.

In the kitchen, Eddie tosses his letters on the breakfast nook's table and lights a cigarette. He throws his match into a large glass ashtray on the kitchen counter and turns on the radio. Shirley and Lee are singing, "I'm Gone".

Jill enters the room as Eddie is thinking, "Sounds like our station."

"I love the songs on that station," Jill comments. "They have such feeling. Joan introduced me to rhythm and blues the day she left the hospital. She said this was the favorite station for you two."

"Yeah. It was," Eddie reminisces. "You really think we can pull this off?"

Jill is carrying a packet of letters, a yellow legal pad and two pencils. "Don't get faint-hearted on me now." She smiles warmly, puts her things on the table next to Eddie's letters, brings the ashtray over and sits down. She takes one of her long cigarettes out and lights up. "Why don't you pop us a couple of beers and come sit down. I do some of my best literary work at this little table." They both laugh.

During the afternoon, while going over their letters together, Eddie opens his letter that Joan refused. He reads it to Jill.

"That's uncanny," she declares. "I think with the limited knowledge you had at the time, you struck the mother lode. Joan's developed a morbid fear of the devil and hell at that damn school."

"She's usin' the place as a hideout, I guess," Eddie agrees.

"I think our chances are improving. I suggest that you take your letter with you, along with your list of religions and those other notes you showed me." Jill pauses. "Your thoughts on logic."

Eddie goes to the refrigerator, gets two beers and opens them. He returns to the table, gives one beer to Jill and takes a long drink out of the other. "If you feel confident, maybe some it it'll rub off on me," he states. "I'm goin' up against Notre Dame."

"I'm betting on you, Eddie." Jill takes a hit of her beer. "Eddie?"

"Yes?"

"Do you still have any of that stuff for your hair? That nice-smelling pomade?"

"Dixie Peach? Sure. Plenty. I had no reason to use it in Alaska." He smiles. "No Joan."

"I think it would be a good idea to use some tomorrow, when you go to see Joan."

Eddie laughs. "Don't worry, Jill. I'll lay it on. Joan loves it."

Jill looks at her watch. "Six-thirty. A good time to call Sister Maria Dolores about my nephew James." They both laugh.

When Jill hangs up she reflects, "That was fairly easy. Sister could hardly speak. Sounds like she's got laryngitis. But it's all set for tomorrow."

"That was slick work. So far, so good."

Jill laughs. "I got hungry halfway through that call. Eggs okay?"

"Absolutely."

After an excellent cheese omelet made with extra-sharp cheddar cheese from New York, garlic toast and two more beers, Eddie, beat from traveling, says good night to Jill and heads for Joan's room.

Jill stays in the kitchen to finish her beer and cigarette. The Orioles come on the radio, singing, "Maybe it's much too early in the game, oh, but I thought I'd ask you just the same, what are you doing New Year's, New Year's Eve." Jill allows herself a dream. "I'd like to be at a New Year's Eve party at Joan and Eddie's home ... dancing with Slim."

The tune ends. Jill puts out her cigarette, finishes her beer and heads upstairs.

Tomorrow's the big day, she thinks just before falling off to a restless sleep.

In Joan's bed, the smell of her is overpowering. Eddie falls asleep with his head in Joan's lap, on a sunny day at the quarry. He dreams of rescuing Joan from a fire-breathing dragon and awakens hungry, with the sun in his eyes. Showering and shaving in Joan's room gets him as horny as six billy goats and a ram. He dresses and goes downstairs where Jill has buckwheat cakes, Jones Brothers sausage links and coffee waiting for him.

"Good morning, Jill." Eddie sits down at the table. "Can Joan make this kind of a breakfast?"

Jill laughs. "She sure can."

After he finishes eating, Jill gives him a large terrycloth robe. "Get into this," she directs, "and let me freshen up those khakis. They look like you slept in them."

"I did," Eddie confesses. "On the plane."

An hour later, Eddie is driving Jill's Cadillac, heading for Our Lady of the Lakes and Joan. He turns the radio on and "For You I have Eyes" is playing. "The day will come when you'll be mine," The Crickets are singing. Eddie takes this as a good sign.

CHAPTER 37

▼

The Saturday traffic is light and Eddie feels secure backed up with his week-old Alaskan driver's license. *At least I got a couple of good things out of Alaska. A driver's license and a great-lookin' tattoo.* He respects all of the various towns' speed limits, rolling through Ohio. *This bright red Caddy'll attract the man like flies to fresh horseshit,* he thinks. *Besides, I'd rather see Joan after sundown. More romantic.* He lights a cigarette and wonders about Joan.

Joan is honed to a fine edge. A few weeks without the dreams about the devil have brought about some changes. Without the dreams at night, she finds herself not thinking of the devil during her waking hours. She feels much more relaxed, and with the feeling of relaxation come more frequent little flashes of Lust. Not only are the errant thoughts more frequent, they are also of longer duration. Joan says many a Hail Mary as, more than once, a fleeting scene of her first night with Eddie, in her car, parked by the graveyard in Tawas delights her. Sometimes, feeling a gentle breeze, she recalls the breeze riffling the curtains at the Briggs Hotel on her eighteenth birthday, and the way Eddie's hands felt running over her body. She calls these memories "impure thoughts," when she goes to Confession and she wonders why it's so hard not to be a sinner.

Joan added excitement to her mix of emotions, agreeing to meet with Eddie under the alias of Cousin James. Excitement at the thought of running a deception past the Mother Superior mixes with the excitement in the anticipation of seeing Eddie.

Now taking one of her regular Saturday morning walks in the woods, enjoying the autumn colors, she figures, October tenth. Eddie's tour was over eleven days ago. With travel time, this could be the day. I'll go to Confession this afternoon and then pray for help resisting temptation.

The sun is setting when Eddie wheels the Cadillac into the parking lot across from O.L.L. Getting out of the car he checks himself out in the car window's reflection. That's about as clean-cut as I can look. He takes off his shades, tosses them onto the car's front seat, and slams the door. At least I'm not showing up unannounced.

The main gate swings open as he approaches and when he gets to the front door a tiny old nun opens it. Eddie states his business and the nun shows him to the Mother Superior's office.

Sister Anne, standing in for Sister Maria Dolores, shuffles through some papers on her desk, looks at Eddie with a gimlet-eye and states, "Mother Superior is ill. I'm Sister Anne. I thought you'd be here earlier in the day." She looks at the wall clock.

"I'm sorry, Sister. Traffic was tough all the way," he offers with all the reverence he can muster.

Continuing to glare at him icily, Sister Anne continues. "So you're Joan's cousin?"

"Yes, Sister. My mother is Aunt Jill's older sister."

"Where are you going to be stationed?"

"I can't tell anyone." Eddie starts to enjoy the cat and mouse game. "But it's cold, it's remote and it's for two years, Sister." Eddie smiles.

Sister Anne's glacier look melts slightly. "The novitiates are still in the refectory. Sister Margaret will show you to the meditation garden. Dinner will be finished in twenty minutes."

"Thank you, Sister." He follows the old nun down a hall that smells heavily of floor wax to the end and then out a side door to a small garden.

Eddie sits on a stone bench in the far corner of the garden and watches the stars begin to appear. The bench has no back. Typical, he thinks. Just like religious assholes to not want a guy to be comfortable. He looks around the twilight-lit garden. The low boxwood hedges are green, but the rest of the garden is in retreat from autumn. The rose bushes are bare, the flower beds are empty and the grass is turning brown.

There are three statues in the garden; a large one of The Blessed Virgin is in the middle of the garden with a circular path around it, a smaller version of the school's quad statue. In the corner opposite this, he recognizes a statue of Saint Teresa and right next to his bench, looking down on him, is a statue that turns him sullen. It's a statue of a grown-up Jesus, holding a lamb. A metal plaque screwed into its base reads, "The Good Shepherd."

"Good Shepherd, my ass," Eddie mutters aloud, as he plunges into the mental achieves of his grammar school years.

Eddie is a student at Blessed Child Academy. A kid is stumbling through "Three Billy Goats Gruff", ruining the story for Eddie, with Sister Anastasia saying, "Sound it out," every third or fourth word.

Eddie is itching to turn a page or two and get on with the story. He's called on to read and he rips into the story, sailing along.

Eddie, in the garden, sees Eddie, the first grader, smiling. He sees the smile fade as Sister Anastasia stops him short after only four sentences. The nun takes the book away and sternly rebukes him, in front of the whole class, on the grievous sin of Pride and the virtue of Humility. From then on, Eddie fakes ineptness when called on to read. He does this so well that Sister Anastasia, infuriated at the charade, calls on him less and less.

He gets up from the bench and stands looking at the statue. "That was the same year I decided I wasn't one of your fuckin' sheep," he snaps contemptuously at the statue and he recalls another less-than-fond memory from his grammar school skirmishes with authority.

Using books, small tables and green cloth, Sister Anastasia and some of the girls built their own "Hills of Bethlehem" with a stable at its highest point. The stable is stocked with statues of Mary, Joseph and the Wise Men, clustered around the Baby Jesus in the manger.

At the bottom of the hill, lined up almost like racehorses, are twenty spotless, white lambs, each about two inches long and each with a tiny collar with a student's first name and last name's initial.

Eddie recalls Sister Anastasia explaining Advent and the journey of the lambs. "Advent is the time to do penance and to do good works in preparation for the birth of Jesus. As we progress through Advent, the lamb with your name on it will climb the hills of Bethlehem toward the stable according to a pupil's good conduct. Neat homework and good effort are also rewarded, as well as helping the teacher." Her pause stops only a fraction of a second on Eddie, before she continues. "Bad conduct, sloppy, half-hearted homework or an uncooperative attitude can hinder a lamb's progress." Though the nun's pause when he was in her sights was brief, Eddie took note of it.

Colleen O. and Rosemary T. led the pack from the first day. Eddie calls them "Teacher's Pets." Other lambs like John C. and Margaret D. make their way up the hill more slowly, but by the day before Christmas vacation all the lambs are up by the stable happily breathing on the Baby Jesus. Even William R., who Eddie thinks of as "the dumbest kid in the whole world" is up there. Only one lamb remains at the bottom of the hill, Lamb Edward F.

Sister Anastasia gives the kids their lambs to take home. Eddie accepts his lamb silently and out-stares the nun. Holding back tears of rage at the unfairness of school, he blows the dust off his lamb. My sheep turned gray, he broods, and mouths, "Merry Christmas, Sister Anastasia." He does this with a big, false smile.

On the way home, he drops away from his buddies and heads for an alley to crush the lamb beneath his heel. In the alley, Eddie looks in the lamb's eyes and feels sorry for it. "What the hell," he says to the lamb, "I'll take pity on you. Bring you home to Jimmy."

Eddie's father comes home half-loaded and in a bad mood. He and Eddie get into a beef about Eddie eating all his mashed potatoes first, instead of a little bit of each thing on his plate. It escalates. They both lose what Eddie's mother calls "their dirty tempers" and Eddie winds up getting his ass kicked after dinner.

After his father falls asleep, Eddie gives the lamb to Jimmy. Jimmy likes it and names it "Fuzzy."

Eddie looks at his watch, looks back at the statue and continues drifting through his early school days.

He sees himself, the following year, getting the boot from Blessed Child Academy for calling a nun "a son-of-a-bitchin' bastard." Words like "defiant" and "contrary" are used to describe him and he's sent to boarding school. "So that he can get a little respect for authority knocked into him," is the way that Sister Immaculata, the principal at Blessed Child Academy, puts it.

To be admitted to Saint Andrew's Academy, Eddie had to be advanced to the third grade. The school offered no first or second grade classes. Eddie had no trouble passing the test that showed that he was capable of doing the work in third grade, but at seven years old, he was the youngest, smallest boy in a dormitory of seventy boys, ranging from third to sixth grades.

The first day at school, feeling abandoned and angry, Eddie gets his face pushed into the drinking fountain by an older, bigger boy. Eddie explodes. The temper that got him sent to boarding school erupts. He attacks the kid, punching with both hands, screaming, "Son-of-a-bitchin' bastard!" He's still flailing at the kid and the kid is trying to cover up, when Brother Michael, the dormitory's prefect, pulls him away.

"That'll be ten on each hand, Flynn," he proclaims, "Friday afternoon." He writes Eddie's name in a pocket-sized pad and goes back to supervising the dodgeball game.

A kid the same size as the one Eddie went after comes up to Eddie and states, "I'm Duffy. I can beat up every kid in the dorm. Anybody you can't handle, I'll take care of." They shake hands.

Eddie's first Friday punishment session is the toughest. His hands are new to the strap, a piece of ox-blood-colored leather a quarter of an inch thick, 12 inches long and an inch and a half in width. It has good flexibility and Brother John Patrick is an excellent dispenser of corporal punishment when wielding it. He has a flair for the dramatic, slowly opening the drawer that houses the strap. Eddie had been forewarned of this intimidation strategy before his Friday session by Duffy, who said, "He'll open the drawer real slow, to get you all jumpy. Don't fall for it. You're going to get some licks on your hands. It'll hurt and you'll get over it. That's that."

Brother John Patrick is not a big man, but what he lacks in size he makes up for in skill. He has a supple wrist action that achieves maximum results from the strap. He takes no joy in his Friday sessions and some of the students that he sees regularly, like Duffy, cause him to pray, "Lord, I'm not seeing any improvement in this boy, but if it's Thy will, I'll continue to discipline him until I see some improvement in his attitude. Amen."

The first five licks sting, more than really hurt and Eddie offers up his left hand for its first five easily, but the second set of five to his right hand are a different story.

The palm is starting to swell, the sting has turned to pain. It takes all of Eddie's will to put up his right hand for its second set. Only his father's often repeated message, "Stand up and take your punishment like a man, you little bastard," enables him to suck it up, choke down any thought of tears and leave the session with his head up. I'll never quit gettin' even with kids who do stuff to me, he vows, leaving the principal's office. I don't care if I got to show up here every Friday.

Eddie falls in with Duffy and a couple of other kids who Brother Michael calls "Bad Attitude Cases." Duffy shows Eddie how to toughen his palms up, rubbing them on some of the building's brick walls and slapping them against the walls. These palm-conditioning exercises keep Eddie's palm in good shape for his Friday sessions, which Eddie catches almost every second week.

The punishment becomes so meaningless to Eddie that he retaliates to one schoolyard incident while Brother Michael is looking right at him.

Eddie's going for a ball that he and some kids are kicking around. A big kid pushes him, banging him into the wall. This'll be a Tenner. Better make it count. He kicks the kid's shin with full force. He draws blood.

It was worth it, he tells himself, as he listens to Brother Michael order, "That'll be ten on each, Flynn."

Eddie makes the most of his stay at what he and his buddies call "Saint Andy's." In the rec hall, he learns to shoot pool and on the playing fields he learns to be more wily in his paybacks, sometimes delaying them until another day. This delaying tactic cuts Eddie's Friday sessions with Brother John Patrick down to one a month. "I ain't behavin' any better," Eddie tells Duffy, "I'm just gettin' smarter. Gettin' caught less." Brother John Patrick presumes, "I'm seeing less of Flynn. He must be improving."

The death of his father and its resulting change in family finances spring Eddie from boarding school. At his father's funeral, Eddie tries to decide which punishments he liked least, his father's spontaneous acts, or the more structured sessions at Saint Andy's. Doesn't matter now, he concludes. They're both over. I'm almost eleven. Time to grow up. As he watched the casket with his father's body in it get covered with dirt, Eddie declared himself "cool."

The respect for authority that Sister Immaculata hoped would occur at Saint Andrew's never bloomed.

Eddie stares hard into the eyes of the statue of The Good Shepherd. He feels like toppling it. He dismisses the thought and picks up a small stone from the flower bed. He considers, Maybe I'll just knock off a couple of toes, then reconsiders. "Fuck it," he mumbles and throws the stone back in the flower bed. "It's just a fuckin' statue."

Joan comes out of the convent door ten seconds later. Eddie watches her walking toward him. Joan is wearing a black and white over blouse and a black skirt that reaches almost to her ankles, revealing black hose. Black Oxfords and a tight black, hood-like cover on her head complete her outfit.

She looks like a junior nun, Eddie decides. Or the widows at the seven o'clock Mass. All she needs is a fuckin' shawl.

Joan approaches him, almost timidly, a small smile on her face. She don't even walk right anymore, he observes. Lost her swagger.

Joan greets him. "Hello, Eddie." The sound of her voice melts Eddie's negative feelings. Sadness begins to settle on him.

"They gave me thirty minutes to say goodbye."

Anger pushes sadness aside in Eddie's head. Thirty minutes? I ain't seen you in a year and I get thirty minutes to say goodbye? Big fuckin' deal. Thanks for nothin', he thinks, but instead manages a pleasant, "That's nice, Joan. Sure is good to see you again." He almost chokes up, feels the first sign of watery eyes and continues, "Let's sit down and talk a little. Okay?"

Joan sits next to Eddie on the bench and for the first few minutes she rambles on, almost non-stop about her vocation, forgiveness, God's love of all his children, heaven, hell, the devil, atonement and eternity, with Eddie saying nothing more than, "Uh-huh" and "I see."

She finishes by saying, "You know you'll always have a special place in my heart ... and, you'll be in my prayers every day."

That's just a song and dance, Eddie thinks. He pictures Joan rehearsing it and smiles. But he feels like he doesn't have a chance, feels like he wants to quit, give up. The foe looks far too mighty.

Eddie fights down the defeatist feelings. "I didn't come here to say goodbye. Remember the first night I came to dinner at your house?"

Eddie's voice has an edge to it, an edge that Joan vaguely remembers from the night at the Blue Light Inn, when he told the soldier to "Get the fuck out of here before you get hurt." She's never heard Eddie direct this tone of voice toward her. She pulls back from him slightly, involuntarily.

Eddie feels her withdrawal and softens his tone. He smiles. "Remember after dinner, by your car, when I told you that I saw 'Casablanca' and I said Rick was a jerk for givin' up the girl he loved?"

Joan nods.

"Remember what I said next?"

"Not exactly."

"I said I wouldn't give you up for nothin' or nobody."

Joan looks at him sweetly but a little blankly. "I remember some things better than others."

Eddie eases back. "You remember your birthday?"

Joan nods.

"The Briggs Hotel?"

Joan nods. Tiny embers of lust glow faintly.

"Teachin' me to drive at the quarry? Wenona Beach?"

Joan's face reddens. She feels anger start to rise at this challenge to her memory. "Of course, I do," she stammers. "I remember all those things." She flashes the scenes of the Briggs, the quarry and Wenona Beach through her mind and the lust embers brighten a bit.

"I don't mean do you remember them as facts, like William the Conqueror comin' to England in ten sixty-six. What I mean is do you remember your feelin's? I remember how you smelled the first time I held you in my arms, when we were on the Tawas Pier. Gardenias. Mmmm, that was some night."

Joan sees the scene. One of the lust embers flickers, almost flaming. "I don't want to talk about mistakes that I made," she states flatly, "sins and transgressions. I've been forgiven for all of that. That was lust."

"Lust ain't nothin' but the first baby steps toward love, as far as I'm concerned. It was lust that first attracted me to you ..."

Joan interrupts him, "That's awful."

"No. Not really. Let me continue," Eddie presses, "lust is just what religions like the Catholics, Puritans and some others call natural attraction. First comes lust, then comes love. Lust brings people together, love keeps 'em together, or in our case brings a guy back from Alaska."

"You make lust sound like it's quite all right."

"Joan, from the night we met in Tawas, until the night we kissed goodbye for awhile at the hospital, we never lied to each other. We lied to the world, your old man, Becker, teachers, cops, all those people who don't deserve the truth, but we never lied to each other. The three months we had together were like a lifetime. A lifetime in three months and I ain't givin' it up because of fables."

"Fables?"

"You know, Adam and Eve, the serpent and the apple. That kind of stuff."

"You don't believe in the devil?"

"Not for a second, honey. The devil's just an idea religious leaders use to control their followers. Keep 'em scared." Eddie slips a letter out of his pocket. "This is a letter I sent you when you wrote about joinin' the nuns. Okay if I read it?"

Joan is thinking about the phrase "joinin' the nuns." She smiles a little smile and says, "Okay."

Eddie starts reading his letter. He enjoys reading and he gives an animated delivery. When he gets to the part about the tribe on the remote island being denied admission to heaven, Joan pictures Eddie posing the question to the priest and smiles. She feels sorry for the tribe and considers it unfair that they be locked out due to no baptismal certificate.

Then when Eddie reads about the perfect kid, who skips Mass, goes to a picnic, drowns and goes to hell for all eternity, she feels sadness. "Just for one little mistake. It's not fair."

Joan cheers up again when Eddie gets to the part about his mother calling him "A devil from hell, sent to torment me." At the part where Eddie's Uncle Frank tells him if there was a devil, he'd appear to Eddie to tell him what a good job he's doing raising hell, she almost laughs.

Eddie delivers the last three lines of the letter with all the intensity with which they were written. "Please," he continues, "if you wait for me, we'll get married by a priest and I'll go to Mass every Sunday, if that's what it takes to prove that I love you. All my love forever, Eddie." He looks at Joan. She frowns.

"So there's no devil?"

"No devil. Just bullshit and jive." Eddie smiles a big smile.

Joan shakes her head slowly. "Just bullshit and jive? All those nuns and priests are wasting their time on bullshit and jive?"

"Yes." Eddie smiles at her. "And I'll tell you somethin' else. Religion? Pure horseshit. Anyone can start one." Eddie's enthusiasm is on the rise. He takes out his notes. "I wrote some of this stuff down. It's so goofy. Number one, Roman Catholicism, the one that we happened to be born into, wasn't first and it won't be the last. You know, like the Jews were before the Catholics and the Protestants came after. There's probably strange people startin' religions right now for all we know."

Joan enjoys listening to Eddie. He sees the relaxation in her demeanor and steps things up a notch. He continues, "Luther didn't like the Catholic church sellin' indulgences. Bingo! Lutherans. Not that he wasn't right but that's how easy it is to start one up. Henry the Eighth started his own religion because the Pope wouldn't give him a divorce. People in Ireland are still killin' each other thanks to that fat-bellied asshole, but that's a whole other story. You gotta read some Irish history sometime. You're half-Irish. The best half. Your mom's half."

Joan smiles a full smile. Eddie takes heart. "Listen to this bunch." He looks at his notes. In rapid-fire he starts, "Roman gods, Greek gods, Jews, Catholics, Quakers, Presbyterians, Huguenots, Mormons, Episcopalians, Holy Rollers, Christian Scientists, Fundamentalists, Ballpark Preachers, Pentecostals, Snake Worshipers, Moslems, Jehovah's Witnesses, Volcano Worshipers, Seventh Day Adventists, Greek Orthodoxers, Sun Worshipers, Brahmans, Moon Worshipers, Anglicans, Buddhists, Shintoists, Taoists, Confucians, Baptists ..."

Joan interrupts. "I don't see where this is going?"

"Okay, here it is," he says, gently, "and I'm sure you'll get the point. All these religions and many more say they know what happens after we die. And much more important, each one says that they're the one true faith. They call each other infidels, heathens and worse and they're all willing to kill and torture people from other faiths to prove that they are really the only true religion. Joan, I'm sure you see the stupidity of religion. At least you must wonder about it. Don't you?"

"It is funny that there are so many," Joan ventures.

Eddie smiles. "You're startin' to get the joke." He moves in an inch closer to Joan.

"The joke?"

"Yeah. God didn't make man. God is just a name man came up with for somethin' that man can't understand. Tryin' to fill some emptiness inside 'em or somethin'. Most of the time, especially in the olden days, religion was about con men takin' advantage of suckers ... Guess it still is, huh?"

"What about after we die?" Joan is keeping her Lust embers cool.

"Who knows," Eddie replies, "I sure don't. But I know what doesn't come next and that's just as good. Heaven or hell won't be next. No gangs of angels singin' and playin' harps all day, and no guys in red underwear runnin' around the flames of hell pokin' sinners in the ass with a pitchfork."

Joan smiles and Eddie continues, "Look at that sky."

Joan looks up and Eddie begins, "Stay logical with me, now, just common sense." In a mellow, almost conspiratorial tone, Eddie asks, "Is it logical that anyone or anything powerful enough to scatter stars all over the universe, helter skelter, would demand order from a species, on a tiny flyspeck of a planet, when the whole rest of the universe is floatin' along, free and unruly, like boilin' water? Common sense says, the answer is no."

Eddie's feeling pumped up. "Here's somethin' else," he states. "Anything powerful enough to generate a universe sure doesn't want to be worshiped, adored or prayed to. If you're that great, you don't need to be told so by a bunch of ants on an ice cream stick. You already know you're cool and all-powerful." Eddie smiles and moves his head two clicks closer to Joan. She smells the Dixie Peach hair pomade and a faint breeze blows over her embers of Lust.

Joan fights back, hoping to douse her feelings. "It sounds like you lost the faith. Are you an atheist?"

Eddie smiles a warm smile. "No. I'm not sayin' there's no God. I don't know if there is or isn't a God. In fact, I hope there is a God. Everyone wants to live forever. They got a name for guys like me."

Joan jumps in, happy for the diversion from her lustful feelings. "You're called an agnostic," she prompts. "We studied that."

Eddie smiles. "That's right. I'm an agnostic. What's wrong with sayin' you don't know if there's a God or not or what happens after death. To my way of thinkin' sayin' you don't know is better'n tryin' to run a bluff past everyone, sayin' you got all the answers. Especially if your answers are based on books written long ago, when people thought that lightning came from a God named Zeus."

The Dixie Peach is cutting through the incense, floor wax and burning candle odors of Joan's year at Our Lady of the Lakes. Battling against the embers, she demands, "What about eternity?"

"Eternity? I'd say, don't waste your beautiful life worry-ing about eternity. It's been around forever and it ain't gonna go away."

"That's it?"

"That's it for me. My motto is 'Don't worry about eternity, it'll only last for-ever and then it's gone.'" Eddie laughs. "I'm sorry, Joan. I just can't get serious about eternity."

Joan feels more in control of herself. "You've dismissed the devil, all religions and eternity. Is that all that you've got to say?"

"No, it isn't," he replies. "What I really came to tell you is, I love you, Joan and if I'm gonna lose you at least I'm goin' down fightin'. I know I'm up against somethin' that's been around for two thousand years. But just because somethin's old, don't make it right." Eddie looks to Joan for a sign and sees none. He con-tinues, "When I first saw you at that dance it was your beauty that attracted me, that's no lie. But when I got to know you I loved other things about you, your spirit, your refusal to knuckle under to authoritarian assholes, your mind, your sense of humor, your voice." A slight breeze rustles through the embers.

"Remember you and me against the world? One-percenters?"

"I remember that."

Eddie starts to take off his shirt. Joan draws back.

"Don't worry," he reassures her. "I just want to show you my arm." He takes off his shirt, pulls up the sleeve of his T-shirt and flexes his left arm. On his bicep is a big new tattoo of two red hearts, an arrow piercing them and a ribbon across each. One ribbon says, "Eddie" and the other says, "Joan." Underneath the hearts are the words, "One-percenters."

Joan looks at the tattoo, flashes back to the night they parked by the Saginaw River, after the fight at the Blue Light. We went from there to Rostonkowski's, she remembers, and a small flame flickers in lust's embers. She says nothing.

"Okay, so you don't like it." Eddie shucks back into his shirt.

Oh, but I do like it, Joan thinks, I like it very much. Her mind is racing, flip-ping back and forth between dogma and memories of times with Eddie. Eddie sits back down next to her and extends his right hand, palm upward to her. "Would you put your hand in mine for just a little second, Joan?"

Joan puts her left hand in Eddie's hand. The warmth of his hand sends a charge running through her. Sister Cecelia's talk on eternity is echoing in another part of her mind. The aroma of Eddie's hair is soaking her brain. Small flames are dancing in lust's lively embers.

"Picture a huge steel ball the size of the earth," Sister Cecelia instructs, "and once every hundred million years a fly comes by and lands on it. By the time that steel ball is worn down to nothingness from the friction of the fly's feet skidding on it during landings, eternity will just be beginning." Her mind shifts gears from the nun's eternity tale to the idyllic days with Eddie at Rostonkowski's Lodge, back to the torments of hell promised in one of Father Quinn's Sunday sermons, to Wenona Beach, to Benediction, to the Flame Show Bar, to the picture of The Blessed Virgin on her convent wall. The nearness of Eddie, the feel of his hand, makes Joan feel sensuous. She squeezes his hand slightly. Joan's embers erupt into bright yellow, red and blue flames.

Joan turns her face toward Eddie. He kisses her lightly. She opens her mouth wide to receive his tongue. Just like receiving Communion, she thinks. Eddie runs his hand up under her blouse and her nipple is hard. Every ember of lust in her slumbering campfire explodes into a multi-colored starburst. She relaxes and spreads her legs. Eddie puts his hand up her skirt and doesn't stop until it rests on her pussy.

"Oh, Eddie," she sighs. "Fuck eternity."

Eddie slips her panties off, gets out of his trousers and boxers and gives Joan what he'd call "a pretty good fuck" right on the patch of dead grass directly in front of and under the gaze of the statue of The Good Shepherd.

While Joan sneaks back into her room to retrieve her few possessions, Eddie looks at the statue and says, "You win some, you lose some. At least I didn't knock your toes off." He smiles thinking of Joan, wonders about getting through the main gate and speaks to the statue, once again. "You got a big flock, so don't you begrudge me one little lamb. One beautiful little lamb.'

In her room, Joan takes the pillowcase off her pillow, throws her underwear, her shoes, a blouse and a sweater into it. She takes her skirt, her raincoat and her Alaskan jacket out of the wardrobe and tosses them on her bed. She puts her toothbrush and toiletries in the pillowcase and is about to add her jewelry, cards, mementos and stationery to the pillowcase's load, when she realizes, "I better leave a note, so they don't think Eddie kidnapped me."

She sits at her desk. "Saturday night," she thinks, "Barbara's doing the laundry."

Dear Barbara,

You've been a wonderful friend, but I'm going to marry Eddie. He's back and I'm still in love with him. Please tell Sister Cecelia about Eddie. I know she'll understand. I don't think she was ever truly convinced that I had a vocation. She was right, I didn't. Thank her for me. Please accept these rosary beads that my granny gave me for my First Communion. I know you like them and I know you'll use them.

Love, your very good friend,

Joan

P.S. Tell Sister Cecelia, I'll mail the pillowcase back when I get home.

Joan leaves the note on the desk under the rosary, throws the rest of her stuff into the pillowcase, scoops up her clothes from her bed and she's back in the garden with Eddie in five minutes.

"I left a note saying I'm going home," she whispers. "So they won't think you kidnapped me."

"Smart girl." Eddie kisses her. "What're we gonna do about that big gate?"

"Follow me." Joan leads Eddie. They hurry through the garden's side gate, out onto the front lawn, hugging the building to stay out of sight of the Mother Superior's window, until they get to a spot near the gatehouse.

"There's a manual control in there," Joan instructs. "I've seen Sister Cecelia use it."

"Okay," Eddie directs, "here it is. When I pop that lever, you start runnin'. The gate'll be openin' by the time you get there. Head for your mom's car. I'll be right behind you."

"My mom's car?"

Eddie smiles. "You bet. She missed you as much as I did."

They move through the gate, across the road and into the Cadillac, slick as a fox and a vixen.

Eddie drives off the lot quietly and heads down the empty county road. "Oh Eddie, this is so exciting." Joan is bubbling. "I'm going to change clothes."

Eddie laughs. "It is kinda like a jailbreak, ain't it?"

"I forgot how much fun it was, being with you." Joan takes off her head-covering. Her hair is back, shorter, but as black and luxurious as before her accident.

"Man, your hair came back like a champ." Eddie runs his hand through it.

Joan gets out of her other things and sits there in her bra, panties and black stockings for a moment or two before she pulls her sweater and skirt out of her pillowcase, along with her yellow high heels. "These are my only civvies," she remarks when she's got everything on, and they both laugh.

"And Eddie, I really do like your tattoo."

"I knew you would."

"Did it hurt?"

"Naw. It was like gettin' a haircut."

"One more thing." She pulls her necklace out of the pillowcase, fastens it around her neck, throws the pillowcase onto the back seat and slides over, next to Eddie. She turns the radio on and The Flamingos are just getting into "That's My Desire".

"I saw a good-looking auto court in Ohio. We can stop there and call your mom," Eddie offers. "Then, I'm gonna throw a really good hump into you."

"Oh Eddie." Joan pushes him playfully. "You're so romantic."

They spend a restful, happy night together at the Tick-Tock Auto Court and get off to an early start. Driving through the western fringe of Cleveland, listening to Gospel music on the local R&B station, Eddie looks over at Joan. She's smoking, reading his letter and smiling. I can't believe I got her back, he thinks as he stops at a red light to let some kids all dressed up for church pass.

Joan looks up from her letter and sees the kids. Eddie asks, "You want to stop and go to Mass, honey?"

Joan takes a drag off her cigarette.

"I meant what I said at the end of that letter, about gettin' married in church and goin' to Mass every Sunday." The light turns green. Eddie presses the gas pedal gently. There's no traffic behind him, so he just pokes along.

"I can park on one of these side streets. It's a nice neighborhood."

Joan blows out a long stream of smoke. It bounces off the dashboard and rolls up the windshield. "You know what I'd really like, Eddie?"

"You name it."

"What I'd really like would be to get married in Tawas, by the Justice of the Peace, just like we planned."

"Really?"

"Really."

"No church?"

"No church, no priest." Joan is thoughtful. She stubs her cigarette out in the ashtray. "You're right. I have no idea what happens after we die, and neither does anyone else."

Eddie eases the Cadillac up to speed. "That's my motto, honey. Who gives a shit what comes next, as long as we've got now?"

CHAPTER 38

▼

Monday morning, Jill gives Joan and Eddie her car keys and three hundred dollars, and tells them, "If you want to get married on Saturday, you've got things to do. I'm going to spend the day on the phone."

Joan and Eddie drive to Tawas, take care of business with the Justice of the Peace and then pay a surprise visit on Bob and Sandy. They discuss their wedding plans and get some news about the 646th. Bob tells them that Arbo, DiNessi and Brownie are gone, along with most of the guys on the old crew. Sandy tells them that Bob's a crew chief and that she's pregnant.

"Wait'll I tell Major Ross you're back," Bob shouts as he drives off at 3:30 for swing shift.

Sandy kisses and hugs them goodbye a few minutes later, saying, "See you guys Saturday," as they leave her driveway.

On their way back to Joan's, they cruise past the Blue Light, don't see Slim's Olds and decide not to stop.

After dinner, Eddie calls his mother to invite her to the wedding. She begs off, claiming prior commitments and the short notice of the event as reasons. She expresses her dismay with them not getting married in the church and just as she's ready to say, "It's as good as no marriage at all," Eddie catches Jill's eye. He interrupts, "Mom, I'd like you to speak to the mother of the bride."

Jill takes the phone and starts telling Mrs. Flynn how fortunate she feels that Joan was able to find Eddie, a real gentleman and a son that any mother could be proud of. She offers Eddie's mother a round trip airline ticket to Detroit, but Mrs. Flynn's business commitments are genuine. "A bunch of cosmetics execs are in town," she tells Jill and she thanks her.

"Your future daughter-in-law would like to say 'Hi.'" Jill hands the phone to Joan, who immediately goes into ecstasies over Eddie. She tells Mrs. Flynn how much she's looking forward to meeting her and passes the phone back to Eddie.

"I'm really quite surprised," Mrs. Flynn states, "that a woman of such obvious refinement and good breeding would allow her daughter to even keep company with you, let alone marry you. The little girl sounds lovely, God help her. The two of them must see something in you that I don't. Be good to Joan, she sounds sweet, and I'll be praying that you get back to God."

"Thanks, Mom," Eddie replies and he hangs up. "Well, my mother likes you two." Putting his arm around Joan's waist he says to Jill, "My mom can't understand how such a refined, well-bred lady as you can allow your lovely daughter to marry the likes of me."

"Neither can I," Joan adds, and they all laugh.

Tuesday, Wednesday and Thursday are devoted to furious shopping, and on Friday morning Jill takes off by herself. "I've got a few loose ends to tie up," she almost sings, heading for the door.

"What loose ends?" Joan asks.

"Just a couple of little surprises." Jill laughs. "See you two at dinner."

The following morning, Joan and Eddie get married in Tawas, with Bob and Sandy standing up for them and Jill taking pictures.

Joan is wearing an almost identical outfit to the one she wore the night of her wreck. Eddie, dressed as he was for Joan's birthday party, is wearing his blues, with his Ike jacket open and a white pleated shirt, but his bow tie and cummerbund are pale blue instead of maroon and his black suede loafers are brand new.

After the wedding Jill suggests, "Why don't we all go down to the Blue Light and celebrate."

At the Blue Light, Joan expresses surprise at the many cars and motorcycles parked on the lot so early on a Saturday. Jill smiles. "'Loose end' number one, honey."

Jill parks. Bob pulls up, parks next to her, and Jill leads them all to the entrance. She opens the door. All the blue lights are lit. The mirror ball is rotating and the baby spot is shining on it. Blue and white streamers and silver-foil bells are hung. Blue and white balloons are taped to the walls and a buffet table, loaded with roast beef, roast turkey, ham, shrimp, assorted cheeses, breads, spreads and salads is set up along the far wall. The centerpiece of the table is a tasteful, three-tier wedding cake, with an airman for a groom instead of the little guy in the tux.

Standing at the end of the buffet table, between it and the jukebox, are Dave and Trash. They are watching Slim. It's noon.

Slim, wearing a powder blue tuxedo, greets the wedding party at the door. Amid hugs and handshakes, Slim waves to Dave. Trash punches up the juke and Lonnie Johnson starts to sing "Tomorrow Night".

Slim leads everyone in applause for the married couple. Alone on the dance floor, Joan and Eddie glide around, doing their own steps and turns.

Two girls smile and wave as Eddie and Joan dance past their table. "That's Dreamboat and Joy," Joan comments. "Mom and I met them when we were here."

"Good work, honey. I'm seein' a lot of faces out there I can't hook a name on. Man, I wasn't sure if we'd ever dance to this tune again. We're actually fuckin' married."

"Fuckin'-A," Joan answers, dropping her "g." They both laugh and go into a turn. Going through their turn, Eddie gets a 360° view of the crowd. He sees Big-Bob, Dutch and Spot-Shot. He sees McKinny with Sally. He sees Peterson and Davis from his old radar crew, some other guys from the base and three tables of Oscoda and Tawas girls, as well as other Cobras and guys from the 646th sprinkled around.

"We're gonna be shootin' the shit all afternoon, honey," Eddie declares as the song ends.

During the afternoon, Joan and Eddie find out a few things and meet some new people. They find out that McKinny was snapped out of the motor pool and back into Radar Ops the same afternoon that Major Ross took over the 646th, and that two weeks later, Sumner was shipped to Johnson Island.

They find out that Rita is now Trash's full-time old lady and that the good-looking, tall, blonde girl hanging all over Dave is called "Slats." They also are told that ever since Jon gave Becker's Buick that gravel shower he's been called "Stones."

Sally catches the bridal bouquet, looks at McKinny and exults, "It's about time." McKinny opens another beer and smiles.

Big-Bob catches Joan's thrown garter, puts it on his wrist and announces, "Kind of tight." Joan tells him that catching the garter means he's going to get married and Big-Bob laughs. "I can't do that." He grins. "I'm already married to my Hog."

At three o'clock, Major Ross and his wife come by with the best news of all, a teletype from Selfridge AFB stating that Airman Basic Edward Flynn is assigned to the 646th AC/W Squadron, per the major's request upon completion of said airman's 30-day leave. Orders to follow.

Major Ross and his wife hang around, dancing to the blues tunes and drinking to the jump tunes. Every guy from the 646th finds a moment to come by and say, "Hi, Major, afternoon, ma'am." They share a bottle of champagne and Major Ross drinks a couple of double Scotches with Slim. At 5:30, he and his wife leave. On his way out, he tells Eddie, "If you're a couple of days late reporting in, don't sweat it."

About three minutes before six o'clock, Jill touches Joan's arm. "I'm feeling a little light-headed, honey. Need some air."

"Let's go outside," Joan encourages. She and Eddie go out to the parking lot with Jill.

Jill takes a few deep breaths. "Ahhh. That was just what I needed." Jill smiles. "What time is it, Eddie?"

Eddie looks at his watch. "Just about six."

A brand new black Chevy coupe comes wheeling onto the lot and parks right in front of them. A salesman gets out, leaving the front door open and revealing zebra-skin upholstery. The salesman reports to Jill, "Six o'clock, ma'am, your car."

"Thank you, Alex," Jill responds. "Go on in and have some dinner, something to drink. I'll get you a ride back to the dealership."

Jill looks at Joan. "'Loose end' number two."

"Oh Mom." Joan hugs Jill.

"It's a stick shift and it's got the big engine, just the way you like."

"Oh Mom, what a great wedding present."

Eddie hugs Jill. "Thanks for the beautiful wheels, Jill. And thanks for havin' Joan."

At eight o'clock, saying their goodbyes as they leave the still-in-progress party, Eddie tells Jill of his plan for the honeymoon trip. "I'm keepin' Joan guessin' until we get started in the morning. You know how she loves surprises."

"Who loves surprises?" Joan asks as she moves up behind Eddie. She looks at Jill. "He told you, didn't he?"

Jill laughs. "Let me speak with you for a second, honey." Over her shoulder, she says to Eddie, "Girl stuff."

"I'm going to wish you a happy honeymoon right now, dear." Jill smiles. "I'm going to stay over tonight. Not make that drive. I've had a bit of champagne."

"Slim?"

"Slim," Jill smiles, bigger.

Joan takes both of Jill's hands in hers. "He's so nice. Oh Mom, I'm so happy for you!"

"Well, we'll see," Jill remarks. "Here's a house key. Just lock up when you leave and keep it. I have another." She turns. "Eddie, here's three hundred to help on your trip. If you need more, call. That's an order." They all laugh.

Eddie hugs Jill. "We'll send cards, Jill," he promises. "Thanks for everything."

Out on the parking lot, Joan and Eddie approach the car. "You drive, honey," Eddie urges. "Break it in right."

They get into the car. Joan gets herself settled behind the wheel, cranks the engine, depresses the clutch, slips the shift lever into first and revs the engine a few times. Sliding her foot off the clutch while stomping on the gas pedal, Joan rips through first and second, laying a smoking, burning trail of rubber forty feet long. She gets into third, kicks the car up to seventy, eases back to sixty-five and cruises down Highway 23, with Eddie cheering her on.

EPILOGUE

▼

Monday morning at 10 AM, while Jill is still sleeping in Slim's big bed, Joan is easing the new car out of the driveway. She's smiling and happy. "Okay, Eddie, you said you'd tell me our mystery destination the minute our wheels left the drive," she insists. "Let's have it.'

"How about Chicago?"

"Chicago?" Joan can't hide her disappointment. "I've been there."

"Then we'll go through Saint Looie." Eddie smiles and sings, "Joplin, Missouri, Oklahoma City is mighty pretty, you'll see Amarillo, Gallup, New Mexico, Flagstaff, Arizona ..."

Joan interrupts him. She's beaming. "Oh Eddie, we're going to drive Route 66."

"Yeah, from stem to stern," he boasts. "You're gonna spit in the Pacific. I figure we better drive Route 66 while it's still there."

"While it's still there? Where's it going?"

"I dunno. An old trucker named Hank said Route 66'll be gone in thirty or forty years. Funny guy, huh?"

"Yeah."

"Claimed he drove a million miles."

"You believe him?"

"He sure looked it," Eddie answers, and they laugh.

Joan and Eddie do a round-trip on Route 66, staying at some of the places where Eddie stayed before and eating at some of the same spots. He introduces Joan to little, yellow peppers in Oklahoma City and to the Ranger at the Lazy Z

Motel. They send postcards to Jill from every town mentioned in "Get Your Kicks on Route 66".

They get back to Michigan with three days to spare, rent a house north of Oscoda, a block from where Captain Becker and his wife lived before Becker got shipped to Greenland, and settle down.

December 31st, 1953, New Years Eve, twenty minutes before midnight. While slow dancing with Jill at Joan and Eddie's New Year's Eve party, listening to the Orioles singing "What Are You Doing New Year's Eve", Slim asks Jill to marry him. Jill accepts and thinks, Sometimes dreams come true.

February 14th, 1954, Saint Valentine's Day. Slim and Jill get married. "We've been engaged since last year," Slim jokes. Getting married on Valentine's Day was his idea. "Long engagements don't make sense at our age," Jill tells Joan. They use the same Justice of the Peace that married Joan and Eddie. Joan and Eddie stand up for Slim and Jill.

March 19th, 1954. Joan and Sandy get postcards from Laura: scenes of New Orleans. One says, "Honeymooning" and the other card says, "At last!" Both cards are signed Mrs. Staff/Sergeant Norman Stanton.

April 1st, 1954, Sandy gives birth to Robert Edward Porter. Mother and baby both doing well.

July 23rd, 1954. Jill Sandra Flynn is born. 6 pounds and 6 ounces. She was conceived at the Lazy Z Motel. Joan and Baby Jill are both doing fine.

August 1st, 1954. Eddie gets promoted to airman third class. He can't remember if it's the third or fourth time.

October 6th, 1954. Eddie receives an honorable discharge from the Air Force. He does not receive a re-enlistment talk.

December 10th, 1954. Bob gets discharged. He does get the re-enlistment talk, which he enjoys, but he chooses to go into business with Slim and Eddie.

December 15th, 1954. HIGHWAY 23, CUSTOM CARS AND RODS opens for business. It's a combination used-car lot, garage, speed equipment store and body shop. Dave and Trash are kept busy full time as mechanics. Spot-Shot is an excellent artist and the guys use him for special paint jobs like flames or cobras.

Drop in sometime. The place is about a mile north of The Saginaw Farms Esso Station on Highway 23.

THE END

About the Author

Jan. 1, 1931	Conceived on New Year's Eve by a Catholic couple practicing the Rhythm System. Dad drank a lot and wouldn't take "NO!" for an answer.
Oct. 1, 1931	Happy Birthday to me. Grew up in Morningside Heights, in New York City. Great fun.
June 1948	Graduated Cardinal Hayes H.S. and went to work at the New York Journal-American as a mail clerk.
Oct. 1950	Korea misbehaving. Turn 19 and join the air force. Texas, Biloxi, Michigan, Alaska and California. My

rank changes, up and down. Honorable Discharge in 1954 with one stripe and NO re-enlistment talk.

t. 1954 — Back to the old neighborhood and work at the Journal-American, selling used car ads over the phone. Meet Marlene.

Nov. 1956 — Off to California with Marlene. Get married and work various sales jobs, 3 years selling Yellow Pages advertising, about a year at the L.A. Mirror-News selling classified ads, and brief stints peddling desert land, modeling courses and aluminum siding before drifting into selling cars.

Jan. 1961 — Start of the "Auto Years". I sold Pontiacs, Fords, and then Volkswagens.

Nov. 1962 — Son, Packy born.

July 1964 — Son, Dennis born.

Oct. 1, 1964 — Quit drinking alcohol. Wow!

June 1966 — Move from L.A. to Newbury Park. Sheep graze next door to us.

June 1969 — End of Auto Years. Burned out.

June 1970 — Goodbye suburbs. Bulldozers have replaced sheep. Gas stations and convenience stores are appearing.

June 1972 — Nixon looks like a lock. Goodbye U.S.A. Hello, Trinidad and Tobago. Beautiful 9 months. Trinidad denies work permit.

March 1973 — On to Vermont, to run the kitchen at a rustic private school for kids who are not living up to their parents' great expectations. Leave 2 years later due to "Creeping Preppiness". Go to work at a textile mill, 7pm to 7am shift. Noisy but fun.

Jan. 1983 — Work on The Thicke Of The Night Show as a researcher. Make a few TV appearances.

The 90's

Thanks to nepotism, I worked 2 years on The Georg
Carlin Show, writing two episodes during that time.
have 3 screenplays and thirty short stories as well as a
TV series pilot, none of them going anywhere but they
are written. That's it for now.

351

e
l

978-0-595-42639-3
0-595-42639-5